Lord Lytton

Pamphlets and Sketches

Lord Lytton

Pamphlets and Sketches

ISBN/EAN: 9783337010959

Printed in Europe, USA, Canada, Australia, Japan

Cover: Foto ©Andreas Hilbeck / pixelio.de

More available books at **www.hansebooks.com**

PAMPHLETS AND SKETCHES.

PAMPHLETS

AND

SKETCHES

BY

THE RIGHT HON. LORD LYTTON

LONDON
GEORGE ROUTLEDGE AND SONS
THE BROADWAY, LUDGATE
NEW YORK: 416 BROOME STREET
1875

PREFATORY NOTE TO THE KNEBWORTH EDITION.

THE half-dozen pieces comprised in this volume are given for the most part in the chronological order in which they originally appeared.

The Letter upon the Political Crisis of 1834 had an extraordinary success at the time of its first publication, enjoying, besides this, the repute of having considerably influenced the General Election, which immediately afterwards led to a change of government.

How it was that the "Confessions of a Water-Patient" came to be written at all may be here explained. Mr. Harrison Ainsworth having, in 1845, purchased the *New Monthly Magazine*, applied to Sir Edward Lytton, with whom he had long been on terms of intimacy, and who had himself been a former editor of that periodical, to aid his new enterprise with a contribution. In compliance with this request, these Experiences of the Water Cure were jotted down in the form of a letter addressed to Mr. Ainsworth, as editor of the *New Monthly*. Grateful for so welcome a contribution, the romancist of "Rookwood" begged his brother author's acceptance of two antique suits of armour, which still adorn the banqueting-hall at Knebworth.

As for the "Letters to John Bull," which appeared from the press in 1851, they were the vindication of the writer's views as an agriculturist and a politician, or, as he expressed it by his signature, as a landlord and a labourer—views consistently maintained by him during seventeen years consecutively. The publication of these Letters was chiefly important to himself, as preparing the way for his return to the House of Commons (after an absence from it of eleven years) in his capacity as the Conservative member for Hertfordshire.

The "Life of Schiller" originally appeared as a prefix to the translations of the poems and ballads of the great German lyrist, when, in 1845, they were first collected together, after their piecemeal issue in the pages of *Blackwood's Magazine*. Similarly the essay illustrative of the "Causes of Horace's Popularity," having first appeared as a contribution to Maga, was, in 1849, placed, by way of Introduction, before Lord Lytton's unrhymed but rythmical version of the Odes and Epodes published by the Messrs. Blackwood.

The concluding pages in this volume, now first identified as from the hand of "Bulwer," appeared anonymously nearly forty years ago, that is, in 1838, in the first volume of the *Monthly Chronicle*. As an elaborate disquisition upon the Art of Fiction, penned in mid-career by one of the great masters of that art, it will, doubtless, be turned to with something of the same interest with which the reader might turn to a treatise of Paganini on the structure of a Straduarius, or to one by Sebastian Bach upon the subtleties of counterpoint.

CONTENTS.

PAMPHLETS AND SKETCHES.

THE PRESENT CRISIS.

A LETTER TO A LATE CABINET MINISTER.*

"But, my Lords, how is the King's Government to be carried on ? "—*The Duke of Wellington on the Reform Bill.*

"The general appearance of submission . . . . encouraged the King to remove from office the Marquis of Halifax, with whose liberal opinions he had recently, as well as early, been dissatisfied. As the King found that Halifax would not comply with his projects, he determined to dismiss him before the meeting of Parliament."—*Mackintosh's History of the Revolution,* chap. ii.

My Lord,—The Duke of Wellington has obtained many victories, but he never yet has obtained a victory over the English People !—That battle has now to be adventured ; it has been tried before, but in vain. On far worse ground the great Captain hazards it again ; for his first battle was to prevent giving power to the people ; the power obtained, his second is to resist it. It is the usual fate of fortunate warriors, that their old age is the sepulchre of their renown. No man has read the history of England without compassion for the hero of Anno's time. Marlborough in his glory, and Marlborough in his dotage ; what a satire in the contrast ! With a genius for war, it may be, equal ; with a genius in peace, incontestably inferior ; with talents far less various ; with a knowledge of his times far less profound ; with his cunning and his boldness, without his eloquence and his skill, the Duke of Wellington has equalled the glory of Marlborough,—is he about to surpass his dotage ?

* [Originally published in 1834 as an 8vo pamphlet.]

Marlborough was a trickster, but he sought only to trick a court; has the Duke of Wellington a grander ambition, and would he trick a people? "Like chimneys," said the wise man, "which are useful in winter and useless in summer, soldiers are great in war, and valueless in peace." The chimney smokes again!—there is a shout from the philosophers who disagree with the wise man, "Sée how useful it is!"—but it smokes because it has kept the soot of the last century, and has just set the house in a blaze!—the smoke of the chimney, in this instance, is only the first sign of the conflagration of the edifice.

Let us, my Lord, examine the present state of affairs. Your Lordship is one of that portion of the late Ministry which has been considered most liberal. Acute, far-seeing, and accomplished, with abilities, which, exercised in a difficult position, have been singularly successful in the results they achieved, your Lordship is among those whose elevation to the Cabinet was hailed with a wider satisfaction than that of a party—and so short a time has elapsed between your accession and retirement, (expulsion would be the proper term,) that you are but little implicated in the faults or virtues of the administration, over whose grave I shall endeavour, in the course of this letter, to inscribe a just and impartial epitaph. I address to you, my Lord, these observations, as one interested alike in the preservation of order, and the establishment of a popular government—there may be a few who wish to purchase the one at the expense of the other; you wish to unite them, and so do I. And we are both confident that such is yet the wish,—nay more—the assured hope, of the majority of the English people.

The King has dissolved Lord Melbourne's Administration, and the Duke of Wellington is at the head of affairs. Who will be his colleagues is a question that admits of no speculation. We are as certain of the list as if it were already in the Gazette. It is amusing to see the now ministerial journals giving out, that we are not on any account to suppose, that it must necessarily be a high Conservative cabinet. God forbid so rash a conjecture! "Who knows," say they, "but what many Whigs—many Liberals, will be a part of it! We are only waiting for Sir Robert Peel, in order to show you, perhaps, that the Government will——*not* be Tory!"* So then, after all the Tory abuse of the Whigs—after all the assertions of their unpopularity, it is nevertheless convenient to insinuate that some of these most abominable men may yet chequer and relieve the too expectant and idolatrous adoration with which the people would be imbued for a Cabinet purely Conservative! The several ambrosias of Wellington and Londonderry, of Herries and Peel, would be too strong for mortal tastes, if blended into one divine combination—so they might as well pop a Whig or two into the composition, just to make it fit for mankind! The hypothesis may be convenient—but, unhappily, no one accepts it. Every man in the political world who sees an inch before his nose, is aware, that though his Grace may have an option with respect to measures, he has none with respect to men. He may filch away the Whig policy, but he cannot steal the Whigs themselves without their consent. And the fact is notorious, that there is not a single man of liberal politics—a single man, who either belonged to the late government, or has supported popular measures, who will take office under the Duke of Wellington, charm he never so wisely. It is said, my Lord, by those who ought best to know, that even Lord Stanley, of whom, by the unthinking, a momentary doubt was entertained, scorns the very notion of a coalition with the Conservatives—a report I credit at once, because it is congenial to the unblemished integrity and haughty honour of the man. The Duke of Wellington, then, has no option as to the party he must co-invest with office—unless, indeed, he strip himself of all power—abdicate the post of *chef*, and send up to his Majesty the very same bill of fare which has just been found so unpalatable to the royal tastes. This is not exactly probable. And we know, therefore, even before Sir Robert Peel arrives, and whether Sir Robert Peel take office or whether he do not,—we know that his Grace's colleagues, or his Grace's nominees, can only be the dittos of himself—it is the Farce of Anti-Reform once more, by Mr. Sarum and his family—it is the old company again, and with the old motto "Vivant Rex et Regina!" Now-a-days, even in farces, the loyalty of

---

* "It is possible his Grace may think that some of the Whig leaders who are abroad, or absent from London, are likely to form useful components of a new administration."—*Standard.*

the play-bill does not suffice to carry the public.   Thank
God! for the honour of political virtue, it *is*, and *can* be,
no compromise of opinions!—no intermixture of Whigs
and Tories!—not a single name to which the heart of the
people ever for a moment responded will be found to relieve the well-known list of downright, thorough, uncompromising enemies to all which concedes abuse to the
demands of opinion.   Your Lordship remembers in Virgil
how Æneas meets suddenly with the souls of those who
were to return to the earth they had before visited, after
drinking deep enough of oblivion ; so now how eager—how
noisy—how anxious wait the Conservative shadows, for the
happy hour that is to unite them to the substance of place.

—Strepit omnis murmure campus! *

how they must fret and chafe for the appointed time!—
but in the meanwhile have they drank of the Lethe ?   If
they have, unhappily the world to which they return has
not had a similar advantage; they are escaped from their
purgatory before the appointed time—for the date which
Virgil, and we, gave them, in order completely to cleanse
their past misdeeds, was—a thousand years! In the meanwhile there they stand! mistaken, unequivocal!—Happy
rogues—behold them, in the elysium of their hopes, perched
upon little red boxes, tied together by little red strings—

"· · · · · Iterumque in tarda reverti
Corpora; quæ lucis miseris tam dira cupido!" †

Well may the Times and the Tories say they will be "an
united Cabinet :"—united they always were in their own
good days of the Liverpool ascendancy—united to take
office at every risk—to seize all they can get—to give
nothing that they can refuse!—My God! what delight
among the subordinate scramblers to see before them once
more the prospect of a quarter's salary !—They have been
out of service a long time—their pride is down—they are
willing to be hired by the job ;—a job too of the nature of
their old services ; for, without being a prophet, one may
venture to predict that they will have little enough to do

* [And all the plain buzzes with their humming noise.]
† [And enter again into inactive bodies; what direful love of the light
possesses the miserable beings !]

for their money! When working-day commences with the
next session of Parliament they will receive their wages
and their discharge. They have gone into sinecures again!
honest fellows! they are making quick use of the Poor
Law bill—in which it is ordained that able-bodied paupers
out of employ should be taken in doors for relief! And
yet I confess, there is something melancholy as well as
ludicrous, in the avidity of these desperadoes.—The great
Florentine historian informs us, with solemn indignation,
(as something till then unheard of in the corruption of
human nature,) that in the time of the plague there were
certain men who rejoiced, for it was an excellent time for
pillage!—the people perished, but the brigands throve!—
And nothing, we might imagine at first, could exceed the
baseness of those who sought to enrich themselves amidst
the general affliction. But on consideration, we must deem
those men still baser who do not find—but who create—
the disorder;—and who not only profit by the danger of
the public—but in order to obtain the profit, produce the
danger!—For, my Lord, there are two propositions which
I hold to be incontestable:—first, that the late resolution
of the King, if sudden in effect, was the result of a previous and secret understanding, that the Tories would
accept office; and that his Majesty never came to the determination of dismissing my Lord Melbourne, until he
had ascertained, mediately or immediately—(it matters not
which, nor how long ago)—that the Duke of Wellington
was not only prepared to advise the King as to his successor, but could actually pledge himself to form a Ministry.

I grant that this is denied, though feebly, by the Conservative journals, but to what an alternative would belief in
that denial reduce us! Can we deem so meanly of the
royal prudence, as to imagine that the King could dismiss
one Government, without being assured that he could form
another? In what an awful situation would this empire
be placed, could we attribute to his Majesty, with the
Tory tellers of the tale, so utter a want of the commonest
resources of discretion,—so reckless and improvident a
lunacy!

But it may be granted, perhaps, that the King was aware
that the Duke of Wellington *would* either undertake to
form a Cabinet, or to advise his Majesty as to its forma-

tion, whenever it should please the King to exercise his undoubted prerogative in the dismissal of Lord Melbourne, and yet be asserted that neither that understanding nor that dismissal was the result of intrigue. Doubtless! Who knows so little of a Court as to suppose that an intrigue is ever carried on within its precincts? Is not that the place, above all others, where the secret whisper, the tranquil hint, the words that never commit the speaker, the invisible writing and automaton talking of diplomacy, are never known! It is never in a Court that an intrigue is formed; and the reason is obvious—because they have always another name for it! There was no intrigue then. Why should there be one? The King might never have spoken to the Duke of Wellington on the subject—the Duke of Wellington might be perfectly unaware of what time or on what pretext Lord Melbourne would be dismissed; and yet the King might, and must, (for who can say a King has not common sense?) have known that the Duke would accept office whenever Lord Melbourne was dismissed; and the Duke have known, on his part, that the King was aware of that loyal determination. This is so plain a view of the case, that it requires no state explanations to convince us of it, or persuade us out of it.

The Duke, then, and his colleagues were willing to accept office: on the knowledge of that willingness the King exercised his prerogative, and since we now see no other adviser of the Crown, it is his Grace alone whom we must consider responsible for the coming experiment, which is to back the House of Lords against the Representatives of the People.

I hold it as a second and incontestable proposition, that in this experiment there is danger, were it only for Ireland —the struggle has begun—the people have not been the first to commence—they will be the last to leave it. It is a struggle between the Court and the People. My Lord, recollect that fearful passage, half tragedy, half burlesque, in the history of France, which we now see renewed in England—when Mirabeau rose up in the midst of an assembly suddenly dissolved, and the nation beheld the *tiers état* on one side, and —— the Master of the Ceremonies on the other!

The Duke of Wellington is guiltless of the lore of history,

not so his colleagues. I will concede the whole question of danger in the struggle about to be—I will subscribe to the wisdom of the experiment—I will renounce liberty itself— if Sir Robert Peel, so accomplished in letters—if Sir George Murray, so erudite in history, will but tell us of a single instance in which the people, having firmly obtained the ascendant power,—having held that power for two years, have, at the end of that period, spontaneously re-signed it. The English people have the power now, in their elections—an election is at hand—there is no army to awe, no despot to subdue, no enemy to embarrass them— will they, of their own accord, give back that power to the very men from whom they have wrenched it? The notion is so preposterous that we can scarcely imagine the design of the new Cabinet to rest with the experiment of a new Parliament: it would seem as if they meditated the alter-native of governing without a Parliament at all—as if they would hazard again the attempt of the Stuarts; as if the victor of Waterloo were already looking less to the conduct of the electors than to the loyalty of the army. In fact, this is not so wholly extravagant an expectation as it may seem. The Tories fear the people—why should the people not fear the Tories? They call us desirous of a revolution—why may we not think they would crush that revolution in the bud, by a despotism? Nor, for politicians without prin-ciple, would the attempt be so ridiculous as our pride might suppose. It seems to me, if they are resolved to govern us, that the sword would be the best sceptre. A resolute army, well disciplined, and well officered, with the Duke of Wel-lington at the head, would be a far more formidable enemy to the people than half a score hack officials in the council, and a legion of smooth-faced Conservatives, haranguing, bribing, promising,—abusing known reformers, and pro-mising unknown reforms, to the " ten-pound philosophers" from the hustings: the latter experiment *is* ridiculous, the former is more grave and statesmanlike. If a Londonderry would have advised his Majesty to call in the Duke of Wellington, a Machiavelli would have told him in doing so to calculate on the army. Folly in these days, as in all others, can only be supported and rendered venerable by force.

As yet we are lost in astonishment at the late changes:

we are not angry, we are too much amused, and too confident of our own strength to be angry. So groundless seems the change, that people imagine it only to be fathomed by the most recondite conjectures. They are lost in a wilderness of surmise, and yet, I fancy, that the mystery is not difficult to solve.

Let us for a moment leave Lord Althorp out of the question; we will come to him by-and-by. Let us consider the question of reforming the Irish Church. England has two prominent causes of trouble: the one is the state of Ireland, the other is her House of Lords. Now it is notorious that we cannot govern Ireland without a very efficient and thorough reform in the mighty grievance of her church ; it is equally notorious that that reform the House of Lords would reject. We foresaw this—wo all knew that in six months the collision between the two Houses would come —we all knew that the Lords would reject that reform, and we all felt assured that Lord Melbourne would tell the King that he was not fit to be a minister if he could *not* carry it. There is the collision! in that collision which would have yielded? Not the House of Commons. All politicians, even the least prophetic, must have foreseen this probability, this certainty. His Majesty (let us use our common sense) must have foreseen it too. Doubtless, his Majesty foresaw also that this was not the sole question of dispute, which his present administration, and his present House of Commons would have been compelled by public opinion to raise with the Hereditary Chamber, and his Majesty therefore resolved to take the earliest decorous opportunity of preventing the collision, not by gaining the Lords, but by dismissing the Commons, and he now hopes, by the assistance of the leader of the House of Lords, to make the attempt to govern his faithful subjects, not by the voice of that chamber they have chosen for themselves, but by that very assembly who were formerly in the habit of choosing for them. It is an attempt to solve our most difficult problem, an attempt to bring the two Houses into harmony with each other ; but it is on an unexpected principle.—There is an anecdote of Sheridan, that walking home one night, not altogether so sober as he should be, he was suddenly accosted by a gentleman in the gutter, considerably more drunk than himself. " For the love of God, help me up!" cried the stranger. "My dear Sir," hiccuped Sheridan, "that is out of the question. I cannot help you up; but (let us compromise the matter) I will lie down by you!" The House of Lords is in the gutter—the House of Commons on its legs—the matter is to be compromised—the House of Commons is not to help up the House of Lords, but to lie down by its side! Fate takes from us the leader of the Liberals in one House;—to supply the place, his Majesty gives us the leader of the Tories in the other. Prophetic exchange! We are not to make our Lords reformers, but our representatives cease to be so! Such is the royal experiment to prevent a collision. It is a very ingenious one; but his Majesty has forgotten that Gatton and Lostwithiel are no more. In the next election this question is to be tried, "ARE THE PEOPLE OF ENGLAND TO BE GOVERNED ACCORDING TO THE OPINION OF THE HOUSE OF LORDS, OR ACCORDING TO THE PRINCIPLES OF THEIR OWN REFORM!" That is the point at issue. Twist, pervert, construe it as you will—raise whatever cries in favour of the Church on one hand, or in abuse of the Whigs on the other, the question for the electors is;—will they, or will they not, choose a House of Commons that shall pass the same votes as the Lords, and that shall not pass votes which the Lords would reject? After having abolished the Gattons, will they make their whole House a Gatton?

Supposing then the King, from such evident reasons, to have resolved to get rid of his Ministers, at the first opportunity,*—suddenly Lord Spencer dies, and the opportunity is afforded. There might have been a better one. Through-

---

* And the *Standard* (Nov. 20th), the now official organ (and certainly an abler or a more eloquent the ministers could not have), frankly allows that the King has long been dissatisfied with the government—and even suggests the causes of that displeasure.

"Lord Grey's administration," it says, "was at first perfect—(indeed! that is the first time we have heard the concession from such a quarter)—or if altered, altered only for the better by its purification from the *to-all-intolerable!* Earl of Durham." But this halcyon state soon ceases, because liberal measures creep in, and chief among the causes of the King's dislike to his ministers, and therefore to the Commons, is, first, the Irish Church Bill, which the reader will remember was rejected by the House of Lords—*the bill*, not the *rejection of it*, is mightily displeasing to the King; and secondly, that change in the Irish Coercion Bill which allowed his Majesty's Irish subjects a Jury instead of a Court-Martial. This is termed by the *Standard*—"the Coercion Bill mangled into a mere mockery."—We may see what sort of mangling we are likely to have.

out the whole history of England, since the principles of a constitutional government, and of a responsible administration, were established, in 1688, there is no parallel to the combination of circumstances attendant upon the present change. A parallel to a part of the case there may be, to the whole case there is none. The Cabinet assure the King of their power and willingness to carry on the government: the House of Commons, but recently elected, supports that Cabinet by the most decided majorities; the Premier, not forced on the King by a party, but solicited by himself to accept office; a time of profound repose; no resignation tendered, no defeat incurred—the revenue increasing—quiet at home—peace abroad; the political atmosphere perfectly serene :—when lo, there dies a very old man, whose death every one has been long foreseeing—not a minister, but the father of a minister, which removes, not the Premier, but the Chancellor of the Exchequer, from the House of Commons to the House of Lords ! An event so long anticipated, does not confound the Cabinet. The premier is not aghast, he cannot be taken by surprise by an event so natural, and so anticipated, (for very old men *will* die!) he is provided with names to fill up the vacant posts of Chancellor of the Exchequer, and Leader of the House of Commons. He both feels and declares himself equally strong as ever; he submits his new appointments to his Majesty. Let me imagine the reply. The King, we are informed, by the now ministerial organs, expresses the utmost satisfaction at Lord Melbourne and his Government; he considers him the most honourable of men, and among the wisest of statesmen. Addressing him, then, after this fashion—

> " He does not affect to dissemble his love,
> And *therefore* he kicks him down stairs."

" My Lord :—you are an excellent man, very—but old Lord Spencer—he was a man seventy-six years old; no one could suppose that at that age, an Earl would die! You are an admirable minister, I am pleased with your measures; but old Lord Spencer is no more. It is a sudden, an unforeseen event. Who could imagine he would only live to seventy-six ? The revenue is prospering, the Cabinet is strong—our allies are faithful, you have the

House of Commons at your back, but alas! Lord Spencer is dead! You cannot doubt my attachment to Reform, but of course it depended on the life of Lord Spencer? You have lost a Chancellor of the Exchequer; you say, you can supply his place;—but who can supply the place of the late Lord Spencer? You have lost a leader of the House of Commons; you have found another on whom you can depend; but, my Lord, where shall we find another Earl Spencer, so aged, and so important as the Earl who is gone! The life of the government, you are perfectly aware, was an annuity on the life of this unfortunate nobleman—he was only seventy-six! my love of liberal men, and liberal measures, is exceeding, and it was bound by the strongest tie,—the life of the late Lord Spencer. How can my people want Reform, now Lord Spencer is dead? How can I support reforming ministers, when Lord Spencer has ceased to be? The Duke of Wellington, you must be perfectly aware, is the only man to govern the country, which has just lost the owner of so fine a library, and so large an estate. It is true, that his Grace could not govern it before, but then Lord Spencer was in the way! The untimely decease of that nobleman has altered the whole face of affairs. The people were not quite contented with the Whigs, because they did not go far enough; but then—Lord Spencer was alive! The people now will be satisfied with the Tories, because they do not go so far, for —Lord Spencer is dead! A Tory ministry is necessary, it cannot get on without a Tory parliament; and a Tory parliament cannot be chosen without a Tory people. But, ministry, parliament, and people, what can they be but Tory, after so awful a dispensation of Providence as the death of the Earl of Spencer? My Lord, excuse my tears, and do me the favour to take this letter to the Duke of Wellington."

Well, but it may be said, that it was not the death of this good old man, that so affected the King's arrangements; it was the removal of Lord Althorp from the Commons. "What, is not that cause enough?" cry the Tories. About as much cause as the one just assigned. "What, did not Lord Melbourne himself say, at the retirement of Lord Grey, that the return of Lord Althorp was indispensably necessary to his taking office?" Very possibly. But there is this little difference between the two cases; in the one, Lord Melbourne said, he could not carry on the government without Lord Althorp as leader of the Commons; and in the other, he assured the King, that he could. The circumstances at the time which broke up Lord Grey's government, were such as raised the usual importance of Lord Althorp to a degree which every one saw must subside with the circumstances themselves. In the first place, it was understood, that Lord Althorp left the government, rather than pass an unpopular clause in the Coercion Bill, the passing of which certain circumstances rendered doubly distasteful to his mind; that this led to the resignation of Earl Grey, and that Lord Althorp felt a natural and generous scruple in resuming office after that resignation. The Members of the House of Commons came to their memorable requisition, because they looked upon Lord Althorp's resignation, as the consequence of his popular sentiments. They feared the vacancy he created could be filled only by a man of less liberal opinions, and they felt his return, in such circumstances, would be for the popular triumph, as his secession might be but a signal for a change of policy. Such were the circumstances under which Lord Melbourne, at that time, considered Lord Althorp's return to the leadership of the Commons as necessary to the stability of the government. But what circumstances in the late changes are analogous to these? Is Lord Althorp now removed from office by popular sentiments, which rendered his return necessary for the triumph of his sentiments—not the use of his talents? Is the Cabinet broken up? Is the House of Commons declaring, that not even death shall tear it from its beloved leader? What absurdity, to follow out the parallel! Lord Althorp was called by the death of his venerable father to the House of Lords. His loss created no alarm for an alteration in our policy, broke up no cabinet, and disturbed no measures; the prime minister was perfectly resigned to the event, and perfectly prepared with his successor—a successor of the same principles, and if of less conciliatory manners, of equal experience, more comprehensive knowledge, and greater eloquence.* The King has a right to exercise his prerogative—no one dis-

* In the best informed political circles it is understood that Lord John Russell would have led the House of Commons and had the conduct of the Irish Church Bill. Mr. Abercromby would have taken charge of the Muni-

putes it. It is only a misfortune that other ministers have not also fathers of seventy-six! Old Sir Robert, good Lord Mornington—would that *they* were alive!

And having now to all plain men shown how utterly burlesque is the whole pretext of the dismissal, and the whole parallel between Lord Althorp's former retirement and present elevation, let us turn again from the reason of the change to the change itself.

There are some persons simple enough to imagine that though the Tory government may imply Tory men it does not imply Tory measures; that the Duke of Wellington, having changed his sentiments (no, not his sentiments,—his actions)—on the Catholic question, will change them again upon matters like—the reform of the Protestant Church, the abuses of corporations, perhaps even triennial parliaments, and the purgation of the pension list! There are men, calling themselves reformers, and blaming the Whigs as too moderate in reforms, not only vain enough to hope this, but candid enough to say that a government thus changing—no matter with what open and shameless profligacy—no matter with what insatiate lust of power, purchased by what unparalleled apostacy—that a government, thus changing, and therefore thus unprincipled, ought to receive the support of the people! They would give their suffrage to the Duke of Wellington upon the very plea, that he will desert his opinions; and declare that they will support him as a minister, if they can but be permitted to loathe him as an apostate.

My Lord, I think differently on this point. Even were I able to persuade myself that the new Tory government would rival or outbid the Whigs in popular measures, I would not support it. I might vote for their measures, but I would still attempt to remove the men. What! is there nothing at which an honest and a generous people should revolt, in the spectacle of ministers suddenly turned traitors by the bribe of office—in the juggling by which men, opposing all measures of reform when out of place, will, the very next month, carry those measures if place depends upon it? Would there be no evil in this to the morality of the people? Would there be no poison in this

cipal Reform. Names that on these questions in particular would have shown that the government were in earnest in their measures.

to the stream of public opinion? Would it be no national misfortune—no shock to order itself, (so much of which depends on confidence in its administrators,) to witness what sickening tergiversation, what indelible infamy, the vilest motives of place and power could inflict on the characters of public men? And to see the still more lamentable spectacle of a Parliament and a Press vindicating the infamy, and applauding the tergiversator! Vain, for these new-light converts, would be the cant excuses of 'practical statesmen attending to the spirit of the age'—'conforming to the wants of the time'—'yielding their theories to the power of the people;' for these are the very excuses of which they have denied the validity! If this argument be good for them in office, why did they deny, and scorn, and trample upon it out of office? far more strong and cogent was it when they had only to withdraw opposition to measures their theories disapproved, than when they themselves are spontaneously to frame those measures, administer them, and carry them through. There could be but one interpretation to their change—one argument in their defence, and that is,—that they would not yield to reforms when nothing was to be got by it; but that they would enforce reforms when they were paid for it—that they would not part with the birthright without the pottage, nor play the Judas without the fee! I do not think so meanly of the high heart of England as to suppose that it would approve, even of good measures, from motives so shamelessly corrupt. And, for my own part, solemnly as I consider a thorough redress of her "monster grievance" necessary for the peace of Ireland, a reform of our own Church, and our own Corporations, and a thorough carrying out and consummation of the principles of our reform, desirable for the security and prosperity of England, I should consider these blessings purchased at too extravagant a rate, if the price were the degradation of public men—and the undying contempt for consistency, faith, and honour—for all that makes power sacred, and dignity of moral weight—which such an apostacy would evince. Never was liberty permanently served by the sacrifice of honesty.

But this supposition, though industriously put forward by some politicians, unacquainted with what is best in our English nature, is, I think, utterly groundless. I do not attribute to the Duke of Wellington himself too rigid a political honesty. He, who after having stigmatized one day the Reform Bill, could undertake to carry it the next, may be supposed to have a mind, which, however locked and barred, the keys of state can open to conviction. But, let it be remembered, that his Grace stood then almost alone. All that was high and virtuous of his party refused to assist in his astonishing enterprise. From Sir Robert Peel to Sir Robert Inglis—from the moderate to the ultra-Tory—every man who had tasted the sweets of character, recoiled from so gross a contamination. His three days' government fell at once. Now he is wiser—doubtless he has formed a government—doubtless, he has contrived to embrace in it the men who refused before. I believe, for the honour of my countrymen, that they have not receded from their principles now, any more than they receded then. And those principles are anti-reforming.

This is, then, their dilemma: either they will prosecute reform, or they will withhold it—either they will adhere to their former votes, or they will reverse them: in the one case, then, people of England, you will have uncompromising anti-reformers at your head,—in the other, you will have ambitious and grasping traitors. Let them extricate themselves from this dilemma if they can!

But, in fact, they have not this option. They are committed in every way to their old principles; they are committed, first, to their own party, and secondly, to the King. Were they as liberal as the Whigs, their friends would desert them, perhaps his Majesty would dismiss them. Their friends are the High Church party. High Church is the war cry they raise—High Church the motto of their banner. What is the High Church party? It is the party that is sworn to the abuses of the Church. Its members are pledged body and soul to the Bishops, and the Deans, and the Prebends, and the Universities, and the Orangemen of Ireland. They may give out that they think a great Church Reform is necessary; vague expression! what is great to their eyes would be invisible to ours. Will they—let us come to the point, and I will single out one instance—will they curtail the Protestant Establishment of Catholic Ireland? They have called the attempt " spoliation ; " will they turn " spoliators ? "—If so, they lose their friends, for no man supposes that the Tory churchmen have a chemical affinity to the Duke of Wellington—they have no affinity but that of interest: if he offend their interests, he offends the party. Let him but say, " that church has no congregation, but it gives 1500*l.* a year to the parson; I respect property—the property of the people—and they shall cease to pay, after the death of the incumbent, for receiving no benefit;" and all the parsons of the country are in arms against him! What a moment to suppose that he could do justice in such a case, —with the cheers of the Orangemen, and the ravings of Londonderry, and Roden, and Wicklow ringing in his ears! *

As for the claims of the Dissenters, who can imagine they will be attended to by the man who has called them atheists? He may swallow his words, but can he swallow his friends of the colleges? He cannot lose his great permanent support, the Church, for a temporary and hollow support which would forsake him the moment he had served its purpose.

The Corporations—what hope of reform there? Every politician knows the Corporations are the strongholds of Toryism, and many of the truest liberals supported the government till the Corporation reform should be passed, in order to see, safely carried a measure against Toryism, only less important than the Reform Bill. To reform the Corporations will be to betray his own fortresses. Is the Duke of Wellington the man to do this?

But it is not to isolated measures that we are to look—the contest is not for this reform or the other—the two parties stand forth clear and distinct—they are no parties of names, but parties of opposite and irreconcilable interests. With the Duke of Wellington are incorporated those who have an interest in what belongs to an aristocratic, in opposition to a popular goverment, and he can concede nothing, or as little as possible, calculated to weaken the interests of his partizans. He is the incarnation of the House of Lords in opposition to the voice of the House of Commons.

* See too the extracts from the Duke's speeches appended to this letter. And while I am correcting these sheets (Friday, Nov. 21), in the Report of the Conservative Dinner in Kent, it is pleasing to find that the supporters of the Duke of Wellington are of opinion that the cause of THE GREAT SINECURE OF IRELAND, is the cause of all England! Very true—but one is the plaintiff in the *cause*, the other the defendant!

Were he then a Reformer, the people would despise him, his friends would desert,* and we may add, the possibility that the King would dismiss him.

His Majesty, we are assured, has no personal dislike to the late premier : he lauds him as the most honourable of men—he blows up his government, and scatters chaplets over the ruin. It was not a dislike to his person, but to his principles that ensured his dismissal. Perhaps, had that accomplished and able minister. condescended ' to palter in a double sense '—to equivocate and dissemble, to explain his means, but to disguise his objects, he might still be in office. But it is known in the political world that he was an honest statesman—that whatever was his last conference with the King, he did not disguise in *former interviews* that reform must be an act as well as name— that a government to be strong must be strong in public gratitude and confidence—and perhaps, with respect to the particular reform of the Irish church, he may have delicately remarked, that the late Commission sanctioned by the King was not to amuse but to satisfy the people—that if its Report furnished a list of sinecure livings, there would be no satisfaction in wondering at the number—that to ascertain the manner and amount of abuses is only the prelude to their redress. This is reported of Lord Melbourne. I believe it, though not a syllable about any reform might have been introduced at the exact period of his removal. These, then, were the sentiments that displeased his Majesty, and to these sentiments he preferred the Duke of Wellington. He chose these new ministers because they would do less than his late ones. He can only give them his countenance so long as they fulfil his expectations.

I pass over as altogether frivolous and absurd the tittle-tattle of the day. The King might or not be displeased at the speeches of Lord Brougham,—true, they might have offended the royal taste, but scarcely the royal politics—Heaven knows they were sufficiently conservative and sufficiently loyal;—they were much of the same character as those his Majesty might hear whispered, not declaimed, from his next chancellor at his own table. Such as they

---

* But he might suppose that the measure which lost a Tory would gain a liberal. Yes, for that measure only. The friend would be lost for ever, the enemy gained but for a night.

were, they had nothing to do with his Majesty's resolve —if they had, he would have sent, not for the Duke of Wellington, but the Earl of Durham! I pass over with equal indifference the gossip that attacks the family of his Majesty. I know enough of courts to be sensible that we, who do not belong to them, are rarely well informed as to the influences which prevail in that charmed orbit; and I am sufficiently embued with the chivalry of an honest man not to charge women with errors of which they are probably innocent, and of the consequences of which they are almost invariably unaware. I can even conceive that were it true that his Majesty's royal consort, or the female part of his family, were able to exercise an influence over state affairs, they would be actuated by the most affectionate regard for his interests and his dignity. The views of women are necessarily confined to a narrow circle: their public opinion is not that of a wide and remote multitude. They are attracted, even in humble stations, by the "solemn plausibilities" of life—they feel an anxious interest for those connected with them, which often renders their judgment too morbidly jealous of the smallest apparent diminution of their splendour or their power. To imagine that the more firmly a monarch adheres to his prerogatives the more he secures his throne, is a mistake natural to their sex. If such of them as may be supposed to advise his Majesty did form and did act on such a belief, to my mind it would be a natural and even an excusable error. Neither while I lament the resolution of the King, am I blind to the circumstances of his situation. Called to the throne in times of singular difficulty—the advisers of his predecessor, whose reign had been peaceful and brilliant, on one side—a people dissatisfied with half reforms on the other—educated to consider the House of Lords at least as worthy of deference as the popular will —disappointed at finding that one concession, however great, could not content a people who demanded it, but as the means to an end—turning to the most powerful organ of the Press, and reading that his liberal Ministers were unpopular, and that the country cared not who composed its government—seeing before him but two parties, besides the government party—the one headed by the idol of that people he began to fear, and the other by the most illustrious supporter of an order of things which in *past times* was the most favourable to monarchy;—I cannot deem it altogether as much a miracle as a misfortune that he should be induced to make the experiment he has risked. But I do feel indignation at those—not women, but men— grey-haired and practical politicians, who must have been aware, if not of its utter futility, of its pregnant danger; by whose assistance the King now adventures no holiday experiment.—For a poor vengeance or a worse ambition they are hazarding the monarchy itself; by playing the Knave they expose the King. "There are some men," says Bacon, "who are such great self-lovers, that they will burn down their neighbour's house to roast their own eggs in the embers." In the present instance their neighbour's house may be a palace! For this is the danger— not (if the people be true to themselves) that the Duke of Wellington will crush liberty, but that the distrust of the Royal wisdom in the late events—the feeling of insecurity it produces—the abrupt exercise of one man's prerogative to change the whole face of our policy, domestic, foreign, and colonial, without any assigned reason greater than the demise of old Lord Spencer—the indignation for the aristocracy, if the Duke should head it against Reform— the contempt for the aristocracy if the Duke should countermarch it *to* Reform—the release of all extremes of more free opinions, on the return which must take place, sooner or later, of a liberal administration;—the danger is, lest these and similar causes should in times, when all institutions have lost the venerable moss of custom, and are regarded solely for their utility—induce a desire for stronger innovations than those merely of reform.

"Nothing," said a man who may be called the prophet of revolutions, "destroys a monarchy while the people trust the King. But persons and things are too easily confounded, and to lose faith in the representative of an institution, forbodes the decease of the institution itself." Attached as I am by conviction to a monarchy for this country—an institution that I take the liberty humbly to say I have elsewhere vindicated, with more effect, perhaps, as coming from one known to embrace the cause of the people, than the more vehement declamations of slaves and courtiers—I view such a prospect with alarm. And not the less so, because Order is of more value than the Institutions which are but formed to guard it; and in the artificial and complicated affairs of this country, a struggle against monarchy would cost the tranquillity of a generation.

We are standing on a present, surrounded by fearful warnings from the past. The dismissal of a ministry too liberal for a King—too little liberal for the people, is to be found a common event in the stormiest pages of human history. It is like the parting with a common mediator, and leaves the two extremes to their own battle.

And now, my Lord, before I speak of what ought to be, and I am convinced will be the conduct of the people, who are about to be made the judge of the question at issue, let me say a few words upon the Cabinet that is no more. I am not writing a panegyric on the Whigs—I leave that to men who wore their uniform and owned their leaders. I have never done so. In the palmiest days of their power, I stooped not the knee to them. By vote, pen, and speech, I have humbly but honestly asserted my own independence; and I had my reward in the sarcasms and the depreciation of that party which seemed likely for the next quarter of a century to be the sole dispensers of the ordinary prizes of ambition. No matter. I wanted not their favours, and could console myself for the thousand little obstacles, by which a powerful party can obstruct the parliamentary progress of one who will not adopt their errors. I do not write the panegyric of the Whig, and though I am not one of those who can be louder in vituperation when the power is over, than in warning before the offence is done, I have not, I own, the misplaced generosity to laud now the errors which I have always lamented. It cannot be denied, my Lord, or at least *I* cannot deny it, that the Whig government disappointed the people. And by the Whig government I refer to that of my Lord Grey. Not so much because it did not go far enough, as with some ill judged partizans is contended, but rather because it went too far. It went too far, my Lord, when its first act was to place Sir Charles Sutton in the Speaker's chair,—it went too far when it passed the Coercion Bill—it went too far when it defended Sinecures—it went too far when it marched its army to protect the Pension list. —It might have denied many popular changes—if it had

not defended and enforced unpopular measures.—It could
not do all that the people expected, but where was the
necessity of doing what the people never dreamt of?
Some might have regretted when it was solely Whig—
but how many were disgusted when it seemed three parts
Tory! Nor was this all—much that it did was badly
done: there was a want of practical knowledge in the
principle and the details of many of its measures—it often
blundered and it often bungled. But these were the faults
of a past Cabinet. The Cabinet of Lord Melbourne had
not been tried. There was a vast difference between the
two administrations, and that difference was this—in the
one the more liberal party was the minority, in the other it
was the majority. In the Cabinet of the late Premier, the
weight of Sir John Hobhouse, Lord Duncannon, and the
Earl of Mulgrave was added to the scale of the people.
There was in the Cabinet just dissolved a majority of men
whose very reputation was the popular voice, whose names
were as wormwood to the Tories, and to whom it is amusing
to contrast the language applied by the Tory Journals
with that which greeted "in liquid lines mellifluously
bland," the luke-warm reformers they supplanted. Lord
Melbourne's Cabinet had not been tried—It is tried now
—The King has dismissed it in favour of the Duke of
Wellington! His Majesty took the earliest opportunity
and the faintest pretext in the royal power to prove that
he thought it more liberal than the Cabinet which preceded
it. If some cry out with the Tories—"Nay, what said
Lord Brougham at the Edinburgh dinner?" the answer is
obvious. Without lending any gloss to the expressions of
that singular and unfortunate speech, it is enough to
remind the people that Lord Brougham, though a great
orator and a great man, able to play many parts, cannot
fill up the whole *rôles* of the Cabinet. Three other Cabinet
ministers were present, Sir John Hobhouse, Mr. Ellice,
Mr. Abercromby. Did they echo the sentiments of Lord
Brougham? No; they declared only their sympathy with
the sentiments of Lord Durham. They too lamented every
hour that passed over "recognized and unreformed abuses;"
they adopted Lord Durham's principle as their own. The
Chancellor, since he quoted so reverently the royal name,
may have uttered the royal sentiments, but three of his

colleagues before his very face uttered only the sentiments which were those of the people when they elected a re-formed parliament for the support of reforming ministers. By these three speakers, and not by the one speaker, are we to judge, then, in common fairness of what the government would have done. The majority of the Cabinet were of the principles of these speakers. Had even Lord Brougham been an obstacle to those principles when they came to be discussed in the Cabinet, Lord Brougham would have succumbed and not the principles. Of the conduct of that remarkable man it is not now necessary to speak ; nor is it by these hasty lines, nor perhaps by so unable a hand, that so intricate a character can be accurately and profoundly analysed. When the time comes that may restore him to office, it will be the fitting season for shrewder judges of character than I am, to speak firmly and boldly of his merits or his faults. At present it is no slight blame to one so long in public life—so eminent and so active—to say that his friends consider him a riddle: if he be mis-construed, whose fault is it but his own? When the Delphic oracle could be interpreted two ways, what wonder that the world grew at last to consider it a cheat!

With Lor dMelbourne himself, it was my lot in early youth to be brought in contact, and, though our acquaint-ance has now altogether ceased, (for I am not one who seeks to refresh the memories of men in proportion as they become great,) I still retain a lively impression of his pro-fundity as a scholar—of his enthusiasm at generous senti-ments—and of that happy frame of mind he so peculiarly possesses, and of which the stuff of Statesmen is best made, at once practical and philosophical, large enough to con-ceive principles,—close enough to bring them to effect.* Could we disentangle and remove ourselves from the pre-sent, could we fancy ourselves in a future age, it might possibly be thus that an historian would describe him :—
"Few persons could have been selected by a king, as prime minister, in those days of violent party, and of constant

---

* I imagined him susceptible only to the charge of indolence, and I once imputed to him that fault. On learning from those who can best judge, that in office at least the imputation was unjust, I took, long since, the opportunity of a new edition to efface it from the work in which the impu-tation was made.

change, who were more fitted by nature and circumstances to act with the people, but for the King. A Politician probably less ardent than sagacious, he was exactly the man to conform to the genius of a particular time;—to know how far to go with prudence—where to stop with success; not vehement in temper, not inordinate in ambition, he was not likely to be hurried away by private objects, affections, or resentments. To the moment of his elevation as premier, it can scarcely be said of his political life that it affords one example of imprudence. 'Not to commit himself,' was at one time supposed to be his particular distinction. His philosophy was less that which deals with abstract doctrines than that which teaches how to command shifting and various circumstances. He seldom preceded his time, and never stopped short of it. Add to this, that with a searching knowledge of mankind, he may have sought to lead, but never to deceive, them. His was the high English statesmanship which had not recourse to wiles or artifice. He was one whom a king might have trusted, for he was not prone to deceive himself, and he would not deceive another. His judgment wary—his honour impregnable. Such was the minister who, if not altogether that which the people would have selected, seems precisely that which a king should have studied to preserve. He would not have led, as by a more bold and vigorous genius, Lord Durham, equally able, equally honest, with perhaps a yet deeper philosophy, the result of a more masculine and homely knowledge of mankind, and a more prophetic vision of the spirit of the age, might have done; he would not have *led* the People to good government, but he would have marched with them side by side."

Such, I believe, will be the outline of the character Lord Melbourne will bequeath to a calmer and more remote time. And this is not my belief alone. I observe that most of those independent members who had been gradually detached from the Cabinet of Lord Grey, looked with hope and friendly dispositions to that of his successor. In most of the recent public meetings and public dinners where the former Cabinet was freely blamed, there was a willingness to trust the later one. And even those who would have wreaked on the government their suspicions of the Chancellor were deterred by Lord Durham's honest eulogium on the Premier. This much then we must concede to the Melbourne administration. First, it went a step beyond Lord Grey's, it embraced the preponderating, instead of the lesser, number of men of the more vigorous and liberal policy. The faults of Lord Grey's government are not fairly chargeable upon it. Men of the independent party hoped more from it.

Secondly, by what we know, it seems to have been in earnest as to its measures, for we know this, that the Corporation Reform was in preparation—that the Commission into the Irish Church had produced reports which were to be fairly acted upon—that a great measure of justice to Ireland was to be based upon the undeniable evidence which that Commission afforded of her wrongs. We know this,—and knowing no more, we see the Cabinet dissolved,—presumption in its favour, since we have seen its successor!

But, my Lord, if we may speak thus in favour of that Cabinet which your abilities adorned, and in hope of the services which it would have rendered us, we must not forget that we are about in the approaching election, to have not the expectation of good government, but the power of securing it. We must demand from the candidates who are disposed to befriend and restore you, not vague assurances of support to one set of men or the other, to the principles of Lord Grey or those of Lord Melbourne, but to the principles of the people. Your friends must speak out, and boldly—they must place a wide distinction, by candid and explicit declarations, between themselves and their Tory antagonists. Sir Edward Sugden said at Cambridge that he was disposed to reform temperately all abuses. The Emperor of Russia would say the same. Your partizans must specify what abuses they will reform, and to what extent they will go. The people must see, on the one hand, defined reform, in order to despise indefinite reformers on the other. Let your friends come forward manfully and boldly as befits honest men in stirring times, and the same people who gave the last majority to Lord Grey, will give an equal support to a cabinet yet more liberal, and dismissed only because it was felt to be in earnest. I know what the conduct of all who are temperate and honest among reformers ought to be. It is the cry of those who have compromised themselves with their constituents in their too implicit adherence to the measures of Lord Grey, that "All differences must cease—Whig and Radical must forget their small dissensions—all must unite against a common enemy." A convenient cry for them; they are willing now to confound themselves with us, to take shelter under our popularity!—For we, my Lord—and let this be a lesson to the next Parliament—we are safe. Of us who have not subscribed implicitly to Lord Grey's government—of us who have been more liberal than that government—of us who have not defended its errors, nor, what was worse, defended the errors of its Tory predecessors,—I do not believe that a single member will lose his seat! The day of election will be to us a day of triumph. We have not enjoyed the emoluments and honours of a victorious party—we have not basked in the ministerial smiles—we have been depreciated by lame humour, as foolish and unthinking men, and stigmatized by a lamer calumny as revolutionary Destructives. But we had our consolation—we have found it in our consistency and our conscience—in our own self-acquittal, and in the increased esteem of our constituents. And now they need our help! Shall they have it? I trust yes! We can forgive jests at our expense, for nobody applauded them, and they were not echoed, my Lord, by the majority of the Cabinet. One man might disavow us—one man might not enter our house nor travel by our coach, (it is not we who have now pulled down the house, or upset the conveyance!) but three of his colleagues asserted our principles, and we felt that there spoke the preponderating voice of the ministry. I trust, and I feel assured, that we shall forget minor differences, when we have great and ineffaceable distinctions to encounter. I trust that we shall show we are sensible we have it now in our power to prove that we fought for no selfish cause—that we were not thinking of honours and office for ourselves—that we shall show we wished to make our principles, not our interests, triumphant;—willing that others should be the agents for carrying them into effect. This should be our sentiment, and this our revenge. All men who care for liberty should unite—all private animosities, all partial jealousies should be merged. We should remember only that some of us have advocated good measures more than others; but that, the friends of the New Ministry have opposed all. Haroun Alraschid, the caliph of immortal memory, went out one night disguised, as was his wont, and attended by his favourite Giaffer ;—they pretended to be merchants in distress, and asked charity. The next morning two candidates for a place in the customs appeared before the divan. The sultan gave the preference to one of them. "Sire," whispered Giaffer, "don't you recollect that that man only gave us a piece of silver when we asked for a piece of gold?" "And don't you recollect," answered Haroun, "that the other man, when we asked for a piece of silver, called for a cudgel?"

Looking temperately back at the proceedings of the Whigs, we must confess that they have greater excuses, than at the time we were aware of. "Who shall read," says the proverb, "the inscrutable heart of kings?" We could not tell now far the Monarch was with us: rumours and suspicions were afloat—but we were unwilling to believe them of William the Reformer. We imagined his Majesty, induced by secret and invisible advisers, might indeed be timid, and reluctant; but we imagined, also, that the government, by firmness, might bias the royal judgment to a consistent and uniformly paternal policy. Many of us, (though, for my own part, I foresaw and foretold* that the Tory party, so far from being crushed, were but biding their time, scotched not killed)—many of us supposed the Tories more humbled and more out of the reach of office, than the Cabinet, with a more prophetic vision, must have felt they were. With a House of Lords, which the Ministers had neither the power to command nor to reform—with a King, whose secret, and it may be stubborn inclinations, are now apparent,—surrounded by intrigues and cabals, and sensible that the alternative of a Tory government was not so impossible as the public believed, we must, in common candour, make many excuses for men, who, however inclined to the people, had also every natural desire to preserve the balance of the constitution—to maintain the second chamber, and to pay to the wishes of the King that deference, which, as the third voice of the legislature, his Majesty is entitled to receive.

* England and the English.

Add to this, if they resigned office, the King would have had the excuse he has not now : he would have had no alternative but a Tory Cabinet! It is true, however, that so beset with difficulties, their wisest course would have been to remember the end and origin of all government— have thrown themselves on the people and abided the consequences—and that, my Lord, is exactly what I believe your colleagues and yourself intended to do, and it is for that reason you are dismissed. A few months will show, a few months will allow you to explain yourselves; but I should not address to your Lordship this letter—I should not commit myself to a vain prophecy—I should not voluntarily incur your own contempt for my simplicity, if I had not the fullest reason to believe, that the occasion is only wanting to acquit yourself to the public.

Considering these circumstances with candour — the situation of the last ministry—the dissolution of the present, and the reasons for that dissolution ; considering also the first enthusiasm of the Reform Bill, which induced so many members, with the purest motives, to place confidence in the men who had obtained it ;—we shall find now excuses for much of whatever temporising we may yet desire for the future to prevent: and to prevent it must be our object at the next election.

On all such members of the Whig majority as will declare for the future for a more energetic and decided conduct, so as to lead the government through counteracting obstacles, and both encourage, if willing, and force it, if hesitating, to a straightforward and uncompromising policy, the electors cannot but look with indulgence. Such candidates have only to own on their part, that any dallying with " recognized abuse " has been the result not of inclination, but of circumstance, and the difficulties of circumstance will be at once remembered. For those who will not make this avowal, whatever their name, they are but Tories at heart, and as such they must be considered. This is what the late Cabinet itself, if I have construed it rightly, must desire ; and if we act thus, with union and with firmness, with charity to others, but with justice to our principles, we shall return to the next Parliament a vast majority of men who will secure the establishment of a government that no intrigue can undermine, no oligarchy supplant;

based upon a broad union of all reformers, and entitled to the gratitude of the people, not by perpetually reminding it of one obligation, but by constantly feeding it with new ones. Of such a Cabinet I know that you, my Lord, will be one; and I believe that you will find yourself not perhaps among all, but among many of your old companions, and no longer without the services of one man in particular whose name is the synonym of the people's confidence. Taught by experience,* there must then be no compromise with foes—no Whig organ holding out baits of office to Sir Robert Peel—no speeches of "little" having a successor in "less"—no crowding popular offices with Tory malcontents—no ceding to an anti-national interest, however venerable its name—no clipping to please the Lords—no refusing to unfurl the sail when the wind is fair, unless Mrs. Partington will promise not to mop up the ocean!

At present we are without a government; we have only a dictator. His Grace the Duke of Wellington outbids my Lord Brougham in versatility. He stands alone, the representative of all the offices of this great empire. India is in one pocket, our colonies in the other†—see him now at the Home Office, and now at the Horse Guards; Law, State, and Army, each at his command—Jack of all trades, and master of none—but that of war;—we ask for a cabinet, and see but a soldier.

Meanwhile, eager and panting, flies the Courier to Sir Robert Peel!—grave Sir Robert! How well we can picture his prudent face!—with what solemn swiftness will he obey the call! how demurely various must be his meditations!—how ruffled his stately motions at the night-and-day celerity of his homeward progress! Can this be the slow Sir Robert? No! I beg pardon; *he* is not to discom-

---

* And we have the assurance from one of the organs of the late ministers, in an article admirable for its temper and its tenets, that this lesson is already taught. "The leaders of the liberal party must have at last learned the utter futility of every attempt to conciliate the supporters of existing abuses—they must now know that secret enmity is ever watching the occasion of wounding them unawares, and that the public men who would contend against it can only maintain themselves by exhibiting a frank and full reliance on the popular support, and meriting it by an unflinching assertion of popular principles."—*Globe, Nov.* 17.

† "His grace will superintend generally the affairs of the government, till the return of Sir Robert Peel." So says the *Morning Post*. But the *Post* is very angry if any one else says the same.

pose himself. I see, by the papers, that it is only the Courier that is to go at " minute speed "—the Neophyte of Reform is to travel "by easy stages"—we must wait patiently his movements—God knows we shall want patience by and by; his stages will be easy enough in the road the Times wishes him to travel!

The new political Hamlet!—how applicable the situation of his parallel!—how well can his Horatio, (Twiss,) were he himself the courier, break forth with the exposition of the case—

> . . . . "Fortinbras *
> Of unimproved mettle hot and full,
> Sharks up a list of *brainless* resolutes
> For food and diet to some enterprise,
> That hath a stomach in't, which is no other,
> As it doth well appear unto the state,
> But to recover for us by strong hand,
> And terms compulsatory, our—' offices.'
> . . . . This, I take it,
> Is the main motive of our preparations,
> The source of this our watch, and the chief head
> Of this post-haste and romage in the land!

> [*Enter the Ghost of the old Tory Rule.*]

> "'Tis here—'tis here—'tis gone!"

[*Now appears Hamlet himself, arms folded, brow thoughtful.—Sir Robert was always a solemn man!*]

[*Enter the same Ghost of Tory Ascendancy, in the likeness of old Sir Robert.*]

> "My father's spirit in arms!
>
> . . . .
> Thou com'st in such a questionable shape,
> That I will speak to thee. . . . . . Tell,
> Why thy canonized bones, hearsed in death,
> Have burst their cerements."

Whereat good Horatio wooingly observes—

> "It beckons you to go away with it."

Our Hamlet is in doubt. The Tory sway was an excellent thing when alive, but to follow the ghost now, may lead to the devil; nevertheless, Horatio says, shrewdly,

> "The very *place* puts toys of desperation,
> Without more motive, into every brain!"

---

* Fortinbras, Anglice "Strong Arm "—literally "the Duke."

The temptation is too great, poor Hamlet is decoyed, and the wise Marcellus, (the Herries of the play,) disinterestedly observes,

> " Let's follow ! "

Alas ! we may well exclaim, then, with the soft Horatio,

> " To what issue will this come ? "

And reply with the sensible Marcellus, who sums up the whole affair,

> " Something is rotten in the state of Denmark ! "

We need not further pursue the parallel, though inviting, especially in that passage, where to be taken for a rat, is the prelude to destruction. Leave we Hamlet undisturbed to his soliloquy,

> " To be, or not to be—that is the question."

And that question is unresolved. Will Sir Robert Peel commit himself at last—will he join the administration—will he, prudent and wary, set the hopes of his party, the reputation of his life, on the hazard of a die, thrown not for Whigs and Tories—but for Toryism, it is true, on the one hand, and a government far more energetic than Whiggism on the other, with all the chances attendant on the upset of the tables in the meanwhile ? The game is not for the restoring, it is for the annihilation of the *juste milieu !* If he joins the gamesters, let him ; we can yet give startling odds on the throw. But may he see distinctly his position ! If he withdraw from this rash and ill-omened government, if he remain neutral, he holds the highest station in the eyes of the country, which one of his politics can ever hope to attain. It is true, that office may be out of his reach, but to men of a large and a generous ambition, there are higher dignities than those which office can bestow. He will stand a power in himself—a man true to principle, impervious to temptation ; he will vindicate nobly, not to this time only, but to posterity, his single change upon the Catholic Emancipation ; he will prove that no sordid considerations influenced that decision. He will stand alone and aloft, with more than the practical sense, with all the moral weight of Chateaubriand—one whom all parties must honour, whose counsels must be respected by the most liberal, as by the most Tory, cabinet.

Great in his talents—greater in his position—greatest in his honour. But if he mix himself irrevocably with the insane and unprincipled politicians, who now seek either to deceive or subdue the people, he is lost for ever. That ministry have but this option, to refuse all reform and to brave the public, or to carry, in contempt of all honesty, measures at least as liberal as those which he, as well as they, opposed when proceeding from the Whigs. Will he be mad enough to do the one—will he be base enough to do the other? Can he be a tyrant, or will he be a turncoat? His may be the ambition which moderate men have assigned to him—an ambition prudent and sincere:—His may be a name on which the posterity that reads of these eventful times, will look with approval and respect;—on the other hand, the alternative is not tempting—it is to be deemed the creature of office, and the dupe of the Duke of Wellington! Imagine his situation, rising to support either the measures which must be carried by the soldiers, or those which would have been proposed by the Whigs— bully or hypocrite;—what an alternative for one who can yet be (how few in this age may become the same!) a great man! And this too, mainly from one quality that he has hitherto carried to that degree in which it becomes genius. That quality is Prudence! all his reputation depends on his never being indiscreet! He is in the situation of a prude of a certain age, who precisely because she may be a saint, the world has a double delight in damning as a sinner. Sweet, tempted Innocence, beware the one false step! turn from the old Duke! list not the old Lord Eldon! allow not his Grace of Cumberland (irresistible seducer!) to come too near! O Susanna, Susanna, what lechers these Elders are!

But enough of speculation for the present on an uncertain event. We have only now to look to what is sure and that is a New Parliament.* They hint at the policy

* Since writing the above, it seems to be a growing opinion among men of all parties, that if Sir Robert Peel join the Ministers, they *will* meet Parliament—for the sake of mutual explanations!—But the Duke is a prompt man, and loves to take us by surprise—we must be prepared!

Addendum to Third Edition.—And now we have additional reason to be prepared, and to acknowledge how little to-morrow can depend on the reports of to-day.

"We owe it to our readers to acknowledge that we have much less hope of a dissolution of parliament being dispensed with than we had on Saturday.

of trying this: let them! I think they would dissolve us the second day of our meeting!

And now, my Lord, deviating from the usual forms of correspondence, permit me, instead of addressing your Lordship, to turn for a few moments to our mutual friends—the Electors of England.

I wish them clearly and distinctly to understand, the grounds and the results of the contest we are about to try. I do not write these lines for the purpose of converting the Conservatives—far from me so futile an attempt. With one illustrious example before our eyes, what man of sense can dream of the expediency of attempting to convert our foes? I write only to that great multitude of men of all grades of property and rank, who returned to the Reformed Parliament its vast reforming majority. Thank God, that electoral body is as yet unaltered. Who knows, if it now neglect its duty, how long it may remain the same! I have before spoken, Electors of England, of what seems to me likely to be your conduct. But let us enter into that speculation somewhat more minutely. There are some who tell us that you are indifferent to the late changes, and careless of the result,—who laugh at the word "Crisis" and disown its application. Are you yourselves, then, thoroughly awakened to your position, to the mighty destinies at your command? I will not dwell at length upon the fearful anxiety with which your decision will be looked for in Foreign Nations; for we must confess, that engrossed as we have lately been in domestic affairs, Foreign Nations have for us but a feeble and lukewarm interest. But we are still the great English people, the slightest change in whose constitutional policy vibrates from corner to corner of the civilized world. We are still that people, who have grown great, not by the extent of our possessions, not by the fertility of our soil, not by the wild ambition of our conquests; but, by the success of our

The caballing of the metropolitan members, and a repetition of the kind of display made on Friday at Stroud, may render it impossible for any government, not prepared to sacrifice the King, to go on with the present House of Commons."—(*Standard*, Nov. 24.) Let other than the metropolitan members cabal! Let there be other displays than those at Stroud. We see the force attached to these demonstrations; we have no cause to fear a dissolution: the threat does not awe us;—we would not sacrifice the King, and therefore we would rescue him from his advisers.

commerce, and the preservation of our liberties. The influence of England has been that of a moral power, not derived from regal or oligarchic, or aristocratic ascendancy; but from the enterprise and character of her people. We are the Great Middle Class of Europe. When Napoleon called us a *bourgeois* nation, in one sense of the word he was right. What the middle class is to us, that we are to the world!—a part of the body politic of civilization, remote alike from Ochlocracy* and Despotism, and drawing its dignity—its power—its very breath—from its freedom. The Duke of Wellington and his band are to be in office : for when we are met with the cry, "Perhaps the Duke himself will not take office at all," what matters it to us whether he be before the stage or behind the scenes— whether he represent the borough himself, or appoint his nominees—the votes will be the same !—The Duke and his band are to be in office ! what to the last hour have been their foreign politics ?—wherever tyranny the grossest was to be defended—wherever liberty the most moderate was to be assailed—there have they lent their aid ! The King of Holland trampling on his subjects was "our most ancient ally," whom "nothing but the worst revolutionary doctrines could induce us to desert." Charles X. vainly urging his Ordinances against the Parliament and the Press at the point of the bayonet, was an "injured monarch," and the people "a rebellious mob." The despotism of Austria is an "admirable government"—with Russia it is "insolence" to interfere in behalf of Poland. Miguel himself, blackened by such crimes as the worst period of the Roman empire cannot equal, is eulogized as "the illustrious victim of foreign swords." Not the worst excesses that belong to despotism, from the bonds of the negro to the blood of a people, have been beneath the praises of your present government—not the most moderate resistance that belongs to liberty has escaped their stigma. This is no exaggeration ; chapter and verse, their very speeches are

* Ochlocracy, Mob-rule ; the proper antithesis to democracy, which (though perverted from its true signification) is People-rule. Tories are often great ochlocrats, as their favourite mode of election, in which mobs are bought with beer, can testify. Lord Chandos's celebrated clause in the Reform Bill was ochlocratic. Ochlocracy is the plebeian partner of oligarchy, carrying on the business under another name. The extremes meet, or, as the Eastern proverb informs us, when the serpent wants to seem innocent, it puts its tail in its mouth !

before us, and out of their own mouths do we condemn them. Can we then be insensible, little as we may regard our more subtle relations with foreign states—can we be insensible to the links which bind us with our fellow-creatures; no matter in what region of the globe? Can we feel slightly the universal magnitude of the interests now resting on our resolves? Believe me, wherever the insolence of power is brooding on new restraints, wherever—some men, "in the chamber of dark thought," are forging fetters for other countries or their own—there is indeed a thrill of delight at the accession of the Duke of Wellington! But wherever Liberty struggles successfully, or suffers in vain—wherever Opinion has raised its voice—wherever Enlightenment is at war with Darkness, and Patience rising against Abuse—there will be but one feeling of terror at these changes, and one feeling of anxious hope for the resolution which you, through whose votes speaks the voice of England, may form at this awful crisis. Shall that decision be unworthy of you?

If we pass from foreign nations to Ireland, (which unhappily we have often considered as foreign to us,) what can we expect from the Duke of Wellington's tender mercies? Recollect that there will be no peace for England while Ireland remains as it is. Cabinet after Cabinet has been displaced, change after change has convulsed us, measures the most vital to England have been unavoidably postponed to discussion on Bills for Ireland; night upon night, session upon session of precious time have been thrown away, because we have not done for Ireland what common sense would dictate to common justice. I have just returned from that country. I have seen matters with my own eyes. Having assuredly no sympathy with the question of Repeal, I have not sought the judgment of Repealers—of the two, I have rather solicited that of the Orangemen: for knowing by what arguments misgovernment can be assailed, I was anxious to learn, in its stronghold, by what arguments misgovernment can be defended. And I declare solemnly, that it seems to me the universal sentiment of all parties, that God does not look down upon any corner of the earth in which the people are more supremely wretched, or in which a kind, fostering, and paternal government is more indispensably needed. That people are Catholic. Hear what the Duke of Wellington deems necessary for them.

" The object of the government, (for Ireland,) after the passing of the Roman Catholic Relief Bill, should have been to do all in their power to conciliate—whom ? The Protestants ! Every thing had been granted to the Roman Catholics that they could require ! "—*The Duke of Wellington's Speech. Hansard*, p. 950, vol. xix. 3rd Series. Everything a people groaning under each species of exaction that ever took the name of religion can require ! This statement may delight the Orangemen, but will it content Ireland ? that is the question. As for the Orangemen themselves, with their Christian zeal, and their Mahometan method of enforcing it ;—with their—" here is our Koran," and " there is our sword,"—they remind us only of that ingenious negro, to whom his master, detecting him in some offence, put the customary query—" What, sir, do you never make use of your bible ? "—" Yes, massa, me trap my razor on it sometime ! " So, with these gentlemen, they seem to think that the only use of the bible is to sharpen their steels upon it !

The story of the Negro recalls us to the Colonies : what effect will this change have upon the fate of the late Slave Population ? By our last accounts, the managers, instead of co-operating with the local authorities, were rather striving to exasperate the Negroes into conduct, which must produce a failure of that grand experiment of humanity.— The news arrives,—(just before Christmas too,—what a season !) the managers see in office, the very men, who not only opposed the experiment, but who prophesied the failure :—they know well, that if the failure occur, it is not *to them*, that the new government will impute the blame— they know well that a prophet is rarely displeased with the misfortunes he foretells. Is there no danger in all this ? And shall we be told that this is no crisis ? that there is nothing critical in these changes—nothing to reverse or even to affect our relations with Ireland, the Colonies, and the Continent—nothing that we should lament, and nothing that we should fear ?

And now, looking only to ourselves, is there nothing critical in the state of England ?

You must remember that whatever parliament you elect

will have the right of remodelling that parliament! The same legislative power that reformed can un-reform. If you give to the Duke of Wellington a majority in the House of Commons, you give him the whole power of this Empire for six years. If a liberal House of Commons should ever go too far, you have a King and a House of Lords to stop the progress. If a conservative House of Commons should go too far in the opposite extreme, who will check its proceedings? You may talk of public opinion—you may talk of resistance—but when your three branches of the legislature are against you, with what effect could you resist? You might talk vehemently—could you act successfully;—when you were no longer supported by your representatives,—when to act would be to rebel! The law and the army would be both against you. How can you tell to what extent the one might be stretched or the other increased? Vainly then would you say, "In our next parliament we will be wiser;" in your next parliament the people might be no longer the electors! There cannot be a doubt but that, if the parliament summoned by the Duke be inclined to support the Duke, the provisions of the Reform Bill will be changed. Slight alterations in the franchise—raising it where men are free, lowering it where men can be intimidated, making it different for towns and for agricultural districts, working out in detail the principles of Lord Chandos, may suffice to give you a constituency of slaves. This is no idle fear—the Reform Transformed will be the first play the new company will act, if you give them a stage—it is a piece they have got by heart! Over and over again have they said at their clubs, in public and in private, that the Reform Bill ought to be altered.* They

---

* And Lord Strangford seems to speak out pretty boldly at the Ashford dinner. "It was true that among the institutions of the country, there was something that might be amended and improved, but there was much more that required to be placed in its pristine state of purity. That that would come to pass he felt sure, when he saw so many around him thinking as he did," &c. Pristine state of purity! But what so pure as the rotten boroughs? What so pure as the old parliamentary system? And if the restoration of these immaculate blessings depends upon seeing "many around him who thought as he did," where will his Lordship find those of that philosophy, except in the party now in power? It matters not what Lord Strangford meant should be restored to its pristine purity. He may say it was not the old parliamentary system. What was it then? Is there a single thing which the Reformed Parliament has altered that the people wish to see restored to "its pristine purity?" But then we are told that

may now disavow any such intention. Calling themselves reformers, they may swear to protect reform. But how can you believe them ? "Abu Rafe is witness to the fact, but who will be witness for Abu Rafe ?" * By their own confessions, if they call themselves reformers, they would be liars ; if they are false in one thing, will they not be false in another? Are they to be trusted because they own they have been insincere ? If we desire to know in what light even the most honourable Tories consider public promises, shall we forget Sir George Murray and the dissenters ? Do not fancy they will not hazard an attempt on your liberties—they will hazard it, if you place the House of Commons in their hands. Whatever their fault, it is not that of a want of courage. You talk of Public Opinion—history tells us that public opinion can be kept down. It is the nature of slavery, that as it creeps on, it accustoms men to its yoke. They may feel, but they are not willing always to struggle. Where was the iron-hearted Public Opinion, that confronted the first Charles, threw its shield round the person of Hampden, abolished the star-chamber, and vindicated the rights of England, when, but a few years afterwards, a less accomplished and a more unprincipled monarch, sent Sydney to the block—judges decided against law—Parliament itself was suspended—and the tyrant of England was the pensioner of France ? The *power* of public opinion woke afterwards in the reign of James II. but from how shameful a slumber—and to what even greater perils than that of domestic tyranny, had we not been exposed in the interval ! Nothing but the forbearance of the Continent itself saved us from falling a prey to whatever vigorous despot might have conceived the design. With the same angry, but impotent dejection with which Public Opinion beheld the country spoiled of its Parliament —its martyrs consigned to the block—its governors harlots, and its King a hireling—it saw, unavenged, the Dutch fleet riding up the Thames,—the war-ships of England burnt before the very eyes of her Capital,—and "the nation," to

we are not to judge the Duke by the language of his supporters. By what are we to judge of him then ? Either by their language or his own : it is quite indifferent which. But perhaps Tory speeches are like witches' prayers, and are to be read backwards !

* Gibbon.

quote even Hume's courtly words, "though the King ever appeared but in sport (!) exposed to the ruin and ignominy of a foreign conquest." Happily, Austria then was not as it is now—profound in policy, stern in purpose, indomitable in its hate to England; Russia was not looking abroad for conquests, aspiring to the Indian Empire, and loathing the freemen who dare to interfere for Poland. We were saved, but not by your Public Opinion! You may boast of the nineteenth century, and say, such things cannot happen to-day; but the men of Cromwell's time boasted equally of the spirit of the seventeenth, and were equally confident, that liberty was eternal? And even at this day have we not seen in France, how impotent is mere opinion? Have not the French lost all the fruits of their Revolution? Are not the Ordinances virtually carried? and why? Because the French parted with the power out of their own hands, under the idea that public opinion was a power sufficient in itself? When the man first persuaded the horse to try (by way of experiment) the saddle and bridle, what was his argument?—"My good friend, you are much stronger than I am; you can kick me off again if you don't like me—your will is quite enough to dislodge me;—come—the saddle—it is but a ride, recollect!—come, open your mouth—Lord have mercy, what fine teeth!—how you could bite if I displeased you. So so, old boy!"—What's the moral? The man is riding the horse to this day!—Public opinion is but the expression of the prevalent power. The people have now the power, and public opinion is its voice; let them give away the power, and what is opinion?—*vox*, (indeed,) *et præterea nihil*—the voice and—nothing more!

It is madness itself in you, who have now the option of confirming or rejecting the Duke of Wellington's government, to hesitate in your choice. They tell you to try the men; have you not tried them before? Has not the work of reform been solely to undo what they have done? If your late governments could not proceed more vigorously, *who opposed them ?*

> " Hark! in the lobby hear a lion roar;
> Say, Mr. Speaker, shall we shut the door?
> Or, Mr. Speaker, shall we let him in,
> To—try if we can turn him out again!"

You may say, that amongst the multiplicity of candidates

who present themselves, and amongst the multiplicity of their promises, you may be unable to decide who will be your friends, who not. You have one test that cannot fail you. Ask them if they will support the Duke of Wellington. If they say "Yes, if he reform," you will know that they will support him if he apostatizes. He who sees no dishonour in apostacy, waits but his price to apostatize himself. "Away," said Mr. Canning, long since—"Away with the cant of measures, not men. The idle supposition, that it is the harness, not the horses that draw the chariot along." "In times of difficulty and danger, it is to the energy and character of individuals, that a nation must be indebted for its salvation!"—the energy and character! Doubtless, the Duke has at present energy and character! I grant it; but if he exert in your behalf the energy, will he keep the character? or if he preserve his character, how will you like his energy?

Recollect that it is not for measures which you can foresee that caution is necessary, it is for measures that you *cannot* foresee; it is not for what the Duke may profess to do, but for what he may dare to do, that you must not put yourselves under his command. Be not led away by some vague promises of taking off this tax, and lowering that. The empire is not for sale! We, who gave twenty millions to purchase freedom for the negro, are not to accept a bribe for the barter of our own. One tax too may be taken off, but others may be put on! They may talk to you of the first, but they will say nothing of the last! Malt is a good thing, but even malt may be bought too dear. Did not the Tories blame Lord Althorp for reducing taxation too much? Are they the men likely to empty the Exchequer? To drop a shilling in the street was the old trick of those who wanted to pick your pockets! Remember that you are not fighting the battle between Whigs and Tories; if the Whigs return to office, they must be more than Whigs; you are now fighting for things not men—for the real consequences of your reform. In your last election your gratitude made you fight too much for names; it was enough for your candidates to have served Lord Grey; you must now return those who will serve the people. If you are lukewarm, if you are indifferent, if you succumb, you will deserve the worst. But if you exert yourselves once more, with the same honesty, the same zeal, the same firm and enlightened virtue as two years ago ensured your triumph, —wherever, both now and henceforth, men honour faith, or sympathise with liberty, there will be those who will record your struggle, and rejoice in its success. These are no exaggerated phrases: you may or may not be insensible to the character of the time;—you may or may not be indifferent to the changes that have taken place—but the next election, if Parliament be dissolved by a Tory minister, will make itself a Date in History,—recording one of those ominous conjunctions in " the Old Almanack" by which we calculate the chronology of the human progress.

And, my Lord, that the conduct and the victory of our countrymen will be, as they have been, the one firm and temperate, the other honourable and assured, I do, from my soul, believe. Two years may abundantly suffice to wreck a Government, or convert a King—but scarcely to change a People!

I have the honour to be,

My Lord,

With respect and consideration,

Your Lordship's obedient servant,

E. LYTTON BULWER.

London, Nov. 21, 1834.

CONFESSIONS OF A WATER-PATIENT,[*]

IN A LETTER TO W. HARRISON AINSWORTH, ESQ., EDITOR
OF THE "NEW MONTHLY MAGAZINE."

——◆——

DEAR MR. EDITOR,—I am truly glad to see so worthily
filled the presidency of one of the many chairs which our
republic permits to criticism and letters—a dignity in
which I had the honour to precede you, *sub consule Planco,*
in the good days of William IV. I feel as if there were
something ghost-like in my momentary return to my ancient haunts, no longer in the editorial robe and purple,
but addressing a new chief, and in great part, a new assembly: For the reading public is a creature of rapid
growth—every five years a fresh generation pours forth
from our institutes, our colleges, our schools, demanding,
and filled with, fresh ideas, fresh principles and hopes:
And the seas wash the place where Canute parleyed with
the waves.

All that interested the world, when to me (then Mr.
Editor, now Mr. Editor's humble servant) contributors addressed their articles—hot and seasoned for the month, and
like all good articles to a periodical, " warranted *not* to
keep," have passed away into the lumber-room, where those
old maids, History and Criticism, hoard their scraps and
relics, and where, amidst dust and silence, things old-
fashioned ripen into antique.

The roar of the Reform Bill is still, Fanny Kemble is
Mrs. Butler, the "Hunchback" awaits upon our shelves the
resuscitation of a new *Julia;* poets of promise have become
mute, Rubini sings no more, Macready is in the provinces;
" Punch " frisks it on the jocund throne of Sydney Smith,
and over a domain once parcelled amongst many, reigns
"Boz." Scattered and voiceless the old contributors—a
new hum betrays the changing Babel of a new multitude.

Gliding thus, I say, ghost-like, amidst the present race,
busy and sanguine as the past, I feel that it best suits with
a ghost's dignity, to appear but for an admonitory purpose;
not with the light and careless step of an ordinary visitor,

* [Originally published in 1845 in the "New Monthly Magazine," from
which it was shortly afterwards reprinted as a duodecimo of 98 pages.]

but with meaning stride, and finger upon lip. Ghosts, we know, have appeared to predict death—more gentle I, my apparition would only promise healing, and beckon not to graves and charnels, but to the Hygeian spring.

And now that I am fairly on the ground, let us call to mind, Mr. Editor, the illustrious names which still over-shadow it at once with melancholy and fame. Your post has been filled by men, whose fate precludes the envy which their genius might excite. By Campbell, the high-souled and silver-tongued, and by Hook, from whom jest, and whim, and humour, flowed in so free and riotous a wave, that books confined and narrowed away the stream; to read Hook is to wrong him.

Nor can we think of your predecessors without remembering your rival, Hood, who, as the tree puts forth the most exuberant blossoms the year before its decay, showed the bloom and promise of his genius most when the worm was at the trunk. To us behind the scenes, to us who knew the men, how melancholy the contrast between the fresh and youthful intellect, the worn-out and broken frame; for, despite what I have seen written, Campbell when taken at the right moment, was Campbell ever. Not capable, indeed, towards the last, of the same exertion, if manifested by those poor evidences of what is in us, that books parade, but still as powerful in his great and noble thoughts, in the oral poetry revealed by flashes and winged words, though unrounded into form.

And Hook jested on the bed of death, as none but he could jest. And Hood! who remembers not the tender pathos, the exquisite humanity, which spoke forth from his darkened room? Alas! what prolonged pangs, what heavy lassitude, what death in life did these men endure!

Here we are, Mr. Editor, in these days of cant and jargon, preaching up the education of the mind, forcing our children under melon-frames, and babbling to the labourer and mechanic, "Read, and read, and read," as if God had not given us muscles, and nerves, and bodies, subjected to exquisite pains as pleasures—as if the body were not to be cared for and cultivated as well as the mind; as if health were no blessing instead of that capital good, without which all other blessings—save the hope of health eternal—grow flat and joyless; as if the enjoyment of the world in which we are, was not far more closely linked with our physical than our mental selves; as if we were better than maimed and imperfect men; so long as our nerves are jaded and prostrate, our senses dim and heavy, our relationship with Nature abridged and thwarted by the jaundiced eye, and failing limb, and trembling hand —the apothecary's shop between us and the sun!

For the mind, we admit, that to render it strong and clear, habit and discipline are required;—how deal we (especially we, Mr. Editor, of the London world—we of the literary craft—we of the restless, striving brotherhood) —how deal we with the body? We carry it on with us, as a post-horse, from stage to stage—does it flag? no rest I give it ale or the spur. We begin to feel the frame break under us;—we administer a drug, gain a temporary relief, shift the disorder from one part to another—forget our ailments in our excitements, and when we pause at last, thoroughly shattered, with complaints grown chronic, diseases fastening to the organs, send for the doctors in good earnest, and die as your predecessors and your rival died, under combinations of long-neglected maladies, which could never have been known had we done for the body what we do for the mind—made it strong by discipline, and maintained it firm by habit.

Not alone calling to recollection our departed friends, but looking over the vast field of suffering which those acquainted with the lives of men who think and labour cannot fail to behold around them, I confess, though I have something of Canning's disdain of professed philanthropists, and do not love every knife-grinder as much as if he were my brother—I confess, nevertheless, that I am filled with an earnest pity; and an anxious desire seizes me to communicate to others that simple process of healing and well being which has passed under my own experience, and to which I gratefully owe days no longer weary of the sun, and nights which no longer yearn for and yet dread the morrow.

And now, Mr. Editor, I may be pardoned, I trust, if I illustrate by my own case the system I commend to others.

I have been a workman in my day. I began to write and to toil, and to win some kind of a name, which I had the ambition to improve, while yet little more than a boy. With a strong love for study of books—with yet greater desire to accomplish myself in the knowledge of men, for sixteen years I can conceive no life to have been more filled by occupation than mine. What time was not given to action was given to study; what time not given to study, to action—labour in both! To a constitution naturally far from strong, I allowed no pause nor respite. The wear and tear went on without intermission—the whirl of the wheel never ceased.

Sometimes, indeed, thoroughly overpowered and exhausted, I sought for escape. The physicians said, "Travel," and I travelled. "Go into the country," and I went. But at such attempts at repose all my ailments gathered round me—made themselves far more palpable and felt. I had no resource but to fly from myself—to fly into the other world of books, or thought, or reverie—to live in some state of being less painful than my own. As long as I was always at work it seemed that I had no leisure to be ill. Quiet was my hell.

At length the frame thus long neglected—patched up for awhile by drugs and doctors—put off and trifled with as an intrusive dun—like a dun who is in his rights—brought in its arrears—crushing and terrible—accumulated through long years. Worn out and wasted, the constitution seemed wholly inadequate to meet the demand.

The exhaustion of toil and study had been completed by great anxiety and grief. I had watched with alternate hope and fear the lingering and mournful death-bed of my nearest relation and dearest friend—of the person around whom was entwined the strongest affection my life had known—and when all was over, I seemed scarcely to live myself.

At this time, about the January of 1844, I was thoroughly shattered. The least attempt at exercise exhausted me. The nerves gave way at the most ordinary excitement—a chronic irritation of that vast surface we call the mucous membrane, which had defied for years all medical skill, rendered me continually liable to acute attacks, which from their repetition, and the increased feebleness of my frame, might at any time be fatal. Though free from any organic disease of the heart, its action was morbidly restless and painful. My sleep was without refreshment. At morning I rose more weary than I laid down to rest.

Without fatiguing you and your readers further with the *longa cohors* of my complaints, I pass on to record my struggle to resist them. I have always had a great belief in the power of WILL. What a man determines to do—that in ninety-nine cases out of the hundred I hold that he succeeds in doing. I determined to have some insight into a knowledge I had never attained since manhood—the knowledge of health.

I resolutely put away books and study, sought the airs which the physicians esteemed most healthful, and adopted the strict regimen on which all the children of Esculapius so wisely insist. In short, I maintained the same general habits as to hours, diet (with the exception of wine, which in moderate quantities seemed to me indispensable), and, so far as my strength would allow, of exercise, as I found afterwards instituted at hydropathic establishments.

I dwell on this to forestall in some degree the common remark of persons not well acquainted with the medical agencies of water—that it is to the regular life which water-patients lead, and not to the element itself that they owe their recovery. Nevertheless I found that these changes, however salutary in theory, produced little, if any, practical amelioration in my health.

All invalids know, perhaps, how difficult, under ordinary circumstances, is the alteration of habits from bad to good. The early rising, the walk before breakfast, so delicious in the feelings of freshness and vigour which they bestow upon the strong, often become punishments to the valetudinarian. Headache, langour, a sense of weariness over the eyes, a sinking of the whole system towards noon, which seemed imperiously to demand the dangerous aid of stimulants, were all that I obtained by the morning breeze and the languid stroll by the sea-shore.

The suspension from study only afflicted me with intolerable *ennui*, and added to the profound dejection of the spirits. The brain, so long accustomed to morbid activity, was but withdrawn from its usual occupations to invent horrors and chimeras. Over the pillow, vainly sought two hours before midnight, hovered no golden sleep. The absence of excitement, however unhealthy, only aggravated the symptoms of ill-health.

It was at this time that I met by chance, in the library

at St. Leonard's, with Captain Claridge's work on the "Water Cure," as practised by Priessnitz, at Graafenberg. Making allowance for certain exaggerations therein, which appeared evident to my common sense, enough still remained not only to captivate the imagination and flatter the hopes of an invalid, but to appeal with favour to his sober judgment.

Till then, perfectly ignorant of the subject and the system, except by some such vague stories and good jests as had reached my ears in Germany, I resolved at least to read what more could be said in favour of the *ariston udor*, and examine dispassionately into its merits as a medicament.

I was then under the advice of one of the first physicians of our age. I had consulted half the faculty. I had every reason to be grateful for the attention, and to be confident in the skill of those whose prescriptions had, from time to time, flattered my hopes and enriched the chemist. But the truth must be spoken—far from being better, I was sinking fast. Little remained to me to try in the great volume of the herbal. Seek what I would next, even if a quackery, it certainly might expedite my grave, but it could scarcely render life—at least the external life—more unjoyous.

Accordingly I examined, with such grave thought as a sick man brings to bear upon his case, all the grounds upon which to justify to myself an excursion to the snows of Silesia. But I own that in proportion as I found my faith in the system strengthen, I shrunk from the terrors of this long journey to the rugged region in which the probable lodging would be a labourer's cottage,* and in which the Babel of a hundred languages (so agreeable to the healthful delight in novelty—so appalling to the sickly despondency of a hypochondriac), would murmur and growl over a public table spread with no tempting condiments.

Could I hope to find healing in my own land, and not too far from my own doctors in case of failure, I might indeed

* Let me not disparage the fountain head of the water-cure, the parent institution of the great Preissnitz. I believe many of the earlier hardships complained of at Graafenberg have been removed or amended; and such as remain, are no doubt well compensated by the vast experience and extraordinary tact of a man who will rank hereafter amongst the most illustrious discoverers who have ever benefited the human race.

solicit the watery gods—but the journey. I who scarcely lived through a day without leech or potion!—the long—gelid journey to Graafenberg—I should be sure to fall ill by the way—to be clutched and mismanaged by some German doctor—to deposit my bones in some dismal church-yard on the banks of Father Rhine.

While thus perplexed, I fell in with one of the pamphlets written by Doctor Wilson, of Malvern, and my doubts were solved. Here was an English doctor, who had him-self known more than my own sufferings, who, like myself, had found the pharmacopœia in vain—who had spent ten months at Graafenberg, and left all his complaints behind him—who, fraught with the experience he had acquired, not only in his own person, but from scientific examination of the cases under his eye, had transported the system to our native shores, and who proffered the proverbial salu-brity of Malvern air and its holy springs, to those who, like me, had ranged in vain from simple to mineral, and who had become bold by despair—bold enough to try if health, like truth, lay at the bottom of a well.

I was not then aware that other institutions had been established in England of more or less fame. I saw in Doctor Wilson the first transporter—at least as a physician —of the Silesian system, and did not care to look out for other and later pupils of this innovating German school.

I resolved then to betake myself to Malvern. On my way through town I paused, in the innocence of my heart, to inquire of some of the faculty if they thought the water-cure would suit my case. With one exception, they were unanimous in the vehemence of their denunciations.

Granting even that in some cases, especially of rheuma-tism, hydropathy had produced a cure, to my complaints it was worse than inapplicable—it was highly dangerous—it would probably be fatal. I had not stamina for the treatment—it would fix chronic ailments into organic disease—surely it would be much better to try what I had not yet tried.

What had I not yet tried? A course of prussic acid! Nothing was better for gastrite irritation, which was no doubt the main cause of my suffering! If, however, I were obstinately bent upon so mad an experiment, Doctor Wilson was the last person I should go to. I was not deterred by all these intimidations, nor seduced by the salubrious allurements of the prussic acid under its scientific appellation of hydrocyanic.

A little reflection taught me that the members of a learned profession are naturally the very persons least disposed to favour innovation upon the practices which custom and prescription have rendered sacred in their eyes. A lawyer is not the person to consult upon bold reforms in jurisprudence. A physician can scarcely be expected to own that a Silesian peasant will cure with water the diseases which resist an armament of phials. And with regard to the peculiar objections to Doctor Wilson, I had read in his own pamphlet attacks upon the orthodox practice sufficient to account for—perhaps to justify—the disposition to depreciate him in return.

Still my friends were anxious and fearful; to please them I continued to inquire, though not of physicians, but of patients. I sought out some of those who had gone through the process. I sifted some of the cases of cure cited by Doctor Wilson. I found the account of the patients so encouraging, the cases quoted so authentic, that I grew impatient of the delay. I threw physic to the dogs, and went to Malvern.

It is not my intention, Mr. Editor, to detail the course I underwent. The different resources of water as a medicament are to be found in many works easily to be obtained,* and well worth the study. In this letter I suppose myself to be addressing those as thoroughly unacquainted with the system as I was myself at the first, and I deal, therefore, only in generals.

The first point which impressed and struck me was the extreme and utter innocence of the water-cure in skilful hands—in any hands, indeed, not thoroughly new to the system. Certainly when I went, I believed it to be a kill or cure system. I fancied it must be a very violent remedy —that it doubtless might effect great and magical cures— but that if it failed, it might be fatal.

Now, I speak not alone of my own case, but of the immense number of cases I have seen—patients of all ages— all species and genera of disease—all kinds and conditions

* The works of Drs. Johnson, (of Stansted-Berry,) Weiss, Wilson, Gully, &c., as well as that of Capt. Claridge.

of constitution, when I declare, upon my honour, that I never witnessed one dangerous symptom produced by the water-cure, whether at Doctor Wilson's or the other hydropathic institutions which I afterwards visited.

And though unquestionably fatal consequences might occur from gross mismanagement, and as unquestionably have so occurred at various establishments, I am yet convinced that water in itself is so friendly to the human body, that it requires a very extraordinary degree of bungling, of ignorance, and presumption, to produce results really dangerous; that a regular practitioner does more frequent mischief from the misapplication of even the simplest drugs, than a water doctor of very moderate experience does or can do, by the misapplication of his baths and friction.

And here I must observe, that those portions of the treatment which appear to the uninitiated as the most perilous are really the safest,* and can be applied with the most impunity to the weakest constitutions; whereas those which appear, from our greater familiarity with them, the least startling and most innocuous,† are those which require the greatest knowledge of general pathology and the individual constitution. I shall revert to this part of my subject before I conclude.

The next thing that struck me was the extraordinary ease with which, under this system, good habits are acquired, and bad habits relinquished. The difficulty with which, under orthodox medical treatment, stimulants are abandoned, is here not witnessed.

Patients accustomed for half a century to live hard and high, wine-drinkers, spirit-bibbers, whom the regular physician has sought in vain to reduce to a daily pint of sherry, here voluntarily resign all strong potations, after a day or two cease to feel the want of them, and reconcile themselves to water as if they had drunk nothing else all their lives. Others, who have had recourse for years and years to medicine,—their potion in the morning, their cordial at noon, their pill before dinner, their narcotic at bedtime, cease to require these aids to life, as if by a charm.

Nor this alone. Men to whom mental labour has been

* Such as the wet-sheet packing.
† The plunge-bath—the Douche.

a necessary—who have existed on the excitement of the passions and the stir of the intellect—who have felt, these withdrawn, the prostration of the whole system—the lock to the wheel of the entire machine—return at once to the careless spirits of the boy in his first holiday.

Here lies a great secret; water thus skilfully administered is in itself a wonderful excitement, it supplies the place of all others—it operates powerfully and rapidly upon the nerves, sometimes to calm them, sometimes to irritate, but always to occupy.

Hence follows a consequence which all patients have remarked—the complete repose of the passions during the early stages of the cure; they seem laid asleep as if by enchantment. The intellect shares the same rest; after a short time, mental exertion becomes impossible; even the memory grows far less tenacious of its painful impressions, cares and griefs are forgotten; the sense of the present absorbs the past and future; there is a certain freshness of youth which pervades the spirits, and lives upon the enjoyment of the actual hour.

Thus the great agents of our mortal wear and tear—the passions and the mind—calmed into strange rest,—Nature seems to leave the body to its instinctive tendency, which is always towards recovery. All that interests and amuses is of a healthful character; exercise, instead of being an unwilling drudgery, becomes the inevitable impulse of the frame braced and invigorated by the element. A series of reactions is continually going on—the willing exercise produces refreshing rest, the refreshing rest willing exercise.

The extraordinary effect which water taken early in the morning produces on the appetite is well known amongst those who have tried it, even before the water-cure was thought of; an appetite it should be the care of the skilful doctor to check into moderate gratification; the powers of nutrition become singularly strengthened, the blood grows rich and pure—the constitution is not only amended—it undergoes a change.*

* Doctor Wilson observed to me once, very truly I think, that many regular physicians are beginning to own the effect of water as a stimulant who yet do not perceive its far more complicated and beneficial effects as an alterative. I may here remark, that eminent physicians are already borrowing largely from the details of the water-cure—recommending water to be drunk

The safety of the system, then, struck me first;—its power of replacing by healthful stimulants the morbid ones it withdrew, whether physical or moral, surprised me next; that which thirdly impressed me was no less contrary to all my preconceived notions. I had fancied that whether good or bad, the treatment must be one of great hardship, extremely repugnant and disagreeable. I wondered at myself to find how soon it became so associated with pleasurable and grateful feelings as to dwell upon the mind amongst the happiest passages of existence.

For my own part, despite all my ailments, or whatever may have been my cares, I have ever found exquisite pleasure in that sense of *being* which is, as it were, the conscience, the mirror, of the soul. I have known hours of as much and as vivid happiness as perhaps can fall to the lot of man; but amongst all my most brilliant recollections I can recall no periods of enjoyment at once more hilarious and serene than the hours spent on the lonely hills of Malvern —none in which nature was so thoroughly possessed and appreciated.

The rise from a sleep sound as childhood's—the impatient rush into the open air, while the sun was fresh, and the birds first sang—the sense of an unwonted strength in every limb and nerve, which made so light of the steep ascent to the holy spring—the delicious sparkle of that morning draught—the green terrace on the brow of the mountain, with the rich landscape wide and far below—the breeze that once would have been so keen and biting, now but exhilarating the blood, and lifting the spirits into religious joy; and this keen sentiment of present pleasure rounded by a hope sanctioned by all I felt in myself, and nearly all that I witnessed in others—that that very present was but the step—the threshold—into an unknown and delightful region of health and vigour;—a disease and a care dropping from the frame and the heart at every stride.

But here I must pause to own that if on the one hand the danger and discomforts of the cure are greatly ex-

fasting—the use of the sitz, or hip-bath, &c. But these, however useful as aids in the treatment of maladies, cannot comprehend that extraordinary alterative which is produced by the various and complicated agencies of water, brought systematically, unintermittingly, and for a considerable period, to bear, not only upon the complaint, but the constitution.

aggerated (exaggerated is too weak a word)—so, on the other hand, as far as my own experience, which is perhaps not inconsiderable, extends, the enthusiastic advocates of the system have greatly misrepresented the duration of the curative process. I have read and heard of chronic diseases of long standing cured permanently in a very few weeks. I candidly confess that I have seen none such. I have, it is true, witnessed many chronic diseases perfectly cured—diseases which had been pronounced incurable by the first physicians, but the cure has been long and fluctuating.

Persons so afflicted who try this system must arm themselves with patience. The first effects of the process are indeed usually bracing, and inspire such feelings of general well-being, that some think they have only to return home, and carry out the cure partially, to recover. A great mistake!—the alterative effects begin long after the bracing—a disturbance in the constitution takes place, prolonged more or less, and not till that ceases does the cure really begin.

Not that the peculiar "crisis," sought for so vehemently by the German water-doctors, and usually under their hands manifested by boils and eruptions, is at all a necessary part of the cure—it is, indeed, as far as I have seen, of rare occurrence—but a critical action, not single, not confined to one period, or one series of phenomena, is at work, often undetected by the patient himself, during a considerable (and that the later) portion of the cure in most patients where the malady has been grave, and where the recovery becomes permanent. During this time the patient should be under the eye of his water-doctor.

To conclude my own case: I stayed some nine or ten weeks at Malvern, and business, from which I could not escape, obliging me then to be in the neighbourhood of town, I continued the system seven weeks longer under Doctor Weiss, at Petersham; during this latter period the agreeable phenomena which had characterised the former, the cheerfulness, the *bien être,* the consciousness of returning health vanished; and were succeeded by great irritation of the nerves, extreme fretfulness, and the usual characteristics of the constitutional disturbance to which I have referred. I had every reason, however, to be satisfied with the care and skill of Doctor Weiss, who fully deserves the reputation he has acquired, and the attachment entertained towards him by his patients; nor did my judgment ever despond or doubt of the ultimate benefits of the process.

I emerged at last from these operations in no very portly condition. I was blanched and emaciated—washed out like a thrifty housewife's gown—but neither the bleaching nor the loss of weight had in the least impaired my strength; on the contrary, all the muscles had grown as hard as iron, and I was become capable of great exercise without fatigue; my cure was not effected, but I was compelled to go into Germany.

On my return homewards I was seized with a severe cold, which rapidly passed into high fever. Fortunately I was within reach of Doctor Schmidt's magnificent hydropathic establishment at Boppart; thither I caused myself to be conveyed; and now I had occasion to experience the wonderful effect of the water-cure in acute cases; slow in chronic disease, its beneficial operation in acute is immediate. In twenty-four hours all fever had subsided, and on the third day I resumed my journey, relieved from every symptom that had before prognosticated a tedious and perhaps alarming illness.

And now came gradually, yet perceptibly, the good effects of the system I had undergone; flesh and weight returned; the sense of health became conscious and steady; I had every reason to bless the hour when I first sought the springs of Malvern. And, here I must observe, that it often happens that the patient makes but slight apparent improvement, when under the cure, compared with that which occurs subsequently. A water-doctor of repute at Brussels, indeed, said frankly to a grumbling patient, "I do not expect you to be well while here—it is only on leaving me that you will know if I have cured you."

It is as the frame recovers from the agitation it undergoes, that it gathers round it powers utterly unknown to it before—as the plant watered by the rains of one season, betrays in the next the effect of the grateful dews.

I had always suffered so severely in winter, that the severity of our last one gave me apprehensions, and I resolved to seek shelter from my fears at my beloved Malvern. I here passed the most inclement period of the winter, not only perfectly free from the colds, rheums, and catarrhs, which had hitherto visited me with the snows, but in the enjoyment of excellent health; and I am persuaded that for those who are delicate, and who suffer much during the winter, there is no place where the cold is so little felt as at a water-cure establishment.

I am persuaded, also, and in this I am borne out by the experience of most water-doctors, that the cure is most rapid and effectual during the cold season—from autumn through the winter. I am thoroughly convinced that con-sumption in its earlier stages can be more easily cured, and the predisposition more permanently eradicated by a winter spent at Malvern, under the care of Doctor Wilson, than by the timorous flight to Pisa or Madeira. It is by harden-ing rather than defending the tissues that we best secure them from disease.

And now, to sum up, and to dismiss my egotistical re-velations;—I desire in no way to overcolour my own case; I do not say that when I first went to the water-cure I was afflicted with any disease immediately menacing to life—I say only that I was in that prolonged and chronic state of ill-health, which made life at the best extremely precarious —I do not say that I had any malady which the faculty could pronounce incurable—I say only that the most eminent men of the faculty had failed to cure me. I do not even now affect to boast of a perfect and complete deliverance from all my ailments—I cannot declare that a constitution naturally delicate has been rendered Herculean, or that the wear and tear of a whole manhood have been thoroughly repaired.

What might have been the case had I not taken the cure at intervals, had I remained at it steadily for six or eight months without interruption, I cannot do more than con-jecture, but so strong is my belief that the result would have been completely successful, that I promise myself, whenever I can spare the leisure, a long renewal of the system.

These admissions made, what have I gained meanwhile to justify my eulogies and my gratitude?—an immense accumulation of the capital of health. Formerly, it was my favourite and querulous question to those who saw much of me, " Did you ever know me twelve hours without pain or illness?" Now, instead of these being my constant companions, they are but my occasional visitors. I compare my old state and my present to the poverty of a man who has a shilling in his pocket, and whose poverty is therefore a struggle for life, with the occasional distresses of a man of £5000 a year, who sees but an appendage endangered, or a luxury abridged.

All the good that I have gained, is wholly unlike what I have ever derived either from medicine or the German mineral baths: in the first place, it does not relieve a single malady alone, it pervades the whole frame; in the second place, unless the habits are intemperate, it does not wear off as we return to our ordinary pursuits, so that those who make fair experiment of the system towards, or even after, the season of middle age, may, without exaggeration, find in the latter period of life (so far as freedom from suffering, and the calm enjoyment of physical being are concerned) a second—a younger youth! And it is this profound conviction which has induced me to volunteer these details, in the hope (I trust a pure and kindly one) to induce those, who more or less have suffered as I have done, to fly to the same rich and bountiful resources.

We ransack the ends of the earth for drugs and minerals —we extract our potions from the deadliest poisons—but around us and about us, Nature, the great mother proffers the Hygeian fount, unsealed and accessible to all. Wherever the stream glides pure, wherever the spring sparkles fresh, there, for the vast proportion of the maladies which Art produces, Nature yields the benignant healing.

It remains for me to say, merely as an observer, and solely with such authority as an observer altogether disinterested, but, of course, without the least pretence to professional science, may fairly claim, what class of diseases I have seen least, and what most, tractable to the operations of the water-cure, and how far enthusiasts appear to me to have over-estimated, how far sceptics have under-valued the effects of water as a medicament.

There are those (most of the water doctors especially) who contend that all medicine by drugs is unnecessary— that water internally and outwardly applied suffices, under skilful management, for all complaints—that the time will come when the drug doctor will cease to receive a fee, when the apothecary will close his shop, and the water-cure bo adopted in every hospital and by every family.

Dreams and absurdities! Even granting that the water-cure were capable of all the wonders ascribed to it, its process is so slow in most chronic cases—it usually requires such complete abstraction from care and business—it takes the active man so thoroughly out of his course of life, that a vast proportion of those engaged in worldly pursuits cannot hope to find the requisite leisure, There are also a large number of complaints (perhaps the majority) which yield so easily to a sparing use of drugs under a moderately competent practitioner, that the convenient plan of sending to the next chemist for your pill or potion can never be superseded, nor can I think it desirable that it should be. Moreover, as far as I have seen, there are complaints curable by medicine which the water-cure utterly fails to reach.

The disorders wherein hydropathy appears to me to be the least effectual are, first, neuralgic pains, especially the monster pain of the Tic Doloreux. Not one instance of a cure in the latter by hydropathy has come under my own observation, and I have only heard of one authentic case of recovery from it by that process. Secondly, paralysis of a grave character in persons of an advanced age. Thirdly, in tubercular consumption. As may be expected, in this stage of that melancholy disease, the water-cure utterly fails to restore, but I have known it even here prolong life, beyond all reasonable calculation, and astonishingly relieve the more oppressive symptoms.

In all cases where the nervous exhaustion is great, and of long standing, and is accompanied with obstinate hypochondria; hydropathy, if successful at all, is very slow in its benefits, and the patience of the sufferer is too often worn out before the favourable turn takes place. I have also noticed that obstinate and deep-rooted maladies in persons otherwise of very athletic frames seem to yield much more tardily to the water-cure than similar complaints in more delicate constitutions; so that you will often see, of two persons afflicted with the same genera of complaints, the feeble and fragile one recover ,before the stout man with Atlantic shoulders evinces one symptom of amelioration. I must add, too, generally, that where the complaint is not

functional, but clearly organic, I should deceive the patient
if I could bid him hope from water more than what drugs
may effect—viz., palliatives and relief. But medical
science is not always unerring in its decisions on organic
complaints, and many that have been pronounced to be
such, yield to the searching and all penetrating influences
of water.

Those cases, on the other hand, in which the water-cure
seems an absolute panacea, and in which the patient may
commence with the most sanguine hopes, are, First, rheu-
matism, however prolonged, however complicated. In this
the cure is usually rapid—nearly always permament.
Secondly, gout.

Here its efficacy is little less startling to appearance than
in the former case; it seems to take up the disease by the
roots; it extracts the peculiar acid, which often appears in
discolorations upon the sheets used in the application, or
is ejected in other modes. But here, judging always from
cases subjected to my personal knowledge, I have not seen
instances to justify the assertion of some water doctors
that returns of the disease do not occur. The predisposition—the tendency, has appeared to me to remain. The
patient is liable to relapses—but I have invariably found
them far less frequent, less lengthened, and readily susceptible of simple and speedy cure, especially if the habits
remain temperate.

Thirdly, that wide and grisly family of affliction classed
under the common name of *dyspepsia*. All derangements
of the digestive organs, imperfect powers of nutrition—
the *malaise* of an injured stomach, appear precisely the
complaints on which the system takes firmest hold, and in
which it effects those cures that convert existence from a
burden into a blessing.

Hence it follows that many nameless and countless complaints proceeding from derangement of the stomach, cease
as that great machine is restored to order. I have seen
disorders of the heart which have been pronounced organic
by no inferior authorities of the profession, disappear in
an incredibly short time—cases of incipient consumption,
in which the seat is in the nutritious powers; hæmorrhages,
and various congestions, shortness of breath, habitual
fainting-fits, many of what are called improperly nervous

complaints, but which, in reality, are radiations from the main ganglionic spring; the disorders produced by the abuse of powerful medicines, especially mercury and iodine, the loss of appetite, the dulled sense, and the shaking hand of intemperance, skin complaints, and the dire scourge of scrofula—all these seem to obtain from hydropathy relief —nay, absolute and unqualified cure, beyond not only the means of the most skilful drug doctor, but the hopes of the most sanguine patient.*

The cure may be divided into two branches—the process for acute complaints—that for chronic; I have just referred to the last. And great as are there its benefits, they seem commonplace beside the effect the system produces in acute complaints. Fever, including the scarlet and the typhus, influenza, measles, small-pox, the sudden and rapid disorders of children, are cured with a simplicity and pre-cision which must, I am persuaded, sooner or later, render the resources of the hydropathist the ordinary treatment for such acute complaints in the hospitals.

The principal remedy here employed by the water-doctor is the wet-sheet packing, which excites such terror amongst the uninitiated, and which, of all the curatives adopted by hydropathy, is unquestionably the safest—the one that can be applied without danger to the greatest variety of cases, and which I do not hesitate to aver can rarely, if ever, be misapplied in any cases where the pulse is hard and high, and the skin dry and burning.

I have found in conversation so much misapprehension of this very easy and very luxurious remedy, that I may be pardoned for re-explaining what has been explained so often.   It is not, as people persist in supposing, that patients are put into wet sheets and there left to shiver. The sheets, after being saturated, are well wrung out— the patient quickly wrapped in them—several blankets tightly bandaged round, and a feather-bed placed at top;

* Amongst other complaints, I may add dropsy, which, in its simple state, and not as the crowning symptom of a worn-out constitution, I have known most successfully treated; cases of slight paralysis; and I have witnessed two instances of partial blindness, in which the sight was restored. I have never seen deafness cured by hydropathy, though I believe that one of the best German treatises on the Water Cure, at Graafenberg, was written by a Prus-sian officer, whom Preissnitz relieved from that not least cheerless of human infirmities.

thus, especially where there is the least fever, the first momentary chill is promptly succeeded by a gradual and vivifying warmth, perfectly free from the irritation of dry heat—a delicious sense of ease is usually followed by sleep more agreeable than anodynes ever produced. It seems a positive cruelty to be relieved from this magic girdle in which pain is lulled and fever cooled, and watchfulness lapped in slumber.

The bath which succeeds, refreshes and braces the skin, which the operation relaxed and softened. They only who have tried this, after fatigue or in fever, can form the least notion of its pleasurable sensations, or of its extraordinary efficacy; nor is there anything startling or novel in its theory.

In hospitals, now, water-dressings are found the best poultice to an inflamed member; this expansion of the wet dressing is a poultice to the whole inflamed surface of the body. It does not differ greatly, except in its cleanliness and simplicity, from the old remedy of the ancients—the wrapping the body in the skins of animals newly slain, or placing it on dunghills, or immersing it, as now in Germany, in the soft slough of mud-baths.* Its theory is that of warmth and moisture, those friendliest agents to inflammatory disorders.

In fact, I think it the duty of every man, on whom the lives of others depend, to make himself acquainted with at least this part of the water-cure :—the wet sheet is the true life-preserver. In the large majority of sudden inflammatory complaints, the doctor at a distance, prompt measures indispensable, it will at the least arrest the disease, check the fever, till, if you prefer the drugs, the drugs can come—the remedy is at hand wherever you can find a bed and a jug of water ; and whatever else you may apprehend after a short visit to a hydropathic establishment, your fear of that bugbear—the wet sheet—is the first you banish.

The only cases, I believe, where it can be positively mischievous is where the pulse scarcely beats—where the vital

* A very eminent London physician, opposed generally to the water-cure, told me that he had effected a perfect cure in a case of inveterate leprosy, by swathing the patient in wet lint covered with oil skin. This *is* the wet sheet packing, but there are patients who would take kindly to wet lint, and shudder at the idea of a wet sheet!

sense is extremely low—where the inanition of the frame forbids the necessary reaction;—in cholera, and certain disorders of the chest and bronchia; otherwise at all ages, from the infant to the octogenarian, it is equally applicable, and in most acute cases, equally innocent.

Hydropathy being thus rapidly beneficial in acute disorders, it follows naturally that it will be quick as a cure in chronic complaints in proportion as acute symptoms are mixed with them, and slowest where such complaints are dull and lethargic—it will be slowest also where the nervous exhaustion is the greatest. With children, its effects can scarcely be exaggerated; in them, the nervous system, not weakened by toil, grief, anxiety, and intemperance, lends itself to the gracious element as a young plant to the rains.

When I now see some tender mother coddling, and physicking, and preserving from every breath of air, and swaddling in flannels, her pallid little ones, I long to pounce upon the callow brood, and bear them to the hills of Malvern, and the diamond fountain of St. Anne's—with what rosy faces and robust limbs I promise they shall return — alas! I promise and preach in vain — the family apothecary is against me, and the progeny are doomed to rhubarb and the rickets.

The water-cure as yet has had this evident injustice,—the patients resorting to it have mostly been desperate cases. So strong a notion prevails that it is a desperate remedy, that they only who have found all else fail have dragged themselves to the Bethesda Pools. That all thus not only abandoned by hope and the College, but weakened and poisoned by the violent medicines absorbed into their system for a score or so of years,—that all should not recover is not surprising!

The wonder is that the number of recoveries should be so great;—that every now and then we should be surprised by the man whose untimely grave we predicted when we last saw him meeting us in the streets ruddy and stalwart, fresh from the springs of Graafenberg, Boppart, Petersham, or Malvern.

The remedy is not desperate; it is simpler, I do not say than any dose, but than any course of medicine—it is infinitely more agreeable—it admits no remedies for the complaints which are inimical to the constitution. It bequeaths none of the maladies consequent on blue pill and mercury —on purgatives and drastics—on iodine and aconite—on leeches and the lancet. If it cures your complaint, it will assuredly strengthen your whole frame; if it fails to cure your complaint, it can scarcely fail to improve your general system.

As it acts, or ought, scientifically treated, to act, first on the system, lastly on the complaint, placing nature herself in the way to throw off the disease, so it constantly happens that the patients at a hydropathic establishment will tell you that the disorder for which they came is not removed, but that in all other respects their health is better than they ever remember it to have been.

Thus, I would not only recommend it to those who are sufferers from some grave disease, but to those who require merely the fillip, the alterative, or the bracing which they now often seek in vain in country air or a watering place. For such, three weeks at Malvern will do more than three months at Brighton or Boulogne; for at the water-cure the whole life is one remedy; the hours, the habits, the discipline — not incompatible with gaiety and cheerfulness (the spirits of hydropathists are astounding, and in high spirits all things are amusement) tend perforce to train the body to the highest state of health of which it is capable.

Compare this life, O merchant, O trader, O man of business, escaping to the sea-shore, with that which you there lead — with your shrimps and your shell-fish, and your wine and your brown stout—with all which counteracts in the evening, the good of your morning dip and your noonday stroll.

What, I own, I should envy most, are the feelings of the robust, healthy man, only a little knocked down by his city cares or his town pleasures, after his second week at Dr. Wilson's establishment—yea, how I should envy the exquisite pleasure which he would derive from that robustness made clear and sensible to him;—the pure taste, the iron muscles, the exuberant spirits, the overflowing sense of life.

If even to the weak and languid the water-cure gives hours of physical happiness which the pleasures of the grosser senses can never bestow, what would it give to the strong man, from whose eye it has but to lift the light film

—in whose mechanism, attuned to joy, it but brushes away the grain of dust, or oils the solid wheel!

I must bring my letter to a close. I meant to address it through you, Mr. Editor, chiefly to our brethern—the over-jaded sons of toil and letters—behind whom I see the warning shades of departed martyrs. But it is applicable to all who ail—to all who would not only cure a complaint, but strengthen a system and prolong a life.

To such, who will so far attach value to my authority, that they will acknowledge, at least, I am no interested witness—for I have no institution to establish—no profession to build up—I have no eye to fees, my calling is but that of an observer—as an observer only do I speak, it may be with enthusiasm—but enthusiasm built on experience and prompted by sympathy ;—to such, then, as may listen to me, I give this recommendation : pause if you please—inquire if you will—but do not consult your doctor. I have no doubt he is a most honest, excellent man—but you cannot expect a doctor of drugs to say other than that doctors of water are but quacks.

Do not consult your doctor whether you shall try hydropathy, but find out some intelligent persons in whose shrewdness you can confide — who have been patients themselves at a hydropathic establishment. Better still, go for a few days—the cost is not much—into some such institution yourself, look round, talk to the patients, examine with your own eyes, hear with your own ears, before you adventure the experiment. Become a witness before you are a patient; if the evidence does not satisfy you, turn and flee.

But if you venture, venture with a good heart and a stout faith. Hope, but not with presumption. Do not fancy that the disorder which has afflicted you for ten years ought to be cured in ten days. Beware, above all, lest, alarmed by some phenomena which the searching element produces, you have recourse immediately to drugs to disperse them. The water-boils, for instance, which are sometimes, as I have before said, but by no means frequently, a critical symptom of the cure, are, in all cases that I have seen, cured easily by water, but may become extremely dangerous in the hands of your apothecary.*

* I have no prejudice, as I have before implied, against the *use* of drugs,

Most of the few solitary instances that have terminated fatally, to the prejudice of the water-cure, have been those in which the patient has gone from water to drugs. It is the axiom of the system, that water only cures what water produces. Do not leave a hydropathic establishment in the time of any " crisis," however much you may be panic-stricken. Hold the doctor responsible for getting you out of what he gets you into; and if your doctor be discreetly chosen, take my word he will do it.

Do not begin to carry on the system at home, and under any eye but that of an experienced hydropathist. After you know the system, and the doctor knows you, the curative process may probably be continued at your own house with ease—but the commencement must be watched, and if a critical action ensues when you are at home, return to the only care that can conduct it safely to a happy issue.

When at the institution, do not let the example of other patients tempt you to overdo—to drink more water, or take more baths than are prescribed to you. Above all, never let the eulogies which many will pass upon the *douche* (the popular bath), tempt you to take it on the sly, unknown to your adviser. The *douche* is dangerous when the body is

though, despite their more merciful and sparing administration during the last twenty years, I venture, with such diffidence as becomes one practised upon, not practising, to hint an opinion, that they are still applied more frequently than is warranted by their success on the complaint, or their effect on the constitution. But I am quite sure that a patient can rarely, with impunity, be at once under a water doctor and a drug doctor; and that the passage from the first to the last, requires the greatest nicety and caution. A physician, however skilful, who not only has not witnessed, but is inclined to deride that commotion which is produced in the system, especially on the nerves, by vigorous hydropathic treatment, can scarcely be aware of its nature and extent, nor how frequently medicines, quite innocuous with an ordinary patient, may become dangerous, misapplied to one fresh from a long course of hydropathy. Dr. Weeding, of Ryde, it is true, sometimes unites drugs with the water-cure. As I never witnessed his treatment, so I can say nothing as to its effects. But granting them to be such as to warrant his departure from hydropathic theory and practice, it is one question whether a water-doctor, thoroughly acquainted with his own system, and minutely studying its effects on a particular patient, may or not, with advantage, occasionally administer drugs, and another question, whether a physician, wholly unacquainted with the water-cure, can be reasonably expected to deal, from his ordinary pathological experience, however great, with the peculiar symptoms produced by a system of which he knows nothing, or with a constitution rendered by the same system acutely sensitive to drugs, and in which a critical excitement, wholly out of his range of practice is probably at work.

unprepared—when the heart is affected—when apoplexy may be feared. After you leave the establishment, be slow and gradual in your return to all habits that require much intellectual labour, or subject you to much nervous harassment ; be slow, also, in your return to habits that necessitate late hours. If you drink wine or fermented liquors at all, be sparing in your first recurrence to them. Well for you if you adhere throughout life to water as your ordinary beverage, and make wine but your occasional luxury. At all events, let the constitution slowly *settle* back—do not *hurry* it back—to artifice from Nature.

For your choice of an establishment you have a wide range. Institutions in England are now plentiful, and planted in some of the loveliest spots of our island. But as I only speak from personal knowledge, I can but here depose to such as I have visited, I hear, indeed, a high character of Doctor Johnson, of Stansted-Berry, and his books show great ability. Much is said in praise of Doctor Freeman, of Cheltenham, though his system, in some measure, is at variance with the received notions of hydropathists. But of these and many others, perhaps no less worthy of confidence—such as the magnificent establishment at Ben Rhydding, in Yorkshire ; that at Grasmere, under Doctor Stumm ; and that at Ryde, in which Doctor Weeding seeks to unite hydropathy with drugs, &c., &c.—I have no experience of my own. I have sojourned with advantage at Doctor Weiss's, at Petersham ; and for those whose business and avocations oblige them to be near London, his very agreeable house proffers many advantages, besides his own long practice and great skill.

To those who wish to try the system abroad, and shrink from the long journey to Graafenberg, Dr. Schmidt, at Boppart, proffers a princely house, comprising every English comfort, amidst the noble scenery of the Rhine, and I can bear ready witness to his skill ; but it is natural that the place which has for me the most grateful recollections, should be that where I received the earliest and the greatest benefit, viz., Doctor Wilson's, at Malvern ; there even the distance from the capital has its advantages.

The cure imperatively demands, at least in a large proportion of cases, abstraction from all the habitual cares of life, and in some the very neighbourhood of London suffices to produce restlessness and anxiety. For certain complaints, especially those of children, and such as are attended with debility, the air of Malvern is in itself Hygeian. The water is immemorially celebrated for its purity—the landscape is a perpetual pleasure to the eye—the mountains furnish the exercise most suited to the cure—"*Man muss Gebirge haben*," "one must have mountains," is the saying of Preissnitz.

All these are powerful auxiliaries, and yet all these are subordinate to the diligent, patient care—the minute, unwearied attention—the anxious, unaffected interest, which Doctor Wilson manifests to every patient, from the humblest to the highest, who may be submitted to his care. The vast majority of difficult cures which I have witnessed, have emanated from his skill. A pupil of the celebrated Broussais, his anatomical knowledge is considerable, and his tact * in diseases seems intuitive; he has that pure pleasure in his profession that the profits of it seem to be almost lost sight of, and having an independence of his own, his enthusiasm for the system he pursues is at least not based upon any mercenary speculation. I have seen him devote the same time and care to those whom his liberal heart has led him to treat gratuitously as to the wealthiest of his patients, and I mention this less to praise him for generosity than to show that he has that earnest faith in his own system, which begets an earnest faith in those to whom he administers; in all new experiments, it is a great thing to have confidence, not only in the skill, but the sincerity, of your adviser.—His treatment is less violent and energetic than that in fashion on the continent. If he errs, it is on the side of caution, and his theory leads him so much towards the restoration of the whole system, that the relief of the particular malady will sometimes seem

* I use the word "tact" advisedly; for I think the medical profession will bear me out in the observation, that a certain quality, which I can describe by no other word, is as valuable, as it is rare in practice, and often makes the precise and scarce describable difference between one physician and another. To this Dr. Wilson joins a remarkable acuteness in his predictions as to the nature and termination of complaints, which (as no man is less a charlatan) he, no doubt, owes in much to his knowledge of the human frame, and his careful education as a practitioner,—but towards which, I suppose, as in all other gifts, a natural faculty guides the acquired experience.

tedious in order to prove complete. Hence he inspires in those who have had a prolonged experience of his treatment a great sense of safety and security. For your impatient self, you might sometimes prefer the venture of a brisker process—for those in whom you are interested, and for whom you are fearful—you would not risk a step more hurried.

And since there is no small responsibility in recommending any practitioner of a novel school, so it is a comfort 'to know that whoever resorts to Doctor Wilson will at least be in hands not only practised and skilful, but wary and safe. He may fail in doing good, but I never met with a single patient who accused him of doing harm. And I cannot help adding, that though Mrs. Wilson does not interfere with the patients, it must be gratifying to such ladies as resort to Malvern to find in her the birth and manners of a perfect gentlewoman, and the noiseless solicitude of a heart genuinely kind and good !

Here then, O brothers, O afflicted ones, I bid you farewell. I wish you one of the most blessed friendships man ever made — the familiar intimacy with Water. Not Undine in her virgin existence more sportive and bewitching, not Undine in her wedded state more tender and faithful than the Element of which she is the type. In health may you find it the joyous playmate, in sickness the genial restorer and soft assuager. Round the healing spring still literally dwell the jocund nymphs in whom the Greek poetry personified Mirth and Ease. No drink, whether compounded of the gums and rosin of the old Falernian, or the alcohol and acid of modern wine, gives the animal spirits which rejoice the water-drinker.

Let him who has to go through severe bodily fatigue try first whatever—wine, spirits, porter, beer—he may conceive most generous and supporting ; let him then go through the same toil with no draughts but from the crystal lymph, and if he does not acknowledge ¦that there is no beverage which man concocts so strengthening and animating as that which God pours forth to all the children of nature, I throw up my brief.

Finally, as health depends upon healthful habits, let those who desire easily and luxuriously to glide into the courses most agreeable to the human frame, to enjoy the morning breeze, to grow epicures in the simple regimen, to become cased in armour against the vicissitudes of our changeful skies—to feel, and to shake off, light sleep as a blessed dew, let them, while the organs are yet sound, and the nerves yet unshattered, devote an autumn to the water-cure.

And you, O parents! who, too indolent, too much slaves to custom, to endure change for yourselves, to renounce for awhile your artificial natures, but who still covet for your children hardy constitutions, pure tastes, and abstemious habits—who wish to see them grow up with a manly disdain of luxury—with a vigorous indifference to climate—with a full sense of the value of health, not alone for itself, but for the powers it elicits, and the virtues with which it is intimately connected—the serene, unfretful temper—the pleasure in innocent delights—the well-being that, content with self, expands in benevolence to others—you I adjure not to scorn the facile process of which I solicit the experiment. Dip your young heroes in the spring, and hold them not back by the heel. May my exhortations find believing listeners, and may some, now unknown to me, write me word from the green hills of Malvern, or the groves of Petersham, "We have hearkened to you—not in vain."

Adieu, Mr. Editor, the ghost returns to silence.

LETTERS TO JOHN BULL, Esq.*

"Et RECREAVERUNT vitam, legesque rogârunt." †
LUCRET. l. vi. 3.

LETTER I.

DEAR AND RESPECTED JOHN,—Although I deeply sympathise with your natural vexation at the troubled state of your Town Household in Downing Street, and although at other times, I might have much to say upon the disorders of that establishment, yet at this moment your rural affairs appear to me in a condition so bad and unpromising, as to claim all the attention which you can spare from your just quarrel with the Pope, and your hospitalities to the strangers you have invited to your Barmecide's feast on the banks of the Serpentine.

I bear no ill-will, my dear John, to your present servants, they are horrible plagues to you, it is true,—but servants always are. I believe many of them to be extremely intelligent,—I am sure that they are as honest as day. All they want is a comfortable situation—wages no object. And that, somehow or other, the situation is not comfortable, seems perfectly clear; for though they've expressed themselves ready to go, yet, when it comes to the point, nobody else appears anxious to step into their shoes. It used not to be so, my dear John : I remember the time when you could not discharge a servant from Downing Street but what his face was as long as my arm, and you had plenty to choose from, amongst applicants who were thoroughly up to their business.

For this domestic dilemma of yours, so wounding to your pride and destructive to your peace, no doubt there are many causes; but I suspect that the one most serious is this—you have allowed your town servants to regulate all

* [Originally published in 1851 as an 8vo pamphlet.]
† [And they renewed or remodelled life and secured or established laws.]

your country affairs, and they know just as much about them as—common sense might have told you! They have thus got the poor land, on which, sooner or later, you are doomed to fall back for the expenses of housekeeping, into such a deuce of a mess, that I don't wonder they are willing to shift to others the task of hearing the complaint, and contriving the remedy ; while those who might otherwise be disposed to succeed, have the wit to perceive that it will be no easy matter to undo what is done, or restore what is —undone. For, unhappily, in the dispute so inevitably created between your town and country establishments, the neighbours of each have been called in to take part in the quarrel; and the question is, how to give content to the one side, without making the servants' hall too hot to contain the other.

This I believe to be the true state of things. And this, my dear John, it behoves you to consider with that freedom from prejudice and passion which should characterise the head of a family when its peace is disturbed by dissensions.

There drop we the metaphor, and enlarge the scope of our views.

That the existing government cannot last as it is now composed, all men seem to admit. We may galvanise the lifeless muscles,—we may give to the worn-out frame the grimace and convulsion of simulated vitality; but the animal spark has fled. We feel that the body is only kept above ground for the purpose of philosophical experiment, and are quite indifferent to the shocks it receives or the gashes inflicted on it, because we say to ourselves, " It is a dead thing practised upon for a short time for the sake of the living."

Whether this Government, by some gentle metempsychosis, shall pass into another much resembling itself,—or whether the party it embraces shall rise into vigour and power as an antagonistical principle to some Government by which my Lord Derby may boldly replace it,—is a speculation that I leave to the hopes and the fears of others. I shun in these Letters all mere party questions. I stand alone from all party. I will not attack the Minister. I will not panegyrise the rival. I leave to those whose support, as the representatives of manufacturing and urban populations, Lord John Russell unhesitatingly preferred to all terms with the agricultural constituencies,—the grateful task to extenuate his merits, and enforce his offences. To me his name is identified with the memory of imperishable services; and I feel too much regret to differ from him, not to be reluctant to blame. If in him could yet be supplied what appears to me the main want of the time, there is no man I should be so proud—what?—to follow as a Leader? No. To support as a Conciliator. What the time now demands is, not the Leader; it is the Conciliator. Wherever I turn, I dread the chance of a chief who is to represent all the passions of class or the selfishness of interests,—wherever I turn, I see cause to desire that the Coming Man may covet, not the bays of the conqueror, but the oak wreath of the citizen.

Is it not so, my dear John?—pause and reflect! Carry your eye from these figures in the front; examine the vast background that lies beyond. Is it simple strife between two parties, in which each requires the strong hand and fierce heart of the captain, that meets your survey, and solicits your preference?—No: everywhere you behold divisions between classes; jealousies, and feuds between national interests; and victory, pushed too far by the one against the other, will be a victory achieved over the country itself by its own sons, far worse than the fears of Lord Ellesmere could ever anticipate from the fleets and hosts of the foreigner. Penetrate the smoky atmosphere through which rise the tall chimneys of countless factories; examine the heart of those mighty towns, in which all theories that affect the interests of labour are discussed with the passions which numbers speed and inflame; where the spirit of an eternal election agitates the mass of the everlasting crowd—say, if there be not yet reserved for the Coming Man the consideration of social questions which no Factory Bill has yet settled; which no Repeal of the Corn Laws, after its first novelty is worn away, can lull into rest; and tell me whether it be better for the solution of these that the Man shall come as the leader or the conciliator? What are become of our sanitary regulations? Where are the reforms in the law? Doomed to "lie in cold obstruction, and to rot," till statesmen have time to conciliate, and till we can look to the forum and not find it a battle-field.

What have we done to regain the affections and arrest the ruin of our West Indian colonies ?   What is the nature of the emigration now pouring into Australia and America ? Friendly to the mother country, or carrying thence all the bitterness engendered by that scorn of complaints which has compelled expatriation ?   If our colonies are to be our foes or our friends, our weakness or strength, all depends on whether the Coming Man shall be the leader of a party or the conciliator of discontents that may dissolve an empire.

Look to the state of the Church, with a schism that threatens far more peril to its future integrity and well-being than the petty questions of surplice and gown, which inflame congregations, and trouble the peace of bishops. So much of learning, of earnestness, of zeal, rising with each generation of Churchmen, that leaves the college for the pulpit, against the popular feeling, clashing with it, warring on it, and remaining within the camp, under its separate banner of mutiny, or deserting to the Roman Gonfalon, with all the arms of controversy it had found in the very arsenal which Oxford had established against the foe. "*Atque, atque accedet muros Romana juventus.*"— " And more and more Rome's youth invades our walls." Woe to the Church, and woe to the peace of our religious community, if we are to have our statesmen of the laity appear as leaders for or against these spiritual factions of the Bianchi and Neri, in a war of which texts and citations are the ostensible weapons!   A Minister who has the confidence, not only of the Church, but of the main body of Protestant belief, might possibly be able to conciliate—if not, time and common sense will ultimately settle—these disputes, as they have hitherto settled all disputes among the clergy, where they are not whirled away and mixed up with the party passions of politicians.   Behold the vast question of Popular Education, checked in the Legislature by the rival jealousies of Church and Dissenter, but daily and hourly, without-side the walls of Parliament, occupying the thoughts of intelligent men, who see not only, in the want of education, an element of crime and misery, but who see in education itself, unless it be taken up in a noble and fitting spirit, evils as great as can befall society, if intellectual cultivation (limited to the extent that it must be when you deal with large masses whose destined employment is manual labour) is to be held a thing wholly different and apart from moral instruction and religious discipline. Who, regarding popular education in its comprehensive application to states,—who, knowing the statistical fact, that whereas with us the larger proportion of criminals can neither read nor write, in France the larger proportion of the worse sort of criminals possesses even more than that elementary instruction;*—who does not hope that some statesman may arise, with the happy art to conciliate Church and Dissent, and to insure to the rising generation those early lessons which not only quicken the thought, but guide the conduct?

Carry your gaze across the Channel—look at Ireland. Long distracted from the true objects of civilisation by the genius of one leader—Heaven preserve her from another! Consider there the differences affecting the very core of society, which hitherto you have so vainly struggled to adjust. Recall the late famine there — contemplate the vast diminution in the produce of the soil, which your laws, intended to prevent the recurrence of such famine, have already effected; while Ireland at least has no foreign commerce that can be supposed to recruit the capital that is lost to the land. Recall, too, the toil it has cost to the wisest to harmonise religious distinctions with due regard

---

* By the elaborate tables of M. Guerry, it would seem not only that this applies to individual cases, but that in those *départemens* of France in which the average of education is highest, it is found, almost invariably, that crimes, against both life and property, are the most relatively numerous; and crimes against life especially, rarest in some districts, such as Limousin and Brittany, where the people are most ignorant. Beaumont and Tocqueville, in their works on Crime in America, have also rather startled us with the remark, that "they cannot attribute the diminution of crime in the northern states to instruction, because in Connecticut, where there is more instruction than in New York, crime increases with terrible rapidity." It is obviously needless to say that such facts prove nothing against popular instruction; but they do prove that popular instruction alone does not suffice for the ends required from it; that it cannot be safely dissociated from direct moral and religious cultivation. A critic in the *Edinburgh Review*, in noticing these Letters, asserts that M. Guerry's tables, which were published some years ago, have been explained away; and that, though crime may have been found most in educated districts, it was not among the educated part of their population. But M. Guerry, who is one of the most illustrious statists in Europe, visited England this very year, and in an address at the great meeting of our men of science, repeated and enforced the inferences drawn from his tables, refuted the explanations on which the reviewer relies, and brought forward new facts in support of his proposition, "that mere mental education has not been found to diminish crime."

to the conscience of both, between Protestant Britain and Roman Catholic Ireland—then see this new brand which the Pope and his Cardinal have flung amongst the smouldering fires of recent rebellion—and who does not sigh, " May the Coming Man be the Peace-maker ! "

Conciliation!—this is in all times, and all lands, the master-art of the administrator. As the vehement advocate once raised to the bench becomes the impartial judge, so he who in opposition is the leader, in office should become the arbiter. And that authority has ever been the firmest which reconciles the differences of each with the order and progress of all. Difficult task, and rarely undertaken!—but wisdom is difficult, and firm administrations are rare.

So far, my dear John, methinks I have your approval;— nay, had I the voice of the orator, here perhaps I might bo flattered by your cheers. There remains yet a class and an interest, towards the propitiation of which there is more doubt of a fair hearing. Nevertheless, I deliberately approach that subject; for I honestly think that here the conciliator is the most immediately needed. I speak of the class which cultivate the land we live in; I speak of the interest which comprises a vast mass of the real property of the country—an interest which supports the bulk of our poor; which maintains the clergy and defrays the costs that uphold civilisation in rural districts; which, whether it be or be not disproportionately taxed, does at all events contribute towards the State to so large an amount, that it cannot be materially injured nor depressed by any change in the law, without affecting the very capital upon which depend the income of the fund-holder and the solvency of the nation.

Now, O dear and respected John, when we survey this important tribe of your family—pretty well united in the complaints of distress, and in the assertion of its cause—do you think we may say that this is precisely the class in the kingdom to which we can safely refuse attention, and which we will thrust out of the pale of all paternal and beneficent legislation ?

But, hark !—it seems to me that I hear a loud and derisive outcry. "Pooh !—Stop your ears, John ! This gentleman, who is in reality a vampire, wants to open the question of the Corn Law.   Don't listen to him ; that question is settled.   The law is passed—once passed, it cannot be repealed.   As well talk of repealing the Reform Bill ! "

You scratch your head, John ; you look puzzled ; but still you listen to me : for a moment's reflection tells you that there is all the difference in the world between a question of constitutional change, and a question of political economy or fiscal arrangement.   It is rare, indeed, that a law which serves to popularise a Constitution, or advance democracy, is repealed.   But even that has been done in times the most agitated, where the public expediency seemed to require it.   You yourself, John, once advanced into a republic, and drew back into monarchy as fast as you could.   Again, you once transacted your affairs through a triennial parliament, yet you very soon made a retrograde movement, and are still compelled to grant a seven years' lease to the occupiers of St. Stephen's, notwithstanding all the arguments of the National Reform League to prove that lease a great deal too long for your interests as landlord.   You have only to look to the Foreign News in the *Times* to see that it was but as the day before yesterday, compared with your long life, when universal suffrage was proclaimed in France ; and but as yesterday that a law has been passed which shakes off a weighty per-centage from the suffrage so recently created.   And the whole history of Europe for the last few years does little more than chronicle the sudden enactment and as sudden repeal of charters and constitutions which wise-heads declare to be the irrevocable advance of entire populations.   You know, therefore, that even a political step backward has been taken, sometimes because of the brute force of a despot—but sometimes, also, as the voluntary choice of a nation.   The *Sed revocare gradum** applies to progress, not towards the region where we all wish to go, but to its dismal antipodes.   It is only the first step to the infernal regions which Virgil so emphatically implies that mortal man can never recall.   But, bless your heart, my dear John, as to changes and rechanges in commercial regulations, in duties and non-duties upon produce, raw and manufactured,—what man in his senses, or with no more knowledge of history than he could pick up at a grammar-school, ever dreamed that laws affect-

* [But to retrace the step.]

ing them were not, by their very nature, experiments, and
the most liable of all laws to revision or repeal? "Ay—
but corn—the staple of food—the big loaf?" The very
thing, my dear John, of all others, that your experience
tells you has been most subject to the mutability inherent
to affairs mundane and mortal.

What, did we never try this experiment before? Why,
throughout all the dark ages, the importation of foreign
corn was substantially free. For about five hundred years
that experiment was tried; and much good it did to commerce and manufactures—much good it did to the condition
of the people; and well it prevented fluctuations, scarcity,
and famine! Free importation of corn! The duration of
that experiment extends through the history of our barbarism. From the dawn of civilisation dates the record of
Protection : it commenced under the dynasty of the House
of York, in which commerce was first especially honoured
and upheld—in which, under a king who himself was a
merchant,* began the sagacious favour to the trading
middle class, as a counterpoise to armed aristocracy, that,
under the more tranquil intellect of Henry the Seventh,
created the civil powers ruling modern dominions; and
that Protection, thus first admitted in theory, but long de-
feated in practice, can hardly be said to have been vitally
and resolutely incorporated in our national system till the
very era that confirmed our constitutional freedom, and
saw the rise of Great Britain to the rank it now holds
amongst nations—the reign of William the Third.

Well, this Protection, first vigorously enforced at the
Revolution of 1688,† lasted for the best part of a century;

* Edward IV.—"King Edward went beyond all the contemporary sove-
reigns in commercial transactions. He owned several vessels, and, like men
whose living depended on their merchandise, exported the finest wool, cloth,
tin, and the other commodities of the kingdom, to Italy and Greece, and imported their produce in return by the agency of factors or supercargoes."—
Macpherson's Annals of Commerce. In one sense of the word, it was very
injurious to merchants to have a royal competitor, who paid no duties; but
his example served very much to increase the power and dignity of the mercantile order; and during his reign that order gained the authority which
enabled Henry the Seventh to found a middle class on the ruins of the
Feudal system.

† In 1463, reign of Edward the Fourth, importation was legally prohibited
until the home price reached that at which exportation ceased, viz., 6s. 8d.
a quarter (money of that period); but, as Mr. M'Culloch observes, "the
fluctuating policy of the times prevented these regulations being carried

"and under it," says the commercial historian, "the commerce and manufactures of the country were extended to an unprecedented degree." The country wished then, as now, to have some return to the system of those blessed five centuries of Free Trade in corn; and in 1773 a law was passed which a few years ago would have satisfied, I suspect, Manchester itself; for foreign wheat was permitted to be imported on paying a nominal duty of 6*d.* whenever the home price was at or above 48*s.* per quarter. The Nation tried that plan for about eighteen years, and then what did it do?—this England that the newspapers tell us "never goes back!"—why, it went back, of course! And the price at which foreign importation could take place at 6*d.* was raised in 1791 from 48*s.* to 54*s.*; while under 50*s.* the home producer was protected by a duty of 24*s.* 3*d.* And observe this date, 1791! Was that a period when the temper of the times was peculiarly submissive, and inclined towards political retrogression? It was a time more democratic than this—a time when the spirit of the first French Revolution was at work through all the great towns of the empire. "But the people cried out? There were riots, rebellions, for the sake of the big loaf?" Not a bit of it, my dear John! The people were a sensible people, as the English are in the long run: they had tried their experiment—did not like it; "And," says Mr. M'Culloch, with a candid sigh, "there was a pretty general acquiescence in the act of 1791."

"Pretty general acquiescence!"—the admission is satisfactory in extent, but lukewarm in expression: the truth is, that no more popular act passed throughout the whole reign of George the Third.

And yet "laws against protection are never repealed! as well repeal the Reform Act!—England never goes back! —A law about corn is as fixed as the nod of Jove!" And all the while you are going back to the reigns of the Nor-

into full effect, and, indeed, rendered them in a great measure inoperative."

The subsequent law that imposed prohibitory duties on the importation of wheat, till the price rose to 53*s.* 4*d.*, and a fixed duty of 8*s.* between that price and 80*s.*, was enacted eighteen years before the great Revolution that placed William the Third on the Throne; but "the want of any proper method for the determination of prices went far to nullify the prohibition of importation."—M'Culloch. Protection against importation cannot be said to have been vigorously and systematically carried out before the reign of William.

man and Plantagenet! and insisting on the stability of experimental legislature upon the very article and in the very mode upon which the History of Civilisation abounds the most with precedents of change!

I read, indeed, in very popular and influential journals—I hear, indeed, from grave authorities "speaking in their place in Parliament"—that "all sensible men" are of one opinion upon this point; that to doubt for a moment a dogma of the *Corn Law Catechism* is to forfeit one's claim to understanding. Were it an actual fact that the opinion of "sensible men" was thus forcibly expressed, I confess to you frankly, my dear John, that it would not, as a matter of logic and reasoning—as a proof upon which side lies *the truth*—have the slightest weight upon my convictions. And it never ought to have the slightest weight on the convictions of the man who calls himself a reformer in politics, or a student in philosophy; for is there a simple question of reform in the laws, or a single principle now maintained in philosophy, which has not had at one time nearly all who, in their own day, were called "sensible men," dead against it? The "sensible men" of their age were, at one time, for burning the Lollards and drowning old women with bleared eyes and hook noses—nay, theorems in sciences far more positive than Political Economy professes to be—in Astronomy, in Chemistry—which, not twenty years ago, all "sensible men" were agreed on, are now maintained to be errors. The history of Truth is the history of her opposition to "sensible men." And Truth would never have advanced one step from the wilds of the savage, if those who sought for her traces had paused a moment to ask of her "whereabout" from the public opinion of their day. But not to go further than the very subject before us, pray were not the great majority of "sensible men," even though favouring Free Trade, against a total repeal of the Corn Law some dozen years ago? And when you—the Free-Traders—so exultingly taunt my Lord Derby that, on the recent resignation of the present ministers, he could not form a cabinet of statesmen in favour of a fixed duty of five shillings—pray is it ten years ago that you could not maintain a cabinet in favour of a fixed duty of eight? All your argument as to the fashion of opinion being wholly on your side, would prove nothing more than the changeability of such fashion, so far as the positive truth of the question at issue is concerned. If wholly correct, however, I allow that, whether the doctrine itself be true or false, it would present on your side the argument of tyrants—Might, if not Right. And public opinion is, I allow, to the legislator, though not to the mere seeker of truth, an adversary against whom it were idle to hoist the banner and flourish the sword.

But I have lived long enough to find out that there are two Publics—a Public invisible, with "airy tongues that syllable men's names," much quoted in newspapers, much referred to by members of Parliament;—and another Public that is visible and tangible, that we meet in street and club, in market and shop; and I cannot say I find this latter Public of the same mind as that first mentioned and mythical Public, with which neither you nor I, nor any creature of flesh and blood, ever comes into positive contact. I have as wide a range of acquaintance as most people, amongst all ranks and all classes; and whether I talk with the statesman, the man of the world, the abstruse thinker, whose task it is to master these topics, or with the merchant, the man of business, and the intelligent tradesmen, I find a very large proportion who are in favour, certainly not of prohibitory duties, not of a reversal of the general policy involved in our tariffs, but of a moderate fixed duty upon foreign grain. And, moreover, amongst those not in favour of attempting such a modification of the law, I find at least half who are far from disliking the notion of that said fixed duty in itself—far from doubting its beneficial effects, if it could be carried; but who merely doubt whether that incorporeal essence, the other Public, will be disposed to accept it. And, though it may seem strange to persons less acquainted with the inconsistencies of mankind than it has been my professional lot, as a writer, to make myself, I positively aver, that among those who, thus seen in the streets, and talked with in tranquil nooks, either favour a fixed duty altogether, or wish the other metaphysical Public might so favour it, I find no small number of the very men who enjoy, by votes in Parliament or paragraphs in print, the reputation of being "sensible and enlightened," and go the whole loaf with Mr. Cobden!

The Corn Law settled! No! Free-traders and Protectionists alike feel in their heart of hearts that it is not settled; that it is not in the power of this Parliament to settle it. Many large portions of the constituent body, many agriculturists themselves, were induced, by the calculations of great authorities, to consent to what was called an experiment. Those calculations have been tested; and it is now not on the speculative probabilities, but on the experiment itself, that the agriculturists at least desire to pass their opinion. There has been a Parliament with faith in the prophecy; there must be a Parliament to decide on the nature of its fulfilment. "It is one thing," said the shrewd Arab, "to believe the assurance of Mahomet that he can move a mountain, and another thing to say before the kadi that the mountain has been removed."

Let there be fair play. Let THIS be the question at the hustings. Do not try, by a new Reform Bill, cut and carved so as to adjust the franchise to a particular party question; so as to create a constitution for the purpose of enforcing an experiment in political economy—do not try, by a proceeding so obviously disingenuous, either to silence the expression of the complaint you have occasioned, by the uproar of recruits to the aggressors, or represent the man who contends that one class of his countrymen is wronged, as an enemy to the claim of another class not yet enfranchised. This great and solemn question of an extended suffrage should be approached in a spirit free from what, at this moment, must warp justice on either side; viz., the heated jealousy of town and country—agriculture and manufactures. The Corn Law, the cry of the day, should be really settled, ere a question that may affect the duration of the empire can be fairly considered.

And now, my dear John, before I proceed further, let me humbly and respectfully seek to remove from your mind an impression which, if entertained by you, as it is by many of your family, would go far towards deadening any attention that you may condescend to pay to the remarks that I proffer. It is industriously represented that to question Free Trade, is to abandon Freedom itself; that such sceptics are to be classed with the dust and shadow of defunct Toryism ; that a man who doubts whether a fiscal law does not injure a large class of his countrymen, more than it will, in the long run, benefit any other, is to be considered a recreant to all those noble principles which, comprehended in the word Liberty, exalt the character of a people, and widen the basis of states. By the air that we breathe, John, at least do not do the author of these pages that signal injustice ! Perhaps, in his day, he has rendered some service to Freedom—some service to the party from which he has at present the misfortune to differ. Dear as were to him, in the ardour of youth, the principles of political freedom, they are no less dear to him in the maturity of manhood. And time has only strength-ened his belief that you can select from no class in the community a man who has so fervent and absolute a sym-pathy with the People as THE WRITER, who is compelled, in every thought and in every study, to look to that People as the tribunal of the worth of his labours, and to hope in its ultimate judgment for the enduring reward of all.

But I own to you, O my honoured and somewhat anti-quated John ! I own to you, that the school in which I learned to love liberty seems now as old-fashioned as yourself. For I learned that love in the school of the great patriots of the Past ; I learned to connect it inseparably with love of country ; and it would really seem as if a new school had arisen, which identifies the passion for freedom with scornful indifference for England. And when, in a popular meeting, which was crowded by the friends of the late Corn-Law League, and at which one of the great chiefs of that combination presided, an orator declared, in reference to the defences of the country, that " he thought it might be a very good thing for the people if the country were con-quered by the foreigner ;" and when that sentiment was re-ceived with cheers by the audience, and met with no rebuke from the Paladin of Free Trade seated in the chair, I felt that, however such sentiments might be compatible with Free Trade,—in the school in which I learned to glow at the grand word of Liberty, they would have been stigmatised as the sentiments of slaves. Yet more recently and more notoriously, when Sir James Graham, who, it now seems, is the " Coming Man " of the Free-Traders, introduced into an address to the Commons of England a significant menace of the will and the power of the soldiers;* and when that menace was not drowned by the indignant outburst, but hailed by the exulting cheers, of a party professing affection for civil freedom, I own again, that, in the school in which I learned that liberty rested upon law, the barest allusion to the armed force of a standing army as a parliamentary argument would have been deemed an outrage on the senate, and applause given to such allusion the last degradation that could debase the representatives of citizens. Another high authority in Free Trade—nay, the very author of the *Corn Law Catechism*—uttered, not long since, a sentiment equally worthy the loyalty of an officer and the patriotism of an Englishman :—"I would rather," said Colonel Thompson, " see a foreign army in possession of London six weeks, than see the Protectionists for six weeks in possession of those benches." † What! prefer the sword of the foreign conqueror to the vote of legislators elected by the free choice of the native !—No, such is not the school in which I learned to love liberty, and these are not the authorities I will consent to acknowledge as guides to the free men of England.

But, in truth, my dear John, you have only to open your eyes in order to recognise the plain fact, that there is no reason why a man should not be a very democrat in politics, if he so please, and an ultra-protectionist in trade. The Americans are as free and as progressive a people as one can well suppose to exist, but they have evinced no peculiar affection for Free Trade. The French seem pretty well disposed to go all lengths in democracy, but they still maintain rather strict notions as to the value of Protection. The principle, therefore, of Free Trade may be wise or not; but it is indisputably clear, when we look to other nations, that it is perfectly consistent with the freest opinions on politics, to have very exclusive notions as to national trade.

It is not, then, incompatible with freedom to believe that

* "The time has arrived when the truth fully must be spoken. There is not a soldier who returns to England from abroad that does not practically feel that his daily pay is augmented,—that he has a cheaper, larger, and a better mess,—and that he enjoys greater comforts; and he also knows the reason. Now, Sir, I entreat my honourable friends who sit below me to be on their guard."—*Speech of Sir James Graham, Privy Councillor and ex-Cabinet Minister, in the Parliament of Great Britain,* 1851.

† Speech of Col. Thompson, M.P., April 2, *à propos* of a County Franchise !

there may be circumstances in which it is expedient to protect articles of home produce from the competition of the foreigner. But is it so wholly incompatible with wisdom? Must I be totally without intelligence and instruction, if I doubt every article in the *Corn Law Catechism?* Do the arguments against me rest upon propositions as clear as those in Euclid, or are they confirmed by the preponderating authorities of history?

Looking first to the logic employed by these Free-trading denouncers of fallacies, is there any coincidence between the premises and conclusions? Has there been a general concurrence amongst modern Free-Traders as to even the effect of the recent law upon the price of bread—the amount of importation? The League Circular asserted that the Corn Law "compelled us to pay *three times* the value for a loaf of bread." Mr. Cobden, on the contrary, exclaimed in his speech at Winchester, "The idea of low-priced corn is all a delusion; provisions will be no cheaper." Colonel Torrens, Mr. Villiers, the Manchester Chamber of Commerce, concurred in the assertion that the first object of the Corn Law was to raise the price of corn above its natural level. And yet Mr. James Wilson, considered the most learned authority of all the repealers, thus denounces—what? the fallacies of the Protectionists? No—the especial and most popular fallacies of his own Free-trading friends! Thus saith Mr. Wilson in his work on *The Influence of the Corn Laws:*—"Our belief is, that, if we had had a free trade in corn since 1815, the average price of the whole period, actually received by the British growers, would have been higher than it has been; that little or no foreign grain would have been imported; and that if, for the next twenty years, the whole protective system shall be abandoned, the average price of wheat will be higher than it has been for the last seven years, or than it would be with a continuance of the present system."

Here, then, in the first great principle, viz., the cheapness of food, and the lowness of prices—here, then, we have the most contradictory deductions from the same premises. Fallacies there must be somewhere, but they are not here those of the Protectionists. Here, it is one Corn Law repealer who answers another. It is the old story of Munchausen: the tiger jumps down the jaws of the crocodile;

the crocodile is strangled by the tiger. What and who alone remains safe, challenging our convictions, insisting on our belief? Munchausen!

I come next to the question—so important to labour—the ultimate effect which the repeal of the Corn Laws is to have upon wages. Do we arrive at any better agreement in opinion amongst those gentlemen who so despise the understanding of all who differ from them? I turn to the speeches of Mr. Villiers. I know there that I shall find the evidence of an acute, subtle, and honest intellect—and I find that just as the Protectionists venture still to say, the cheapening of bread must sooner or later produce the cheapening of labour. On the necessity of lowering wages —ay, and not in agricultural districts, but in manufacturing towns—on the necessity of lowering them in order to compete with the foreigner, Mr. Villiers rests half his case. And yet, what says his fellow political economist, Colonel Torrens? Exactly the contrary: "The true cause of low wages is high food ; for then mechanical power is brought more and more in competition with human labour, and the operative will be employed at wages reduced to the slavery point."

" The repeal of the Corn Laws must lower the wages," says Mr. Villiers. "It must raise them," says Colonel Torrens. Every fact, real or supposed, adduced by the Manchester Chamber of Commerce, tended to show the necessity of conforming to the low wages of the Continent. And again, Mr. James Wilson, who has a kind word and coaxing lure for every class, fells the Manchester Chamber of Commerce with this knock-down prediction, "We are therefore of opinion that, in the event of a free trade in corn, the price of labour in this country would rather be increased than diminished."

The farther we advance in the polemics of Free Trade, the more the perplexity gathers : not a result but has its separate Free-trading prophet, and not a prophet that does not belie his brother. "Will rents fall?" murmurs the timid landowner. "Fall? of course, you vampire!" cries the Manchester Chamber of Commerce ; "you have been living on the capital of the farmer ever since the peace." "Certainly they will fall," says Mr. Villiers, with polite indifference to so small a calamity.

"Fall?—they will rise!" exclaims Colonel Torrens. "They will rise," says Mr. W. W. Whitmore, who was a very popular prophet in his day. "Pooh! don't believe them, my dear vampire," argues that dear, good Mr. Wilson; "my object in removing these Corn Laws is to increase the value of your land!"

The farmer puts *his* question, "Will these horrible prices last for ever; and how many quarters of grain are likely to be imported?"

And straight, therewith, arises such a discord of contradictory answers, all equally positive, and equally contradictory, that poor Chawbacon, if he have any animal desire still to have bacon to chaw, thinks it best to escape from the hubbub, and stick to his old motto, "Live and let live in the land we live by."

Now, my dear Free-Traders, own that the honestest vampire who ever set out on his travels in search of an understanding, has had very little chance to find it amongst you! Shall he be enlightened with Mr. Villiers? then he can't be enlightened with Mr. Wilson. How can he get rid of his fallacies, when every opinion he picks up in exchange from one Free-Trader is remorselessly condemned as a fallacy by the rhetoric of another.

The question settled! Why, it was settled on the faith of logic like that I have quoted. And those who believed with one set of Free-Traders, are perhaps undeceived by the results foretold by another. But, if you say, fairly, "Oh, we own this was an experiment on which no one could calculate"—can you add, "We have history and experience on the side of the general good effects of Free Trade?" When one hears you so confident in your assertions, one would be tempted to believe that, under all circumstances, and in all nations, the prosperity of trade has been found to depend upon its freedom; that all departments of commerce wither under protection, and expand in the open air of competition. But when we turn to history, we find nowhere sufficient facts to prove the prosperity of commercial nations under a system of perfectly free trade, while we have abundant facts to prove the prosperity of the greatest commercial states in the history of the world under systems of protection. The longest pre-eminence in commerce ever enjoyed by a state, since

Carthage, is that of Venice—the earliest commercial city in our modern era. For five centuries this little community maintained a trading ascendency, which is one of the marvels of human annals. With little natural advantages, and under a wretched form of government, Venice was the most illustrious navigator, the most renowned manufacturer, of the globe. All the other contemporaneous maritime powers of earth combined, scarcely equalled the Venetian commerce from the thirteenth to the fifteenth century. Under what system arose her greatness? Free Trade?— No; under a system that grasped at monopoly, and intrenched itself under every imaginable rigidity of protection.* Our accounts of the ancient trade of Genoa are less ample than those of Venice; but they leave no doubt, at least, that in its palmiest time it was guarded with the laws most opposed to the enlightenment of Free-Traders. So jealous were the Genoese of competition that they stipulated with kings to banish their mercantile rivals. Thus they requested the King of Sicily, A.D. 1156, to expel from his territories the merchants of Provence and France. And the fierce commercial strife which lasted for nearly two hundred years between Venice and Genoa was decided in favour of Venice—how?—by her wisdom in opening her markets? Oh no—by her good luck in securing the monopoly of the trade of the Black Sea, and becoming, by the revolution of the Eastern Roman Empire, the master of markets that she most rigidly protected. And how did Genoa, for a short time, regain the ground she had lost in her struggle with Venice?—by reversing her commercial policy, and abjuring her villanous systems of Protection? Oh no—by upsetting the Latin Empire, and obtaining from the Greek she restored, the keys of the Black Sea, and the principal part of the monopoly which had enriched the Venetians. If we go back to the commerce of the Ancient World, and strive to pierce the obscurity which wraps its economical regulations, we find nothing to sanction the assertion that Protection is injurious, or unshackled competition essential, to the prosperity of Commerce. Athens was the most considerable commercial state of Greece. Much, at the first glance, appears to favour the Free-

---

* DARU, *Histoire de la République de Vénise ;* unrivalled as an authority on this State.

Traders, in our information respecting the old delight and teacher of the world. The necessities of the soil, and the magnitude of the population, obliged Athens to favour to the utmost extent the importation of corn. Unquestionably, the early stimulus to maritime enterprise, which could not but goad a people living on the shore, and driven betimes to search elsewhere for their food, tended to sharpen the activity and intellect of the Athenians, and, as I have elsewhere observed,* made one secret of their after greatness. But I apprehend that it made also a main cause of their after downfall. They paid dear for their Egyptian corn. All the regulations of their ablest statesmen, all the severities of their most stringent laws, all the power of their vigilant fleets, could not save them from the greatest fluctuations in the price of corn. In vain were the Attic promontories garrisoned for the protection of ships bringing corn to the Piræus; in vain the City of the Violet Crown sought to make herself the granary of the world. All her arts and all her genius could not save her from the distresses which attend the country that depends on the foreigner for the food of the population. Scarcity at Athens was only to be met, and that partially, by provisions incompatible with modern empires; viz., ample storehouses and gratuitous distribution of corn. Fluctuations greater than have ever been known under a system of protection, no policy could prevent. And it is possible that this necessity to seek elsewhere, not only empire, but one market to counterbalance the vicissitudes of another, contributed to the fatal ambition by which Athens eventually lost both political freedom and maritime supremacy. Her population that gathered round the fleets of Nicias saw, in the anticipated conquest of Sicily, not only an addition to the empire, but fresh corn-supplies for the Piræus.

But Athens was a free trader for corn, because her necessities made her so. Athens was not a free trader where national interests and national policy suggested prohibition. She would not export the timber, which might supply her rivals with shipping, to be used against herself; she would not export the weapons for which her manufactories were renowned, to arm an enemy; she would not import the commodities of hostile states, nor give her

* *Athens, its Rise and Fall,* vol. i.

markets to Bœotia and Megara. "In brief," as Boeckh justly observes, "the Athenians did not avoid any restriction of commerce, so long as it appeared profitable to them." *

Holland has been a free trader in corn. She required the provision her own soil could not adequately supply; but though in this respect Holland has been held out to us by Free-Traders as an example. Holland was not, in her greatest day, what is meant by a Free-Trader. In that branch of commerce on which she mainly herself depended, —her fisheries,—Holland was jealously restrictive. Her commerce with India was carried on through the monopoly of a company, and, no doubt, to her disadvantage. But what was the main cause of the commercial eminence of Holland? She herself was one monopoly. Her greatness was in the feebleness of her rivals. Her judicious tolerance to religion, her hospitable reception of all aliens and strangers, might certainly assist towards the accumulation of her wealth; or, to use the words of her own merchants, " make the cause that many people not only fled thither for refuge with their whole stock in ready cash, and their real valuable effects, but also settled and established many trades, fabrics, manufactures, arts, and sciences in the country." But the great and paramount cause of Dutch prosperity in the seventeenth century was the absence of competition. The absence of the very principle which you allege is vital in all cases to the healthful action of trade and barter! Let Mr. M'Culloch here speak for himself: " During the period when the Republic rose to great eminence as a commercial state, England, France, and Spain, distracted by civil and religious dissensions, or engrossed wholly by schemes of foreign conquest, were unable to apply their energies to the cultivation of commerce, or to withstand the competition of so industrious a people as the Dutch. They, therefore, were under the necessity of allowing the greater part of their foreign, and even of their coasting trade, to be carried on in Dutch bottoms, and under the superintendence of Dutch factors. But after the accession of Louis Fourteenth, and the ascendency of Cromwell had put an end to internal commotions in France and England, the energies of these two great nations began to be directed to pursuits of which the Dutch had hitherto

* Boeckh's *Public Economy of Athens*, Book i.

enjoyed almost a monopoly. . . . The Dutch ceased to be the carriers of Europe without any fault of their own." *

Hitherto, then, the Dutch had enjoyed a virtual monopoly. Their greatness was the absence of competition—it declined as competition arose. It is so distinctly stated in the luminous Dissertation drawn up from the communications of their own merchants. Here, then, was Holland, with all the advantages attributed to a thorough free trade in corn, which could nevertheless not keep its pre-eminence when other nations began to compete; and its commerce declined mainly from two causes—competition and great taxation. Will free trade in corn suffice to remedy those causes in other countries? No! Home taxation and foreign competition!—these are the enemies to England now as to Holland before. Free trade in corn could not preserve to Amsterdam its ascendency,—free trade in corn cannot give monopoly to Manchester.

I argue not in exclusive favour of Protection. I say, simply, that those who attribute all advantages to the opposite system have not facts sufficient to render their theory indisputable; that in all the commercial States in the history of the world, the policy of Protection has been admitted—more or less stringent, according to the expediency of the State; that the duration of commercial eminence in the most restrictive of all modern States, Venice, was more than double that of the most liberal of all modern States, Holland; that England has grown up into the greatest commercial commonwealth now existing, under systems of Protection; that under systems of Protection the rivals she has to encounter, in America, in Germany, in France, flourish and increase; that even our cotton manufacture, "that hardy child of Free Trade," was shown, before a Committee of the House of Commons, to have increased in the years between 1812 and 1826 in the ratio of only 270 per cent., while the cotton manufacture of France, "that sickly offspring of Protection," had increased in the ratio of 310 per cent.; and this in spite of French duties, the most really injudicious, on raw cotton and iron. "The increase," says Mr. Porter,† "has since gone forward with at least equal speed, the quantity of cotton used by the

<hr>

* *Commercial Dictionary*—Art. "Amsterdam."
† *Progress of the Nation*, Sect. ii. c. 3, "Manufactures."

manufacturers of France in 1843 having been equal to 132,000,000 of pounds, being about 70 per cent. addition in ten years, and about 22½ per cent. of the quantity used in the same year in the United Kingdom." And if we ask the cause of this progress in France, I suspect we shall soon find the "reason why." It is that she excludes the competition to which you so vainly invite her. In fine, no man can anywhere discover in history that Protection has been the cause of decline in any commercial State; the cause invariably has been found to be in the awakened energies of other countries; the pre-eminent state has lost its monopoly, through the competition of fresh rivals, in lands less taxed. It is quite true, that the judicious and tempered opening of some particular branch of trade, *over* protected, may often give it fresh stimulus and vigour; this was signally the case with the English Silk Trade; but it is equally true, that Protection to a certain, sometimes to a high, degree is necessary to other branches of trade at particular epochs. Nay, let us take the Silk Trade itself. There was a time when it was expedient to repeal the prohibitions, which gave to our silk manufacturer the monopoly of the home market; but there was a time when, without those prohibitions, the Silk Trade would have been without any market at all. The law of prohibition was enacted in 1765. Let any man look back, and see the comparative perfection of foreign looms at that period, and say, whether it would have been possible for the English manufacturer to have competed with his continental rival. What does Mr. Porter* himself remark on this head:—"By this prohibitory law, the English silk manufacturers were legally secured in the exclusive possession of the home market; from which, in the then imperfect condition of the manufacture, they would have been driven by the superior fabrics of foreign looms." The true reason why the prohibition finally failed was, that silk is an article against the importation of which prohibition is in vain. The smuggler stepped in, and redressed the market. But as long as the prohibition was effective, the manufactory thrived, and the operative had from 30*s.* to 40*s.* a week. When, in the beginning of the present century, the smuggler became formidable, the manufactory drooped and

* *Progress of the Nation*, Sect. ii. c. 2.

wages fell: it was then expedient to remove a useless prohibition. The smuggler was a more terrible rival than the Lyonnese. But the manufacture really rose while the protection was *de facto* strict, and fell exactly in proportion as the prohibition, though legally the same, became practically inoperative. The silk trade, when Mr. Huskisson legislated for it, was precisely in that state when an opened market gave stimulus and refreshed vitality; in 1765, an opened market, as Mr. Porter himself owns, would have destroyed it. Again, take the German States included in the Prussian League: they begin to compete with the English manufacturer; but with all their advantages of cheap food and cheap labour, could they do so, if not protected? What does our friend Mr. Porter say, too, on this head?—"At present it is only through the imposition of considerable import duty on the German States that their cotton goods are able in any way to compete with English fabrics." And what does he add?—"But it is altogether impossible to say how long this state of things may continue; and it may reasonably be expected that the German artisans will in time acquire a degree of skill and experience which, aided by the lower cost of subsistence in Germany as compared with England, will render their rivalry formidable to Manchester and Paisley—at least in neighbouring countries, if not in more distant parts of the world!" What! this formidable rivalry against our cotton manufacture—"that hardy child!" Is the rivalry, too, a "hardy child," growing up under Free Trade? No!—under a system of Protection, without which, Mr. Porter himself tells us, the Germans "are not able in any way to compete with our fabrics!"

It is clear, therefore, that what is one man's meat may be another man's poison. It is natural that the Manchester manufacturer should be desirous of competing with the German; it is natural that the German should, at present, beg to be excused; it is natural that the Cracovian corn-grower should be desirous of competing with the English; it is natural that the English corn-grower should be unwilling to have that honour thrust upon him. A State can adopt no dogma for universal application, whether of Protection or Free Trade. In those branches in which it produces more or better supplies at less cost, it must naturally court Free Trade; in those branches where its produce is less or its cost greater than that of its neighbours, it must either consent to the certain injury, the possible ruin, of that department of industry, or it must place it under Protection. Free Trade, could it be universally reciprocal, would therefore benefit Manchester *versus* Germany, and injure Lincolnshire *versus* Poland. The English cotton manufacturer thoroughly understands this when he says, with Mr. Cobden, "Let us have Free Trade, and we will beat the world!" But the world does not want to be beaten! Prussia, France, and even America, prefer "stupid selfishness" and protected manufactures to enlightened principles and English competition. When the English manufacturer says, "he wants only Free Trade to beat the world," he allows the benefit of Protection to his rivals, and excuses them for shutting their markets in his face.

But whether Free Trade be, in all cases, right or wrong, every one has allowed that we can't have it. To Free Trade, fairly and thoroughly carried out, there are more than fifty million obstacles to be found—in the Budget.*

That we must lay certain duties on certain foreign articles of general consumption, and cramp the home producer by the iron hand of the exciseman, are facts enforced upon our attention every time the miserable man doomed to hold the office of Chancellor of the Exchequer goes through the yearly agonies of his financial statement. Free Trade, too, in the proper acceptation of the term, by all the laws of grammar and common sense, requires two parties to the compact—the native and the foreigner. Between you and me, John, I see no hope of the foreigner. I wish, however, to raise no argument upon this, against the policy of our tariffs. Reciprocity may be good; but I allow that it is not essential. Wherever it is for our interest to open our markets, it would be idle to wait till the foreigner, against his idea of his interests, opened his own. All that I would observe is, that such one-sided liberality may be judicious and politic, but it has no right to the appellation of Free Trade.

But the name matters little; and the real question that

* " To expect that the freedom of trade should ever be entirely restored to Great Britain is as absurd as to expect that an Oceana or Utopia should ever be established in it."—ADAM SMITH's *Wealth of Nations*, Book iv. c. 11.

now opens before us is the special application of a special principle to the commodity of grain.

Free Trade at present means the free importation of foreign corn ; and that is the question I proceed to consider. In doing so, I shall make no declaration of war on political economy. I will not refuse to it the name which its professors arrogate for it—a science—though I cannot hold with M. Say that it has been investigated on the Baconian principle of philosophy—viz., the inductive. I do not think that it has proceeded from the collection, examination, and weighing of the largest number of experiences, and then, and not till then, deducing thence its general maxims. For obviously, were it so, we should not find such notable differences as I have shown in anticipations amongst its disciples,* nor so startling a disparity between

* If two men of the acuteness of Mr. Villiers and Mr. Wilson were studying any natural science according to the inductive philosophy, they would not differ as to facts produced by certain agencies, though they might differ widely as to the nature and inherent principle of the agencies themselves. They would both agree, for instance, that heat expands bodies ; but the one might contend that the nature of heat was an accident, and the other a substance, as philosophers have disputed from the time of Bacon to this day : they would, doubtless, come to a like result as to a proposition on the specific gravity of a fluid, though as to the cause of fluidity in bodies they might be wholly at variance. Mr. Villiers might assert that it depended on the globular form of the particles, Mr. Wilson on the caloric contained between them, or on both combined. For, notwithstanding the centuries that have passed since the experiment of Archimedes on fluid, those questions as to cause are, I believe, still open to discussion. Had they studied political economy in the same way, through induction and experiment, they could never differ as to whether a law like that put in motion by the opening of the home corn-market, through free importation, would raise or lower wages and prices ; though they might fairly differ as to the abstract nature of the principle which produced the effect. But this is precisely the reverse with them, as with all the exclusive students of political economy—they concur wonderfully as to the abstract principles, and differ only as to the results ;—whether political economy yet fails in what is the great and ultimate source of knowledge, viz., "the experience not of one man only, nor of one generation, but the accumulated experience of mankind in all ages ; "* or whether, from the many disturbing elements which society interposes between cause and effect, it cannot be thus inductively followed—certain it is, that they do not, as experimental philosophy demands, "suspend the preconceived notions of what might or ought to be the order of nature in any presupposed case, and content themselves with observing as a plain matter of fact what *is ;* † but rather pursue the opposite and more popular principle condemned by Bacon, viz., "of explaining phenomena according to their own preconceived notions." Now that mode of philosophising which makes sure of the results of a given agency under certain conditions, and reserves to the last the

---

* Herschel's Discourses on Natural Philosophy.   † Ibid.

the fund of its experiences and the rigidity of its dogmas. It has rather, I think, proceeded in "that opposite way" which Bacon[*] has condemned, and in which, according to him, no subtlety of definition, and no logical acuteness, can suffice to avail for the establishment of truth. It has rather commenced with the abstract principles, and then selected the experiences on which to support them—resembling somewhat that ingenious philosopher of whom Condillac informs us, who blessed himself with the persuasion that he had discovered a system that was to explain all the phenomena of Chemistry, and hastened to a practical chemist to communicate his discovery. "Unhappily," said the chemist, "the chemical facts are exactly the reverse of what, in this most luminous and ingenious discovery, you suppose them to be." "Tell me," then cries the philosopher, nothing daunted, "what the facts are, that I may explain them by my system!" But whether or not political economy be a science rather than a system, and a science based upon induction rather than logic, it is a study affording the most valuable suggestions, throwing light upon much that had been hitherto obscure; it is allied to researches with which I have for years been familiar; I have pondered it with attention, I would speak of it with respect; and it is the more my interest to do so now, for I shall rest much of my case on reference to

general maxims to be deduced, (nay, if it never even pretends to ascertain the abstract cause thereof,) can rarely be unsafe. But that other mode of philosophising in which men so able as Messrs. Wilson and Villiers can concur in asserting their absolute knowledge of the abstract principle, and of its infallibility, and yet contend that its application under the circumstances they are agreed on will produce totally opposite phenomena, is obviously always liable to mislead us into very great errors.

[*] Bacon, *Nov. Org.*, Lib. i. c. 19. [Bacon, in the passage here particularly referred to, says: *Duæ viæ sunt atque esse possunt ad inquirendam et inveniendam veritatem :* that is, There are and can be but two ways of investigating and discovering truth. *Altera a sensu et ad particularibus advolat ad axiomata maximè generalia, atque ex iis principiis eorumque immota veritate judicat et invenit axiomata media : atque hæc via in usu est :* that is, The one flies from sense and particulars to the most general axioms, and from these as first principles, and their undisputed truth determines and discovers middle axioms; and this is the way which is in use. *Altera a sensu et particularibus excitat axiomata, ascendendo continentè et gradatum, ut ultimo loco perveniatur ad maximè generalia : quæ via vera est sed intentata :* meaning, The other draws out the axioms from sense and particulars by ascending uniformly, and step by step, so that at last it reaches the most general or comprehensive; and this is the true way, but untried.]

its maxims and the admissions of its authorities. But I must be permitted to observe, that it is a common mistake with the ordinary run of students in political economy, to mistake altogether the nature of that science, and the reservations imposed upon the practical adoption of its principles. Political economy deals with but one element in a state—viz., its wealth; and the soundest political economists will be found cautiously stopping short of what would seem the goal of an argument with some such expression as—"But this belongs to national policy." Political economy goes strictly and sternly, as it were, towards the investigation of the rigid principle it is pursuing; it has only incidentally to do with the modifications which it would be wise to adopt when you apply the principle to living men. Of living men, their passions, and habits, and prejudices, it often * thinks no more than Euclid does when he is demonstrating the properties of a triangle. All this is out of the province of the political economist, and within that of the statesman.

Far from blaming political economy for this, it could not be what it professes to be if it were otherwise. The persons to blame are those who insist on applying all its principles, as if they were describing lifeless things, and not dealing with human beings; and hence innumerable mistakes, made by hasty readers, not only in the application, but we may say also in the comprehension, of the principle itself.

Political economy, for instance, says drily, "It is for the interest of a nation to do so and so." Well, grant that it is so; but every man who has dipped into metaphysics should know that there are different degrees of interest, and sometimes one degree of interest will practically be found to counterbalance the other; just the same as in phrenology, Gall or Spurzheim would say, "Here is a strong

---

* Mr. Senior, indeed, says distinctly that the political economist "is not to give a single syllable of advice, and that his business is neither to recommend nor dissuade, but to state general principles." Mr. M'Culloch, dissenting from this restricted view of the science, yet very properly distinguishes between political economy and politics: while he owns with a candour that proves the largeness of his intellect—"However humiliating the confession, it is certainly true that, owing to the want of information, not a few of the most interesting problems in economical legislation are at present all but insoluble."

impulse to combativeness, but is the man then combative? No; for here are two larger organs of caution and benevolence—that counterbalance the combative faculty."

Bearing in mind this variety of interests or impelling motives, let us take a favourite proposition in political economy, and we will do so in the words of Mr. Mill.

"It is the interest of two nations to exchange with one another two sorts of commodities, as often as the relative cost is different in the two countries." Now I will grant the general proposition; but it will often happen that there is a still stronger interest not thus to interchange particular articles. For instance, Athens manufactures admirable weapons at a cheaper cost than Bœotia; Bœotia produces corn, which Athens very much needs, at a much cheaper cost than Athens. Is it to the interest of Athens to exchange her weapons for the corn? Not if she has cause to dread the hostility of Bœotia, and believes that the weapons she thus sends out will be used with advantage against her freedom and existence. There is an interest to effect exchange with two sorts of commodities, the relative cost of producing them being very different in the two countries, upon the abstract general principle, but, in the special case, a much stronger interest not to furnish Bœotia with weapons.

Take another case. Suppose Germany has lately instituted a cotton manufacture, but produces cotton goods with greater labour (that is, more cost) than England, and England, on the other hand, produces corn at more cost than Germany—Is it for the interest of Germany to exchange her corn for the English cotton goods? No; for, as it has been seen, we have Mr. Porter's assurance that nothing but protective duties can preserve the German cotton manufacture from ruin, as against the English competition. Therefore here, again, though, on the abstract general principle, it is the interest of Germany to exchange with England two sorts of commodities, of which the relative cost is different, yet she has a stronger interest, in the special case, to guard the cotton manufactures, which may ultimately enrich her much more than the price she receives for the corn that she sends into England. So, finally, without in the least disputing the abstract proposition of Mr. Mill, a statesman may well consider, that, seeing the importance to England of a thriving and prosperous agriculture, and all the danger to the State that may be incurred by the impoverishment and disaffection of many millions of his countrymen, there is a greater interest, in the special case, to limit an exchange which may be as injurious, for a time at least, to the British husbandman, as Germany holds it injurious to the German cotton manufacturer. For the political economist deals with the dead principle—the statesman, with the living men.

These distinctions would be perfectly clear to all persons, if they would only regard political economy as they do any other investigation of art or science. First, with regard to the abstract truth of its principles, and next, to the prudence of applying them in each special instance.

Suppose that I write a treatise on Architecture, wherein I geometrically establish the fact that the Parthenon is a most beautiful building. If my neighbour, Squire Hawthorn, who lives in an old-fashioned irregular country-house, as unlike the Parthenon as a house can be, runs to me out of breath, transported to enthusiasm by my admirable treatise,—"My dear sir, I have read your work; you have proved to my satisfaction that no building on earth is so perfect as the Parthenon. Pray, would you advise me to pull down Hawthorn Hall, and build a country-house exactly on the model of which you have so lucidly given the geometrical designs? Shall I turn Hawthorn Hall into a Parthenon? What's your advice?"

"Sir," I should answer, unless I had a sinister interest to answer otherwise, "I am not the proper person of whom to ask that advice; whether it is for your interest to pull down your very irregular old house,—whether, if you did, you would be as comfortable in a Parthenon; and, however beautiful that edifice, find that it could be adapted to the wants of your family and the difference of your climate— whether you could even live in it, without catching your death of cold—are all considerations with which I had nothing to do when I wrote my treatise. My object was but to explain the true principles of Architecture, and establish the excellence of the Parthenon upon geometrical principles!"

Squire Hawthorn would have no right to blame me for having written my treatise and disturbed his mind; but he would be a monstrous great fool if he turned his old hall into a Parthenon!

In this Letter, I trust, my dear John, that I have cleared my way to a fair and candid examination of a subject uppermost in men's minds; that I have shown that there is nothing in that great storehouse of truth called History which should induce us to believe that a fiscal enactment once passed, must be regarded as a law not to be repealed; and that, according to history, such belief can be least entertained on the matter of the very enactment which we are forbidden to question; that there is nothing in the doubt whether absolute Free Trade in corn be desirable, that implies indifference or distaste to freedom in political opinions; that, whether examining the contradictory assertions of the Corn Law repealers, or the records of nations, a man may presume to form a judgment in favour of Protection applied to certain articles of home cultivation and industry without being necessarily excluded from the average understanding of the human biped; that it is obvious, by the admission of the great authorities of Free Trade themselves, that there are circumstances under which a check upon competition, by means of protective duties, is necessary to the article produced; and finally, that, whatever our respect for political economy, it is one thing to accept the general principle, another to enforce its application to each special instance.

Think of all this, my dear John; and having commenced with stating that the policy of the Coming Man should be that of conciliation, now let us see whether it will be just and wise to leave out of that policy the class whose claims I am about to advocate.

Your affectionate well-wisher,
And A LABOURER, though
A LANDLORD.

LETTER II.

MY DEAR JOHN,—I closed my last Letter by subscribing myself " A Labourer, though a Landlord." Why did I arrogate that title? not merely as a boast, though it be one of which I am justly proud. Why? Because, when my main income was derived from my labour, ten years before I was a landlord, I recorded, by my vote in Parliament, the same opinion that I profess now—viz., that a total repeal of the Corn Laws would ultimately prove injurious to the true social interests of this community.

If I have, as a landlord, a landlord's interest in the question, it cannot, therefore, be taken in account against my honesty in the formation of my convictions—let it be taken in account against the motives that still uphold my consistency in the same faith, to whatever extent it may be supposed that self-interest perverts the judgment or misconceives the argument. Yet, even so, it is the law of our land, and the privilege of freemen, for each class to state its own grievance. And were men to be dismissed unheard, because they felt the injury of which they complain, pray tell me what grievance, since the world began, would ever have been redressed?

On the other hand, my dear John, while I believe that my land, which is free from all mortgage, is not of that kind on which the severest loss is likely to be incurred; so, health permitting, I have as a labourer a resource that all landlords do not enjoy—and if my rents should fall, no corn law will affect my pen and my brain,—I can work; I am used to it. Moreover, dear John, you are too fine-hearted a fellow not to own that avarice is rarely the most cogent motive in the ambition of public men. It is something to see myself separated, not by my own change of opinions, but by theirs, from the party with which, in public, I have acted, and the men whom, in private, I have honoured or loved—and on this, as on all matters where conviction is strong and earnest, whatever divides the opinion, estranges the friendship;—it is something for many years, and those spreading over the prime of manhood, to have stood alone and excluded from the noble field of action—Parliamentary life. Had I consented not to compromise, nay, but to conceal, the doubts I entertain, as to the success of the experiment made on the original and primary source of capital,—land,—I should have been at no loss for a seat in Parliament. But I could not accept the experiment as a *fait accompli* until its results were tested, and thus my principles, right or wrong, at least have not furthered my ambition. Nor, if the Free-Traders are right, and the authority of intelligence and the power of numbers are opposed to the views I entertain, is it much to my interests, as a writer, to hazard at once my reputation with the few and my popularity with the many, by plying, with feeble oar, against the strong current of the day?

Wherefore, all these circumstances, *pro* and *con*, balanced fairly one against the other, I trust that I may be exonerated from the suspicion of interests purely sinister and selfish, and that, if my views be erroneous, they will be held those of a man who is accustomed to carry his gaze beyond the map of his estate, and is capable of fears more generous than such as darken the perspective that is closed by an audit-day. And though I have advanced the doctrine that there is nothing which in historical precedent or political science should make us condemn the principle of Protection, as applied whether to land or to manufactures, in certain periods, or under certain conditions, I am inclined to go very far—nay, as far as the most eminent political economists, whom Time acknowledges to be the standard authorities of their school, in the policy of exposing native agriculture to the risk of foreign competition, and of procuring a steady and regular importation of corn, as the best means of extending the market of our manufacturers. I cannot consent, it is true, to say with Mr. Cobden, that the fear of depending solely for the staple of food upon the soil of the foreigner is an exploded fallacy. If it be so, it is a fallacy that was never exploded from the mind of the man who most combined the practical statesman with the political economist—I mean Mr. Huskisson. However else he might have modified the strong opinions that he once expressed upon protection to agriculture, it is notorious to those who best knew him, that Mr. Huskisson never modified, never changed this doctrine, " that in peace the habitual dependence on foreign supply is dangerous. We place the subsistence of our own population not only at the mercy of foreign powers, but also on their being able to spare us as much corn as we may want to buy." Thus said Mr. Huskisson in 1815; and in 1827 he said, "I hold that doctrine now, and think nothing so dangerous to this country as to rely too largely and too frequently on foreign countries for supplies of corn."*

I cannot consent, then, to dismiss the authority of a man like Mr. Huskisson, upon the risk of depending on the foreigner, with the contempt which it inspires in Mr. Cobden; nor do I think that those answers to Mr. Huskisson which he borrows from Mr. Mill, and considers so victorious (viz., " that countries most dependent on their neighbours for grain, have enjoyed the steadiest and least variable market; that if one neighbour withholds his corn others will send it, and that the abundant harvests of one land may atone for the deficiencies of another,") would have been considered by Mr. Huskisson incontestably established by a sufficient number of experiments and facts.   But it is not now my object to dispute those premises, since I am willing to concede the conclusions to which they bring Messieurs Cobden and Mill. And looking to the rapid increase of our population, doubting the results that some anticipate, from bringing our own waste lands into cultivation, seeing the growth and grandeur of our manufacturing interests—knowing that whatever corn we take from the foreigner must increase the sale of whatever cotton or other manufacture the foreigner takes from us—seeing, moreover, that no system of protection, short of prohibition, could prevent our receiving some supplies of corn from abroad, I willingly allow, with Mr. Mill, that the apprehension of future evil should not operate against present good; and cannot prevail against what nature and commerce have made stronger than all arguments, viz., necessity.

I do not, therefore, dispute the policy of opening to foreign corn a constant and regular market in our ports— and of exposing the home producer to a severe competition; but I do maintain that, while you arrogate Mr. Huskisson's authority, you should so far respect his judgment as to take some precaution that, while the supplies of corn from abroad are increased, the supplies grown at home do not

* Mr. Cutler Ferguson, than whom a more honourable and truthful man never existed, said in the debate on Mr. Hume's motion on the Corn Law, 1834:—" I was intimately acquainted with Mr. Huskisson's sentiments on these subjects, and know that to the last it was his opinion that a great country like this should not be subject to foreign powers in the article of food."

incur the risk of being materially diminished—that the competition you invite, while it will tend to lower the price, may serve to stimulate the energies that will augment the quantity; and so, while fitting the farmer for the struggle, save the country from that absolute reliance on the harvests and the will of other States, which I firmly believe could never exist without endangering our political independence as a nation, and subjecting us to more than fluctuations—to scarcities, approaching to famine. Are these sentiments to be despised? "Yes," cries Mr. Cobden, "the men in fustian would laugh them to scorn!" Be it so—it is at Mr. Huskisson they laugh!—the sentiments are his; and I will quote his words in order afterwards, my dear John, to call your attention to a signal proof that his sagacity is already shown to be deeper than that of any of the gentlemen, whether they be clothed in fustian or broadcloth, who laugh at him. Thus says Mr. Huskisson :— "Suppose, as it frequently happens, the harvest in this year to be a short one, not only in this country, but the foreign countries, from which we are fed. What follows? The habitually exporting country, *France*, for instance, stops the export of its corn, and feeds its people without any great pressure. The habitually importing country, England, which, even in a good season, has hitherto depended on the aid of foreign corn, deprived of that aid in a year of scarcity, is driven to distress, bordering upon famine."

Now observe, my Lord John Russell (in arguing lately that the present low prices were to be held no criteria for the future) stated, as a peculiar phenomenon in the case, "that corn had come exactly from the quarter which *no* one had anticipated—viz. France."

Mr. Huskisson, at least, was more far-sighted—it is expressly France that he names as the quarter from which the exports will habitually come. Of this I myself never had a doubt—I said so at the time of the Repeal of the Corn Laws, not induced to that belief by any examination of tariffs and reports, but simply from my personal knowledge of the social habits of the French. It is difficult for an Englishman to imagine how the small French proprietor, usually a peasant, will pinch and save in his household, in order to put monies into his pouch. There is that in the actual property of land, strongly contrasting mere tenure, still more service by hire, which induces the labourer who owns it to push economy into what you, my dear John, would call the self-mortification of the miser. The more corn your farming labouring children can grow, the more they will eat; the more corn *Jacques Bonhomme* can grow, with the better heart he will starve;—it is something not to live upon, but to send away and to sell. And the money goes;—upon mutton and shoes, tobacco and coffee? No, my dear John; upon buying some other half acre of land— which after his death will be equitably subdivided, perhaps among a family of five — from whom the self-pinching system will start anew.* From France habitually you will have corn, but there is no country in the world upon which it is more dangerous to rely for the quantity and steadiness of the supply. Take this year :—suppose that your recent change had been some years in operation—that a great deal of British land, now devoted to corn, had relinquished that grain, as the Free-Traders tell us it ought—that there was a scarcity at home—and in the same year a scarcity in France—or a quarrel with that somewhat irascible country, (which, to do it justice, is always willing to sacrifice self-interest to some touchy crochet of honour,) pray do you think, then, that the men in fustian would laugh Mr. Huskisson to scorn ? Or dare you say that they might not be inclined to exclaim with him—"Let the bread we eat be the produce of corn grown amongst ourselves, and I for one care not how cheap it is — the cheaper the better: cheapness produced by foreign importation is the sure fore-runner of scarcity, and a steady home supply the only safe foundation of steady and moderate prices."

What is it, then, that I ask ? I go much farther than Mr. Huskisson did in 1815; go as far as I believe he ever

* It is thus stated in recent statistical accounts of France, that less butcher's meat is consumed now by its population than there was under the ancient *regime*, when the state of the agricultural peasantry is represented to have been so miserable. And the fact is accounted for (no doubt justly) by the asserters of the social improvement effected by the Great Revolution—in the doctrine that the small subdivisions of land, which have raised the peasant from the serf into the proprietor, have induced habits of extraordinary thrift, and that to maintain his land, and to meet its mortgages, he stints himself much more in the consumption of food than he did, when living totally from day to day without heed of the morrow, upon the wages secured from a master.

went. I subscribe to the expediency of opening our ports
—of greatly increasing our regular importation of corn;—
and all that I ask of the manufacturer is this—Fit the
farmer for the competition you force on him; and, gaining
a great deal, concede a little in return! You say that you
find in Christianity itself a sanction for the maxim to buy
in the cheapest, and sell in the dearest market. There is
another maxim to which the sanction of Christianity is
more generally conceded—"As ye would that men should
do to you, do ye also to them likewise." Your friend, Mr.
M'Culloch, in speaking of the Cotton Trade, and in seeking
to calm any excess of imprudent compassion which might
be excited by the sufferings of the children employed in
the factories, uses these very sensible and conciliatory expressions :—

"The subsistence of 1,400,000 people is not to be endangered on slight grounds. The abuses, even, of such a
business, must be cautiously dealt with ; lest, in eradicating
them, we shake or disorder the whole fabric."

· I concede this proposition in favour of the British
manufacturers of cotton; and I claim that concession in
favour of the British producers of corn.

But in this latter case, it is more than 1,400,000 persons
whose subsistence is involved. I will take the lowest calculations of the proportional agricultural population that I
can find in any Free-Trade authorities; and it is at least a
fourth of the entire population in Great Britain, and considerably more than half the population in Ireland.* And
from these computations I omit altogether one important
item, in wealth at least, if not in numbers—I mean *the
landowners*, classed under the general head of "Persons of
independent means." Take, then, the agricultural population of Great Britain at certainly not less than three millions and a half; add to it the millions similarly engaged
in Ireland. Join to these the landlords "of independent
means ;" and if you refuse to annex to such numbers the
most moderate proportion that can be assigned of that part
of the trading population, such as the ploughwright, the ,

* Mr. Porter calculates from the census of 1841, that the farmers, graziers,
bailiffs, agricultural labourers, &c., are to be assessed at 25·17 per cent. of the
population in Great Britain ; and 66·15 per cent. in Ireland. The landowners (if of independent means) are not reckoned in either computation.

wheelwright, the blacksmith, the farrier—essentially dependent upon the agriculturist—still you will have in Great Britain and Ireland at least eight million persons vitally interested in your laws affecting their produce and its price. Surely, then, I may well exclaim that the subsistence of numbers so far exceeding all the population engaged in the cotton trade, to whom I make a similar concession, should not be hazarded—I will not say on slight grounds, but on grounds that have already called forth one cry of acknowledged distress; and that even if abuse does exist, in such a business you should be as careful of eradicating it, "lest you shake or disorder the whole fabric," as you would of interference with the economy of the cotton trade. Yet how have we dealt with this mighty interest? We have for more than half a century, by repeated acts of our legislation, approved, confirmed, rooted as a very habit of thought into the minds of the cultivators of our soil, the idea that Protection from the foreigner is necessary to their existence. And having ourselves authorised that faith, we have suddenly removed all that we ourselves have told them their very existence required, and brought them into unmitigated competition with lands the most fertile which the world can boast, tilled by populations exempted from the burdens we bear! Just see how differently the Free-Traders dealt with the silk manufacture, which has been so often cited against us in advocating the advantage of foreign competition over protective duties. When, by the advice of Mr. Huskisson, you removed the prohibition of foreign silk goods, beginning in 1824, you left in 1826 an *ad valorem* duty of 30 per cent. on the importation of foreign silk goods. You altered the duty to specific rates per pound, but so calculated upon different kinds of goods as to be equal in most cases to 30 per cent. upon the presumed value, this rate being assumed as the maximum of protection; yet was the duty bounded in effect to 30 per cent.? Far from it: twenty years afterwards, the duties on crape were from 43 to 50 per cent.; on velvet, from 34 to 50 per cent.; on silk net, from 36 to to 58 per cent.; on manufactured bonnets, 145 per cent. I quote from the statement of Sir Robert Peel, on January 27, 1846—eventful day to the agriculturist!

Such was the protection you left to manufactures in silk

when you began to open the trade—such was the protection
you left to them for twenty years. And you still left protection to silk (it exists still) on the very day that you
passed sentence on the corn-grower, and doomed him to
compete, not as the manufacturer of silk does with the
rival inhabitants of a few towns, and meeting that rivalry
with advantages no other land possesses—but wherever in
the universe corn can be sowed in a richer soil, ripened
under a brighter sun, reaped by a cheaper labour. You
were as clearly persuaded of the truth of your abstract
principle of the benefit of free trade in silk as you are in
that of corn; but you applied it in the one case with due consideration of the fact that you were dealing not only with
the interests, but the convictions (and, if you will, with
the prejudices) of human beings; and you have dealt, in
the other case, with as much sternness as if the machinery of
your law operated only upon brute matter. Why, when you
opened the trade in silk, did you leave still to the silk manufacturer duties so protective? Mr. Huskisson stated the
reason, and all succumbed to it—"Because, as our manufactures were burthened by taxation, a protection as against
France was necessary." The reason by which you aided
the competition that was successful in silk, you throw to
the winds when you call forth a far severer competition in
corn. And while you have been thus abrupt and imperious
in enforcing so wholesale and entire a change upon the
business in which many millions are engaged, in what
mode have you shaped your policy so as to soften, at least,
the austerity of your fiat? By all that can soothe irritation, by all that can encourage effort, by all that can
lighten burdens? No. You have done it so that it is
made to bear a character the most galling; made to seem
the triumphant victory of the men who had gone about
from platform to platform to preach a crusade against
those whom your change has afflicted; who had used
language the most derisive to their understanding, the
most inflammatory against their motives: whose favourite
expressions for the owners of the land had been "Vampire"
and "Blood-sucker," and for the occupiers, "Thick-scull"
and "Bull-calf." Very good words, it may be, for a cheer
or a laugh, but not words that make eloquence as per-
suasive as it is "unadorned." And when the chief to whom

this class had committed its interests, and the leader who had so shortly before proposed on its behalf a duty of 8*s*., concurred to ascribe the principal merit of the wholesale change enforced to the head of the Anti-Corn Law League —thereby approving an agitation that had created an *imperium in imperio,* and virtually commending the oratory of abuse which yet rung in the ears and rankled at the hearts of the victims—can you say that you did not make your experiment as intolerable to the spirit of Englishmen as it has been abrupt and trying to the resources upon which so many millions depend ?   The Italian proverb saith, "That it must be a very fine tree to make one pleased to be hung from it."   And a tree more rugged and thorny than that on which you have hung the British corn-grower, certainly never yet was planted by the hand of the legislator.   .

Reflect, too, from whom come these assaults on the very character of those who advocated the protection our habitual legislation had taught to consider essential to their existence ?   Who denounced them as plunderers and robbers, bloodsuckers and vampires ?   The very men who had first introduced protection into the legislature.   Thus says the Father of Free Trade, Adam Smith :—" The merchants and manufacturers seem to have been the original inventors of these restraints upon the importation of foreign goods which secure to them the monopoly of the home market. . . . It was probably in imitation of them, and to put themselves on a level with those who they found were opposed to oppress them, that the country gentlemen and farmers of Great Britain so far forgot the generosity which is natural to their stations as to demand the exclusive privilege of supplying their countrymen with corn and butcher's meat."

And Sir Robert Peel himself, at the very time that he extolled the "unadorned eloquence" which had sought to arouse the country against the class that was struggling for what Sir Robert Peel himself had asserted, during the whole previous period of his career, to be the condition of life to them and of welfare to the commonwealth, still echoed Adam Smith, and said, with the Repeal of the Corn Law in his hand—"*It was the mercantile and manufacturing interest which set the example of requiring protection.*"

Of this there can be no doubt. Our statutes tell us that the policy of protection was introduced on behalf of the manufacturers and merchants, and at their own demand, for centuries before it was accorded to the land.

And if such has been your mode to soothe the pain and to cheer the spirit, where has since been your attempt to lighten the burden?

Nothing can be more true, and nothing more tacitly acceded to by the conscience of the community, than the proposition Mr. Disraeli has luminously stated—viz., that under the system of Protection, offered and insisted on as a counter-equivalent, you have built up your present system of taxation; you remove the equivalent, you will not touch the taxation. Just consider the vast amount of taxes that has been taken off since the war—the manner in which, especially of late years, since 1830, the reductions have been shaped so as to give the greatest relief or the greatest impetus to manufactures; and out of all those millions so dealt with, what, from the passing of the Corn Law in 1815 to the year 1846, has been the amount of taxes, bearing chiefly on agriculture, reduced or repealed? I quote the authority of Mr. Pressley himself before the House of Lords—£985,824!—a relief that appears as nothing, compared with the vast sums which have been cast forth from the revenue to meet the demands of rival interests in commerce and manufactures. And justly so. Why? because during those years the agriculturists had their equivalent—protection! But the protection is vanished from the agriculturist, and the agriculturist stands alone in the community without a due share of relief.

And now, my dear John, as I know you are a lover of fair play, even in fighting your enemies, (if, indeed, wo poor owners and tillers of land are to be so considered,) let us see whether we have had something of good faith to set off against so much severity—let us see whether you would not have been ashamed to have dealt with a Frenchman, when you were at war with him, as your agents have dealt with your own children.

In 1846, Sir Robert Peel, in arguing for Free Trade, observes, "I have always felt and maintained that the land is subject to peculiar burdens." He goes on to argue that the question of Free Trade is one of policy—that of relief to peculiar burdens on those it may affect, one of justice; and he implies as strongly as man can do, that, having decided on the question of policy we should then have to consider the question of justice.

The antithesis was ominous. What Englishman, on reading it, will not say with Burke, "It was with the greatest difficulty that I was able to separate policy from justice. Justice itself is the great standing policy of civil society; and any eminent departure from it, under any circumstances, lies under the suspicion of being no policy at all." But to proceed—

Lord John Russell, in his letter to the Queen, 1846, (read to the House of Commons,) states that the measures which Sir Robert Peel had in contemplation appear to have been "a present suspension of the duties of corn—a repeal of the Corn Laws at no remote period, preceded by diminution of duties—relief to the occupiers of land from burdens by which they are peculiarly affected, so far as it may be practicable." And Lord John adds, in the same letter, an opinion yet more strongly expressed as to the said burdens—"Lord John Russell is prepared to assent to the opening of the ports, and to the fiscal relief which it was calculated to convey. He would have accompanied this proposal with measures of relief to a considerable extent of the occupiers of land from the burdens to which they were subjected."

Now, I ask you, John, as an honest man, whether a distinct and positive pledge of the relief of burdens on land be not hereby and herein held forth as an accompaniment to the repeal of the Corn Laws?—whether many, who in Parliament agreed to such a repeal, must not have been so induced to agree?—whether the country generally would not have been led on to accept the policy, by the persuasion that the justice that was to soften it would be fairly meted out? Well, what has been the fact? Sir Robert Peel removed the protection, and left untouched the burdens he had engaged to release. It is true that he did at the time dwell on some peddling and pitiful mitigations of local burdens—some mitigations of a county rate, on the proportions the land should pay to the gaoler of the prison and the doctor of the pauper, on some trifling extension of the law of settlement. But there was not a man in the country who did not feel that it was not to such miserable doles that Sir Robert Peel could have meant to stint the performance of his solemn engagements to the land, if he had remained in office, and when, having carried his system of policy, his mind would be free to consider freely the question of justice.   Well, Lord John becomes Prime Minister; he accepts the task of maintaining and perpetnating the repeal of the Corn Laws; but surely with it he inherits the pledge to relieve the burdens of the land. Is not this the absolute condition imposed by good faith? And could any man suppose we were afterwards to be met by a doubt if there were any burdens at all?   And if before the enactment of the law, when the sages and prophets of the Corn League predicted that the land would be no sufferer—that rents would rather rise than fall—prices would average 7s. on wheat, where they now average 5s.— farmers rather flourish than decay—agricultural wages rather increase than diminish—if then Lord John thought such concessions of relief to a considerable extent fair and reasonable, how much more have they become so now, when the distress of the cultivator is acknowledged by Lord John himself, and lamented in the speech which is delivered from the throne?   Concessions!   First, reduction on bricks, which benefits certainly urban speculators more than it can at present the unhappy landlord, who has small heart for building new farm premises; and now a further reduction on timber, which, where the landowner has any timber on his property, is another diminution of the income from which he is to contribute new barns and granaries for the corn, which the farmer trembles while he stores!   And this is the way faith has been kept to us, and the pledges of two Prime Ministers fulfilled!

The true question before us is plain.   Will you, or will you not, conciliate this great interest, comprising so much of your capital — this great class, containing so large a share of your population?   Are you to continue to treat the producers of bread, in your own country, as an enemy whom it is necessary or wise thoroughly and resolutely to conquer and put down; or as a vast element in the commonwealth, with whose claims and opinions it is prudent and patriotic to effect some gentle compromise?   And here let me observe that, in all important questions which you have safely and durably settled, you have always (and in all times and countries judicious statesmen always have) shunned to extend too far the victory of one opinion over another. It is the principle of compromise, more or less extended, upon which you have always gone; and hence the stability of your institutions, and the contrast they present to our impetuous neighbours, the French, who, because they push the dogma of the day into the unqualified triumph of a party, obtain nothing that far-sighted men can consider settled, and leave liberty equally endangered by the pressure of the mob and the cannon of the soldier. Your great constitutional changes, where durable, have been compromises—your religious Reformation—your Revolution of 1688—your Reform Bill of 1831—were all compromises between the extremes of opinion. The sole time when you deserted this principle was amidst the passions of the Civil War, when you destroyed a Monarchy, tried for a Republic, gained a Dictatorship, passed at once into reaction, and welcomed back in Charles the Second a despotism more degrading than that which you had successfully resisted in Charles the First. Beware then, how, in dealing with your own countrymen, and in those civil wars which are now fought by the pen or in the senate—beware how you push, too far, even what you consider just on the abstract principle. This total repeal of all Protection, as affecting men whom your previous legislation has tutored, right or wrong, into believing that without Protection there is ruin, is no compromise—it is the extreme opinion urged to its extremest point, and, as I have shown, in its harshest character; it has been attended with insult, with betrayal, with forfeited promises and broken faith.

My Lord John Russell, you are fond of quoting Burke: your scholarship can appreciate the vast range of his knowledge; your experience of men, the common sense that lies under the subtlety of his thought or the glow of his eloquence; and the natural loftiness of your mind, when it rises free from the trammels of party, finds something congenial in that genius which was equally hostile to cruelty and meanness, whether they took the plausibilities of power or usurped the high attributes of freedom. Does your lordship remember these passages, or can you dispute their application?—

" What is the use of discussing men's abstract right to food or medicine? The question is upon the method of procuring and administering them. In that deliberation I shall always advise to call in the aid of the farmer and the physician, rather than the professor of metaphysics." . . .

" The science of government being, therefore, so practical in itself, and intended for such practical purposes, a matter which requires experience, and even more experience than any man can gain in his whole life, however sagacious and observing he may be, it is with infinite caution that any man ought to venture upon pulling down an edifice which has answered in any tolerable degree for ages the common purposes of society, or on building it up again without having models and patterns of approved utility before his eyes."

On these two passages I make but two brief comments—

In the first, Burke would, in deliberating on the method of procuring and administering food, call in the aid of the farmer rather than the professor of metaphysics. It is the farmer whom, in your change, you altogether exclude from your council; and I will show, later, that you have not even on your side the aid of the professor of metaphysics, though you may have the sanction of some of his obscurer disciples.

Look to the second passage. Can you deny that you pull down the whole edifice of protection, which has for ages sheltered the farmer, and which has so far answered the common purposes of society that, to use the words of Sir Robert Peel, " if you convinced us that your most sanguine hopes would be realised, that this country would become the workshop of the world, would blight, through the cheapness of food and the demand for foreign corn, the manufacturing industry of every other country, we should not forget, amid all these presages of complete happiness, that it is under the influence of protection to agriculture, continued for two hundred years, that the fen has been drained, the wild heath reclaimed, the health of a whole people improved, their life prolonged—and all this not at the expense of manufacturing prosperity, but concurrently with its wonderful advancement." *

You pull down this edifice. Where is the " model and

* Speech of Sir Robert Peel, 1839.

pattern of approved utility before your eyes? " Historian that you are, I defy you to find in all history one such model and pattern. I turn to you, my dear Mr. Bull, to your agents and your family, and I say renovate, alter, repair, curtail the edifice—do not wholly pull down. I say you are dealing with men, not machines — fellow-citizens, not foes; conciliate, do not crush; compromise, do not conquer. Have you a compromise? You have, theoretically, two; practically, but one. Theoretically, you have the option of revising your whole taxation, national and local, and readjusting those burdens which, under Protection, you laid or continued to enforce on the agricultural interest : but so arduous is the task of dealing with the most prominent and least disputed of all—the Poor-Rate; so injurious to the condition of the working class, so favourable to the extension of pauperism, does all sound evidence prove it would be to take the rates from local control, and add them to national taxation; and so difficult does it appear to be to restore and enforce the original law—which, declaring that every man should contribute to the support of the poor according to his means, imposed the relief of pauperism upon personal as well as real property—that I believe any systematic and wholesale legislation, which should aim at dividing fairly amongst the community the burdens which now rest unduly on the land, could not be carried into effect. And therefore this compromise with the agricultural interest is not practically in your power. Your difficulty is not diminished by the loud cry of the opposite party, that, in point of fact, no such undue burdens exist; that the land does not bear more than its due proportion—some say, even less; for, if your object is to conciliate, the very discussion of such questions only frustrates that at which you would aim. And—wrangle, cavil, subtleise and special-plead as you may—you cannot convince either owner or occupier that he does not pay taxes which he does not see paid by his neighbour; that the poor-rate collector does not take out of his pocket pounds which the poor-rate collector does not take out of the pockets of a man better off than himself. Nay, the very arguments by which you urge the necessity of repealing the Corn Law bring before him more strik-ingly the injustice of the burden that cripples the competition to which you condemn him. For you say that the old proportions of property are altered, that the manufacturing wealth increases in a ratio far beyond that of the agricultural; and yet this increasing wealth escapes comparatively free from the support of the very population that it forces to produce it! It takes the sinews of the human being, from childhood to decay, and then throws the human machine, when it breaks under its use, upon the alms of that very property to which that human machine has yielded no return, and towards the war against which it has been used as an instrument. Glance at this instance from the evidence given before the Committee of the House of Lords, (on the Burdens on Land). A farmer was examined, and speaks thus :—" The poor-rates on Mr. Heathcoat's factory, in this parish, have averaged £41 0s. 9d. a-year, for the last seven years; on the farm occupied by myself, £58 2s. So that I have paid £17 1s. 3d. a-year more than Mr. Heathcoat. My rental is £300 a-year, and the profits you can imagine; Mr. Heathcoat's profits are reputed to be £40,000 a-year!

Now, observe, if in any time of distress Mr. Heathcoat reduces the number of hands he employs in the produce of his wealth, the men thus thrown out of work fall, not on the factory which their labour has benefited, but on the lands of the parish. The farmer maintains not only the paupers for whom the land has no labour, but those whom the factory flings back upon the land.* Nor, while thus oppressed by the Free Trade, and unrelieved by the burden, can you convince the agriculturists that this Free Trade, which so endangers the returns to his industry in its habitual directions, fairly opens to him fresh fields for his enterprise and invention. You may tell him there are reasons why he should not unrestrictedly sell any sugar he may extract from beet-root; but it is quite clear that those reasons are opposed to Free Trade. You may tell him there are reasons why he should not grow tobacco; but he sees in France that tobacco is a main element in the profits

---

* I cannot here resist quoting the witty " definition of the building called a factory," by Henry Brougham, before that illustrious man was a Corn-Law repealer—" A large building, erected on a comparatively small piece of ground, carrying on the manufacture of two very important articles—cotton and paupers"

of the cultivator, and that portions of his land could grow quite as good tobacco as that which the labouring population poison the air with in France. And if there are reasons why he should not have Free Trade for such experiment, which his climate does not suit, he replies to you that he finds reasons quite as good why Free Trade should not be forced on him in the article to which he is condemned as the staple of his produce, and for which his climate *is* suited.

Suppose that the merchant has hitherto had a monopoly of the markets in India, and by some change in your commercial system he is driven from those markets by foreign competition. He complains, and you say, "Unjust Man, we have done with monopoly;" he then turns his prows towards the North, and you say, "No, there you must not deal." "Why?" "We have permitted to our Colonists a monopoly against you." "Towards the West?" "No, my friend, the products of the West do not suit your way of business, and for very good reasons; we have given to others a monopoly there, too, for which they pay us a very high price!" Suppose this, and then allow me to ask, whether you could continue to read to your merchant a lecture on the blessings of Free Trade? Reverse the case, and what the difference, when the farmer sees Free Trade give to the foreigner his market in corn, and monopoly exclude his fields from beet-root and tobacco?

In dealing with mankind, I say, as said one who understood nations well, "that even if burdens are laid on fairly, you must convince those who suffer that such burdens are fair." I say this without prejudice to the question whether the land is or is not disproportionably burdened. I am ready, if necessary, to go wholly into that consideration. And if I do not do so now, it is, first, because I never yet met a fair and dispassionate thinker who doubted the fact, though he might cavil as to the degree. Secondly, because, at the very time the Corn Law was repealed, the fact of the burdens was admitted by the Minister who repealed it, and the Minister to whom the maintenance of the repeal was intrusted. Thirdly, because the promise of relief to those burdens accompanied the intimation of their repeal; and, without such promise, I *know* that many of the votes Sir Robert Peel obtained to his change of policy would have been withheld. And we have a right, if you tell us that we must submit to the hardship, to hold as unchallengeable, in point of honesty, the pledge that was given to us of relief from the burdens acknowledged by those who inflicted the hardship. Fourthly, because I here argue for the expediency of a compromise; and compromise in the way of relief from taxation, be my assertions ever so true, and any calculations I might found on them ever so accurate, I am convinced that every financier would concur with me in considering wholly impracticable.

The second compromise, and the only one you can actually effect, is to deal in some mode with your customs, that, interfering the least with the good you anticipate from your recent experiment—leaving undisturbed your general tariff —militating not against its main principle, and recommended by the great authorities you have assumed as your guides, may yet be of some benefit to the agricultural producer, and put him in good heart and good humour to befriend the system you have commenced. Such a compromise Lord Derby has proposed, viz., a low fixed duty upon wheat and other grain—a tax upon the foreigner for the benefit of the native cultivator; and the profits of that tax to go in relief of the most odious burden upon all, whether engaged in trade, commerce, agriculture, or manufactures.

In favour of this low fixed duty as a compromise, I submit these considerations to the Free-Trader:—First, That it still leaves you the victory for which you so eagerly contend—the victory over the abstract principle of Protection. I can well conceive a derisive cheer at this sentence. "So the principle of Protection you give up!" My dear fellow-citizens, I am not writing for Protection or Free Trade as abstract principles; I am writing for what I believe, in my conscience, to be the very existence of a generation of human beings, and in deprecation of the consequences which the ruin of one race may entail on generations yet to come. I believe that my principle is right; but this is no question of School Metaphysics, and I will surrender the principle with all my heart, if you will aid me to save the men. The principle, then, of such a tax is a principle of revenue, drawn from duty on a commodity in general use, and introduced into the country from the foreign merchant. It is the same principle you apply to tea, to tobacco, to any other article you might desire to have free, but to which, for the sake of the revenue, you attach fiscal duties. If indirectly it operates as a protection to the cultivator, because it happens that we cultivate grain, and not tobacco or tea, and thereby effects the compromise that it is best for all classes to establish, it is an incidental good which you admit in dealing with other articles of home production. You derive revenue from duties on foreign shoes, boots, gloves, embroidery; you have a duty of 25 per cent. upon artificial flowers, 15 per cent. upon foreign silk; and you defend these duties, not only as sources of revenue, but as some aid against foreign competition to certain classes of your countrymen. Why deprive yourselves of a source of revenue larger than is derived from all these duties put together, because it would aid, during a fearful strain upon its energies, a Class that comprises at least a fourth of your population?

Secondly, the fixed duty carries with it the recommendation of high authority among Free-Traders themselves; and that, if you gainsay this, you may contradict not me, poor Squire and selfish Vampire, but your own authorities, I give you the words of the most eminent enemies of the old Corn Laws, the most illustrious masters of Political Economy.

Hear, first, Mr. Ricardo—no friend to the Landowner. You will see that he admits the policy of the fixed duty, contends for its justice, and even intimates his concession to a duty of 10s.—double that which Lord Stanley in these times has suggested.

"The growers of corn are subject to some of these peculiar taxes, such as tithes, a portion of the poor-rate, and perhaps one or two other taxes, all of which tend to raise the price of corn and other raw produce equal to these peculiar burdens. In the degree, then, in which these taxes raise the price of corn, a duty should be imposed on its importation. If from this cause it be raised 10s. per quarter, a duty of 10s. should be imposed on the importation of foreign corn, and a drawback of the same amount should be allowed on the exportation of corn. By means of this duty and this drawback, the trade would be placed on the same footing as if it had never been taxed; and we should be quite sure that capital would neither be injuriously, for the interests of society, attracted towards nor repelled from it. . . . . . . If importation was allowed, an undue encouragement would be given to the importation of foreign corn, unless the foreign commodity were subject to the same duty equal to tithes, or any other exclusive tax as that imposed on the home grower."

Thus says Mr. Ricardo. Hear, next, Mr. Poulett Thomson, afterwards Lord Sydenham, speaking against the Corn Laws in 1834:—

" He concluded that a fixed duty of from 8s. to 10s. the quarter, under which foreign corn could at all times come into the market of this country at a moderate price, would have prevented this occurrence (fluctuation) and the consequent loss. . . . . .

" He would not dispute that the Landowners had a claim to a certain degree of protection. His right honourable friend had quoted Mr. Ricardo as if he was with him, and against the imposition of a fixed duty ; but he would find that the authority of Mr. Ricardo, was against him on that point. Mr. Ricardo proposed the adoption of a certain fixed duty as being a full and sufficient compensation to the landowners. Let them adopt that plan. By the adoption of such a plan as that of a fixed duty, there was no doubt that the revenue would be a gainer, and he would not object to appropriate the amount of duty thus received towards affording that relief to the landowners to which they should prove themselves entitled."

But you say, whatever these eminent men may have thought *then* of a fixed duty, in 1846 they would have been for the total repeal now enforced on us. Yet surely, if there be one person who may guide us as to their probable opinion, had they been spared to us in 1846, it is the great living disciple and elucidator of Adam Smith and Ricardo, the most learned and profound of all our surviving masters in the Free-Trade school of this science of Political Economy. Thus says Mr. M'Culloch, writing in 1849, three years after the enactment, but before the serious distress that has befallen the agriculturist :—

"At the same time, we are ready to admit that we should have preferred seeing this question settled by imposing a low fixed duty of 5s., 6s., or 7s. a quarter on wheat, and other grain in proportion, accompanied by a proportionate drawback. We make this statement on general grounds, and without any reference to the peculiar burdens that affect the agriculturists, though these should neither be forgotten nor overlooked. In scarce years, a duty of this description would fall wholly on the foreigner, without affecting prices or narrowing importation; for in such years the prices of corn are wholly determined by demand or supply, without reference to the cost of the corn, including therein any reasonable duty with which it may be charged. The latter is then, in truth, deducted from the profits of the foreign grower or merchant; and its repeal would not sensibly affect prices. But while, in scarce years, when importation is necessary, the influence of a low duty is thus innocuous, it would lessen or prevent importation in unusually abundant years, when the home supply is sufficient. The drawback by which it is supposed to be accompanied would then also come into play, and facilitate exportation; so that their conjoined effect would be to hinder the overloading of the market, and consequently to prevent prices falling so low as to be injurious to the agriculturists and those dependent on them. And it must be borne in mind that the distress of the agriculturists never fails to react on the other classes. When the former are involved in difficulties, the demand for the products of the loom and of our colonial possessions, are proportionally diminished; so that the market is glutted with manufactured goods, sugar, &c., as well as with corn. It is, indeed, uniformly found that the injury that is thus inflicted on the manufacturing and trading part of the community very much exceeds all that they gain by the temporary fall in the price of raw produce. It is plainly, therefore, a capital mistake to suppose that the duty and drawback now referred to would be advantageous only to the agriculturists: they would redound quite as much to the advantage of the other classes. And though this were less certain than it appears to be, still, in a matter of such importance as the welfare of agriculture, and of those dependent thereon, a wise Government should be extremely cautious about taking any step, of the consequences of which it is not fully assured." * This, then, is the opinion of Mr. M'Culloch on the abstract merits of the

* M'Culloch's *Pol. Econ.*, pp. 548, 549, 4th edit., p. 49.

question; and though I grant that this eminent person doubts whether, as "Government had, in 1846, to deal with an irritated and unreasoning populace, it might not have been better to make an end of the matter than to prolong by any system, however well devised, the pernicious trade of agitation;" yet, as the chief reason he states for so preferring concession to wisdom is, that the agriculturists had "little to apprehend" in the change, I think we have a fair right, now that, in 1851, the cause for apprehension is proved to be so grave, to appeal to the country to decide between "an unreasoning" clamour and the principle which this master of the science declares would "not only be for the advantage of the agriculturists, but redound quite as much to the advantage of the other classes."

You tell me, O inflexible Repealers, in defiance of Mr. M'Culloch, that this moderate fixed duty is a miserable boon to the agriculturist, not worth his contending for. So much the better for you, if you can effect such a compromise, and secure yourselves, upon terms so easy, against the reaction that is always liable to follow extremes. You may tell me that this does not carry out your abstract principle to the utmost; but I have proved to you, at least, that the most illustrious asserters of your abstract principle have advocated the very compromise thus proposed. And if, after all, it does not go to the full length to which you would urge your theory, consider, all you who are intelligent among my manufacturing opponents—consider, I pray you, whether in this, as in all other affairs of life, where you deal between man and man, you do not gain more, in security to what you have obtained, in exemption from hostility upon other points affecting your interests, than you lose by your trifling concessions! Reflect, that but a very few years ago you would have delightedly hailed the compromise now submitted to you. Lord J. Russell tells us in the House of Commons, that, had his proposal of an 8s. fixed duty been accepted, the Free-Traders would have been satisfied, and the Corn Law League dissolved! And think, too, how you obtained your triumph—by what combination of circumstances, rare and unprecedented:—by a famine in Ireland—the prospect of a famine in England—the influence of a great man now no more—the changed opinions of Representatives, excusing change by calculations on prices that have proved erroneous, or the pledges of Ministers that have not been redeemed; regard and number the votes upon the opposite benches,—calculate somewhat on the prospect of a majority, in the ensuing Parliament, composed of men whom your obstinate refusal to listen to a question they deem so vital to their interests must make as obstinate as yourselves in regard to your own,—recollect that even in this Parliament, upon the question that "something should be done for the land," you have barely escaped by a Majority of Fourteen,*— own that, in the present balance of parties, legislation, according to your own principles, is impeded by the rallying point you leave to all who own that "Something must be done,"—and say whether, as wise and far-sighted men, you had not better seize this time to settle a dispute, which, believe me, is not settled now, by the consent of your opponents to terms more advantageous than those that, but for extraordinary circumstances, would, a short time ago, have so contented yourselves.

What say you, John! am I not right in my counsel? Did ever one great class in your family refuse all terms with another, and not live to repent it?

I close this letter, to give you time to turn to your History:—Do so, and I can doubt not your answer.

Yours, &c.

LETTER III.

BUT it is said to the agriculturist, "You have suffered distress before; therefore you must learn to suffer it now: you complained when enjoying a high protection duty; we cannot attend to your complaints, if you suffer when that duty is repealed. In 1835, for instance, your average prices were as low as now, in 1851. Why tease us to death with your lamentations?"

O disingenuous, if plausible adversaries, who denies that, ever since Triptolemus invented the plough, the agriculturist has been subjected to great casualties and hard

---

* A majority which, on Mr. Disraeli's motion, April 11th, (debated since the first edition of these Letters,) has been decreased to thirteen.

trials? He is engaged in a constant war with the soil and the elements, and they will sometimes prove more than a match for him. Is that any reason why you should unfit him still more for the struggle? In 1835, prices were low from the abundance of the harvest; they are low now, because you have suddenly brought against the agriculturist the granaries of the world. Your argument only goes to this—that, because he is liable to temporary distress, therefore you will create for him a distress that shall be permanent; and that since he complains of other elements which, in certain seasons, conspire against continuous prosperity to his labour, he has no right to complain when you add a new one which threatens, in all seasons, to render labour without hope of its reward. Because a man has groaned aloud in a fit of the gout, is it a reason that he should not complain if he is dosed to death by ratsbane and arsenic ?

But competition is to do wonders ! Competition does much when the competitors are fairly pitted, and I grant that there is some truth in the old boast that, if one Englishman is not a match for three Frenchmen, at least he will try his best to be so; but you do not raise the spirit —you crush it—if the odds are thoroughly unequal. You may stimulate the combative nature of the Englishman if you set three Frenchmen against him; but if, in addition to the Frenchmen, you add the Dane, the German, the American, the Russian, the Pole, the stoutest Anglo-Saxon who ever existed is likely to give up the battle. To tell the British agriculturist, whose most triumphant marvels of skill have been shown in extracting rich crops from the fens of Lincolnshire or the sands of Norfolk, that he must compete with the most fertile corn soils of the globe—that, met at all sides by excisemen and tax-collectors, he must compete with men free from those drawbacks on his profits —that, having literally thrown upon him the burden of two-thirds of all the poor of his country, he must compete with men to whom a poor-rate is unknown, and who have no check either from the charity of the Legislature or the habits of the labourer upon the minimum of wages—is to tell him that from which his common sense revolts, and which only insults, with the insinuation of cowardice, the courage which you deprive of all hope.

The cotton manufacturer, you say, does not require Protection. Why should the manufacturer of corn? Just an egregious query! If, where ten pieces of cotton were demanded before, I ask the cotton manufacturer to produce me a hundred, or I must cease to pay him any price for the ten pieces that remunerate his labour, he most thankfully accepts the order, and the hundred pieces are produced. There is no limit to the supply that, by the help of the steam-engine and the coal which the mines beneath his own soil afford to the mechanism he employs— no limit to the supply that he can yield to your demand; but if I say to the corn manufacturer, the agriculturist, "Where you grew five quarters of wheat to your acre, you must now grow twenty; or you cannot be paid the price that remunerates the production of the five"—can the agriculturist make the same answer? Can the clod-crusher and harrow wring from the land more than the land can bear? Can the manure that the farmer lays on the soil give to the plough the horse-power that coal gives to the steam-engine? The difference between the two is plain and obvious. The supply of the cotton pieces is inexhaustible, of the acres is limited. The extra demand upon the one is wealth, upon the other is ruin.

"Farm high," you say—"Farm high!" and there ends all your philosophy of relief. To farm high means keep plenty of stock, and buy plenty of artificial manure; in other words, increase your gross expenditure in order to increase your net income—adventure your capital in the hope of a return. Excellent advice! As a landowner, it is not my interest to gainsay it. But allow, at least, that two things are necessary to induce even men so abtuse as, in your superior wit, you deem the poor farmer, to follow your recommendation. First, you must not diminish the capital; and, secondly, you must allow the speculator a reasonable hope that a return is likely to follow the expenditure. But, even if I were to grant assent to a favourite saying of yours, that this is but the period of transition, it is during that period of transition that you are wasting rapidly away the very capital on which you are to depend, in order to bring you through it. And I appeal to any farmer if it be not true that, in cultivating his land, he is now sacrificing his capital. It is not only that the tenant has been paying, in some cases all, in nearly every case a large portion, of his rent out of his capital, and not from the returns of the farm; but even yeomen and proprietors (I don't mean the mere amateur farming squires, who, with the laudable desire of encouraging the breed of stock, and trying various experiments on Model Farms, rarely make or look to a profit—but proprietors farming as practical farmers, and with no rent to pay) find that the first drain that is needed is the—drain on their bankers.

It is frightful to think of the degree of agricultural capital lost for ever to the country, at the very time in which you tell us that capital is our only chance of ultimate salvation.

And if this high farming be indeed the sure remedy, how happens it that those very districts where high farming has been carried to its acme, has extorted the admiration of foreigners, and ranks amongst the triumphs of national enterprise and skill—how comes it that those are precisely the districts from which the complaints are the loudest, and their justice most conceded by the Government itself? The Lothians, Norfolk, Lincolnshire—surely you cannot say to the cultivators of these districts, when they tell you that they are cultivating at a loss, and that they anticipate their ruin:—"Gentlemen, go home and farm high!"

I remember that in 1846 I predicted to the Lincolnshire agriculturist that he, above most cultivators, would suffer, and that his suffering would tell quickly upon the labouring population, where, in other counties, the distress of the farmer would be slow in reaching the labourer. "It is," I then said, "in proportion to the cost upon the soil, and not to the quality of the produce grown upon it, that the farmer will suffer by a fall in price below profits. You, who produce such crops by artificial manures, who consume so much upon guano and bones, you will be the first to find how small and minute would be the benefit of any reduction in rent compared to your great cost in cultivating. And as free competition must affect the gross profits of your land, so the larger the expenses in proportion to the profits, why, the greater you must be the sufferers in any great fall of prices. Suppose A. B. has a certain farm, for which he pays £300 a-year, and has for his own profit as tenant £300 a-year also, but his land, being not originally fertile, is brought into high cultivation by artificial means, and it therefore requires an expenditure of three times the net profit, viz. £900, in order to yield the said rent to the landlord, and the said return to the farmer: in all, the sum risked in the cultivation is £1500 a-year. But suppose C. D. has another farm, on which he too pays £300 a-year; has also £300 a-year for his personal profit; but, the soil being light and fertile, requires an expenditure of only £400 to realise the said rent, and return the said farmer's profit: in all, the sum risked on this farm is but £1000 a-year.

It is perfectly clear, therefore, that the loss occasioned by low prices on these two farms—though at the same rent, and yielding at fair prices the same average profit—is not the same: the loss upon one affects an annual expenditure of £1500, upon the other of only £1000.

And it is clear, also, that in this case the greater loss may fall upon the tenant who farms the highest. Now, if the "strain on his capital compels him to withdraw a certain amount of the labour he had hitherto employed, or if he devotes more attention so some produce demanding less labour than wheat, it is clear, also, that the labourer will be affected by the loss on the higher farming in proportion to the greater loss of the farmer." It has proved thus :— And while the farmer of Lincolnshire is so great a sufferer, you find also that in Lincolnshire the President of the Board of Trade himself confessed that pauperism had largely increased.

We have been told that such lands, not paying the cost of culture, should go out of cultivation. But much of these lands, in the triumph of art over soil, is the very perfection of husbandry. Condemn the fens of Lincolnshire, the sands of Norfolk, to go out of cultivation! It would be to condemn at once enterprise and skill—condemn the noble conquest of man over matter. "Return to pasture!" cry some. Return to comparative barbarism! Return to pasture, and throw hundreds and thousands of labourers out of employ!—diminish the product that is the wealth of your country!—and relinquish large tracts from which the industry and art of successive generations have extracted the food of men—to such desolate sheepwalks and rabbit-haunts as a Ceorl of old might have tended for

Athelstanes and Cerdics! Is it you, the friends of labour and civilisation, of the progress of nations—is it for you to say this? Let me not think it.

Farm high! Farm high! I agree with you. Only help, only encourage us to do so! Away with the fear of throwing land out of cultivation, and back into pasture. Away with it, I say! But, O Manufacturers! if we must throw aside the staff, and yet keep the fardel, do not ask us to perform in a day the pilgrimage which it has taken your class years to accomplish. The last protection was not taken from cotton itself until, by the avowal of the Cotton Manufacturers, it was no longer required! Farm high! Farm high! Yes, but do not forget, that before you affected farming operations by your Corn Law, you affected them by the tariff introducing foreign cattle and meat. And I am sure that I speak the sentiments of a very large proportion of the most spirited agriculturists when I say, that you could not have more interfered with the success of the experiment which was to depend upon high farming to bring us through the "transition" consequent on the repeal of the Corn Law, than by the previous discouragement to high farming in the loss upon cattle. Many a high farmer, dependent on his turnip and bean crops, looked less to the yield of corn than the price of his mutton and beef. I do not say that the sudden fall in the price of meat is not a great boon to the consumer; but it obviously entailed a heavy loss on the farmer, on the very article which constitutes the pith and root of high farming, and at the very time when he had need of all his resources to face the prices to which grain has been since subjected. The object of the high farmer is to sell off every year large quantities of fat meat; without this, it is not high farming. And if he does this at a loss, why, of course, his loss must be great in proportion to his obedience to your command, "Farm high, and don't trouble us." *

Nevertheless, I neither hope nor ask that you should

* Thus Adam Smith, in one of his most valuable chapters, (Book I. Chap. XI.,) proves briefly and clearly the effect of the price of cattle upon the cultivation of land, and says, "Of all the commercial advantages, however, which Scotland has derived from the union with England, this rise in the price of cattle is perhaps the greatest. It has not only raised the value of all highland estates, but it has been perhaps the principal cause of the improvement of the low country."

alter the tariff; and by degrees I believe that the farmer will, more than he now expects, readjust his speculations on cattle. If he must sell the fat cattle cheaper, he can also buy the lean cheaper; and to the farmer now entering on business, there will be far less demand on his capital in the first purchase of stock. But as yet the difference between the purchase of the lean cattle (especially bullocks), and the price at which the farmer sells them when fattened, does not, spite of all reductions on oilcake and forage, cover the costs of feed—as yet, therefore, he still is a loser in proportion to the capital so employed. And for the generation with whom you are dealing, it is impossible to deny that the fall in the price of meat * was a terrible blow to the resources with which high farming was to meet the repeal of the Corn Law. Excellently well has the terse old Satirist described the present condition of the farmer who cultivates with spirit, and sells at a loss :—

> ————"Jam crescit ager, jam crescit ovile,
> Jam dabitur—jam jam! donec deceptus et exspes
> Nequicquam fundo suspiret nummus in imo!"

> "Now teems the field, and now augments the fold;
> What gains await! what harvests shall be told!
> Now—the return—now—now! 'Alas!' he sighs,
> 'So low the prices—hang it, they must rise!'
> 'Try Lawes' manure—' . . . . He tries it. 'Well the grain?'
> 'Good.'—'Then why sad?' 'It don't manure Mark Lane!'
> Thus the crops flourish, thus the funds decay,
> Till the last pound—improves itself away!"

No! Just before the change in your policy there was, indeed, every prospect that could gratify those who advocate agricultural improvement. Under this system of protection, now so condemned, British agriculture had made the most rapid and striking advances. Mr. Porter, in adducing his calculations of our produce in grain, and in showing in how small a degree this country had hitherto been dependent on foreigners, in ordinary seasons, for a due supply of our staple article of food, says :—"It is not, however, with this view that these calculations are brought forward, but rather to prove how exceedingly great the increase of agricultural production must have been to have thus effect-

---

* The large importation of cured meat has had a greater effect upon prices here than the importation of cattle.

nally kept in a state of independence a population which has increased with so great a degree of rapidity."

Just before the change, nothing could equal the zeal and cordiality with which farmers and squires were entering into all that could increase our produce, and improve our agricultural art. And now how inert and lifeless are all the discussions which then provoked so keen and animated an interest! I appeal to any man conversant with agricultural meetings, or what is contemptuously called "the Agricultural Mind," whether all that relates to scientific experiment has not receded before the dread of this competition which you tell us should stimulate science. Nay, even those vexed questions between squire and tenant, out of which our common enemies would make subjects of quarrel, such as the removal of superfluous field and hedgerow timber, the fair opening of land to sun and air, the destruction of rabbits and hares, and, where guarantee is given of the capital and spirit of the farmer, the system of securer tenure by lease—all questions that were about then amicably to be settled, are now comparatively lost sight of in the general feeling, "Pooh, these are trifles; can we continue to live by the land we till?"

I say, fearlessly, that whereas a moderate competition, such as a fixed duty might produce, would have been a stimulant to improvement: improvement has been arrested by a competition carried to an extent which does not stimulate energy, but engender despondence.

"But we never contended, never expected," say my Lord John Russell and our sympathising enemy, the Chancellor of the Exchequer, "that either landowner or occupier would not go through a sharp period of distress; ultimately both will profit by the general prosperity of all classes, and the increase of population. The weal of the country requires the change from the old system. This is a Period of Transition; you must go through it. Hold your tongues, and Heaven be with you!"

A Period of Transition. Well, but what to? To the ultimate growth of our population? A prospect pleasing, no doubt, but exceedingly distant. The generation that complains passes to the grave, while the generation that is to redress the complaint emerges from the nursery. We have not only to look to the growth of population here, but the growth of corn throughout that small occupant of space commonly called The Earth. And while we are waiting for the little Johns and Thomases at present supplied at the pap-boat, and with whom, as they rise inch by inch, profits are to rise also, we are to continue to sell at a loss, pay for the paupers our ranks will recruit, and the gaols to which the transition is hurrying our footsteps—transition to penury, to destitution, to despair, disaffection, hatred of the Legislature which dooms us, and indifference to the safety of the State, whose prosperity is invoked as the cause of our own destitution. For this general prosperity is unwisely and invidiously held up to our eyes in contrast to our sufferings. And when you tell Hodge, the farmer, that he ought to be extremely well satisfied because Smith, the calico-printer, is growing a rich man at his expense, my own private and honest opinion is, that you are making Hodge a very dangerous enemy to Smith. I confess, that if I had to reconcile a man to the contemplation of bankruptcy, I should not say to him, "My dear sir, be comforted with your present state of transition by the gratifying survey of your neighbour's prosperity. You grow thin, it is true; but how plump is the gentleman next door? You, to save yourself from the *Gazette*, are selling off at dead loss your stock in trade; but then, how agreeable it is for others to buy your articles a bargain! Think of that, and be consoled. Instead of selfishly regarding your own poverty, fix your delighted eyes on the wealth of all the rivals who are buying for sixpence what it cost you a shilling to produce." Human nature is human nature; and that is not the way to soothe its sorrows or soften its passions. But, you say, this general prosperity will ultimately benefit us as a part of the public. We deny that this prosperity can long be general, if you continue to destroy what all true political economists acknowledge to be the primary source of the national wealth. A transition state!—a transition in which so vast an interest is concerned! You allow it must be one of distress; will you do nothing to render it less violent and abrupt? I have granted your premises, that a change in the old law was rendered necessary. I have no desire to return to large protective duties, or the principle of a sliding-scale. But is there no medium? Would not a moderate fixed duty secure the true objects at which your policy would aim, and gradually bring about the transition to which it is necessary to subject so large a class of your population, so immense an amount of your national wealth? The transition, even then, will be sharp enough. But you will at least give to it the consoling effect of your obvious desire to sympathise and conciliate. You will appear to be dealing amicably with your own countrymen. You will appear to remember that when you say, " Sacrifice your interests to those of the community," the men you address can be counted as millions in that community itself ! By a fixed duty you obtain—I repeat it—the great principle you contend for. The sliding-scale checks or forbids importation at certain prices. The fixed duty leaves the market always open, with but a slight toll on the foreigner—a toll to which he will soon, when it is regular and unalterable, conform his dealings, and will as little operate against his bringing his corn habitually to your ports, as the toll which the farmer pays on the turnpike to the neighbouring town operates against his conveying his droves there for sale. A low fixed tax upon the seller, to whom you extend a new range of customers, will never be found to interfere with his business; it diminishes a little his profits, and the competition to which you admit a world will compel him to take that diminution to himself, rather than add to the cost of the article—except in times when prices are unusually low. I say, indeed, that a small fixed duty, accompanied by a proportional drawback, must be better for all classes of labour; for it must render prices much less fluctuating than that total repeal of all duty which you have enacted. And great, yet brief, fluctuation in prices is the worst demoraliser you can create in the habits of your people. In whatever country corn has been imported free, I will undertake to show that fluctuations have been more extreme than ever they have been in England, even under the worst operations of the old excessive duties; * whereas—I here

* Whatever the faults of the old Corn Law, fluctuations in price, taken by a series of years, were less extreme in England than in any other country. From 1815 to 1838, the highest variation in England was 140 per cent. We all cried out pretty loudly at this variation; but what was it elsewhere during the same period?

<pre>
          In Bordeaux   .   .   .   .   . 260 per cent.
          In Rotterdam   295   „
</pre>

once more quote Mr. M'Culloch—"it may, we think, be concluded, on unassailable grounds, that were the ports constantly open under a moderate fixed duty and an equivalent drawback, extreme fluctuation of prices would be very rare."

"But," say our adversaries, "why should we think that these prices don't pay the cost of culture? Did not you grumble years ago at prices which now seem a dream? At the end of the war, did you not contend for eighty shillings a quarter, where you would now be rejoiced to contemplate fifty?"

And that cry comes from gentlemen who call themselves political economists! Why, what, according to your theory, is the origin of rent?—(I mean in the scientific sense of the word.) Does it not always presuppose "some anterior soil for which no rent is paid, as a test of comparison?" "Is it not the excess of produce upon any given quality of soil, by comparison with another quality worse than itself?" Thus, "as inferior land is brought into cultivation, rent rises, and with rent prices,"—"the higher price of corn being caused by the necessity under which every increasing population is placed of cultivating inferior land, or of being starved."

Well, then, during the war, every inducement was given to bring under cultivation lands previously waste. It was the avowed object of the Legislature to encourage to the utmost the home production of food. Vast tracts of land were thus reclaimed and tilled—an immense capital thus buried in the soil. Necessarily, prices rose at that time, assisted by a long depreciation of the currency; capital was invested on the calculation of such prices; and while the expense of bringing into tillage fens and heaths was at its height, no

In Prussia Proper	212 per cent.
In Brandenburg	248 ,,
In Saxony	269 ,,
In Westphalia	334 ,,

Any comparison between protected England and unprotected Holland, as to fluctuations, was so in favour of the former that the Free-Traders were forced to push to the extreme an explanation, that it was because England was protected that the prices in Holland so fluctuated;—an argument that, so exaggerated, is obviously untenable. In Athens, under free importation, fluctuations to 300 per cent. were common. And during those centuries, when in England grain was unprotected, variations were so great that there were seasons when even the middle class could not purchase bread.

doubt the farmer really required much higher remunerative prices to sustain his engagements, and save him from bankruptcy, than at a period when this inferior land had been rendered artificially fertile, and produced, perhaps, thirty bushels per acre where it had before produced ten. I believe it to be perfectly true that 80s. then would have been required to remunerate the farmer, where now 50s. might suffice. But the Corn Law of 1815, in forbidding free importation till home-grown wheat reached that price, was no doubt most absurd and impolitic; it held out a hope that could not be realised. Two years of extraordinary high prices—1817 and 1818—induced rash and sudden returns to the inferior tillages, before gradually abandoned. Bold risks of fresh capital in agricultural improvements, "for improvements almost always follow a rise in prices," and the increased supply thus obtained, combined with plentiful seasons, sunk the price of wheat six years afterwards (in 1824) to an average of 43s. 3d. I do not argue for duties like these, nor duties that are based on a similar system; but it is not the less true that the Legislature, during the war, had encouraged such applications of capital to husbandry as high prices for a certain period (till the return to the capital began to show itself) alone could repay—and that large numbers of farmers were left broken and bankrupt by the energy and enterprise which (honour to their spirit, and, alas, for their calamities!) added millions upon millions to the wealth of their country.* Very different are the circumstances under which the farmer now assesses the average of his remunerative prices. The present race of agriculturists are profiting by the improvements effected and the sacrifices undergone by their predecessors. You have no longer to

---

* "The progress of agricultural improvement, which, during the late war, had been extremely rapid, was retarded for a few years by the sudden and heavy fall of prices that took place after the peace; but since 1825, it has been rapid beyond all former precedent. Estimating the increase of population in Great Britain since 1770 at eight millions, and taking the average annual expenditure of each individual on agricultural produce at £8, it will be seen that the immense sum of sixty-four millions a-year has been added to the value of the agricultural produce of Great Britain since 1770."— *M'Culloch's Appendix to Smith's Wealth of Nations*—Art. *Corn Laws and Corn Trade.* And it is the class that, in less than a century, enriched the nation by sixty-four millions a-year, which is to be represented as possessing an interest adverse to the community!

calculate the first cost of bringing waste lands under tillage, but the after cost of maintaining them ; and if you take soils brought into the finest cultivation, from which now all is obtained that can be wrung from them, and find that, despite all that the economists effected by the tariff, the present prices cannot pay for the cost, what prospect remains but the retrogression of husbandry, or the ruin of at least the generation that have buried their substance in the furrows traced by the ploughshare, and to whom "persisting is as fatal as give o'er ?"

Here, my dear John, arise a new crowd of opponents; for while the more popular and numerous sect of our adversaries rejoice in their convictions that prices must, on the long run, continue at least thus low, another, more serene and lofty—disdaining what Mr. Sidney Herbert designates "the clap-trap cry of cheap bread"—reply, "But why deem that the repeal of the Corn Law will have this effect upon prices ? Why believe that there is any connection between the prices you suffer from, and the importation we invite ? This year there are exceptional causes at work, et cetera ! et cetera ! Plough away, and sow on ! Depend on it, that, take an average of years, all things will come right, and prices be no lower than they were before the change."*

Thus asserts my Lord Grey—an authority that I always hear with respect, and question with diffidence ; for Lord Grey is an original thinker, no parrot repeater of phrases, and certainly no trite dealer in clap-traps. But while he maps out the air, I place before me the chart of the world; and, without pausing to inquire if the causes of agricultural distress are this year exceptional or not, I see on that chart all reason to think that every year fresh causes must rise as the foreigner brings fresh lands into tillage, opens new roads to the sea, and widens the range of the taxless and

---

* In an average of years I don't doubt that there will be found, under wholly unlimited importation, sudden, brief, and excessive rises in price; but these will be found more hurtful than profitable to the generality of farmers. They will profit only monied speculators, with other resources than their land wherefrom to meet periodical payments, whether of rents, rates, or tithes, and weekly payments of labour. They may come at a time when the general farmer has nothing to sell, and operate only against him in what he has to buy and to pay away. They may help the landlord in keeping up his rents, and the clergyman in his corn commutation, by a reference to averages; but to the farmer they will be worse than useless.

greedy competitors, with whom your poor farmers, dear
John, are to sharpen scythe and wit to contend. I have
said before, that the prospect of such competition, wholly
unmitigated, does not stimulate the British producer—it
only disheartens him. But it is clear whom it does stimulate, and that is the—Foreigner! And when I have been
told that among these special causes is the importation
from France, which your wise men did not choose to foresee
—why, I know as a fact that, the moment you opened your
ports, you suddenly and marvellously increased in France
that impetus in agricultural improvement which you as
suddenly checked at home; that a large increase of corn as
pure surplus over habitual consumption has been obtained,
and is in active progression on the lands of that country;
that whatever France wants not for its own population it
will sell, no matter the price, for all beyond consumption
is gain; and sell here, for this is its only market for the
surplus your bribe has created.

"No matter," says my Lord John; "be the prices of
corn high or low, all I contend for is, that it should be the
natural price!"—And therewith he is cheered.

Oh, my Lord John, that sophism might do very well for
the mere tyros in political economy, who exchange all
knowledge of the complex relations of men for the pedantry
of set terms and phrases; but is it worthy a statesman of
your rank?

Natural price!—why, what is the natural price? (*id est*,
the central price to which other prices are continually
gravitating). Adam Smith states it thus:—"When the
price of any commodity is neither more nor less than what
is sufficient to pay the rent of the land, the wages of the
labour, and the profits of the stock employed in raising,
preparing, and bringing it to market according to their
natural rates, the commodity is then sold for what may be
called its natural price." If that is what your lordship
means by a natural price, give us that, and we are satisfied
—it is exactly what we contend for. But if by natural
price you mean, that, by the introduction of a foreign
element, prices are to be reduced below their cost, such ceases
at once to be the natural price, scientifically treated; for
the natural price means, as Adam Smith proceeds to define
it—what it costs the person who brings it to market, in-

cluding his profit at the ordinary rate of profits—where ?
Five thousand miles off ? In Poland or Russia ?—No !—
" In his neighbourhood." * If you reply, " I mean by a
natural price that to which the competition, not of the
neighbour, but of the foreigner, five thousand miles off,
drives you down," I reply again, that if that is what you
mean, by the natural price—if you forget or disdain the
fact that the natural price varies in different communities
according to the varying degree of labour (*i.e.* capital)
employed to produce it — then, I say, with the natural
price, as you esteem it, give us at least a natural—taxation !

A Latin author has pithily said :—

" Life is like swimming—he fares the best who carries least weight about
him."

When Leander swam across the Hellespont, no doubt he
was *in puris naturalibus ;* but let us suppose that some experimental philosopher, a lover of Nature, coaxed a rival
to swim against Leander, burthened with tunic and cloak,
two great stones in his pocket, and a couple of paupers
tied to his back, I don't think it would have been quite
fair for the sage to say to the rival, " Swim away, my good
friend ; I have no doubt that you'll outswim Leander; but
whether you do, or whether you don't, all I can say is, that
I'll not lend you a cock-boat, nor throw you a tub, for
there's nothing so natural as swimming."

" Natural ! yes," the poor rival might gasp, ere he " gra-
vitated to the centre"—in other words, went to the bottom
—" natural to that fellow Leander, for he has nothing but
nature to carry. But I've got a tunic and cloak, two great
stones in my pockets, and two paupers as heavy as lead on
my back. Is that the natural way to swim over the Hellespont ?"

Leander gains the shore ; that is natural ! The competitor is drowned ; that also is natural ! The philosopher
contemplates the result with philanthropical pleasure, and
walks off to his dinner, saying, " What stimulates exertion
like rivalry ? But, O Jupiter ! how could you suffer that
man to be drowned in gravitating to the centre ? There is
nothing so natural as swimming !"

* ADAM SMITH, *Wealth of Nations,* Book i., c. 7.

"Well, well! Talk as you will," cry those gentlemen, who only think of a farmer as an abstract proposition, and who have the same vague idea of a landlord that the poets had of a harpy—"Talk as you will; if the landed interest does suffer, and very likely it does, it is all one to the farmer. Mr. Ricardo, a great thinker, and a very eminent stockbroker, and therefore, of course, practically acquainted with all details upon farming, assures us that the farmer himself, honest fellow, can't be any ways injured. It is only a loss to the landlords. They must lower their rents; and there will be an end of all grievance."

Happy, indeed, could the question be so easily settled! Yet, even then, not so light an affliction to the community itself as these gentlemen too rashly imagine. Reduction of rents cannot happen without the depreciation of the property from which the rents are derived—a depreciation of so vast a proportion of the real property of the country—a depreciation of the land throughout Great Britain and Ireland! Would that be so paltry an evil? Would the evil affect the landlord alone? Does he not spend these rents of his amongst the community? Can you impoverish the man who spends money without impoverishing those upon whom he spends it? When you talk of this reduction so lightly, do you sufficiently consider that a reduction of rents is a very different thing in amount from a diminution, nominally the same, on an income derived from the Funds? and how largely what may seem but a moderate reduction must operate on the surplus the landlord has to spend upon trade? Suppose the landlord gives back to his tenants 10 per cent. on his *gross* rental: when you consider all his ordinary drawbacks as a landowner—the tithes that he pays for the grounds, &c. in his own occupation—his own poor-rates, and other local burdens—the incumbrances (I will not say mortgages, but such as probably some jointure or annuity, provision for younger children, &c.) with which most estates are more or less charged, that 10 per cent. on his gross rental will probably amount to at least 20 per cent. on his net income.* And he must be an imprudent and reckless vampire indeed if he do not in-

* I do not believe there are ten properties in a hundred where a reduction of 10 per cent. on the gross rental could be set down at so low a figure as 20 per cent. on the net income.

stantly reduce his dealings with his neighbour, and spend so much the less upon some other classes of the community. But if it should come to a time when the landlord must reduce on his gross rental 25 per cent., and must face the enormous effect which that would have on his *net* income, what trade in the kingdom would not sensibly feel the loss of so large and necessary a retrenchment of expenditure upon the part of the landed proprietors of the country?   That a considerable proportion of proprietors would go abroad is a natural supposition; and, in addition to the pecuniary loss thus entailed on the general community, there would also be that social loss in our rural districts occasioned by numerous absentees amongst a class whose members, whatever their faults, have never been accused by any reasonable and fair antagonist of indifference to the welfare of those who live immediately around them.

And what is this class of men, whose affliction it is so pleasant to contemplate?   What injury have they inflicted on our social system, or what inroads have they made on our freedom, that we should cry with complacency, "No evil; they alone are the victims?"   They are the men of whom all true political economists have spoken with grateful reverence ; whose prosperity the fathers of the science have regarded as the paramount interest in the State; they are men to whom the history of this land assigns the chief merit when a tyrant was to be humbled, or a foeman defied. "While," says thus, with noble truth, a Free-Trader himself, "while other aristocracies have been the sycophants of courts, they have borne the chief burdens of the State ; they have given to the State their service, their blood, and their treasure."*   Take we the loftiest in birth and possessions, are they banded together, like oligarchs in Venice, as the opponents to progress; or, like those Greek nobles justly branded by Aristotle, have they entered into vows against the Demos—the people?   No: wherever you turn to our records, in the front of each march towards social improvement and political freedom, your chiefs have been ever the landed proprietors of England, or the children whom they have reared.   Through the cycle of progress they stand out in each era—Magna Charta, Protestant Re-

* Speech of the Rt. Hon. Sidney Herbert, Feb. 9, 1851.

formation, the first resistance to Charles the First, the martyrdom under Charles the Second, the Revolution of 1688, Catholic Emancipation, the Reform Bill—in each the pioneers and achievers have been the sons of the soil. And even where, as in this very repeal of the Corn Law, their virtual representatives in the Upper Chamber have yielded from what you assert to be fear, the fear at least was generous and noble—the fear of patriots and citizens—lest they might seem to oppose what the statesman they trusted had told them the people demanded, and hazard the peace of their country by even a suspicion that their policy could be debased to their pecuniary interests. And who, in this victory, on which you now plume yourselves, who were the chiefs before a Peel was converted, or a Cobden arose? Who? A Villiers, a Fitzwilliam, a Sponser, a Russell, a Seymour, a Howard. And a glorious thing it is for England that the aristocracy thus never stands distinct and apart in one phalanx for interest and privilege ; that it is so indissolubly fused and commingled with all shades of the people, that men as powerful and noble are found on the popular side as can grace the patrician : and when you would seize, as some tangible substance to confront and oppose, the aristocratic element in our civilisation, it escapes and eludes you, lost in the free air that you breathe, or but seen in the light that encircles you !

Yet it is not the titled aristocracy of our order from whom you derive the more ordinary social advantages; it is rather the men by whom the loss that you so placidly contemplate will be chiefly felt—the smaller proprietors, amongst whom is subdivided a far greater share of the land ; who reside, for the most part, on the domains that they improve, amongst the population that their surplus immediately supports or enriches ; the class that we call the Gentry, who in other countries are Nobles—in this, more proud of their place with the Commons. It is they who communicate to the middle class in which they hold station that hardy patriotism which is inseparably connected with attachment to the soil, the notions of honour, of stout independence, of just pride of character, of contempt for all meanness, that constitute what we mean by the word, for which the tongue of no other land has a synonym, GENTLEMAN. For myself, I hold it my proudest distinction to belong by habit and profession to a class even nobler than they—and to which they have largely contributed—the Labourers of Literature; but, next to that honour, I am not ashamed to confess the pride which I cherish that by birth and rearing I belong to the owners of Land. And if in my childhood I was ever reminded of the centuries in which my forefathers had dwelt on the soil, it was only to impress on me the lesson of deeper love to my country, and warm me to that ambition to render her service, and link my name with her language, which has coloured my life and dictated my labours.

To the class of gentry the words of the sternest of all political economists emphatically apply :—" It is also in a peculiar manner the business of those whose object it is to ascertain the means of raising human happiness to its greatest height, to consider which is that class of men by whom the greatest happiness is enjoyed. It will not probably be disputed that they who are raised above solicitude for the means of subsistence and respectability, without being exposed to the vices and follies of great riches; the men of middling fortunes; in short, the men to whom society is indebted for its greatest improvements, are the men who, having their time at their own disposal, freed from the necessity of manual labour, subject to no man's authority, and engaged in the most delightful occupations, obtain, as a class, the greatest sum of human enjoyment. For the happiness, therefore, as well as the ornament of our nature, it is peculiarly desirable that a class of this description should form as large a proportion of the community as possible. For this purpose it is absolutely necessary that population should not, by a forced accumulation of capital, be made to go on till the return to capital from the land is very small. To enable a considerable portion of the community to enjoy the advantages of leisure, the return to capital should be large." *

Mr. Mill is here arguing on the proportions of population and capital; but the argument holds equally good to the object in view—viz., a return of capital from the land: and whether that return be diminished by a law of nature or a law of Parliament, the same evil is created, so far as affects the happiness of society.

* MILL, *Elements of Political Economy.*

But would, indeed, that the loss were, or could be confined to the landowner! Can any man go into one country market, or one farmer's club, and still adopt so preposterous a fallacy?

Believe me, that farmers, whatever contempt may be entertained for their understanding, have the same knowledge where the shoe pinches, which characterises all human beings who stand upon shoe-leather. To use an Italian proverb—

"The tongue touches where the tooth aches."

And were it but a question for the landlord, the rural districts would resound, not with cries of Protection, but entreaty or clamour for the reduction of rent. Yet who does not know that the most ardent of Protectionist landlords scarcely represents the passionate fervour of the occupier; that, obstinate as you may think the county members in Parliament, they rather repress than excite the impatient groan of their constituents! and that, wherever the corn-law agitator has now the satisfaction to point to some rancour professed by the farmers against the landlords, it is where the farmers contend that the landlords do not sufficiently enter into their grievance, and can never sufficiently participate their loss?

Any one in the least acquainted with the principle upon which farm rents are assessed, must know how little any possible reduction of rent can meet the depression complained of in the price of agricultural produce. I will endeavour to put this clear before the reason of the un-initiated.

We have nothing here to do with the scientific theory of rent; and I suspect that many popular errors, which Ricardo would have been the first to condemn, have arisen from confounding the distinction between rent, scientifically defined, and rents, as practically existing.*

* No writer, perhaps, is more subjected to dangerous misinterpretation by inconsiderate readers than Mr. Ricardo. He is constantly applying scientifically, or according to his peculiar use of terms, words that convey to the general reader totally different meanings. Thus, in his whole Chapter on Profits, upon a matter of the most vital importance, he has misled many into opinions wholly at variance with positive facts. Why? Because, as Mr. M'Culloch remarks, "he did not in his investigations in that chapter, understand the term in the sense in which it is understood in the ordinary business of life. In his own point of view, his doctrine with respect to

Rent is a thing unknown in a newly-settled country—nay, in a country where only the best soils are cultivated. It begins when cultivation is extended to inferior lands; it increases according to the extent in which such lands are brought into tillage, and diminishes according as their culture is relinquished. Such is the theory generally adopted by political economists.

Rent, scientifically considered, is the sum paid for the inherent and natural properties of the soil, and is entirely distinct in its origin from the sums paid for all buildings, improvements, and local advantages produced by civilisation, (such as the neighbourhood of towns and markets, roads, facilities of carriage, &c.)

But as it is utterly impossible to distinguish in practice between this original rent paid solely for the soil, when first brought under the plough, and the sum added thereon for all subsequent improvements—so, in every instance, at present, the two are confounded under the general word *rent*. And the sum paid to that landlord, under that title, is assessed on all the profits of the farm, natural or acquired. Now let us see how, in practice, any surveyor or land agent apportions the rent, (using the word in the popular sense, as all practical men understand it.*)

When a farm is to be let, and the rent to be assessed, the first calculation is the gross profits, and the next the outgoings and the probable expenses of cultivation. There, then, remains the net produce, from which the farmer takes one share as the remuneration for his labour and capital; the landlord another share, including or deducting the tithes.

Formerly the gross produce used to be divided into three parts; one-third allowed for the general expenses of farming, one for the farmer's maintenance and profit on capital, and the third remaining was devoted to taxes, tithes, assessments, and—rent. It would appear by the evidence of Mr. Bradley, the eminent land-surveyor, before the Com-

---

profit is unexceptionable; but practically it is of little or no value, and may lead, unless the sense in which he understood it be always kept in view, to the most erroneous conclusions."—*M'Culloch on Rent, appended to his edition of Adam Smith.*

* See Donaldson's corrected edition of *Bayldon's Art of Valuing Rents and Tillages*, &c.—(a deservedly popular and standard authority.)

mittee of the House of Lords on the Burdens of Land, that this mode of apportionment still commonly exists in Yorkshire. But the difference of localities, the nature of soil, the proportions of grass-land, the distinction between light soils and clay (so considerable when the relative expeuses of cultivation are estimated), all serve to render more complicated what was formerly this simple mode of computation; and the improved cultivation of land, while increasing the gross produce, increases also the expenses of cultivating. As far as my own experience goes, I should say that the gross produce was generally now divided into five portions rather than three (unless where land is very fertile), that three-fifths went to the expenses, rates, and taxes; one-fifth to the maintenance and remuneration of the farmer, and the remaining fifth to the tithes and rent.*

More or less competition among tenants, and peculiar circumstances independent of produce, may, in special cases, somewhat enhance or somewhat diminish the sum thus received for rent; but, as a general rule, the relative proportion, whether under three, five, or more divisions of gross produce, will be found to prevail; and there is not

* In poor clay lands, the landlord has not so large a share, and the farmer somewhat a larger one; for in these, the expenses being nearly as great as upon light soils yielding much more, a larger proportion must be set upon the cost of tillage; a somewhat larger proportion to the return of the farmer, who requires little less capital to work the less productive than the more productive—and of course the landlord's proportion is smaller. In the county in which I reside, there are many farms in which the landlord's rent is not more than a seventh of the gross produce.

Mr. De Quincy (*Logic of Political Economy*), who, to a mind habituated to metaphysical and abstract investigations, adds what is rare in political economists—a knowledge of the practical concerns and interests of husbandry —justly observes: "It has been accidentally Ricardo's ordinary oversight to talk of rent as if this were the one great burden on the farmer of land, whereas so much greater is the burden in this country from the capital required, that Mr. Jacob (well known in past times to the British Government as an excellent authority) reports the proportion of capital to rent needed in ordinary circumstances as very little less than four to one. From fifty-two reports made to a Committee of the Lords in the year before Waterloo, the result was, that upon one hundred acres, paying in rent no more than £161 12s. 7d., the total of other expenses was £601 15s. 1d. per annum. And in some other cases—as, for instance, in bringing into tillage the waste lands technically known as poor clays—the proportion required for some years appeared to be much greater—on an average, three times greater—so that the capital would be ten or eleven times as much as the rent." This may explain to the Free-Trader why the farmer required such high remunerative prices in 1815.

an experienced valuer or land-surveyor who will not allow that in all cases it is from the net or the surplus profit that the farmer gets his maintenance and the landlord his rent.

On the other hand, it is perfectly clear that any gain or any loss on the gross produce is the gain or loss of the tenant, whether he hold on a lease or from year to year: the landlord does not raise his rent when prices are high, and he does not, except in special cases, reduce it when prices are low. Prices, therefore, belong to the speculation of the farmer when he enters on the farm; it is him that their fluctuations must immediately affect: and any general alteration of rent can only be made, not on the average of one or two years, but on the average of a certain series of years. Therefore, if there is a reduction on the gross profit, it must, at all events for a time, fall on the profits of the farmer; though, doubtless, if long continued, the reduction will extend to the rent of the landlord.* To what extent that reduction of profits to the farmer has gone, since the free importation of foreign corn, I am convinced that our countrymen in towns cannot be aware, or they would be rather startled at the patience than callous to the complaints of those upon whom this vast experiment has been so ruthlessly tried.

My table is covered with accounts of tenant-farmers; in many of them the whole amount of their share of profit on time and capital is absorbed—in some, considerably more —in few, less than half. But as I do not wish, my dear John, to fatigue your attention by minute arithmetical details—and as, to make such statements perfectly fair and clear, they ought to be numerous, selected from various districts under different modes and degrees of cultivation, and would thus swell these epistles beyond all readable length, I reluctantly postpone the enforcement of my posi-

---

* "The occasional and temporary fluctuations in the market price of any commodity fall chiefly upon those parts of its price which resolve themselves into wages and profit. That part which resolves itself into rent is less affected by them. A rent certain in money is not in the least affected by them, either in its rate or its value. In settling the terms of the lease, the landlord and farmer endeavour, according to their best judgment, to adjust that rate, not to the temporary and occasional, but to the average and ordinary price of the produce."—ADAM SMITH, *Wealth of Nations*, Book i., c. /— *Price of Commodities.*

tions by the vouchers before me. I will promise, however, that, if the question of relief may be allowed to rest on the proof of the generality and amount of the distress among farmers, I will produce evidence thereof in the minutest detail, with all balance of each possible saving effected by the recent tariffs and diminution of wages, that shall bear the severest test of the most lynx-eyed Free-Trader.

Meanwhile, one short appeal to common sense will suffice. Suppose that I have a farm on which not only rent has been computed, but my capital has been invested, on the calculation of the averages whereon the Tithe Commutation was based, those being what the statesmen who procured the Repeal of the Corn Law stated would be the averages on the continuance of which they reckoned.* According to averages, this farm, on the Four-Course System, produces me—

		£	s.	d.
348 quarters, at 56s. per quarter. . . .		974	8	0
And 435 quarters of barley, at £1 11s. 8d. per quarter.		688	15	0
		£1663	3	0

See what the same produce me at the present prices—

	£	s.	d.
Wheat, 348 quarters, at the average of Christmas 1850, viz., 40s. 3d. per quarter.	700	7	0
Barley, 435 quarters, at £1 3s. 6d., ditto . .	511	2	6
	£1211	9	6

My gross loss on wheat and barley, by the fall in price, amounts to £451 13s. 6d.

I am speaking here of a farm which I well know,† the

* Sir Robert Peel said in 1842, " With reference to the probable remunerating price, I should say, that for the protection of the agricultural interest, if the price of wheat, allowing for its natural oscillations, could be limited to some such amount as between 54s. and 58s., I do not believe that it is for the interest of the agriculturist that it should be higher. Take the average of the last ten years, excluding from some portion of the average the extreme prices of the last three years, and 56s. would be found to be the average. I cannot say, on the other hand, that I am able to see any great or permanent advantage to be derived from the diminution of the price of corn beyond the lowest amount I have named."

† It is obviously unnecessary for the present purpose of illustration to enter into more detail. The quick Free-Trader will probably say, " But from how many acres do you get these quarters of grain? Could you not produce a greater number of bushels per acre by higher cultivation?" A

rent of which is but £435, exclusive of tithes, and on which the farmer's net profit was calculated at the same sum, the remainder being sunk on the cost of cultivation. Therefore the gross loss exceeds the rent on the one hand, and the farmer's net profit on the other? But there are savings in the reduced cost of seed, wages, &c. ? Certainly, to a considerable amount; but this farm (a turnip farm) was an excellent stock-farm. I have already shown how the reduced price of meat affected those profits on which the farmer was to meet the loss upon corn; and I do ask you, my dear John, (if you have not entirely forgotten all rural affairs,) to consider how it is possible that any economy and saving in seeds, and in wages, keep of horses, housekeeping of farmer, (computed to the uttermost farthing,) can render this gross loss on corn and on barley—added to all preceding and continued loss upon cattle—otherwise than appalling to the mind, and ruinous to the purse, of the farmer? What can any probable or possible reduction of rent do here? What would be 10 per cent. on the rental (viz., between £40 and £50) in counterbalance to a deficit of hundreds?

In the first stage of the depression at which we are arrived, the loss, as I before stated, falls mainly upon the occupier. As yet the landowner has been enabled fairly to say—"I never called upon you in prosperous seasons for an increase of rent; and one or two failing seasons you must bear as a just set-off to your advantage in the good. We are told by some that there are exceptional causes to the present prices; we are not without hopes held forth by others that the Legislature will interpose on our behalf. We were assured that this repeal of the Corn Law was an experiment; and certainly the consent of many was obtained to it by the calculations held out by the great authorities in favour of it—that we should still retain remunerating prices. We don't mean to say that there was an absolute

very fair question, but not at present to the point. Either the land is already in the highest state of cultivation, or it is not. If it is, it can yield no more bushels without impoverishing the soil: if it is not, the farmer would reply frankly, "Sir, you are right: my land could produce a greater number of bushels by the help of a much greater cost in stock and artificial manures; and under the stimulus of a fair competition I might so have risked my capital. But I dare not do so now, at these prices; and indeed all my neighbours who have been thus applying to their land the utmost extent of their capital, in artificial manures or large purchases of stock, find that these prices don't pay the cost of increasing the produce."

promise or contract on a subject on which there was no experience to base a guarantee; but as these great authorities have been, as yet, egregiously mistaken in their calculations, we have a fair hope that, in another Parliament, a great portion of such as those authorities influenced will do us the justice to reconsider the question. Such reduction of rent, meanwhile, as I could make, while in the aggregate most serious to me, would, subdivided amongst yourselves, scarcely be felt."—So think or say some. Others return the 10 per cent., and scarcely felt it is by the occupier—severely, often, no doubt by the owner.

Well, grant that this depreciation continues—that landlords' rent and farmers' profit are to be re-assessed on an average of years, (according to such prices)—grant that, in consequence of the savings from cost effected by the tariff and in wages, the farm upon which £451 were lost in barley and wheat is only lowered in annual value £200 a-year of net profit, and that landlord and farmer divide that loss between them—still it is not only a question of rent; the landlord will lose about a fourth of his gross farm-revenue therefrom, or at least 35 per cent. of his net income; but the farmer must also lose a fourth of his profits in return to his capital. And the error into which uninformed theorists have fallen on this point will be found, I think, clearly explained in the note I append.*

* Political economists are quite right in practice, as well as theory, in supposing that rent comes from the surplus profit; but those of Mr. Ricardo's school err in treating the farmer's share as if that did not, also, by uniform practice, come from the surplus profit also. They have argued, for instance, as if on a farm paying £435 a-year rent, and returning for the tenant's profit, say £435 a-year also—there was, in consequence of low prices, a loss in gross profit of £200—the landlord would take that loss all on himself by lowering the rent to that amount—whereas by the invariable practice of surveyors and land agents, and by the usages of custom, a re-assessment would divide that loss between the farmer's profit and the landlord's rent. We shall see in the next page that there are many disturbing circumstances which would long prevent the landlord's share of loss being so large as the farmer's; but in no case of re-assessment, as a general principle, would his rent fall, but what the farmer's profit on the capital he has expended must fall also. The working out of this principle becomes yet more clear, if we look to the practice in other countries, where the landlord's share is not positively based upon what we call rent. Thus, for instance, it is very common abroad, in France and in Italy, for the landlord and farmer to share the net annual profits between them, the farmer finding the requisite capital and paying all the expenses. These shares are sometimes in equal moieties; sometimes where the ground is fertile and the expense light, the landlord's share of profit is much more than the moiety. Generally (in spite of what is said to the contrary) it is

Grant that you mulct the landlord and the tenant equally to a fourth of their income—the fourth of the yearly proceeds from the principal part of the real property of the nation is gone from those not only who spend it, but those upon whom it was spent.

Whichever way we look to the question, £200 loss upon a farm that yielded £435 rent is lost to the community—whether subtracted for the most part from the profits of the farmer, or equably divided between him and the landlord—all those upon whom that sum were expended, must to that amount feel the loss. Extend that loss throughout the country, and say if it is to be despised—or if it be *only* a question of rent.

Meanwhile many circumstances concur to delay for a considerable period any fall of rents proportionate to the loss of the occupier. The landlord, be he ever so benevolent and desirous to meet the times, has against his concessions the check of his absolute ruin; to the majority of the larger landed proprietors, with hereditary burdens, a reduction of 20 per cent. on the gross rental would wholly absorb the net income. A large proportion of proprietors on a smaller scale, habitually resident in the country, and acquainted with rural management, would prefer cultivating a considerable portion of their land themselves to reductions which they could not bear without resigning, not luxuries, but comforts, and crippling the means of education to their children. For though the land, if let, might not yield enough for adequate rent to the landlord, and adequate return to the tenant, yet, taken in hand by the owner, it might well yield enough when there was only *one* share, instead of *two*, to be taken from the produce. On the other hand, while the landlord has the check of his ruin against material reduction, the farmer is urged by the

larger than in England, inasmuch as there are not the same exclusive deductions from the landlord's profit. Now here it is at once obvious, that all loss of net profit falls on the tenant as well as the landlord; and so it does in England, because, though here the rent simplifies the contract, the same common-sense principle prevails in practice—viz., that *both* landlord and tenant are paid out of net profit. And the reason why, in England, the first loss falls exclusively on the farmer is also obvious. He, by the payment of a fixed rent, becomes not only the sharer of profit, but the speculator in its variations. He has all the extra gain in the good year, and therefore sustains all the loss on the bad, until, as I before said, by a long continuation of the bad years, a re-assessment is made to the joint loss of both parties.

fear of his ruin into struggling on to the last, rather than throw up the farm on which he has sunk all his capital. The existing race of farmers cannot, as a class, have the resource of other occupation ; and there will be always found competitors for a vacant farm as there are for a theatre, though both farm and theatre may be a losing concern.

> "'Tis credulous hope that nurtures life, and whispers
> Some kind ' to-morrow '—if we droop to-day.
> 'Tis hope that nerves the tiller of the soil,
> And bids him trust the corn-seed to the furrow,
> Sure of a usurer's wealth from niggard fields."

A new race, too, continually springs up—the children, perhaps, of traders—liking the hardy life and healthful pursuits of the farmer, willing to trust to the future; having some little extra means, beyond the capital invested on the land; disposed to risk, and for the present resign, their fair share of pecuniary return from the land. They may serve to keep up the rents of the landlord; but do they keep up the present generation of farmers ? Nay, do we not hear it constantly said, with all the complacent *sang froid* of pseudo-political economists, " No doubt the present race of farmers must be swept away, and a new race of more energy and capital must succeed." How then can it be said that this is not a vital question for the existing generation of farmers ? how can you be astonished that they object to being swept away ? Great changes in a commercial system must necessarily occasion great distress and hardship to those the changes affect; but when your changes affect a class so numerous as the living men engaged in agriculture, at least make your changes as mild and as gradual as you can.

But what effect is this loss to both classes of employer, landlord or tenant, to have on the wages of the labourer; or his social condition ? I grant to you frankly that, as yet, the distress is but gradually passing from the first phase in the cycle—viz., the class of the occupier; but must it not soon operate on the labourer to a degree far beyond what it has yet reached in those partial districts, where wages already have been brought below the level of the cheaper prices of food ?

You say wages do not depend on the price of bread, and

you point to instances in manufacturing towns, in which, while the price of bread has fallen, the money rate of wages has not decreased.

It is this very fact that ought to make us beware how we adopt the error into which a cursory reading of the political economists is apt to betray us. They are generally inclined, in the course of argument, to personify the country or community as if it were an individual, and to say such and such things affect the country or interest the community. But this country or community is parcelled out in different classes and interests, and what may affect the one is often very slow in reaching the other.

"The cost of food is," no doubt, (as Mr. M'Culloch observes,) "the main regulator of wages" in the long run. But for a considerable time it may regulate wages in the agricultural districts, and not affect them in the manufacturing, and *vice versâ*. And for this very obvious reason, which comprises one of the fundamental doctrines of political economy—Wages rise and fall not only in money value, but in actual value, in proportion to the ratio between the population and the Capital which employs it.* Wages will rise not only in countries, but in particular districts, according as the capital in those districts increases faster than the population; and fall in proportion as the capital is decreased in ratio to the population.

Whenever therefore capital, which, as Mr. Mill truly says, is nothing more than "the result of savings," is diminished in the agricultural districts, wages must fall. But certainly you have left the farmer no savings! His capital is diminished, and diminishing; and, by the inevitable law of political economy, the wages given to the population he employs must proportionally decrease, so long as that population increases or remains stationary. Now, as Mr. M'Culloch has shown, (*Pol. Econ.*, p. 413,) when wages decline in consequence of a diminution of the capital apportioned to their payment, the supply of labourers does not immediately decline; and therefore, for a certain time, wages may fall in the agricultural districts, and not in the manufacturing, if the capital in the one, as proportioned to the population is diminished, and is not diminished in the

* MILL, *Political Economy*, Sect. ii., chap. 2, on wages. M'CULLOCH, *ibid.*, Part III.—*On the Distribution of Wealth.*

other.   By degrees that portion of the surplus agricultural population which is not removed by mortality or emigration is draughted off to the manufacturing towns, and diminishes wages there by increasing the supply of labour.   The comparatively better wages in the manufacturing towns could not be permanent, because it is an axiom in Political Economy that ultimately both "profits and wages on land regulate those in manufacturing communities."   Meanwhile, if the capital devoted to the land be not repaired, the consequences upon wages become more and more serious and threatening.   For, again, Political Economy tells us that agricultural wages rise in proportion as capital is employed in bringing inferior soils into cultivation, and the concomitant necessity of additional cost on the good. And therefore, as either inferior soils are abandoned, or less cost devoted to the good, wages continue to fall; and hence it is that "the cost of food is the main regulator of wages."

Now, to what depth a fall of wages, caused by permanent diminution of capital, in ratio to the population, may descend, Mr. Mill shall inform us :—"How slow soever the increase of population, provided that of capital is still slower, wages will be reduced so low that a portion of the population will regularly die from the consequences of want." *

. Certainly the farmer does not trouble his head about these theories.   The distress falls first upon him ; he looks round to see what he can save: he comes slowly and reluctantly (for he is a warm-hearted fellow, the British farmer) to a reduction in wages equivalent to the price at which he must sell the main article of food ; but come to it he must at last.   And it is only the fortunate check of the farmer's own burden, the poor-rate, that interposes between the labourer and that absolute want which Mr. Mill predicts to him under the operations of a capital that decreases in ratio to the population.

The distress extends necessarily from occupier and labourer to proprietor, and soon spreads to all the trades with which they have dealt ; and if the foreigner preserve awhile the cotton manufacturer, I know not if that be an adequate counter-balancing advantage, and am tempted to

* MILL, *Polit. Econ.*, p. 58.

exclaim with Lord Chatham, "That state alone is sovereign which stands on its own strength, and hangs not on the will of the foreigner."

But, meanwhile, there is another class most materially affected by the change—a class most essential to the civilisation of the country—I mean the Parochial Clergy. When they were induced, for the benefit of the community, to commute their tithes into a corn rent-charge upon the average of seven years, they were not led to anticipate the time when your law was to deprive them of from twenty to twenty-five per cent. of their income. To that reduction, if free importation continues, and, with it, the present prices, that class of our clergy most worked, and which few will consider as over-paid, must soon submit. And when we remember how the income of these men is, for the most part, devoted—the unostentatious charity they practise, the popular education they so liberally help to elevate and diffuse (compelled, by their residence in the country, to spend what they require for their wants chiefly among the neighbouring traders)—I can conceive nothing more calculated to retard the prosperity and well-being of the rural districts than the impoverishment of that class of gentlemen which applies means the most moderate to services the most useful.

It is true that the clergy profit by the cheaper price in the necessaries of life. But that does not meet the question of justice. For you do not say to the other classes of the community, "In return for such cheapness, we will take away a fourth of your income." The clergyman only profits by that cheapness because you cannot exclude him from the general effects of legislation. But if it be true that he could profit to the amount of from 20 to 25 per cent. by your changes, then the other members of society whom you have not mulcted to that amount profit to the same degree, and relatively to them he is therefore still from 20 to 25 per cent. the poorer.

But it is a very small proportion of the clergy, and indeed of all the middle class, whom a cheaper rate of housekeeping profits to between a third and a fourth of their income.

It profits those whose income is at the lowest, whose families are unusually large, and whose whole income, or nearly so, is spent upon the absolute bread and meat of the household: but this applies less to the clergy and the middle class of gentry than to most men: their chief yearly expenses are not in housekeeping, but in various wants and duties, which your tariffs as yet little reach. There is an insurance on life, or a saving for wife and kindred; charities; doctors; the various accidents which are never anticipated; and, above all, the school bills for children. And if, on the average, you say that the parochial clergyman gains 10 per cent. on his house bills, and will lose 25 per cent in hard money, he has still to thank you for a loss, on a modest income, of 15 per cent., which may materially interfere with the usefulness of his life as well as its comforts.

Nor do I think it a matter of subordinate importance, though it lies latent, acts indirectly, and has been wholly unnoticed, to consider what effect the impoverishment of squire, clergyman, and farmer, will practically have on the quality of instruction to be received by the rising generation;—how far the stinted income of the parents may stint also the education of the sons. At the very time that you say that farmers most need intellectual culture, and call upon them to grapple with new theories and rely upon discoveries in science, you will take away the very power to bestow on their children the culture you enforce. The clergyman will be compelled to lower the standard of education for his sons, the squire that for his; for the first item on which men, pushed hard to make both ends meet, retrench, is the school bills of their children. The impoverishment of those classes diminishes the source of intelligence which has been hitherto the richest in its supplies to the nation. For if we look through biography, we shall find that by far the largest proportion of the most eminent men of whom we boast in literature, in science, in the elevated and intellectual departments of action, in all that has enriched our nation with the ideas that constitute its most imperishable wealth, have sprung, not from manufacturing towns, but from rural districts, and claim descent from farmers and yeomen, country squires, and clergymen. I say this in no disrespect to manufacturing communities, certainly in no disparagement of the keen and lively intelligence which such communities arouse and foster, but which it is in the nature of things that such communities should divert either to the pursuit of gain or the contests of politics. The trading and manufacturing Cathaginians were quite as clever as the agricultural Romans, but the Carthaginians were the first nation that had for its proverbial maxim—"Buy at the dearest and sell at the cheapest market;" * and the Romans have left to all time grand thoughts, the memory of great deeds, and the heirlooms of imperishable books; while the Carthaginians, wholly occupied in commerce, and presenting to us an aspect so superb in the sole relation with which political economy professes to deal—viz., the economy of material wealth—the negotiators and factors of the world—contributed as little as might be to the wealth of the mind—to science and art; and a Voyage round Africa, by one of their generals, is the sole contribution still extant of the rivals to Roman power during a dominion that exceeded seven centuries.†

* The following anecdote, recorded by one of the fathers of the Christian Church, (St. Aug. lib. xiii. de Trin., c. 3,) in reference to the maxim we are told to receive as a virtual precept of Christianity, is rather amusing :—"A mountebank promised to the Carthaginians to discover to them their most secret thoughts, if they came on a certain day to hear him. When they had assembled, 'The secret thought of all of you,' said this shrewd fellow, 'is, when you buy, to buy cheap; when you sell, to sell dear.' They all confessed laughing, and with great applause, that he had defined aright—and thus," adds St. Augustine, "confessed themselves—rogues!" The saint there would seem a little too severe if his meaning be not carefully defined. It is a very honest wish to buy cheap and sell dear, provided it is one of the thoughts of men; but if it is the paramount engrossing thought, then I am afraid that Augustine spoke very much—as a saint would do.

† Intellectual education was much restricted in Carthage—Greek, at one time, interdicted. Terence was an African, though it is not clear if he was, properly speaking, a Carthaginian by birth; but he left his country at the age of thirteen, received his education at Rome, and cannot be judged as a Carthaginian writer, though he may, perhaps, be fairly regarded as an example of what Carthaginians might have produced, had their extraordinary intelligence been less confined to buying cheap and selling dear. If Terence be excepted, I am not aware that they are recorded to have produced any other literary works than Hanno's *Voyage*, cited in the text (which is the sole one extant, through the medium of a Greek translation),* except a long trea-

* [This remarkable fragment barely extends to the length of half a dozen pages octavo. Slight though the sketch is, it is pronounced by Montesquieu one of the most valuable remains of antiquity. Its title, Αννωνος καρχηδονιων βασιλευς, κ.τ.λ., may be rendered thus : The Account of the Voyage of Hanno, Commander of the Carthaginians round the parts of Libya beyond the Pillars of Hercules, which he deposited in the Temple of Saturn. It has been translated into Italian by Ramusio, into Spanish by Campomanes, into French by Bougainville, and into English by Thomas Falconer.]

It has been so haughtily asked by Mr. Cobden, what the "landed aristocracy" has contributed to the mental wealth of this country, that we may be forgiven the answer—"More than two-thirds of the greatest men whom your history can boast of!"

But, as here I am contending for the value of sustained education, alike to the proprietor, the farmer, and clergyman of the parish—and as all three, in fact, appertain to the "Agricultural Mind"—may I respectfully ask, whether, from the first date of manufacturers amongst us, with all the wealth they have amassed, with all the laws that have favoured them, their several communities leagued together —and added, if you will, to all the manufacturing populations of Europe—have produced either writers or thinkers, authorities in the law and the state, patriots or heroes, to compare for an instant to those whose fathers were dwellers on our soil, or pastors in our Church?

What writers to compare to Newton, to Bacon, to Boyle; to Addison, to Dryden, to Byron; to Burns; to Gibbon; to Robertson; to Fielding, and to Swift?

What statesmen who will throw into shade, Burleigh, and Cecil; Cromwell, and Clarendon; Walpole, and Chatham; Fox, Wyndham, and Grey?

Where are the patriots or heroes—the doers of deeds— who are to obscure the great images of Hampden and Sidney—of Eliot, of Vane, of Falkland and Derby, of Wellesley and Nelson? Where the Luminaries of Law, that

tise on Agriculture by one of their generals; and after their fall they got up one philosopher, Clitomachus, who attempted to comfort them by essays—a diligent and learned person, whom Cicero says was acute enough for a Carthaginian—(*acutus, ut Pœnus*). We have a fine picture left to us of the great Hannibal, in contrast to his countrymen. When, after the severe conditions imposed by Rome, which ruined their freedom and grandeur, they were lamenting over the necessity of paying the fine from their private fortunes, Hannibal burst out laughing. Chid for his indecorum, he answered, "My laughter is near upon tears. You are lamenting your money, and I thought of the ruin of Carthage."

I must be pardoned this long reference to the great Commercial State of the ancient world, because it stands in contrast to the Greek republics, where, and in Athens especially, though all encouragement was given to foreign commerce, it was carried on by settlers—not the citizens. The Greek republicans were so jealous of political freedom that they did not like to extend the franchise to men who, as dependent on the foreigner, were deemed, right or wrong, by all the Greek sages and legislators, to have an interest apart from, and sometimes paramount to, the domestic and internal welfare of the State.

are to outshine Coke, "the great oracle of our municipal jurisprudence "—Somers, "the chief founder of our constitutional monarchy "—Mansfield, Nottingham, and Erskine;—Cowper, equally famous as lawyer and statesman; or the stainless Camden, "whose name Englismen will honour to the latest generations, for having secured personal freedom, by putting an end to arbitrary arrests under general warrants: for having established the constitutional rights of juries; and for having placed on an imperishable basis the liberty of the press ?"*

All these—sons of the soil or the Church!† We may be proud of such claims on the respect that is due to one *use* of our orders (and that use of the loftiest), and we may justly desire that there should be no diminution in that degree of instruction which the children of those orders may receive for the ornament or strength of generations to come. Nor for them only, but for the whole population, I say, that to lower the standard of education among the classes set apart for that portion of the intelligence of the country not devoted to buying in the cheapest market to sell in the dearest, *is* to lower the standard of idea, and to debase the quality, while it diminishes the degree, of intelligence throughout the whole community;—and that in this question of prices which you would reduce to one of rent—this question affecting so fearfully the means of squire and clergyman—yeoman and farmer—*is* inevitably involved a fall in the standard of education for the rising generation—since the impoverishment of the parent must affect the resources on which the education of the sons will depend.

You may tell us that Adam Smith, however, asserts that merchants and master manufacturers are more intelligent as a body than we plain country squires.—(And their intelligence, indeed, I never dispute; it is only the application of it which can give us, through biography, any claim to superiority.) But while Adam Smith praises their acuteness, observe, my dear John, how he cautions society

* CAMPBELL'S *Lives of the Lord Chancellors.*
† Even Mr. Cartwright, to whose mechanical ingenuity manufacturers owe so much, was the son of a country gentleman; and Mr. Cobden himself, of whose talents no man can doubt, is fond of stating, with some semblance of pride, that he, too, is a child of the land.

against their judgment. And in citing the words of the
great writer upon whom that class which is supposed to
have an interest more peculiarly counter to the agricultural
in the question before us, chiefly relies, I say with sincerity,
that the language of caution employed by Adam Smith is
far stronger than I would have presumed to use :—

"Merchants and master manufacturers, . . . as during
their whole lives they are engaged in plans and projects,
they have frequently more acuteness of understanding
than the greater part of country gentlemen. As their
thoughts, however, are commonly exercised rather about the
interest of their own particular branch of business that that
of the society, their judgment, even when given with the
greatest candour (which it has not been upon every occasion), is much more to be depended upon with regard to the
former of those two objects than the latter. . . . The
interest of the dealers in any particular branch of trade and
manufactures is always in some degree different from, and
even opposite to, that of the public. The proposal of any
new law or regulation of commerce which comes from this
order ought always to be listened to with great precaution,
and ought never to be adopted till after having been long and
carefully examined, not only with the most scrupulous, but
with the most suspicious attention. It comes from an order
of men whose interest is never exactly the same with that of
the public ; who have generally an interest to deceive, and
even to oppress the public ; and who, accordingly, have
upon many occasions both oppressed and deceived it."—
(Adam Smith, Book I., c. xi., *Wealth of Nations.*)

To sum up the authorities from Free-trading political
economists that I have arrayed on the side of justice to
the land, I must here bid you observe, my dear John, how
wholly it has been overlooked, that when Adam Smith
expresses himself in favour of the free importation of cattle
and corn, he does so expressly upon the assumption that that
importation will be so slight as not to injure the farmer. This
is his main and almost sole argument for advising such importation. "If," he says, "importation of foreign cattle
were made ever so free, so few could be imported that the
grazing trade of Great Britain could be little affected by
it."—(Book IV., c. xi.) And he supposes that the importation of lean cattle—which, he says, only could be imported,

M 2

would not interfere with the interest of feeding or fattening countries, only with the breeding. Experience having proved that these assumptions are wholly contradicted by the facts —1st, That the importations of foreign cattle have been very large; 2nd, That not only lean cattle, but meat for market (cured meat alone to at least four times the weight of the lean cattle), has been imported ; 3rd, That the reduced price in meat effected by these importations does interfere with the interest of the feeding and fattening countries, since the price at which cattle are again sold by the farmer does not pay the cost of feeding and fattening ;—the whole of Adam Smith's argument falls to the ground, and he himself, in consistency, would have been compelled to relinquish it, since (in Book I., c. xi.) he had shown it to be absolutely necessary for the improvement of tillage that the "price of butcher's meat, and consequently of cattle, must rise till it gets so high as to become as profitable to employ the most fertile and best cultivated lands in raising food for them, as in raising corn."

In the same chapter (Book IV., c, xi.) he argues for the importation of free corn expressly on the same ground— viz., that "it would very little affect the interest of the farmer in England, since corn is a much more bulky commodity than butcher's meat; since the small quantity of corn imported in times of scarcity ought to satisfy the farmers they had nothing to fear from the freest importation : and since (according to his calculation) the average importation one year with another does not exceed the five hundredth and seventy-one part of the annual consumption." Here again, too, the recent facts being diametrically opposed by experience to the assertion in theory, Adam Smith's argument is lost; and here again he would be compelled in consistency to withdraw it, since, if the free importation does largely affect the capital of the farmer, Adam Smith has expressly stated his opinion, "that the capital employed in Agriculture, not only puts into motion a greater quantity of productive labour than any equal capital employed in manufactures, but in proportion, too, to the quantity of productive labour which it employs, it adds a much greater value to the annual produce of the land and labour of the country, to the real wealth and revenue of its inhabitants. Of all the ways in which a capital can be employed, it is by far the most advantageous to the community." *

This early father of the doctrine of free competition proceeds to admit and to state that "there are two cases in which it will generally be advantageous to lay some burden upon foreign, for the encouragement of domestic, industry.

"The first is when some particular sort of industry is necessary for the defence of the country." He alludes here to the Shipping Interest under the Navigation Act; but it matters not whether the defence be from without or within. A country may be in as much danger from internal disaffection as from a foreign enemy; and there are few, perhaps, who would not think it a less danger for Britain to face a fleet from Russia, than to contend with deep and rankling discontent amongst the owners and occupiers of the British soil.

"The second case" (says Adam Smith) "in which it will be generally advantageous to lay some burden upon foreign, for the encouragement of domestic, industry, is where some tax is imposed at home upon the produce of the latter. In this case it seems reasonable that an equal tax should be imposed upon the produce of the former. This would not give the monopoly of the home market to domestic industry, nor turn towards a particular employment a greater share of the stock and labour of the country than what would naturally go to it. It would only hinder any part of what would naturally go to it from being turned away by the tax into a less natural direction, and would leave the competition between foreign and domestic industry after the tax, as nearly as possible upon the same footing as before it." Therefore, in just equivalent to the taxes on the land (for every tax on the producer, by diminishing his capital, is effectively a tax on the produce), a correspondent tax on the foreign-corn competitor is required.

Thirdly.—Mark this! Even where neither of these cases

* Certain modern political economists contend that this is a very exaggerated estimate of the national value of agricultural capital; but they will observe that that is not here the point in question: the more important Adam Smith considered that capital, the more he would have shrunk from invading it by any of his own theories as to the safety of free importation of agricultural produce, if experience showed that the facts contradicted those theories to the injury of the capital.

may apply, Adam Smith states, " that where, by previous high duties or prohibitions, employment has been extended to a great multitude of hands, humanity may in this case require that the freedom of trade should be restored only by slow gradations, and with a good deal of reserve and circumspection."—(Book IV., c. xi.)

I now hasten to the close. Without entering into mere party and personal questions involving the rise or the fall of Governments; without impugning the motives of the dead, or violating the respect due to the living; with as little of acrimony, I trust, as may be compatible with manly and earnest contest against powerful opponents—I have stated the case of my Clients—I have summoned as my witnesses on their behalf (for a fixed duty at least) the great masters of economical science. The distress they allege is acknowledged from the throne; it is allowed by the Minister. At present, as I have stated, the full weight of distress rests on the occupier. Soon it must extend, not only to clergman and landowner—but to labourer and tradesman. Already in many districts the labourer begins to feel that the cheap loaf entails low wages, and brings him nearer and nearer to the workhouse. In other districts, where wages are not yet lowered to the ratio of prices, the farmer feels the humanity that is akin to his genial nature oozing away, as the wellbeing of the men he employs is adduced as an argument for beggaring the employer. Grand social evil! Hostile interest between masters and men—beware how it spreads too far. Already in rural towns tradesmen begin to feel the change—already say, "Trade is bad; something must be done for the farmer." Ay, that " something." What but the mitigation of your policy can do it? Already the tradesmen in the metropolis, spite of the temporary aid the Grand Exhibition may afford them, begin to complain that gentlemen don't lay out what they did; and many a sturdy Free-Trader behind the counter is already converted by the inspection of his ledger. Common sense is at work amongst all who sell, and is putting this question, which admits but one answer—" Do I save by the baker what I lose by abridging the means of my customers?" And so gradually will that same common sense work, till it reach the manufacturer himself through all its indirect channels,

and prove to him the true value of the Home market, that
he at present despises.

Sooner or later, the movement of distress must pass
through all these phases, if there be a single shred of truth
in the fundamental laws that govern the relations of seller
and buyer, of capital and wages. And if the question of
some relief to the agricultural interest could be delayed till
then, there would be no doubt as to how the constituencies
of the country would decide it. But then, alas! much
greater the difficulty to repair the evil—a vast portion of
the agricultural capital would be irretrievably sunk and
destroyed—the process of restoration would be far more
arduous and prolonged. Feelings of bitterness and desire
of retaliation would have been engendered by distress and
rooted by despair; and I fear that you would have converted the very class most naturally inclined to peace and
order, into the very one most dangerous and disaffected.

Pause, then, before you so resolutely say that you will
not retrace a step of your path—before you close the door
to all conciliation, on so many millions of your suffering
countrymen. I own myself that it is the social considerations inseparably mixed up with this question that weigh
upon me far more than any that can be suggested by the
principles to which mere political economy confines its
survey. And I will own further, that, while pleading for
the cultivator of the land, I carry my sight far beyond his
immediate interest; and I feel, as an Englishman, grave
apprehensions for all the other sections into which the
community is divided.

Grant that you are correct in your general principle, as
political economists; pause as statesmen, pause as patriots,
before you so rigidly apply it.

"All that in the end become evil in example, spring from principles that
were good in the commencement."

Such are the words assigned to Cæsar by an historian,
reared amid those feuds of party and of class which closed
in the corruption of the noblest people and the downfall of
the grandest commonwealth that illustrate the mournful
record of departed nations.

Our foreign trade, the exports of our cotton manufacture, are worthy objects of attention; but they are not the

solo ones. The wealth of a State itself cannot so absorb the attention of a thoughtful Legislator, but what he will also regard the moral and social circumstances by which alone that wealth can be permanently secured. Let me care ever so much for money, it is not only to make money that I must care; I must also look to the safeguards that are to prevent me from losing it.

"Defence," says Adam Smith, "is of much more importance than opulence."

Our debt—the fundholder—the safety of the empire in its actual and necessary defences—all these I must look to as a citizen, as well as to the quantity of cotton I can sell to the foreigner.

The debt—the fundholder! Are any of us so blind to the fact that, ever since Peel's Currency Bill, there has rankled deep in the minds of the agricultural class, which that Bill so gravely affected, a sentiment of injury which it were wise not to irritate too sorely? And though I, myself, reprove that sentiment, and would resist any retaliation which it might engender, there is a man of far more authority than I, who, not very long since, has openly maintained that sentiment to be just; a man at the time clothed with the dignity of a Minister of the Cabinet, and who is now the momentary idol of the party that arrogates the title of "Liberal"—I mean, of course, Sir James Graham.* This powerful orator and distinguished legislator has lately invited us to frankness; pardon me, then, John, if I am frank; for I speak of an evil which, to my mind, is as great as (perhaps it is greater than) all that could fall on the land. Frankly I say, then, this :—

Plunge the whole agricultural class into permanent difficulty and distress, and depend upon it the fundholder will

* "Subsequent events had confirmed the wisdom of the predictions of the Hon. Member for Essex (Mr. Baring). The landlords were obliged to reduce their rents equivalant to the altered value of money; they were obliged to reduce their means of meeting their engagements, while the weight of their fixed engagements, instead of being diminished, was actually increased by the alteration effected in the standard of value. He concurred in what was stated on that point in the Report of the Agricultural Commission of last session. In fact he drew up the report that was agreed to by that committee; he had stated in that report that a matter which, according to the time prescribed for its consideration, might be but a trifling injustice in 1826 and 1827, would be an overwhelming and most indefensible injustice in 1833."—*Speech of Sir James Graham on the Corn Laws*, March 6, 1834.

have cause to tremble—either by loud demands for paper currency, or by a determined resolution to resist the taxes which defray the debt.

First, indeed, under the cry of economy will go those expenses which maintain our navy and protect our shores. And, however welcome to the followers of Mr. Cobden may be the recruits to his financial standard amongst the agricultural members to whom he has before appealed, I do not think that prudent men—nor men who have not lost the love and pride of country, without which no community can endure long—can contemplate without alarm the probability of such a combination of votes in the House of Commons as may reduce the empire of Great Britain to a fourth-rate state, leaving none of the defences which other fourth-rate states concur in maintaining. It was the boast of Themistocles that he knew how to render a small state great. From a modern school politicians have arisen, who seem to make it their boast that they know how to make great states small.*

Look where we will at the consequence of leaving a deep and lasting remembrance of wrong and of insult upon the minds and hearts of a vast number of men—whom no redistribution of the franchise, however artfully arranged, can deprive of numerous representatives connected by the union of a common suffering—and there is cause for the most anxious alarm in all who do not confine their thoughts to the Carthaginian's maxim of " Buy cheap, and sell dear."

You dilate on the blessings of Peace—you cannot prize those blessings too highly; but is there no danger in impressing upon the most high-spirited and martial part of your population the conviction that in war lies their sole chance of return from property and remuneration for labour? You must be conscious that the evil which

---

* Themistocles fulfilled his boast by a policy which appears to have consisted in creating and maintaining a shipping interest and a maritime power —obtaining the sovereignty of the sea ; founding and securing an empire of dependent confederacies ; introducing into his own country the manufactures and arts of the foreigner ; securing to them the markets of Home : protecting their industry where such protection seemed needed ; but not giving to the counsels of those who, by foreign trade, could make themselves independent of the native interests, the preponderant influence in the state. Such, too, was the policy by which England rose ; and such is the policy the new school would reverse from its base to its capital.

modern civilisation has most to apprehend lies, not as of old, in the incursions of the barbarians, but in the struggle and ferment of civilisation itself; that in the heart of your great manufacturing towns works alike all that expedite progress, and all that can threaten dissolution; that thence emerge the dread " *cohors febrium;* " the heated desires for a change never circumscribed in the mild limits of reform; the tendencies to whatever can revolutionise institutions, and substitute for the fair false dreams of Atlantis and Utopia those conditions of labour on which practical society is based. Checked by the inert resistance of the classes that live on the land, this, which is the immemorial and universal spirit of manufacturing communities under all forms of government, is but conducive to improvement. The collision of opinion, when the innovating spirit is opposed and tempered by that which adheres to the ancient forms of constitutional freedom, strikes out those compromises which admit of change, but temper change into harmony with order. It is good for democracy itself that the state should contain a fair proportion of the elements of conservatism. Political liberty could not last a year, if there were not in the community some retentive and tenacious principle which preserves liberty itself from the eternal experiments of fanatics; who, finding no movement of the machine can convey them beyond the reach of toil and of hunger, vent their disappointment at last on the mainspring of the mechanism itself. It is the recognition and establishment of this principle which has rendered hitherto so stable the mighty Republic of America; and has balanced the impatience of men " in crowded cities pent," with the counterpoise of that prudence which is inseparably connected with property in land—that is, where return from the property is safe under systems of order, and only endangered by periods of convulsion. It is this principle alone, though exhibited in its weakest and most inoperative form, which has saved France from Paris and Lyons, and stayed the Communism engendered in urban populations, by the votes of proprietors in land. While, on the contrary, one main cause of the brief duration of all the ancient republics was the preponderance of the urban over the rural classes;—with them there was but one word for the State and the City.

Is there, then, no danger in converting the sole conserv-
ing and retentive classes of the State into those most indifferent to your institutions, and least interested in that
order of things which has condemned them alone to sacrifice and calamity, and denied to them alone all mitigation
of injury?   Consider the incessant fluctuations, from well-
being to adversity, to which that part of your population
dependent chiefly or largely on foreign trade and foreign
competition is exposed.   Consider that at any time, despite
the repeal of the Corn Law, the manufacturing operatives
must be subject to sudden distress; that sudden distress
with them springs at once into loud disaffection; that
they never want the agitator and the leader: And when
you would turn for aid, not to the bayonet of the soldier
(I at least will not speak of that), but to the opinion of
the class on which, of old, without repeal, you could peace-
fully rely, is there no chance that you may find it sullen or
neutral in the senate?—supine or hostile through the land?
It is not that the members of that class would sympathise
with the cause which threatened disorder; it is simply that
they may have ceased to feel interest in the order endangered.   No proprietor, no gentlemen, felt interest in the
cause of the mob that surrounded the Tuileries; they
had only ceased to feel interest in the principles of
government which Louis Philippe represented.   Their
interest did not awake till afterwards, when life was
threatened by the blood-red banner of the terrorist, and
property was proclaimed a theft by the schoolmen of Communism.

Believe me, these are no idle fears; they come from close
observation of the temper of the cultivators and inhabitants
of the land.   Scorn, O Free-Trader, if you will, my views
of your theory; despise me, if you will, as reasoner, logi-
cian, scholar, investigator of historical precedent, or examiner into the theories and abstract principles of science.
But few will deny, however exaggerated in all else be my
reputation as a writer, that, where the reputation has been
the most acknowledged, it rests upon some truth in observing the springs of human action.   It is as the habitual
and long-experienced observer of men that I utter this
warning.   It is my hope and belief that the warning will
not be in vain.

If you say, "Grant that your apprehensions are just as
to the danger from irritation in one class, is there not a
danger as great in provoking the resentment of others
more numerous?   Remember this is a question of exports
to the manufacturer; it is more, a question of the price of
bread to the people."   If you say this, I reply, that I know
and feel most deeply the importance of those considerations
in popular opinion; and, though exports are not in themselves a guarantee of the prosperity of the manufacturer,
nor the cheapness of food an unequivocal test of the physical well-being and social advance of the labouring population, yet I think that Lord Derby has acted wisely, and
shown that, in this respect, he comprehends the duty of
the CONCILIATOR when he has taken Free-Traders themselves
for authorities, and proposed a moderate fixed duty, on
which any rise in price to the farmer cannot, in the judgment of profound economists, raise in practice the price of
the loaf beyond what at least would be immediately coun-
terbalanced by custom to the tradesman—improved home
market to the manufacturer, and rise of wages to the
labourer; a rise, under such a duty, sufficiently slight
to conciliate him who sells his work, sufficiently just
not to ruin him who hires it; a duty, in short, (to
repeat the deliberate opinion of Mr. M'Culloch,) that
would "be innocuous in scarce years, when importation is necessary, and not only be advantageous to the
agriculturist, but redound to the advantage of the other
classes." *

Much misconception prevails when our opponents seem
to confound the consideration of this single claim with a
repeal of the general tariff.   Neither Lord Derby, nor any
chief in his party, has proposed to reverse the commercial
policy commenced, or to interfere with those articles the
greater cheapness of which now diminishes the yearly
expense of the consumer.   It is but on a single article that
it is proposed to raise a revenue on the foreigner, to be
devoted towards a reduction of the most grievous tax on
the national community; and with the indirect consequence, though with the acknowledged view, of relieving a

---

* Refer to the quotation from Mr. M'Culloch, (pp. 125, 126) on the advantages of a fixed Duty to ALL classes.

vast class of our countrymen whom our Legislature condemns to severe trial, and has no other practical means to assist.

Let the agriculturists contrast by their own moderation the vehement intolerance which would deny *all* relief to their distress, and it will be impossible to revive against them, at least to any degree that would justify alarm, the agitation which is held forth as the main argument to prevent concession to what suffering demands as justice, and political economy commends as wisdom. Far more cause for alarm in the despair of hearts hitherto so attached to your institutions, and the progressive decay of an interest so essential to the welfare of all. It is difficult to agitate the humanity of England against distress : And though, as yet, the distress of the agriculturist may have but partially reacted on the rest of the community, enough has been felt to make "sensible men" of every rank rejoice at any reasonable proposition by which it may be mitigated, and separate themselves from the unworthy clamour by which it may be sought to drown the groans of their suffering countrymen.

A moderate fixed duty will still leave to the agriculturist a sufficiently sharp competition with the foreigner; as it will still leave to the manufacturer the regular market assured by the opening of our ports; leave to the general consumer the cheapness effected by the various modifications of our tariffs; and to the labourer it will sustain wages, by sustaining the capital from which wages are derived. To a competition thus mitigated, the farmer will brace all the energies which competition—when it overtasks the strength and sickens the hope—can only enfeeble and relax. Whatever relief to his pecuniary resources this concession—made in time—will afford, greater still will be the stimulus to spirit and courage which comes from all sympathy in human struggles; great the benefit to the agriculturist, greater far to our social fabric, if you diminish the fear with which the son of the soil, the originator of all national capital, now anticipates the future — soften the spirit with which he confronts the present—reconcile class to class—smooth obstacles to progressive legislation—lessen dangers in those crises in which progress is exchanged for convulsion. And, therefore, from the depth of my heart, and moved by interests that sway me far more as patriot than proprietor—as citizen than landowner—I say to the Constituencies of the empire, " Lose not the first occasion to conciliate the cultivators of the land you live in ! "

Forgive, my dear John, this long infliction on your patience; and believe in the truth of

Your loyal and anxious Servant,

A Labourer AND a Landlord,

EDWARD BULWER LYTTON.

PAUL LOUIS COURIER—HIS LIFE AND WRITINGS.

A BIOGRAPHICAL CRITICISM.

LA VERITÉ EST TOUTE A TOUS.[*]

IT has long been my intention to devote some pages of this Journal [†] to the manes of Paul Louis Courier, in the hope of bringing my English readers to a better acquaintance with some of the most remarkable writings, and one of the most extraordinary men that France, in her later day, has produced. Every time has its peculiar representative, and the genius of a single man is often the incarnation of the intellectual character of his cotemporaries. There was only one period in the history of France that could have produced Courier,—he is the man of that period. He gathered once more into a focus those rays of light that had been scattered into a thousand vague refractions by the violent effects of the Revolution. He is the sequel to Voltaire. What Béranger is to verse, Courier is to prose. His life is of no less singular character than his works.

Born at Paris, in 1773, the parentage of Paul Louis Courier was exactly that which was calculated to form in after times the derider of the vices of a *noblesse*. His father was a man of some literary pretensions and of competent wealth ;—he was a *Bourgeois*—an able, witty, intellectual *Bourgeois*. As such he seems to have mixed in the society of the nobles, and to have very narrowly escaped death for his presumption. A certain nobleman of great rank owed our citizen a large sum of money; it was inconvenient to pay it, so he ordered his creditor to be assassinated. True

* [Truth is all to all.]
† [This paper was originally published in the *New Monthly Magazine* for March, 1833.]

that he did not allege the debt as a reason for the proposed murder. He gave a more gallant air to the proceeding, and accused the *Bourgeois* of having seduced his wife. A jealous husband in those days was not common;—but then every husband did not owe the object of his jealousy a considerable sum of money.

If M. Courier escaped death, he did not escape banishment; and he felt himself obliged to become an inhabitant of one of the cantons of Toulouse. He gave himself up to the education of the young Paul Louis. Our hero early developed his peculiar genius,—quick, facile, and impatient. He evinced no turn for the mathematics, but a vehement passion for ancient letters. In these his taste was formed on no very judicious model. He was fond of the Rhetoricians, and considered Isocrates a model. In after life his latent genius was no doubt influenced by these youthful studies. You may trace in his writings all the art of rhetoric, but he studiously avoids its language. He is the only rhetorician in whom simplicity is the most remarkable feature. Those were not, however, the times for Isocrates and rhetoric. The war against France required soldiers for the frontiers, and confined the demand for sophists to the metropolis. Paul Louis entered a school of artillery, and at the age of twenty behold the young officer hastening to join the armies of the Rhine. Never was there a more singular recruit: with considerable valour of constitution, Paul Louis had already formed a most philosophical indifference to glory. Compelled to be a soldier, he walked the stage as an actor who laughs in his sleeve at the wilful delusion of the audience. He saw the paint on the scene, and heard the voice of the prompter; and when the galleries were shouting applause at the effects, our actor was scrutinizing the tricks which produced them. He mixed among that fiery and passionate army, with its boy soldiers and its stripling leader,* like Jaques amidst the gallant foresters of Ardens, for purposes not theirs, and feeding thoughts they could not comprehend. But he was a Jaques without melancholy.

While his young compatriots, all ardent for the new Republic, strove with each other who should advance the

---

* Hoche, the commandant on the Rhine, was twenty-three.

soonest to death for her cause,—while honours showered
daily upon their adventurous emulation,—Courier, never
shunning danger, but never seeking fame, pursued his
separate and strange career,—his genius unknown and his
courses uncheered by the triumphs of success. He studied
much, but the library of a camp is confined, and it was only
among the books which he had read before. His literary
patience was of a peculiar sort : he preferred refreshing his
knowledge in one point to extending it in others. His
diligence was inexhaustible when applied to favourite
models; his apathy extraordinary towards subjects which
did not naturally allure him. He was conscious of this his
intellectual bias, and he speaks of it without affectation.
The philosophical nature of his mind made him in politics
consult the future rather than the past; he had little love,
therefore, for history, and he never mastered its study.
The main defect of his mind was what is the rarest in
men of genius—it was a lack of curiosity! He had a
great tendency to that dispiriting temper which is for ever
damping your ardour with the question of *cui bono?* Yet
in this want of curiosity he was not consistent; and in one
point all the other traits of his character seem strongly
contradicted. He was passionately fond of antiquities; he
would travel miles and court the most imminent dangers
for a sight of some old ruin. And he wandered from the
enthusiastic and ambitious soldiery that now held the territories of the Rhine and the soft Moselle, to pass long
hours among the mouldering convents and shattered towers
in which the dark memory of the middle ages is preserved.
It is assuredly an anomaly in character that a man so indifferent to the history of the Past, should be so attached
to its relics,—that one so derisive of the feudal pomps
should be so wedded to their trophies,—that so little
reverence for the essence of antiquity should be united with
such homage to its externals. I attribute the inconsistency
to early circumstances. As a boy he had been accustomed
to antiquarian researches,—his mind outgrew the passion
for antiquity, but retained the taste for its remains. We
may add to this, somewhat of the gratification of vanity;
for he was not only a diligent but a learned antiquarian;
he was an adept at inscriptions and the erudite mazes of
hieroglyphical conjecture; so that his habits of research

were probably endeared to him by the self-complacence of a triumphant ingenuity.

In this life—brave without glory, and wise without success—Courier passed two years, feeling himself, in that rapid race of honour where he who died not to-day might be a general to-morrow, distanced by his contemporaries, and growing naturally discontented with his station. In 1795 occurred the blockade of Mayence, and at that very time the elder Courier died. His mother was ill and wretched—Paul Louis left the army—left the blockade—and without leave, and with perfect *nonchalance*, returned to France. His filial affection was not, however, perhaps his sole inducement in hazarding the philosophy of desertion. The hardships endured by the French army before Mayence were exceedingly rigorous; they were by no means to the taste of a man who thought renown was no recompense. "It was wonderfully cold there," said the witty soldier; "I thought myself frozen. Never was there a slighter distinction between a man and a crystallization."

The army proclaimed Paul Louis a deserter. Meanwhile Paul Louis shut himself up, and amused his leisure with translating the oration *pro Ligario.* His friends managed to hush up the matter: the young soldier was grateful,— for it enabled him to give a better polish to his translation. The revolutionary war proceeded to its triumph. The star of Napoleon rose above the horizon: the grave melancholy that belonged to the Conventional moralities was broken up. People rushed into feasts and balls. Paul Louis caught the contagion with an avidity natural to his bold and lively temper; and behold him now the gallant and the man of pleasure! Passionately devoted to women, he gave himself wholly up to their society. Young, gay, and with a power of social wit rarely equalled, he became the rage at Toulouse. But his ill fortune pursued him from the camp to the chamber; and an unlucky intrigue made Toulouse no longer a place of security. At the age of twenty-three a man without much difficulty forgives himself these offences: I suspect that he manages to console himself with the same ease! Banished Toulouse, Courier resumed his former career, and he set out to Italy to take the command of a company of artillery.

Italy did not present to the gallant spirit of Courier, intoxicated as it was by the adoration of beauty, and the reverence for departed art, those unmingled sources of delight which earlier and later pilgrims have found amidst its ruins. The severe licentiousness of the young Napoleon was lavishly imitated by his coarser followers : the polished inhabitants of Italy met with no dainty respect from the new successors of the triumphant Gaul. Pillage and Rapine devastated the marble cities and the vine-clad plains. And what to Courier was more bitter than all, the noble relics of antique art, " the breathing canvas and the storied bust," were mangled, defaced, despoiled as the avarice or the ignorance of the hardy conquerors ordained.

Too refined and too classical for his colleagues, Paul Courier deplored these excesses in terms scarcely less eloquent than we find in his later and more elaborate writings. His letters (on this subject) to a Pole of considerable attainments, whose friendship he had acquired at Toulouse, are full of his characteristic graces. Byron's indignation at the rape of the Elgin marbles is tame beside that of Courier at the insulting spoliation of the Italian treasures,—Italy's last triumph,—her consolation in art for her degradation in history. The same cavalier and careless bravery that Courier had evinced on the banks of the Rhine, equally distinguished him among the ruins of Rome. Hated as a Frenchman, exposed day and night to the poignard of the assassin, he yet wandered alone and unguarded in the most solitary and perilous places. His love for antiquities (mingled with the growing passion for adventure, and it may be with a certain romance which his perception of the ridiculous would not allow him to own) was his sole guide. He followed it without fear. With his sabre by his side, he traversed the mountains of Italy, —explored the ruins,—braved the banditti;—Salvator Rosa himself was not more reckless of the poignards of the brigands, whom he afterwards immortalised ;—if Courier was often surprised by them he invariably escaped. He knew well the Italian language ; he was never without a certain bribe to the robber ; and, above all, at that happy age, and with that versatile temper, he possessed the art, better than much gold, which leads us to accommodate ourselves to all men, and supplies the absence of force by the exertion of ingenuity. In the day he sought the mountain passes,—at night he was assailed ;—the next morning he pursued his labours. He never feared the robber,—he never avenged the robbery. A certain generous tone of philosophy made him lenient to these wild banditti. He was a soldier, and he murdered by art; was he to be vindictive to those who robbed by necessity ?

In this eccentric manner, perfecting his mind, enjoying his life, and advancing *not* in his career, our extraordinary hero passed his Italian campaign : it nearly came to a premature termination.

Paul Louis was one of the division left by General Macdonald at Rome. The division capitulated : it was to quit Rome at a certain hour. " *A la bonne heure*," thought Courier; "a last look at the Vatican Library before I depart." What a type of the careless courage of the soldier-student ! He repairs to the Vatican—plunges into study—forgets the hour of departure — and quits the Vatican when he himself is the sole Frenchman left at Rome.

It was a calm, clear, and still evening. Nursing his reveries, Courier walked slowly along the streets of Rome. He was recognised as he passed beneath a lamp. A moment more ; a bullet whizzed by him—missed him—and lodged in the body of a Roman woman. In an instant the city was alarmed—the crowd gathered—Courierdashed through the midst of the mob, and reached the palace of a Roman of his acquaintance : through his aid he escaped. He embarked at Marseilles, and arrived at Paris ; but not without new disasters. On his road he was despoiled of his baggage and his money ; and, what was worse, a pulmonary complaint attacked him, from which he never entirely recovered.

At Paris, however, he renewed his former career of pleasure, but pleasure of a more refined and literary cast. Time had already begun to mellow the Passionate into the Intellectual. He mixed with the learned of his day; he was welcomed by some of the more eminent amongst them. That ambition of a circle, from which no Frenchman is free, animated his powers; and he wrote some works which then were but little known to the public, but are not, for that reason, unworthy of his fame. It often happens among literary men that their best works are neglected, till some *lucky* book gains the author a name; they are then sought for, studied, and admired. Genius revives its own deceased; and the world, once taught to admire an author for one work, lifts the stone from those its neglect has already buried.

From these pursuits and these circles, Courier was aroused by a summons to command a body of artillery stationed in Italy, which now lay supine, and seemingly reconciled, beneath the yoke of Napoleon. Among the softer and more poetical characteristics of Courier's mind, his passion for Italy was not the least remarkable. Not Jacopo Foscari himself loved with a more yearning and filial tenderness the bright air and the genial skies of that divine land. Courier cared nothing for the rank they gave him, and everything for the place assigned to it. He arrived, then, in Italy,—arrived in time to witness one of the most singular farces in the history of the world, and which the pen of more than one memorialist has already rendered so amusing. Buonaparte, tired with being Consul, wanted to be Emperor;—he *was* Emperor. He wanted now to know what the army thought about the change: an order arrived for the taking the opinion of the different regiments. These strokes of policy, where it is advantageous to say "Yes," dangerous to say "No," and wise to say nothing at all, usually succeed. Shakspeare has described their effect admirably in "Richard the Third":—

> "They spake not a word;
> But, like dumb statues or breathing stones
> Stared at each other.   *   *   *
> *   *   *   *   *   *
> When he had done, some followers of mine own,
> At lower end o' the hall, hurled up their caps,
> And some ten voices cried, 'God save King Richard!'
> And thus I took the vantage of those few:
> 'Thanks, gentle citizens and friends,' quoth I."

These lines explain tolerably well the nature and the result of the questions put to the French army.

The great trait of Courier's character was — (I can scarcely translate the word)—*insouciance.* We trace it everywhere—in every action. It curbed his military ardour —*tant mieux;* it chilled his patriotism—*tant pis.* He resisted not the proposal; he continued to serve under

Napoleon; and he contented himself, *en philosophe et à la Française*, with a fine saying and a witticism—"*Etre Buonaparte et se faire Sire! il aspire à descendre.*"* In fact, the essence of Courier's darker and sterner nature was contempt: where he was not indifferent he despised. "Buonaparte loves his rattle; let him have it! The people will obey the puppet. Poor people!—be it so." This was the spirit with which he viewed the nascent despotism. He had the disdain of Cassius, but not his energy. If he had been a contemporary and countryman of Brutus, he would have said the best thing against Cæsar, but have struck no blow. He subscribed to the new dynasty; and amused himself with painting it in some letters of inimitable satire. His course of conduct in this has been vindicated,—I think, without success. The Directory, say his advocates, was a wretched government,—feeble and venal. The Consulship had lasted too short a time for trial. What did you lose by gaining an Emperor? The answer is obvious;—you lost *Hope*. A republic purifies itself naturally,—a monarchy only by great efforts. A republic wants but time,—a despotism wants new revolutions. What was to be hoped from a sway like Napoleon's, which crushed the Press, and resolved all the elements of knowledge into—Military Schools? Paul Courier was a philosopher,—he knew these truths;—but he was a philosopher for himself as well as for others. A better excuse for him is in his position. What could he do?—an undistinguished officer in the artillery, what was his consent to, or his rejection of, the empire of Napoleon? We judge too much in estimating the actions of men, and the good they *might* have effected, by the rank *we* attribute to their intellectual powers, without remembering that it is only when those powers have become acknowledged that their possessors can aspire to play their legitimate part. But patriotism, to be a strong passion, must be a common passion. You cannot inspire the individual, unless you first form the nation; and public integrity in France was at that time at the lowest possible ebb. Despite its false liberty, its laughable citizenship, its terrible republic, France scarcely knew one sound principle of legislation;

* ["To be Buonaparte and to make himself Sire! he aspires to descend!"]

or, after the extinction of the eloquent Girondists, produced one honourable *corps* of men. Courier himself boasted that he was able to show letters from the most eminent men of the empire, who followed, like dogs, the track of the times,—Republicans—Buonapartists—Bourbonists—according as a shilling was to be gained :—" Men who commence their destiny *en sansculottes*, and finish it *en habits de cour*." The success of vice is the discouragement of virtue.

In 1808, Courier, having long and vainly demanded leave of absence to revisit his home, gave in his resignation. He returned to Paris, and proclaimed an eternal renunciation of his military trade.

At this time the wild but solemn fate of Napoleon was rapidly hurrying towards its great, but unrecognised close. His destiny was at its height : and the height of some men is the main step to their fall. Scarce returned from Spain, which his presence alone had almost conquered, he now swept on to the armies gathered by the Danube, which he was to lead to the city of the House of Hapsburg. All Paris was in a paroxysm of excitement, and Courier caught something of the contagion. To understand well the character of this singular man, we must consider him as one fond of studying the peculiar phases and aspects of his kind, and scrutinizing rather than sharing their passions. He looked upon the events which engross and absorb the more vulgar, but warmer spirits, with an artist's inquiring eye. The pomp of empire, the laurels of war, the rewards of ambition, were to him but testimonials of human delusion, and food for a just, and not malevolent, satire ; yet, at this period of his life, his wonted philosophy seems to have forsaken him, and he became one of the worshippers of the Echo. He had never yet served under Napoleon ; he now resolved to do so. He communicated his intention to none of his friends ; he repaired secretly to the army. Having once resigned, his re-admission, according to the military rules of Napoleon, was not easy. He gained access to the tent of a general of the artillery ; and, without any peculiar station, became once more a French soldier.

Something—(I apprehend, in examining his character, his letters, and the common elements of human nature)—

something of sore and mortified feeling, of the consciousness of great powers and a foiled career, had led him to this determination. On his late return to Paris he had found how entirely military reputation engrossed the public voice; his philosophy might, in the main, support him in his obscurity, but not perhaps at all times. *He had had his opportunities, and he had failed!* This was the sole interpretation the public could attach to his career; a bitter verdict to a man of pride and genius, who had not yet found, amidst the depths of an undeveloped intellect, the triumphant answer of self-acquittal. He had arrived too at an age in which a man is often more sensible to mortification than at an earlier period; the season of promise, at the age of seven-and-thirty, is well nigh over, and the world begins to ask for performance. The love, too, of pleasure —of women and of strange adventure—is cooled; and before we resign ourselves to a calm and obscure life, we are often willing to make one sterner attempt than heretofore at glory. Courier, perhaps too, had some sympathy with the genius, if not with the temper and fortunes of Napoleon —the higher minds are attracted toward each other. He thought (this is evident from his letters) that Napoleon might appreciate him. Mocked or slighted by inferior men, he felt his powers, and hoped the penetration of *a great* man might avenge the neglect. Whatever were his motives, Courier joined the camp;—joined—for forty-eight hours! What scenes were crowded into that time.

Hitherto Courier had beheld war by samples, he now beheld it wholesale. Never yet had he seen whole regiments swept away beneath the deadly fires—never yet for his ear had the music of four hundred pieces of cannon risen above a soil of trampled and quivering flesh. Never yet had he fully comprehended the wide vastness of the desolation of War! He himself speaks of the horror, the pity, the disgust which seized him;—a sort of sickness closed around his senses, which were usually so keen—everything passed before him like grotesque phantasmagoria;—he sank, at last, overcome by exhaustion, at the foot of a tree —he recovered not until he was within the walls of Vienna. From that time he required no further conviction of the scourge of war. The theories of life were faint to the practical experience of those terrible hours; nay, he thenceforward even denied genius to generalship; he contended, that all was disorder, and the result chance. He laughed at the phrase—*the art of war;* a great battle conveyed to him the notion of a chaos incompatible with the providence of an intellectual design.

As he sought the campaign, so he left it—abruptly, silently, and with his usual arrogance, as a free agent. He thought to lose the bloody memory of two days in a land that Nature consecrated to love,—and he sought, once more, his favourite Italy.

He took up his abode at Florence, and renewed his studies in Greek literature. But poor Paul Louis was not born under a lucky star, and he could not even study Greek with impunity. His ill fortune led him to read the pastoral romance of " Longus " in manuscript—no trifling affliction in itself —but unhappily, this MS. which was in the Laurentine library, contained a passage to be found in no other printed edition of the tale—nay it supplied a terrible chasm well known to the learned, which has hitherto yawned in a certain part of the romance. Imagine the rapture of the student. With trembling hands he hastened to copy out the passage, and in his ecstacy he contrived to upset the inkstand over the precious passage. The librarians were furious—they swore that he had spoiled the Greek copy on purpose, so that he might pillage its spoils, and be the only one to arrogate the possession. The Frenchman had not perhaps that hardihood of nerve which our periodical critics ultimately bestow upon an English victim. He could not resist unburthening himself in a reply. He addressed this effusion to M. Renouard, Librarian of Paris, and he transferred all the blame from himself to his Italian accusers. His sole crime, he said, was being a Frenchman; and it was not the spilling of ink, but the spilling of blood, that rose in judgment against him. The letter made a noise—attention was riveted to the writer and his inkstand—when lo!—it came out that the copier of " Longus " was the deserter at Wagram. From two such crimes there was no easy escape—but, however, the constitutional dexterity of Courier carried him safe from the result of his constitutional imprudence. Ink, liable to such accidents, was nevertheless considered too dangerous for use, and he was enjoined upon no account to dip his pen into it again. He obeyed the command during his sojourn in Italy. In travel and in study the years rolled on—peace was proclaimed—Buonaparte was at St. Helena—and Paul Louis Courier was married! Two of these events were important enough to the world, the third was not wholly unimportant to Paul Louis Courier!

From this time the wilder portion of life closed for him. The soldier—the adventurer—the wanderer—were no more. He sat himself down in his paternal vineyards, and commenced, in the beautiful seclusion of Touraine, the date of a more bright career. Inspired by the strong disdain which he felt for the rule, weak and violent, of the Bourbons after the Restoration—Paul Courier, in 1816, addressed the two Chambers on behalf of the inhabitants of Luynes, in a short petition of some seven or eight pages, which sufficed, however, to produce a very considerable sensation. This petition is a narrative of the oppression and injustice committed against a village. The narrative of a village was a narrative applicable to all France. When he stated the frivolous grounds of accusation—when he stated the rigour of suspicion—the bigotry of fear—which had converted a village of honest peasants into a herd of discontented and wronged men, he was appealing to the common sense of France, and he was answered at once by the common heart. The style of this petition is simple yet elaborate; biting irony—generous complaint—severe truth —are condensed in periods that remind you of Voltaire, but without Voltaire's affectation. M. Decazes, Minister of Police, courted this new and formidable writer. Courier, in his visits to Paris, visited his salons, and obtained by that complaisance some good for his fellow villagers and himself. That done, he was no more a courtier.

M. Clavier, an Academician, died. Courier demanded admission into the Academy of Inscriptions. He was rejected—he revenged himself by a letter "A Messieurs de l'Academie des Inscriptions et Belles Lettres." This letter contains yet stronger evidence of his powers of irony, than his petition to the two Chambers; but the subject was less popular, and it made less noise. In 1819 he commenced his famous letters to the editor of the "Censor." The publication of these brief and stinging writings brought tho name of Courier into every one's mouth—and inquiry turning, as it is wont to do, when a man begins to attract celebrity,—from the work to the author, found sufficient to interest the public in his person; and thus doubly to increase the charm and fascination of his genius.

This accomplished traveller, this profound student, lived in an obscure village, affecting and proud to affect the simple life and habits of the peasant. His vineyards and his woods were his chief occupation, and yielded him his revenue. He called himself Paul Louis *Vigneron*—he pretended to no superiority over his fellow villagers—he was one of them in all but knowledge. His style happily united the two opposite characteristics he assumed—the scholar and the peasant—at once most classical and most familiar; style irresistible alike to the academy and the market-place. No man ever made elegance so popular, or homeliness so elegant. He polished with great labour, but the polish only rendered the diction and the sense transparent to the dullest comprehension. In 1821 appeared the *Simple Discours*. The occasion was this, it was proposed to purchase the Park of Chambord for the young Duke of Bordeaux. This proposition Courier opposed. Hence the *Simple Discours*.

"If, (he begins this incomparable pamphlet) if we had so much money that we did not know what to do with it —if all our debts were paid—our highways repaired—our poor relieved—and our church (for God before all things) restored, and its windows glazed—I think, my friends, that the best thing we could do with the surplus would be to contribute with our neighbours to rebuild the Bridge of St. Aventin; which, shortening by one good league the distance between us and Tours, would augment the price and the produce of land throughout the neighbourhood. That in my opinion would be the best employment for our superfluous capital,—that is to say, whenever we possess it. But to buy Chambord for the Duke of Bordeaux—I cannot agree to it: no, not even if we had the means. It would be but a bad scheme, in my opinion, for the Duke himself, for us, and for Chambord. If you will listen to me, I will tell you why. It is a holiday, my friends, and we have time to chat over the matter."

In this familiar manner, Paul Louis, *Vigneron de la Cha-vonniere*, throws off his biting truths. He confesses that the courtiers are inclined to the purchase; "but *our* sentiments," saith he, wittily, "are very different from those of the courtiers—they love the Prince in proportion to what he *gives* them—we in proportion to what he *leaves* us."

"The notion is entertained (says the government) of purchasing Chambord by the Commons of France, for the Duke of Bordeaux. The notion is entertained—by whom pray? By the Ministry? No; they would not conceal so beautiful a thought, or content themselves with the mere honour of approval upon such an occasion. By the Prince, then? God forbid that his first idea—his first gleam of reason should be of so singular a character—that the desire of our money should enter his young head, even before the passion for sugar plums and rattles! Do the Commons then entertain the agreeable notion? Not ours certainly on this side of the Loire, &c."

How happily afterwards Courier proceeds to comment on the cant anecdote of Titus!—

"A preceptor—an abbé of the Court, now teaches our young princes the science of history. Be sure he does not forget to make them admire that excellent Emperor Titus, who was so great an adept in the art of donation, that he thought every day was lost in which he did not give something away. So that one never saw him without being made happy—happy, you understand, my friends, with a pension, a sinecure—a handful of the popular money. Such a prince is sure to be adored by all those who are admitted to court, and drive about the streets in their state carriages"—"La cour l'idolatrait—mais le peuple? Le peuple? il n'y en avait pas, l'histoire n'en dit rien . . . . Voila les élémens d'histoire qu'on enseignait alors aux princes."*

To my taste this is the most perfect in point of union between satire and logic of all Courier's works. I know nothing like it in political literature—it is a political library in itself. For this production he was of course

* ["The court idolized him—but the people? The people? There were no people: history said nothing about them. . . Behold the elements of history then taught to princes."]

imprisoned. They punished him for writing truth so well by a fine of three hundred francs, and a confinement of two months. Poor Paul Louis! "Pray God for him!" cries he himself in his address *aux âmes dévotes,*—"may his example teach us never to say what we think of those gentlemen who live at our expense." Courier published a pamphlet relative to his trial, which proved how indomitable wit is against persecution ; and the day of his release from prison they brought him up for a new trial for a pamphlet of the most exquisite composition, called " Petition pour les Villageois qu'on empêche de danser." The peasants had been accustomed to dance every Sunday on the usual spot allotted in the French villages to that amusement. The *Prefet* forbade the dance. Courier demands the restoration of the old and harmless pleasure. Nothing can be more touching than his description of the manners, the good order, the improving morality of his poor neighbours ; nothing more convincing than his arguments on their behalf. They did not think it quite right to imprison a man for wishing the peasants to dance, so this time they let him off with a reprimand. From that date persecution begat its usual result, secrecy ; and Courier contrived to publish, but under a mask—a mask which concealed his name but not his genius. I pass over his " Replies to anonymous correspondents," one of which, the second, contains more eloquent and pathetic passages than any other of his tracts. I pass over the " Livret de Paul Louis," a brilliant sketch, in which, however, the author displays the usual ignorance of a Frenchman on English history, when he observes that literary men have but little knowledge of business, and that Bolingbroke repented of having employed Addison and Steele !—Bolingbroke's bitterest opponents! I pass too over the " Gazette du Village," a polished and most subtle piece of irony. I pass over the few pages contained in the " Pièce Diplomatique," which is supposed to be a letter from Louis of France to the King of Spain, and which at least no Bourbon *could* have written. I come to the most admired—the most laboured—the last of all Courier's writings, the "Pamphlet des Pamphlets." This, I say, is esteemed in France the most perfect and matured specimen of his style. Imagine how wonderful, how expressive that style must be, when we apply the epithets elaborate—finished —even great—to writings scarcely exceeding in length a newspaper article! For my own part, I still hold to my opinion that the "Simple Discours" is the best and fullest of Courier's works—it has more thought and more wisdom than the "Pamphlet des Pamphlets;"—its wit, too, is more racy, and its diction more striking, if less pure. Anything seemingly English in sentiment was at that day sure to be popular in France; and in this pamphlet Courier supposes an English patriot, to whom he attributes a letter to himself,—excellent, indeed, but scarcely characteristic of the tone of English patriots. The merit of the work scarcely strikes upon an English ear; it consists in the eloquence with which Courier vindicates himself from being a pamphleteer—a term of disgrace in the vocabulary of French *bon ton*—a title not discreditable with us, always excepting the refined judgment of my Lord of Durham, who could find nothing worse to say of Bishop Philpotts of Exeter! To an English reader the vindication loses its charm because we feel no venom in the charge. The conclusion, however, of this tract is deeply impressive; it speaks of the shortness of human life—of the eternity of human improvement—of the feebleness of individuals—of the power of the mass. It hath in it a certain solemn and warning voice, preceding as it did the untimely and bloody end of the bold preacher. It reminds us of the deep pathos of those lines, some of the latest that Byron ever wrote, and to which we link the associations of his own death :—

> " Between two worlds life hovers like a star,—
> 'Twixt night and morn upon the horizon's verge;
> How little do we know that which we are!
> How less what we may be! The eternal surge
> Of time and tide rolls on, and bears afar
> Our bubbles."

While Courier was thus occupying the mind of the public, and while he employed his more learned hours in the study of his favourite Greeks, he seems to have shared the ordinary fate of genius ;—he was no prophet in his own country !

A certain fretfulness and acerbity of temper had come upon him with years; always eccentric in his habits, he became gradually morose in his humours; he quarrelled with his neighbours, and was at war with his own household. Much is to be said on his behalf, beyond the common and valid excuse for the peevishness of literary men in overwrought nerves and a feverish imagination. The mind wears the body, and the body reacts upon the temper. This is clear—it is inevitable—we require no waste of sentiment upon so plain a matter. Poor Courier had other excuses; he had done much for his village, and his villagers were ungrateful; this wounded him, and justly. He was not too, I suspect, happy in his marriage; he believed he had cause for jealousy; and to a man so proud the suspicion was no light curse. From the gloom of his obscurity went forth a burning light among the nations, but it came from the midst of discomfort, and the hearth of strife;—petty bickerings, and village annoyances disturbed the serenity once natural to his constitution. His very fame produced him but enemies. He had offended the *Valetaille* of France, and France, in his own words, was *le plus valet de tous les peuples.* But the mortification and the harassment were now drawing to a close—the triumph of genius and the exhaustion of the nerves were alike to cease. He beheld before him the apex of his fame; and he stood, while he gazed, upon the verge of the grave.

On the 10th of April, 1825, Courier left his house—he had spoken but little that day—an evident gloom had hung over him. He was borne back to his door a corpse; —within a few paces from his home he had been found, pierced by some secret bullet, and quite dead. His assassin is unknown to this day. The rash enthusiasts of liberty, often the most illiberal of men, laid the crime on the Jesuits, but without a shadow of proof. One nearest and dearest to himself was, not long since, accused of abetting in the murder, and acquitted. A man of low birth, of whom he had been jealous, was, some time after his death, murdered himself; but eight years have passed, and the sentence of life for life has had no formal record. Peace to his ashes!—they will not rest the less tranquilly, nor will the turf above them be less green, because vengeance is still left in the hands of God!

The countenance of Courier was grave and thoughtful;

the brow high, broad, massive, and deeply marked; his eye somewhat sunk and melancholy—his mouth sarcastic and flexile. His manners varied at various periods of his life. I have met with some who knew him well, and considered him the most delightful of companions. I have known others who considered him the most repellant. In his later days he had transferred the graces from his habits to his style. Perhaps few men, with advantage to the temper, can begin the career of letters late in life. It requires several years to harden us to the abuse, the ingratitude, the wilful misinterpretation, and the gnawing slander we endure from our contemporaries and our rivals. In youth we have years to spare to the apprenticeship; in mature age the pride is more stubborn, and the hope less sanguine.

As a writer Courier must rank amongst the most classical of his language; in vigour, in wit, in logic, he defies all comparison among his contemporaries. They who would learn to what degree the polish and power of style have advanced in France since the peace, should read, not the inflated paradoxes of Chateaubriand, or the extravagant exaggerations of Victor Hugo; but those pages in which Courier has indeed made words things, and in which the plainest truths are conveyed with the most marvellous art. To the strength of Junius he adds the simplicity and the playfulness of Pascal. He fails, however, in imagination, and his thoughts are usually more bold than profound. This is remarkable rather in his literary than his political remains, for popular political writing does not of necessity demand the profound; its merit is often to familiarise, not to invent, truth. In his preface to a new translation of Herodotus, we may especially detect the comparative want of depth in Courier's faculties—comparative, I say, to their power and versatility. He tells us, for instance, that the historical epic must cease for ever when the prose of a language has come to some perfection. He declares that the Greek literature is the *only* one not born of some other literature, but produced by instinct, and the sentiment of the beautiful,—mistakes which could not arise from a want of learning, but from a want of that reflection which stamps even the paradox of a profound intellect; yet the same piece of writing is rich in sentences of beautiful and just criticism. Nothing can be better in its way than his description of courtly translators playing the *petit maître* with the simple language of the Greek;—nothing more true than his warning to his countrymen that the language of poetry is the last to be learnt in academies and courts. "*L'imitation,*" he says finely,—"*l'imitation de la cour est la peste du gout aussi bien que des mœurs.*" *

Courier's style has been compared to that of the Editor of the "Examiner;" but Courier is more free and flowing —more adapted to the popular taste—more familiar and simple. On the other hand, he has not the iron grasp— the novel metaphor—the rich illustration, and the careless *depth* of remark which characterise the most standard and philosophic of our living periodical writers. He reminds us, I think, rather of Sydney Smith, but is less broad and more daring. In fact, his manner is so peculiarly and idiomatically French, that the English writer, who closely resembled him, would write ill.

Paul Louis Courier is then no more!—his bright and short race is run;—the various threads of his desultory and romantic life are prematurely and violently cut short. He has left to mankind not only the evidence of what he has achieved, but the belief of what greater results he had the capacity to accomplish. Living in a time of transition, when the people, passing from a brilliant despotism to a gloomy and imperfect freedom, scarcely know whether to lament the one or to advance the other, his writings tended to destroy the illusion of the despotism, and to instil right notions as to the nature of freedom. No solemn plausibilities of men or of names deceived him. His mockery respected nothing—save the truth. He incorporated, in the form of his constitutional disdain, the popular contempt for the hollowness and profligacy—the venality and the servility—which marked so strongly the character of the French court; a court of slaves and traitors—of sharpers and of cowards—a court of nobles proud without honour, and subservient without loyalty. By expressing the contempt of the people he made their sentiments known to each other; his genius was as a watchword of union, for it

---

* [The imitation of the Court is the blight of taste as well as of manners.]

brought them together. The benefit effected by a bold public writer is this—he acquaints the people, by his own popularity, with the exact strength of the popular sentiment; he thus prepares the common mind, though he may not lead it;—*he* makes the impulse, and Chance the conduct!

THE LIFE OF SCHILLER.*

A BIOGRAPHICAL SKETCH.

CHAPTER I.

FIRST PERIOD.

Schiller's boyhood—His parentage—Early studies and inclinations—His entrance at the Military Academy—His youthful poems, and predilections for the drama.

CLOSE by the village of Lorch, on the borders of Würtemberg, rise the ruins of a castle, the hereditary seat of the Counts of Hohenstaufen. The graves of that illustrious family surround a convent, placed upon a neighbouring eminence, and half hid by venerable limes. Upon another hill, stands an old chapel; below, flows the river Rems, through luxuriant vineyards, and fertile corn-fields. Amidst the ruins of Hohenstaufen, or amidst the graves of its ancient lords, between the years 1765-68, might often be seen two children—a boy and girl,—so strongly resembling each other, as to denote their relationship as brother and sister.† Usually they were seen alone; sometimes with young companions,—sometimes with a man in a military uniform, and in the vigour of life—to whom the boy, especially, listened with avidity, whether he explained the plan upon which the old Castle had been built, or pleased the infant spirit of adventure, by anecdotes of camp and field.‡ More often, perhaps, their companion was a female, of mild exterior, and manners peculiarly gentle, though somewhat grave and serious. And she, too, found in the children, still more especially in the

---

* [Written in 1847 and prefixed to a reprint of Lord Lytton's translation of the "Poems and Ballads of Schiller," which were first collected into a volume in 1845, having appeared piecemeal from month to month in the pages of "Blackwood's Magazine."]

† Hoffmeister, Schwab.   ‡ Hoffmeister.

boy, eager listeners to the talk by which she sought to instruct the understanding, or arouse the fancy. She had tales of witch and fairy to relate;—but, as the children grew older, she preferred rather to please their imagination with verses from Klopstock, Gerhard, and the pious Gellert. More than all—she at once charmed and instructed her young pupils by stories and passages from the Gospel, adapted to their understanding; and their tears flowed betimes at the sufferings of the Redeemer.* Already, perhaps, the scenes which he loved to haunt, and certainly the subjects he was accustomed to hear, had produced strong and deep impressions upon the mind and character of the boy. Already he had conceived a passion for Nature—formed habits of reverie and reflection—and looked forward to the ecclesiastic profession, for which his parents designed him, with a religious and earnest enthusiasm. At eight years old, alone in the woodlands, with a boy about his own age, he exclaimed, "O Karl, how beautiful is it here! All—all could I give, so that I might not miss this joy!" † His very sports partook of his serious character : nothing pleased him more than, by the help of a cap and a black apron, to assume the attire of the priest, mount a stool, and deliver extemporaneous and fervent homilies to an audience consisting of his mother and sisters. From his earliest childhood he was ever delighted to leave his infant games, to join the prayers or Bible lectures of the pious family to which he belonged; and his favourite sister has left a pleasing description of the child at such moments—with his folded hands, his blue eyes raised to Heaven, and the fair hair clustering over the broad forehead which he inherited from his mother. But though from infancy unusually serious, and from infancy, also, impatient of restraint, his temper was sweet, and his disposition full of tenderness and compassion. If he met a poor child in his way to school, he would bestow on him all he had; even his books—his clothes were not sacred from the impulse of his compassion. With all this softness of heart — this love of solitude, and this pious temperament, there was no less manifest a resolute and

* Hoffmeister, Schwab.   † Hoffmeister, Schwab.

determined spirit. He was peculiarly fond of reading Voyages and books of Travels; and the Histories of popular heroes, such as Alexander the Great. He would often exclaim, "I must go into the world!" His reveries were, in short, those that denote not an indolent temper, but an active mind. His musings were not merely day-dreams—they were animated by that zeal for inquiry which usually foretells, in childhood, the career of men destined to think boldly, and love truth. In his seventh year, one evening, during a storm of thunder and lightning, the boy was missed at supper; he was found at last at the top of a tall lime-tree, near the house, enjoying the tempest; and, to quote his own apology, " wishing to see where so much fire in the heavens came from! " *—Such in childhood was the character of Johann Christoph Friedrich Schiller.

His birth placed him in that condition, between wealth and penury—(a condition bordering two classes—the Popular and the Refined), which is perhaps the most favourable to intellectual eminence.

His father, Johann Caspar Schiller, was of humble extraction, the son of a baker, who held the office of Bailiff in the village of Bittenfeld.† He was a man of an adventurous and restless character; stern and severe indeed in manners, but warmly attached to his family, of good abilities, of exemplary probity, and a strong and fervent sense of religion. He had held the rank of Surgeon·in a Bavarian regiment. In 1749, a year after the peace of Aix-la-Chapelle, he married Elizabeth Dorothea Kodweiss, a young woman, born at Marbach (about eight miles from Stuttgart), of parentage suitable to his own; though it is said that her more distant descent could be traced to the noble house of Kottwitz.‡

After his marriage, Caspar Schiller resigned the medical profession; but at the breaking out of the Seven Years' War in 1757, entered the Würtemberg army as ensign and adjutant. It was not till after some years that their union

---

* To this anecdote Schwab gives the weight of his authority.
† Schwab.
‡ Kattwitz, according to Hoffmeister—corrected by Schwab to Kottwitz.

was blessed by children : Elizabeth, the eldest daughter, born 1757 ; Johann Christoph Friedrich, the poet, born at Marbach, Nov. 10, 1759 ;* Dorothea Louise, born two years afterwards ; and Nannette, the youngest.†

When Friedrich Schiller was six years old, his father, then risen to the rank of captain, was sent to Lorch as recruiting officer. Here the boy received the first regular rudiments of education, including Latin, and something even of Greek, from the clergyman of the parish, Philip Moser; whose name and virtues he afterwards immortalised in "The Robbers." His favourite companions were, his eldest sister, and the son of his tutor, Karl Moser. But no observation is at once more true and more hackneyed than that it is to the easy lessons of a mother, men of genius have usually owed their earliest inspiration. Schiller's mother had tastes and acquirements rare in women of her rank : she was a good musician—fond of poetry, and even wrote it; and the gentleness of her temper gave a certain refinement to her manners.

Friedrich Schiller was nine years old when his father 1768. was removed by the Grand Duke to Ludwigsburg, and the boy was entered at the public school instituted at that place. The academical discipline revolted one who had already formed his own desultory modes of self-instruction, and his industry was reluctant and constrained. Still he passed his examinations with credit; was ever one of the first in the Latin class to which he belonged, and received marks of approbation in the four several examinations he underwent before the School Commissioners, at Stuttgart. His character betrayed itself rather with his playfellows than his preceptors. He obtained an ascendancy over them ; and his high spirit would brave those older and stronger than himself, if he suspected any intention to affront him. With his superiors he was reserved and awkward. But what, at this time, chiefly influenced his future fate, was the sight of the theatre at Ludwigsburg—the remembrance of that spectacle, which, according to the fashion of the day, seems to have been a gorgeous spectacle, half opera,

* "A few months later than our own Robert Burns."—*Carlyle.*
† Two other children died soon after birth.

half melodrame, began to colour all his thoughts, and dictate the character of his sports in the hours of play. At the age of eleven, a change was noticeable in his habits; he shrank from the games in 1770. which he had been hitherto amongst the most active. In the playhours he would wander with some friend amongst the neighbouring plantations, and, in those moods of premature gloom and speculation, which so often cloud the dawn of illustrious manhood, complain of present thraldom, and form wild conjectures of future fate. Already he began to throw thought into verse—already he began to meditate the scheme of some elaborate tragedy. But his religious bias was still his strongest, and at 1773. the age of fourteen he still shared the predilections of his parents in favour of the ecclesiastical profession. But now came the first great revolution and crisis of his life.

Karl, Grand Duke of Würtemberg, a luxurious and ostentatious Prince, but one possessed of many excellent qualities, formed the notion of a great National Academy, first instituted at "Solitude," one of his country places,—afterwards transferred to Stuttgart. This establishment was called a Military Seminary, but not confined exclusively to those intended for the military profession.

The majority of the pupils were, indeed, the sons of officers—or even privates—in the Würtemberg Army; but the sons of civilians were admitted also; and suitable instruction was given to students intended for the peaceful profession of the Law. But the school rightly deserved the distinguishing epithet of Military, from the discipline by which it was characterised.

The father of young Schiller had recently been promoted by the Grand Duke to the office of Inspector and Layer-out of the grounds at "Solitude," and was subsequently raised to the rank of Major. But these benefits were not cheaply purchased. The Grand Duke in return desired to send Friedrich Schiller to his Military Seminary. This was tantamount to the rejection of the long-cherished scheme of the clerical profession. After much painful embarrassment, the elder Schiller frankly represented to his Prince the inclinations of himself and his son. The Grand Duke, however, repeated his request, proposed to leave to Friedrich the choice of his studies at the Academy, and promised him, when completed, an appointment in the Royal Service. There was no resisting a petitioner, whose request was in reality a law, and from whose favour was derived the very bread of the family. Friedrich Schiller did not and could not hesitate to sacrifice his own wishes to the interests of his parents. But this renunciation of his young hopes and the independence of his freewill, wounded alike his heart and his pride.

1773. With grief and resentment equally keen, at the age of fourteen he entered the Academy as a student in Jurisprudence. The studies thus selected were, in themselves, sufficiently uncongenial; but to the dulness of the Law Lecture was added the austerity of a corporal's drill. The youths were defiled in parade to lessons, in parade to meals, in parade to bed. At the word " March," they paced to breakfast—at the word " Halt," they arrested their steps—and at the word " Front," they dressed their ranks before the table.* In this miniature Sparta, the grand virtue to be instilled was subordination. Whoever has studied the character of Schiller, will allow that its leading passion was for Intellectual Liberty. Here mind and body were to be alike machines. Schiller's letters at this time to his friend Karl Moser, sufficiently show the fiery tumult and agitation of his mind; — sometimes mournful—sometimes indignant—now sarcastic, now impassioned—weary disgust and bitter indignation are seen through all. The German works, not included in the school routine, were as contraband articles—the obstacles to obtain them only increased the desire: no barrier can ever interpose between genius and its affections. The love of Man to Woman is less irresistible than the love that binds Intellect to Knowledge. Schiller stole, the more ardently because secretly, to the embraces of his mistress —Poetry. Klopstock still charmed him, but newer and truer perceptions of the elements of Poetry came to him in the " Goetz von Berlichingen " of Goethe, with which, indeed, commenced the great Literary Revolution of Europe—by teaching to each nation that the true classical

* Hoffmeister, Schwab, &c.

spirit for each, must be found in the genius of its own Romance. He who would really imitate Homer, must, in the chronicles of his native land, find out the Heroic Age.

Schiller obeyed the impulse of his own frank and courageous mind in an attempt to regain his freedom. A strange custom at the Academy enjoined each pupil, once a year, to draw up and read aloud an analysis of his own character. Schiller seized the first opportunity 1774. thus presented to him, to state that his character was not formed to excel in jurisprudence, but to serve God as a preacher. The confession failed to amend the vocation; but finally he obtained permission to exchange Law for Medicine,—a class for which was superadded to the other academical instructions. The studies for this latter profession were no doubt more congenial to him than those of law, and served, indirectly and collaterally, to enrich the stores of a mind so inquisitive into the operations of Nature. But the discipline in all studies was the same. Had they sought to cure him of Poetry, they would have had but to drill him into being a poet! Meanwhile, he was fast fitting himself for the great destiny to which he was reserved. He devoured the writings of those who were his precursors in German Literature. Wieland's translation of Shakspeare fell into his hands. Nothing more strongly marks the peculiar earnestness of his character—the emphatic distinction between Shakspeare and himself—than the effect which he tells us, in one of his own compositions, the great Englishman produced on him:—"When at a very early age I first grew acquainted with this poet, I was indignant with his coldness—indignant with the insensibility which allowed him to jest and sport amidst the highest pathos. Led, by my knowledge with more modern poets, to seek the poet in his works; to meet and sympathise with his heart; to reflect with him over his object; it was insufferable to me that this poet gave me nothing of himself. Many years had he my entire reverence—certainly my earnest study—before I could comprehend, as it were, his individuality. I was not yet fit to comprehend Nature at first hand!" Nor indeed was Schiller ever able, as Shakspeare, thoroughly to separate himself from his creations. The peculiarities of his mind inclined him, if they did not limit, to the delineation of grave and elevated characters, and his heart, always in unison with his mind, led him to incorporate himself with the beings he invoked; bidding them be serious with his own intellect or ardent with his own emotions.

His friends were few, but they were well selected, and they shared his inclinations, if they had not his genius, for literature. They formed a sort of intellectual fraternity. Each was to compose something, for which all dreamed of publication and fame—one a romance after "Werther;" one a pathetic drama; one a chivalrous imitation of "Goetz von Berlichingen;" Schiller himself (fired by Gerstenberg's "Ugolino") a tragedy, called "The Student of Nassau." This he abandoned afterwards for one of which he composed several scenes, and of which a part yet lives transferred to "The Robbers," viz., "Cosmo de Medicis."

Meanwhile his poetical talent found its first (and the usual) vent in the corners of a periodical 1776-7. Magazine. At the age of sixteen and seventeen appeared in the Suabian Magazine some small poems (very judiciously omitted from the collected editions of Schiller's works), in which the imitation of Klopstock is sufficiently visible. "O, then was I still," he exclaimed later, "but the slave of Klopstock!" Nevertheless, the editor of the Magazine, Balthasar Haug, found promise in the midst of extravagance and bombast, and prophesied that the young poet "would one day do honour to his father-land." *

The more his inclinations grew confirmed, the more sensibly he became alive to the formal tyranny by which they were opposed. No youth was less likely to be corrupted by Voltaire; but bitter was his resentment at the disgrace he incurred, when discovered reading one of Voltaire's works. "O Karl," he exclaims in his correspondence with young Moser, "so long as my spirit can raise itself to be free, it shall bow to no yoke!" In fact, the Man's mind was ripened long before the Poet's genius. Crude, hard, laboured, and extravagant were Schiller's earliest

---

* Schwab, Hoffmeister.

efforts; but the soul from which Poetry springs as a well, clearing itself the more the farther it advances from its source; a soul ever observant of beauty; ever on the search for truth; ever brave in difficulties; ever fierce against restraint; *that* was the same in its large elements, when the Boy, in vehement bombast, declaimed against the blood-stained laurels of a conqueror, as when the Man planted the robust step of Tell on the soil of Switzerland, and drew forth from the obloquy of ages the virgin glory of the Maid of Orleans.

At last this long and terrible conflict between Genius and Circumstance became decisive. The cry of the strong man went forth. The Titan moved beneath the mountain!

CHAPTER II.

IT was precisely that time in Germany when an Author, whatever his defects, might hope for a favourable hearing, provided his genius carried onward the revolution that had already taken place in literature, and sympathised with that more dangerous movement which had begun to disturb society and agitate opinion.

In literature, the old Gallomania, which for half a century had been vigorously opposed by sincere Poets and sturdy Critics,* had become almost extinct, except in the small royal circles where "Seigneur Oreste" and "Madame Hermione" still maintained their ground. The German genius had already arrogated a dynasty, and found in Klopstock an altar and a throne. What Klopstock† *wrote* is comparatively unimportant; what Klopstock *did* is sublime. No matter that his "Messiah" was overrated,—that even his Odes are more tumid with cloud than instinct with fire. Rather a verbal musician than a poet,‡ his poetical imagination is doubtless frigid, and the weakness of his thoughts in vain disguises itself in redundant epithets and syllabic pomp. But he had two other imaginations besides the poetical,—the imagination of the heart,—the imagination of the conscience. He was an enthusiast for his country and his religion. He felt like an honest man, and he wrote like a man in earnest. It has been truly observed, that, after Klopstock, "Germans were no longer ashamed to be German." If he was not absolutely the first to awaken the national spirit, he made it popular with the people, fashionable with the great, ardent in the young, solemn in the pious. There is not a

* Among critics, Bodmer and Breitinger; among poets, von Haller and especially Gellert.

† Born 1724.

‡ One of the greatest of the German critics has observed that Klopstock's odes, to be appreciated, should be accompanied with music—that he wrote, as it were, to tunes and airs.

German poet coming after Klopstock, who is not indebted to him; indebted to him for a German audience—for that prevalent sentiment of patriotism and devotion in the Public without which the Poet sings to lay-figures, not to men. What was begun by Klopstock, was continued, with profounder views and on a grander scale by the illustrious Lessing.* Well does Heine † exclaim, that "Lessing was the literary Arminius, who freed the German Theatre from every foreign domination." Nor the Theatre alone—all German Art was embraced by the vast range of his criticism and the stalwart vigour of his genius. It is impossible to overrate the excellence of Lessing's intellectual nature, and the noble tendencies of his ambition. Though he modestly denied to himself the qualities of the Poet, and though some shallow depreciators have echoed his own assertion, he enters even into prose with the majesty none but Poets can assume. In his "Emilia Galotti" domestic relations are elevated into the sublimest tragic passion. This drama is the German Virginius. No man has ever so happily effected the difficult union of heroic sentiment with modern manners. Greater even as a critic than a creator (and in the former character far more popularly renowned), he served both to place Art in its true sphere, and to enlarge its domain. Manliness was his characteristic in life and in tastes. Like Schiller, he loved to delineate Human Nature in its nobler qualities, and to sympathise with its graver ends, rather than, like Goethe, to dissect its infirmities, or, like Wieland, to trifle with its interests;—the "Werther" of the first disgusted him—the "Agathon" of the last enraged. Lessing had the nationality of Klopstock without his prejudice. If Klopstock were the first National Poet for the Public, Lessing was the great National Writer for the Writers. That a taste for German Poetry should exist, Klopstock was necessary. That Herder, Schiller, and even Goethe, should have been what they were, Lessing must have lived.

But though the influence of Lessing was so profound, it was not of a nature to be widely popular,

* Born 1729.

† " Zur Geschichte der neuern schoenen Literatur in Deutschland."

nor to be clearly comprehended, save by its after-results: and his great career was now approaching to its close. He died in February, 1781, leaving a Public prepared for manly sentiments, for energetic purpose, for genial humanity, in those writers whom his mind had formed.

At the period we enter (about 1780–1), Wieland * stood next to Klopstock in popular opinion. Amiable both in manners and in tastes, of mature years and established fame, if he was less decidedly national than Klopstock and Lessing, he was yet highly influential in the formation of the National Literature. He was also a *First*, an Originator—the first who taught the delicacies of Taste to German strength—the first who taught the various imitators of the Gallic or Grecian Muse how, without imitating, to appropriate—the first in whom learning seemed airy as intuitive observation; and in whom the fancy of a genuine poet, and the fluency of a charming novelist, were blended with the erudition of a scholar, and the elegance of a man who has known the world. Partly French, partly Greek—he is German through all; a German who commenced his education at Paris, and finished it at Athens. We enter not into a discussion of the precise rank Wieland should assume,—a rank too readily conceded at one time, too harshly questioned now. But his influence limited itself to the fancy and the taste—it did not extend to opinions—it did not root itself in passions. His great defect was his want of earnestness and purpose. He may charm and he may refine; but he does not brace the intellect to masculine exertion, nor elevate the imagination to lofty objects. At this time he sat on his careless throne at Weimar, rather to receive homage than to govern. But there were now already labouring into fame three young men; two of whom, at least, were destined not only to wear the robes of sovereignty, but to wield the sceptre—Herder, Goethe, and Johann Heinrich Voss.

The minds of these three men had been formed under the most powerful influence which a Frenchman had ever yet exercised in Germany. Always prone to imitate (as a learned people necessarily must be), the Germans had

* Born 1733.

escaped from the old Gallomania to fall into Grecomania and Anglomania—while one was imitating Theocritus, another was imitating Pope. The English Richardson, who, though less popular in Germany than Fielding, produced a far more profound impression, as, indeed, that greater genius must do wherever the two can penetrate,* may be seen overshadowing the large mind of Lessing himself. The sublime Clarissa, whom Dishonour so noiselessly slays, is the original of the no less sublime Emilia Galotti, who flies to Death from even a sentiment that dishonours. But in vain Klopstock and Lessing had thrown from their pedestals Racine and Corneille—in vain Wieland had given to the Germans a more kindly, if a feebler Voltaire of their own—a new Gallomania had seized the heart, and fevered the brain of the People: "Greek and Briton, all gave way to the influence of ROUSSEAU. Nothing is more interesting to one who seeks with Helvetius to trace the connection and sympathy between social influences and literary tastes, than to contrast the nugatory effect produced in England, with the prodigious effect produced in Germany by this unhealthy Genius. Though, at two great periods in the history of our Literature—that of Elizabeth and that of Anne—the Italian and the French writers have influenced our own, our more illustrious authors have rather reproduced than imitated; and with the single exception of the Sterne-fever, the Literature of Sentiment has never been widely successful with our practical and busy population. But in Germany, always, as we have said, prone to imitate, no imitation was likely to be so contagious as that which combined sentiment with thought. The peculiar habits of life amongst the Germans —the absence for the most part of that active constitutional liberty which, when accompanied with commercial

* The influence of Richardson upon the fiction and poetry of Europe was not only vast at the time, but, enduring still, it must endure for ever. In vain his language grows obsolete, in vain his minuteness has become wearisome, in vain the young race of novel-readers leave him on the shelf—to those somewhat tedious pages turns every genius who aspires to rise in fiction; from them, though with toil and study, can best be learned the art of extracting from the homeliest details the noblest pathos. In "Clarissa" is beheld that true spirit of tragedy which first dispensed with kings and heroes and the paraphernalia of the outward stage—teaching how the compass of all grandeur in fiction can be attained by him who can describe the affection, and comprehend the virtue, of one human being.

pursuits, always tends, overmuch perhaps, to harden and materialise the national mind—do not present to domestic life the counterpoise which the life of the Mart and the Agora effects in England. Books which dispose the mind to abstract reverie or speculation, exercise a greater influence over the Germans than they do over us; a theory appears to them the more seductive in proportion as it is detached from the experience of practical life. Either wholly contented with the existing state of things, or wholly amidst the clouds of Utopia—they want that intermediate standard to which the mass of Englishmen unconsciously refer every suggestion of change or project of reform. The love of liberty, instinctive to all, and especially to nations at once so brave and so lettered as the German, finds that vent in the ideal from which it is precluded by the actual. Hence, while practical liberty amongst the Germans is so confined when compared with ours,* their theoretical liberty—liberty of thought, opinion, and speculation—is infinitely greater. The most religious German will start inquiries which an irreligious Englishman would be afraid to suggest: And the Politician who would shrink from arguing for a Representative Constitution, will luxuriate in the dreams of Republican Fraternity. Precisely the reasons that deadened the influence of Rousseau in England, gave it vitality in Germany, viz., impracticability in politics, and morbidity in romance. Our own active life, that rude, common sense which is acquired with our mother's milk, amidst our world-awake population, would teach even an ordinary Englishman the untruth that forms the ground-work of " The Social Contract," and shock our sense of nature in the eloquence of St. Preux. We know, without reasoning about it, that no Social Contract ever existed, and that no lover, worthy the name, could sit down to make an inventory of furniture five minutes before his first assignation with the woman he professes to adore. But with the Germans the novelty of the political theory concealed its falsehood; the sentiment of the fiction concealed its want of nature. There was much in Rousseau that could not fail to charm and to dazzle the German mind, which, from its own deficient

---

* The reader will remember that this was written in 1847.

experience of agitated and various life, perceived not his ignorance or perversion of nature in character and passion. The Germans could fully comprehend his love and his knowledge of *inanimate* nature; his enjoyment of scenery; his passion for solitude; his power of associating the landscape around with emotions within. Their own fondness for domestic and rural life made them charmed with the primitive simplicity which he held up to admiration. The vast mass of disappointed ambition, which amongst an intellectual population, without he multiform vents of a free constitution, must necessarily be engendered, found a voice and a sickly comfort in Rousseau's disgust of the active world. The ardour for liberty—the revolutionary spirit, awakened in Germany as in France—obtained in the Dreamer of Geneva a representative nearly akin to the amiable and tender character of the Germans. The biting mockery of Voltaire might delight a court and charm a scholar; but the earnest and pious heart of the multitude recoiled from a spirit that desecrated what it attacked, to open itself with dangerous emotion to a spirit that sought to sanctify what it embraced. The laughing philosopher never makes disciples so devoted as the weeping one. With Rousseau rose the great sect of HUMANITY; the school which seeks to lift human nature above convention; which would extract from social life all that is harsh and tyrannous; and (to use the phrase of Seneca) recognise a claim to kindness wherever it looks upon the face of man.

Upon Herder, Goethe, and Voss, the influence of Rousseau produced effects, perhaps equally strong, but widely differing in their nature. Herder* rejected all that in the Genevese was effeminate and egotistical, to seize upon all that was genial and philanthropic. In him arose the true Preacher of Humanity: with Rousseau Humanity was a sentiment; with Herder it became a science. Of a mind thoroughly sound and healthy—of a cultivation vast and various—of a broad common sense which gave life and substance to the boldest speculations, Herder snatched from the weak hands of the French Socialists the great cause which they profaned—viz. the Principle of Human Progress, recognised it through History, illustrated it through Poetry, and reconciled it to Religion as the law of God.

* Born 1744.

P

For Herder the noblest destinies were reserved. By profession a preacher—by energy a citizen—by genius a poet—by piety and wisdom a philosopher and cosmopolite—all that is intellectual in man may be said to have *flowered* in him. With a great inclination towards what is practical in life, which he sometimes regretted he had not more diligently studied in its minutiæ, he combined an innocence of heart in which lay half his strength. "My whole life," he said once, "is the interpretation of the oracles of my childhood." He loved to glean thoughts from the conjectures of childhood—from the wonder of ignorance. Hence he saw in the infancy and youth of nations the beauty and the promise which historians have overlooked. Thus he was the first who gave to Poetry its proper place in the grave and solemn dispensations of the world :—regarding it as the absolute voice that spoke the time and character of a race, he brought into one vast compendium, entitled "The Voices of the Nations," the popular songs of all countries. Amongst the many influences he lived to effect upon his age, is the impetus he gave to that tendency in the German genius, which is called "Universalism." For, as Humanity to Politics, Charity to Virtue, Christianity to Man, so is Universalism to Letters.* That separation between the faculties—that division of mental labour so general elsewhere—in Germany was broken down. The Poet studied Philosophy—the Philosopher Poetry. But most of what Herder lived to effect, was as yet unfulfilled. He was already known as a scholar, an essayist, a victorious prizeman, an eloquent preacher—and in high station and repute at the Court of Weimar. But still he stood somewhat apart from the popular literature of the time; and had rather served to indicate the great

---

* Herder is a very voluminous writer, but the epitome of his mind and his views is to be found in his work on the "Philosophy of the History of Mankind." The work is not without grave faults. It is often incorrect in detail; it too much follows Helvetius in founding authority on the imperfect accounts of travellers and voyagers; it is often displeasingly declamatory in its tone. But its power of generalisation is astonishing. It seizes, as with the grasp of a giant, the immensity of the subject it embraces.. Few works deserve so justly the epithets of *luminous* and *comprehensive*. Readers well acquainted with this work will find many of its ideas, even some of its images, borrowed by Schiller in his later poems, though it would seem unconsciously. Schiller never appears to have been aware of his great obligations to Herder.

change destiued to take place in public taste and feeling, than to dispirit, by his own renown, the ambition of another.

While Rousseau had thus influenced Herder only to grand results; the primitive simplicity, the pastoral family life which Rousseau had held up to admiration amongst the homely Germans, had sunk deep into the mind of a rude young Saxon—Johann Heinrich Voss,* not worthy, indeed, from his mere genius, to be named in the same breath with Herder and Goethe, but still, for many reasons, not meriting the depreciation of Schlegel, and the disdain of Menzel. Low-born, self-educated, a rigid Protestant sectarian, driven for bread to the drudgery of a schoolmaster, Voss is often vulgar in his taste, pedantic in his compositions, prejudiced and intolerant in his polemics. But withal, he is a true German, and a strong man. His services to his language were immense. He enriched it with the wealth of the foreigner; he strengthened it with the cultivation of its own natural resources; he revived the old words of Luther on the lips of Homer. It is well said of Voss that his strength is in his war with obstacles. He hewed his way through poverty into learning; and he cut through rough crags † of diction, till he found out a fount of poetry all his own. But, as yet, Voss was young, —if not obscure, at least but partially known,—and had neither obtained, by harsh and ungrateful controversy, the title of the second Luther, nor given in his "Louise" and his "Idyls" (poems most popular in their time, and thoroughly repugnant to English taste) the pastoral of a Curate's Parlour, and the model to Goethe's "Herman and Dorothea." First, then, already in popular eminence, of the three we have named—first, indeed, of all the younger and rising generation, stood Wolfgang Goethe.‡ Nor had *he* then escaped, perhaps he never altogether escaped, from the influence of Rousseau. In fact, it is the merit of this wonderful man, that his whole nature was especially plastic and impressionable. Every influence of his time stamped itself on his intellect, to be reproduced in new forms by his genius. Does the age incline to sentiment?

---

* Born 1751, two years after Goethe.
† " Versified marble blocks."—*Heine.*
‡ Born 1749, five years after Herder.

he sounas its abysses:—To irony? the sneer of Voltaire seems venomless beside the icy smile of the fiend he calls from hell, to mock at human knowledge, and desecrate human love! Does the age yearn for Pastorals and family life? he turns from courts and the seventh heaven of Poetry to borrow from homely Voss; and ruins him by the riches he extracts from the loan. In his " Werther " he concentrates the history of an epoch in his country,—the epoch of the Rousseau Mania. But though the " Nouvelle Héloïse " is incontestably the origin of " Werther," those* who regard it as a mere copy do it miserable injustice. There is more rhetorical eloquence in one page of the " *Nouvelle Héloïse*," than in the whole of " *Werther*,"—but there is more nature in one page of " *Werther*," than in the whole of the " *Nouvelle Héloïse*." In this, the warmest and most actual of all Goethe's novels—if once overrated, now so unjustly depreciated, which he did right to regret for its moral, which he did wrong to disparage as a proof of his genius—lies the germ of much that, in fiction, its author's riper intellect matured. Here we see that association of homeliness and grandeur which his enemies have called " the Adornment of Commonplace." What Englishman, with his fastidious classical taste, has not ridiculed the contrast of the Hero in the clouds, and the Heroine cutting bread and butter—of the solemnity of deliberate suicide, and the exact description of the top-boots and blue coat in which the unhappy man rushed to the dread Unknown? But considered by a higher art than we learn at college, it is this very homeliness of detail that gives truth to the romance. And this peculiarity Goethe continued, as he advanced in his luminous career, to invest with an unspeakable beauty. It is, in truth, to a very early study of what, while subtlest in the essence, is simplest in the form, that Goethe owes the lucid ease of his after style, and the popularity he secured to flights of imagination which, in a less artful writer, would have left the multitude far behind. Here, too, we see a yet more distinguishing attribute of Goethe, to which we have before alluded—viz. the inclination to describe, not so much the healthful nobleness, as the diseased infirmity, of an intellectual

* Such as Menzel.

character. What he here does in "Werther," he did afterwards in "Clavigo," in the "Elective Affinities," in "Faust,"
and in "Tasso." Menzel, who, whatever may be thought of
his injustice to Goethe, demands the greatest respect for
his honest passion for what is sincere and noble—for his
vigorous sense—for his daring courage—falls into a cant
unworthy of so great a critic, when he accuses Goethe of
confounding vice and virtue, by depicting weak or dis-
honourable characters as interesting and amiable. It is
among the most legitimate, and among the highest provinces of the Poet, to depict those contrasts which subject
him to this charge—to show a vice in the virtuous, and a
virtue in the wicked; and this unquestionable truth in art
once granted, it follows as the very condition of fiction,
that to a hero thus selected, human interest must be given.
You cannot blame a Poet for making a faulty hero interesting, unless you contend that heroes of fiction must be
perfect *—by which dogma you would at once cut off from
the Poet the whole realm of the human heart, and separate
his ethics from the representation of Truth and Nature.
This love, indeed, of probing the sores of character—of
representing the infirmities of intellectual man—was not
more remarkable in Goethe than in Shakspeare; who, in
the whole range of his Dramas, has never presented to us
a single male image of perfect virtue; who, in Macbeth, in
Othello, in Angelo, in Shylock, in Hamlet (the last is so
Goethe-like, that if Shakspeare had never created it one
might predict that Goethe would have done so), lays bare,
with fearful precision, the weakness of the wise—the
crime of the virtuous. It is in vain to deny that our
paramount interest in all these plays is with the erring, or
the infirm. But who shall say that Shakspeare, while
interesting us in the hero, sought to pervert our conscience
into admiring the defect: that it was his object to deco-
rate ambitious murder, or jealous ferocity; licentious
hypocrisy, or implacable revenge; or to womanize the
intellect, and emasculate the will, by all the doubts and
scruples which make up the philosophy of Hamlet?—
Hamlet, that great fountain-head of modern sentiment—

* Or unless you contend, that if a hero is faulty, the author must not make
him interesting; but whatever an author does, he must give it interest.
No author is obliged to be dull.

from which have gushed a thousand rivulets of melancholy and scepticism; Hamlet, that perpetual mirror to minds fluctuating between the Visible and the Unseen, the Actual and the Ideal, the stern demands of uncomprehended duty, and the desire to escape from practical action into visionary self-commune; Hamlet, in whom is shown the mysterious prototype of what man would be with virtue, and with wisdom, but without WILL!

But though Goethe does not seem to us to be blamed for following the tendency of his genius, into directions in which the peculiar delicacy and subtlety of his intellect ensured him such success; and though, a hundred years hence, we believe that what Menzel and other depreciators consider immoral, will not mislead a single imitator, or corrupt a single youth; yet it must be conceded that the *direct* object of his works was not to make Man more manly, and his desires more elevated. We say the *direct* object; for indirectly, and sooner or later, whatever makes man wiser,—nerves his mind, and purifies his emotions; and there may be truth in the theory, that Art is to be cultivated as Art; that the Beautiful must reflect indifferently on its tranquil mirror whatever Convention deems moral or immoral: For, to whatever is really and essentially vicious, the Beautiful itself is opposed;—Convention revolts at the exhibition of the naked form, but foul must be the imagination that finds immorality in the Venus of the sculptor.

At this date, however, Goethe was still scarcely out of his apprenticeship. His greatest works had not been produced. On his " Goetz von Berlichingen," his "Werther," and his " Clavigo," rested the principal columns of the renown he had acquired. These, indeed, had unsettled the public taste, and prepared it for bold innovations; but Goethe had not, like our Byron in a later day, engrossed the general interest in himself, and become the sole representative of a common sentiment. · In that crisis of opinion and of passion preceding the outbreak of the French Revolution, and contemporaneous with the rise of daring speculators and profound inquirers, men required something more than the childlike pietism of Klopstock, the airy elegance of Wieland, or that philosophy of sentiment—that analysis of man's weakness, so apart from sympathy with men's interests, which Goethe had exhibited in "Werther" and "Clavigo." Something indeed was wanting still; something, it is true, which in order to be popular must necessarily partake of the morbid craving, the unsettled spirit, the revolutionary tendency of the time, but which, in order to outlast the hour, must also develop into fuller force, and diffuse through a wider public whatever in Lessing had been earnest, whatever in Herder promised to be humane. There was a great multitude which as yet in Germany had found no voice; which desired to hear its own discontented heart beat in the pulse of some passionate Author, indignant with what was false, and sympathising with what was free. Never, in Germany, had there been a time more favourable to a writer (no matter what his other defects) who, shouldering aside courts and schoolmen, should address himself manfully to men.

CHAPTER III.

AT this time there was published at Mannheim a strange, rugged, fiery melodrame, in which, amidst uncouth masses of extravagant diction,—flashed a spirit true to all the turbulent and unsettled philosophy of the hour—and which seemed destined to announce and to animate the revolution of a world :—" THE ROBBERS " appeared, and the sensation it excited spread through the mind of Germany like fire through flax ;—nor through Germany alone—it produced in France the liveliest enthusiasm ; it even stirred to its depths the calm intellect of England. It was, in fact, the most earnest Revolutionary fiction that had yet revealed what lay hid in the History of the Age.—What the irruption of the old Germans was in the midst of the smooth and decrepit civilisation of Rome,—was the burst of this new German amidst the hollow conventions which under the *ancien régime* less guarded the life of Virtue than entombed her corpse.

"The Robbers" is one sweeping uncompromising defiance of the sober proprieties in which the mature see decorum and the young dissimulation. It is the baseness of the World that makes Karl Moor a criminal. It is in proportion to his exaggerated nobleness that he is unfitted for Society. It is because he is a giant that he cannot live amongst the dwarfs. He commences life with many virtues, and it is the mediocrity of life that turns every virtue into sin. It is his sympathy with poverty and suffering, with the virtuous and oppressed that has banished the Demigod to the rock—and afflicted him with the ever-gnawing vulture.

That a work like this, so conceived, and executed with all the power which can whirl along the passions of the

crowd, must have produced a great deal of mischief at
the time, may be readily allowed. No man can disturb
the settled course of opinion, right or wrong, without
doing evil as well as good.—Whether Genius innovates in
a poem, or Science in a manufacture, some minds in the
one case must be thrown into disorder, some hands in the
other thrown out of employ. But Genius and Science
must still obey the great instincts of their being—the one
still innovate, the other still invent. In the moral constitution of nature, they are the great alterative, the "Sturm-
Bad," which first fevers and convulses, then purifies and
strengthens. But nothing could be farther from the mind
of the Boy from whose unpractised hand came this rough
Titan sketch, than to unsettle virtue, in his delineations of
crime. Virtue was then, as it continued to the last, his
Ideal—and if at the first he shook the statue on its
pedestal, it was but from the rudeness of the caress that
sought to warm it into life.*

The original sketch of this drama Schiller had completed two years before the publication. But he kept it by
him till he had completed his medical studies, towards the
end of 1780, and been appointed by the Duke to the office
of Surgeon to a regiment. He then considered himself
a free agent, and after searching in vain for   1781.
a bookseller to hazard the necessary ex-   Ætat. 22.
penses, he published "The Robbers" at his
own cost.

If the popularity of the work was dazzling, the aversion
it excited in some was as intense as the admiration it
called forth in others. But the most formidable critic was
the Grand Duke himself. This uncouth drama displeased
his taste no less than it revolted his opinions. He sent for
the author, and bade him in future eschew poetry, and
stick to medicine; or, if he needs must write, submit
his productions to the revision of his Prince. It
is easy to sneer at the conduct of the man of power

---

* Goethe himself has somewhere said that the most universal effect of the
highest Genius is to *unsettle;* and certainly it has ever been so where its
effect upon its age could be traced—witness Cervantes, Bacon, Luther,
Milton (especially in his prose works). Shakspeare, not studied in his own
time, has influenced, by unsettling, the literary mind of three Nations at the
least: in our own day, Byron and Wordsworth are, in their several ways,
equal Innovators.

to the man of genius; but the Grand Duke was
scarcely to blame, for there are few individuals now-a-days
whose taste "The Robbers" will not offend, and we may
judge of the abhorrence it excited at that time in others,
besides the Grand Duke, by the words addressed by an
illustrious personage to Goethe, "If I were a God, and
deliberating whether I should create the world, and foresaw that in that world Schiller's "Robbers" would appear,
I would not create it." Meanwhile, however, the young
Poet had commenced a correspondence with the Freiherr
von Dalberg, a nobleman intrusted with the superintendence of the Theatre at Mannheim, and the play was to be
remodelled for the stage. Simultaneously

January,
1782.

appeared many lyrics and minor poems of the
author, contributions to a miscellany entitled
"The Anthology," and set up in concert with some of his
friends. A large portion of these performances, characterised, it is true, by power, though distorted, and originality, though uncouth, still belonged to a very inferior and
coarse school of poetry, known in Germany by the significant title of the "Storm and Stress" *—a school of which
some notion may be gleaned by those who turn to that
later era in our own literature, when the servile herd of
imitators mixed up, on their staring canvas, the sepia of
Matthew Lewis with the gamboge and vermilion of Lord
Byron. Most of these Schiller rejected from the collected
edition of his works; some of those retained have been
wisely corrected and compressed. Such as they were,
however, they added to the sudden celebrity of the writer.
And now, while Germany began to ring with the name of
the young Poet, what was his life? He lodged in a small
apartment, which he shared with a young officer named
Kapff, who had quitted the academy at the same time.
Kapff is said to have been of dissolute habits,† and to
have occasionally misled his wild and impetuous companion
into some irregularities; favoured the more by the general
licence of a town to which the earlier example of the

* The German phrase is thus happily translated by Mr. Carlyle, in one of
his "Miscellaneous Writings."

† Schwab—who rests this assertion against Kapff upon *unprinted*, and,
therefore, very suspicious testimony. Probably poor Kapff lived like most
young soldiers, neither worse nor better.

reigning Duke had given a tone of manners the reverse of austere.* Still such irregularities never degenerated into habit, and were counteracted in their effects upon the mind by Schiller's frequent visits to his excellent family, the tender warnings of his mother, the fortunate narrowness of his finances,† the professional demands upon his time, and that passion for literature, with which systematic indulgence in dissipation and disorder is, it is true, not always incompatible, but to which it is certainly opposed. Above all, perhaps, we must be permitted to believe that the young Poet was saved from more vagrant and unworthy excesses, by that great purifier of youth—First Love. In the same house lodged the widow of a captain, who appears, by all probable accounts, to have been the original of the "Laura," to whom the most impassioned of all his love-verses are addressed. A humorous, but somewhat flippant, friend of Schiller's—Scharffenstein—has described this lady in the same spirit of caricature with which he has treated of the noble image of Schiller himself. He says, "she was not pretty, nor clever; but had something about her, good-natured, *piquant*, and attractive." One of Schiller's biographers hints at unpublished accounts, less flattering; but what is unpublished is necessarily unsifted and unsupported; and we have no evidence whatsoever to invalidate that on which the Poet himself commands our interest for one who could make so vivid an impression on his heart. Schiller was, no doubt, at least as good a judge of beauty and of cleverness as his friend Scharffenstein.

It would be impossible for a critic of common sense to suppose, with certain metaphysical commentators, that this love was merely Platonic. Platonic love in Schiller! As well talk of Platonic love in Burns! The poems themselves, in their very faults, bear internal evidence of the healthful and natural passion of the man, which takes poetry for its vent—not the vanity of the poetaster who would simulate the great passion of man, in order to obtain a vent for his verses.

But whatever this affection, it seems to have burned out from its very fierceness, and (though, years afterwards, the Poet speaks of the resignation of Laura as

---

* Hoffmeister. † Madame von Wolzogen.

the great sacrifice of youth), it was obviously very different from that steady, pure, and permanent attachment which ultimately' made the happiness of his manhood.

At last, on the 13th of January, 1782, "The Robbers" appeared on the stage at Mannheim. The sensation the printed play had produced served to crowd the theatre. Near and far, from Heidelberg and Darmstadt, from Frankfort, Mayence, and Worms, gathered the audience. The play lasted five hours. The success in print was trivial to that upon the stage. The fiery rebellion of thought which it embodied became more startling when animated by the art of the greatest actors of the time,* and hailed by the enthusiasm of spectators, in whom, as everywhere in 1782, the spirit of Revolution was astir.

We can easily imagine the impatient desire of Schiller to witness his own triumph. He went by stealth to Mannheim. In an obscure corner of the crowded house, the author beheld the living embodiment of his own thoughts and passions. He saw himself raised at once into that mighty power—the mover of the hearts of men. He returned to Stuttgart confirmed for life in the vocation his genius had adopted. "If Germany," he wrote to Dalberg on his return, " shall one day recognise in me a Dramatic Poet, I must date the epoch from the last week."

17th Jan. 1782.

But in proportion to the ardour of his inclinations, was the restraint of Schiller's actual life. At Mannheim, he was the freeman, the poet; he returned to Stuttgart to sink again into the subaltern and the subject. Some expressions in the third act of the " The Robbers," reflecting upon the national character of the *Grisons*, gave such offence to the objects of the rude and boyish satire, that their complaint was published in " The Hamburgh Corre-

* Bök acted Karl Moor with prodigious effect: but that is a part which almost plays itself. Iffland, a man of real genius, elevated the disagreeable character of Franz Moor into the dignity of an Iago. His representation of this part seems to have been one of the most perfect as well as one of the most popular triumphs of the stage. His thin figure and meagre countenance, suiting well with the ideal of a formal hypocrite, served to increase the actuality of the personation. Iffland, like Schiller, was commencing his career; he was then about six-and-twenty, according to Schiller's biographers; three-and-twenty according to other authorities, who state his birth to have been in April, 1759.

spondent," and, by the mediation of a man named Walter, who bore some personal grudge to Schiller, laid before the Grand Duke. The result seems to have been a very severe reprimand on the part of the Duke, and a peremptory injunction to Schiller to confine his studies to Medicine—his publications to such as befitted his profession—to abandon all connexion with States under other jurisdiction (meaning Mannheim), limiting his ambition to his calling, and his connexions to his country.* Such a command could not be obeyed by a man urged to resist by the stronger despotism of his own genius. Already new and vast designs were opening to Schiller's intellectual ambition; already he had commenced and proceeded far in the tragedy of "Fiesco;" already meditated a drama on the fate of Don Carlos of Spain. To ask him to renounce these projects was to ask him to renounce the very mind by which they were formed. His first visit to the Mannheim theatre had been undetected or overlooked; he went again in the following May, and was put for fourteen days under arrest. Dangers now beset him; dark and sinister menaces were repeated to him by officious friends, and exaggerated perhaps in their import by the gloom of his imagination. But the dangers in themselves were real and imminent. Before his eyes was the fate of the Poet Schubart,† eight years imprisoned for displeasing the jealousies of Power. What fate could seem more terrible to one drunk with the desire of liberty, and eager to spread the wings of his genius? Stuttgart, nay, all Suabian scenes, as he himself complains, in a letter to Dalberg, "became intolerable and loathed." He could have had but small comfort from his family. His father as yet regarded his notoriety with dislike and fear. He was not a prophet in his own country, nor an honour to his own hearth;—with disgust he saw all around him;—with sanguine self-confidence he cast his eyes beyond. He formed the only resolution natural to his circumstances and worthy of his independence : he resolved to emancipate body and soul both; to fly from Stuttgart, and throw himself on the world.

* Schwab, &c.

† An Appendix to Mr. Carlyle's "Life of Schiller" contains an interesting account of this unfortunate poet.

CHAPTER IV.

AMONGST Schiller's companions was a warmhearted enthusiastic musician, two years younger than himself, named Andrew Streicher. This youth became his confidant. Together they brooded over the future—together they conceived and nursed the project of escape. It had been intended that Streicher should proceed to Hamburgh in the spring of the next year, to take lessons in his art from the celebrated Bach.* He persuaded his mother to consent that the date of this journey should be advanced, and the friends settled that Schiller should bear him company. But Schiller, with all his inexperience, and all his fiery ardour, had that strong sense with which true genius prepares for the fulfilment, even of its wildest schemes. He felt the necessity of providing, from his own talents, the materials for their support. He would not leave Stuttgart till his tragedy of " Fiesco " was nearly completed. In that tragedy lay his fortune and his future. He worked at it night and day—illness seized him, but the work went on. At length it was sufficiently advanced for presentation to the Mannheim Theatre, and the opportunity now offered itself for escape.

The city and its neighbourhood were astir with the visit of the Grand Duke Paul of Russia, and his young Princess, niece to the Duke of Würtemberg. In the midst of these festivities the flight was planned.

It was obviously necessary to conceal from the elder Schiller the designs of the son; the military notions and military duty of the former might not only lead him to forbid, but to disclose them. And the young Poet was

---

* Not the great Sebastian Bach, who died in 1750.

moreover anxious, that whatever the displeasure of his sovereign, it might fall on himself alone—not involve his father. But his eldest and favourite sister was admitted to his confidence;—the little girl who had wandered with the dreaming boy through the ruins of Hohenstaufen, and amidst the pines of Larch, was become a woman, capable of sympathising with the lofty hopes of the adventurous man: and at last, a day or two before the meditated departure, the truth was broken to Schiller's mother. With his friend Streicher, and the wife of the Stage Manager at Mannheim, Madame Meier (whom, as well as the Director Dalberg, the royal festivities had drawn to Stuttgart, but from whom the secret was carefully kept), Schiller for the last time visited his family at "Solitude." He took the opportunity, which his father's absorption in his own account of the royal preparations afforded, to steal with his mother unobserved from the room. After an hour's absence, he returned—alone. The affectionate gaze of Streicher saw what he had suffered in that parting interview, by the redness of his eyes. The important day was now fixed—the 17th of September.

Streicher removed from Schiller's lodging a bundle, containing the dress which was to be substituted for the uniform of the Regimental Surgeon—some linen, and a few books — among which were the works of Haller and Shakspeare. But when Streicher came to fetch Schiller himself—after the return of the latter from his final visit to the Hospital—he found the young enthusiast with Klopstock's Odes in his hands. A favourite ode had given unseasonable inspiration to his own muse, and the impatient musician was forced to wait and hear, not only the seductive ode, but the ode it had called forth. At last all was ready—day passed—night came—Schiller had assumed his disguise; three-and-twenty florins constituted the Poet's wealth, eight-and-twenty the Musician's; two trunks, containing books and apparel—a brace of pistols—and a small clavichord, summed up the effects of the fugitives. At ten o'clock the vehicle which contained the adventurers rolled from Streicher's lodging to the Esslingen Gate (the darkest of all the City Gates), at which the Lieutenant of the Watch was a firm friend of the Poet's. "Halt! who goes there?"

"Dr. Ritter and Dr. Wolf, both bound to Esslingen."
"Pass."

The escape is made. Towards midnight they beheld, at the left, the illuminated Ludwigsburg, like a mount of fire; further on, and at the distance of a mile from their road, they saw the castle of "Solitude," and the neighbouring buildings, lighted up in honour of the Royal visitor. In the clear air, all was so distinctly visible, that the poet could point out to his companion his parents' home; and a suppressed sigh—a soft "O meine Mutter"—escaped him! So fled from the capital of Würtemberg, Friedrich Schiller, "empty"—as, with little exaggeration, he himself has said, "of purse and hope;" esteemed as a rebel by his Sovereign; condemned as a scapegrace by his father; regarded but as an imprudent reckless scribbler, marring his own fair prospects for a vain ambition, by his associates!—He who now visits that capital finds little to arrest his interest—except one colossal statue, in a broad space near the Royal palace; before which his guide will bid him halt to contemplate Friedrich Schiller—the pride of his Fatherland!

The travellers reached Mannheim in safety. They unpacked their boxes, and put on their best clothes; it was a holiday—they were out of the Grand Duke's dominions—they were free! Schiller's hope was in his "Fiesco." In a few sheets of paper lay all that was to give bread to existence, independence to labour, and glory to ambition. Dalberg was at Stuttgart; but Meier, the manager, received them with kindness. When he heard, with astonishment, the bold step Schiller had taken, he urged the expediency of an immediate letter to the Grand Duke. This, indeed, Schiller had already resolved upon. In the small German States, the relation between prince and subject is more parental and patriarchal than in the larger Monarchies of Europe: if the prince be more despotic, the subject can be more familiar. After dinner, to which the young friends were invited by Meier, Schiller withdrew into another apartment, and wrote frankly to his Sovereign; it was a letter at once manly and respectful. He represented how impossible he found it to live upon his professional gains as a surgeon;—his income could only be made sufficient by his literary labours. He prayed for permission to try his fortune for a short time out of the Duke's dominions, and declared his willingness ultimately to return on receiving his Sovereign's pardon. The letter was enclosed to the chief of Schiller's regiment, General Augé, with a petition to present, and to support it. The next day Madame Meier returned from Stuttgart, with the news that Schiller's flight was already notorious; and that it was expected that the Grand Duke would demand the delivery of his person. As Schiller, however, was not a soldier, he could not be treated and reclaimed as a deserter; still it was deemed advisable that he should not show himself till the Grand Duke's answer was received. A letter from General Augé came at last; it preserved perfect silence as to the request Schiller had preferred, and only announced to him the permission, or implied the order, immediately to return. Schiller hastened to reply to the General, that he could not regard the Grand Duke's message as a compliance with his request, which he again respectfully urged. A second letter from the General laconically repeated the purport of the former one. Schiller's pride, his spirit of independence, and his honour became engaged. He could not recall the step which had delivered him from an intolerable bondage : the die was cast, and he resolved, as he himself has expressed it, " to exchange the citizenship of his country for that of the world."

Meanwhile Streicher had fired the manager with his accounts of " Fiesco ; " a day and hour were fixed for Schiller to read his new performance to the more distinguished actors, among whom was Iffland. The young poet commenced his reading,—all listened in silence,—not a word of approbation. At the end of the first act some slipped away ; at the end of the second, the disappointment grew more unequivocal ; and a quarter of an hour afterwards, the poet had lost all his listeners except Iffland. Meier now took aside Streicher, and asked him seriously, " if Schiller really were the author of ' The Robbers ' ? "— " Certainly," said the astonished friend. " Then," answered Meier, " he has exhausted his strength in his first performance." But the manuscript was left with the experienced manager, and the next morning, when Streicher

ropaired, full of painful anxioty, to Meier, he was accosted
with "You are right, 'Fiesco' is a masterpiece!—better
fitted for the stage than 'The Robbers.'" It was
Schiller's Suabian dialect, and his high-pitched monotonous mode of declamation, that had done such injustice to his genius—a perusal of the play excited Meier's
warmest admiration, and Streicher went back to his friend
with the welcome news, that arrangements would be made
to produce "Fiesco" on the stage. Alterations requiring
some time were nevertheless indispensable, and it became
necessary to remove farther from the power of his offended
prince. Warned by letters from Stuttgart, Schiller and
his friend resolved to pass to Darmstadt, near Frankfort.
Their money was nearly gone. Sorely pressed as he was,
Schiller had so tender a consideration for his parents, that
he would not apply to them, lest he might bring upon his
father the suspicion of conniving at his flight. With
enough barely to defray the expenses of their pilgrimage
on foot, the two friends set off one day at noon; rested at
night in a village; resumed their way the next morning
over one of the most striking roads in Europe (the Berg-
strasse); continued their journey for twelve hours; rested
from six in the evening till midnight, when they were
wakened and alarmed by the drums of a revoille. Notwithstanding Schiller felt himself unwell, with the early
morning the journey was resumed; the day was serene and
clear, but Schiller's strength failed his spirit; his step
grew every moment more weary, his cheek more pale: at
last, on entering a wood, he was unable to proceed further;
he laid himself down for an hour's rest upon the grass;
and Streicher, seated on the trunk of a tree, anxious
and sorrowful, watched beside him. The young man,
struggling with his destiny, may take heart for the future
when he contemplates the picture of that wearied sleeper,
homeless and penniless, but already on his path to the
conquest of Destiny itself, and the only throne which no
revolution shakes, and no time decays—in the hearts of
men.

They reached Frankfort at last, and Schiller addressed
a letter to Dalberg:—"When I tell you," he says, "that
I am flying my country, I describe to you my whole fate.
My safety obliged me to withdraw in haste from Stutt-

gart. My sole hopes rested on a removal to Mannheim; there, I trusted, by your Excellency's assistance, that my new drama might enable me to clear myself from debt, and permanently better my condition. This was frustrated through the hasty departure to which I was compelled. I might blush to make such disclosures to you, but I know they do not debase me. If my former conduct—if all that your Excellency knows of my character—can induce confidence in my honour, let me frankly ask your' assistance. Greatly as I need the anticipated profit from "Fiesco," the play cannot be ready for the theatre in less than five weeks. My heart was oppressed—my poetic dreams fled before the sense of my condition. But if at the time specified the play could be ready, and, I trust, worthy,—from that belief I take the courage to ask the advance of what would then be due. I need it, perhaps, more now than I may ever do hereafter. I owed nearly 200 florins when I left Stuttgart. This gives me, I own, more uneasiness than all the care for my future fate. I shall have no rest till in that quarter I am free."

After this letter he was more relieved; and yet, on returning from the post-office to which he took it, he paused on the bridge, beneath which flows the Maine: he gazed long in silence on the river, and said at last, "Which is the deeper, that water or my sufferings?" But no brave man, and no true poet, can remain long despondent in the midst of a world enriched by the activity of his kind, and upheld by the goodness of his Maker. The very sight of that bustling scene; the vessels sailing to and fro; the river gilded by the setting sun; the clear evening air; the fresh and cheerful wave; amidst the smiles of Nature, the evidences of that Nature's subjugation to the will and the power of man—these gradually drew him from his sadness, and re-animated his soul. His very misfortunes, throwing him so wholly on his own resources, quickened his invention, and the next evening he announced to his friend, that he had conceived the plan of a domestic play, entitled* "Louise Miller," which was afterwards completed, and finally became famous under the title of "Cabal and Love."

* According to Madame von Wolzogen (Schiller's sister-in-law), he had, however, first thought of the subject of this play during his military arrest at Stuttgart.

A letter from Meier arrived at last, to say, that while "Fiesco" remained unfit for the stage, Dalberg could not make the proposed advance; that the work must be completed before he could say more. No disappointment could be more cruel. But Schiller bore it undauntedly. He uttered no complaint; not one harsh, one indignant word passed his lips. He prepared only to comply with the condition that was imposed. The friends were reduced to a few small coins, when Streicher received thirty florins, for which he had written to his mother; and with this aid they left Frankfort. A line was, however, first dispatched to Meier, requesting him to meet and agree upon some place in which "Fiesco" might be completed with safety and in repose.

Finally, it was settled that Schiller should take up his residence in an inn at Oggersheim, once more changing his name from Ritter to Schmidt; and here, still accompanied by the devoted Streicher, he shut himself up to compose his glorious taskwork. But so much, while most occupied, did his mind shrink from what was ordained to it, that, instead of completing "Fiesco," his domestic drama of "Cabal and Love" engrossed all his thoughts and labours. Perhaps in a play which sought to prove the tyranny and the prejudice of conventional rank, he found something more congenial to his peculiar condition than the loftier conception of the conspirator of Genoa. The two friends shared one chamber, one bed; the Poet had his play—the Musician his instrument. And Streicher, whom we esteem no less for his self-devotion than Schiller for his indomitable courage, soothed the labours of his friend with the notes of his clavichord. Again their resources were exhausted; again poor Streicher applied to his mother for the money intended for his professional journey to Hamburgh. Necessity then tore Schiller from the new work, and restored him to the old. Early in November "Fiesco" was completed.

But fresh disappointments awaited Schiller. After the suspense of a week, Dalberg reported of "Fiesco" that a part of it was not yet fitted for the stage, and that it must either be rejected or improved. Nothing could be more chilling, more laconic, more heartless, to all appearance, than the reply of this literary courtier. Schiller had been greatly instigated in his flight from Stuttgart by his reliance on Dalberg's professions of esteem and friendship. And now not a word to comfort, much less a florin to support! Before the laborious student rose the sense of a condition thoroughly desolate and alarming—the recollection of his debts at Stuttgart; more than all, the remorse of having implicated his faithful friend in his own ruin. It was evident that Dalberg, with that sympathy which all courtiers have for the grievances of all courts, regarded Schiller as a political offender, and feared to befriend one with whom a Prince was displeased.

Two resources were left: firstly, to find for the two plays a publisher who would advance some money upon their probable profits; and secondly, to take advantage of a generous offer—an invitation which might well put to the blush the niggard heartlessness of Dalberg.

At the Stuttgart Academy, three young men of good birth, named Wolzogen, had been educated contemporaneously with Schiller. The eldest of these, Wilhelm, was afterwards amongst his most intimate friends; their mother, a widow in straitened circumstances, had known and admired the Poet at Stuttgart; she offered him an asylum in a small house she possessed at Bauerbach, about two miles from Meiningen. The advancement of her own sons was in the hands of the Duke of Würtemberg. She hazarded much by receiving into her house the persecuted fugitive; but the magnanimity of her friendship would not take the peril of a good action into account. Thither, then, Schiller resolved to fly. A Mannheim bookseller, named Schwan, advanced upon "Fiesco" sufficient to discharge the debt incurred at Oggersheim, and defray the expenses of the journey to Bauerbach. In a winter's night—the snow deep upon the ground—the generous Streicher bade him farewell; or rather, no word was spoken, no embrace exchanged—a long and silent clasp of the hand was the only token of an affection which had endured so much hardship, and consoled through so much sorrow. "But yet," says Schiller's German biographer, with simple eloquence, "the Musician, after fifty years, was filled with grief when he recalled the moment in which he had left a truly kingly heart—the noblest of the German poets—alone and in misfortune.

CHAPTER V.

Residence at Bauerbach.

As on a December evening, 1782, the wanderer beheld, beneath the old ruins of the Castle of Henneberg, the lights of the scattered houses of the village of Bauerbach gleaming through the deep snow, he felt, as he himself says, "like a shipwrecked man, who struggles at last from the waves." Here, though the family themselves were absent, everything that could comfort and welcome him, awaited. He remained unknown and secure ; a bookseller of eminence at Meiningen (Reinwald), who afterwards married his sister, was admitted to his secret, and cheered his solitude with books and his own society. Sometimes he made a companion of the steward of the property, played with him at chess, or wandered, with him, through the woods which surround that country.* The calm, the security and the solitude were, at first, beneficial to his mind and to his labours. The two plays were completed, and despatched to the bookseller, Schwan. But now, his ardent imagination, having thrown off its tasks, began to prey upon itself. He passed, though for a short time, and with reluctance, into that state common to all good men, in proportion to their original affection for their species— *misanthropy.* No man ever was, in reality, a misanthrope, but from too high an opinion of mankind, and too keen a perception of ideal virtue. "I had embraced," complains Schiller, "half the world, with feelings the most glowing, to find a lump of ice within my arms." † The wild and

---

* A singular anecdote is related by Madame von Wolzogen. One day, in his walk with the steward, Schiller paused in a lonely spot between wild rocks, and was seized with a notion that a dead body lay below. In fact, a poor carrier had been murdered there, and his corpse had been buried in the very place.

† Shortly after this period, on his settlement at Mannheim, he announced his intention of translating Shakspeare's "Timon," and says, "In all Shakspeare there is no piece in which he more loudly and eloquently speaks to my heart—or in which I have learned more of the Science of Life."— *Rhein. Thal. Heft.* 1, s. 13.

desolate scenery around him—the dreariness of winter—
served to increase the gloom that seized him. His prospects
were, in reality, such as might render the hardest sensitive,
and the boldest anxious. The present might be safe, but
at any moment he might be cast again upon the world.
His gratitude to his friends made him feel that his asylum
must be resigned the moment the Grand Duke discovered
it. And, even as it was, could his spirit long bear the
thought of dependence, obscurity, and disguise? Still he
was without a country, still without a career. He
seriously thought of abandoning poetry, and returning to
the medical profession; sometimes the wilder notion of
exile to England—to America—possessed him. This state
of mind was, perhaps, fortunately invaded by a romantic
and hopeless fancy, rather than the love for which he mis-
took it.

Madame von Wolzogen visited Bauerbach.

In Charlotte, the youngest daughter of his benefactress,
Schiller found an image to replace his Laura. He could
not expect encouragement from the mother, nor does it
appear that his attachment was returned by Charlotte;
but he was at that age when feeling is easily awakened,
and as easily misunderstood by the heart which feels it.
The love of youth, before it settles for life, hovers over all
to whom the fancy allures it. The Cupid, with the ex-
panded wings, and the arrow on the string, is but the
false Anteros:—In the true Eros, the wings are folded, and
the bow is broken. Certainly this was the most critical
period in the life of Schiller, moral and intellectual. If
new persecutions, whether of power or of opinion, had now
befallen him, it is at least doubtful whether he would
have ever attained to a name at once so revered and so
beloved—whether indignation and disgust might not, in a
spirit so proud and so impetuous, have ripened into permanent defiance of the world, and its existing orders and
forms.* Who shall say whether it would have been in the
power of Schiller, in the nature of man, to have preserved
the genial purity and kindliness which had been the early
concomitants and softeners of his restless and fiery genius,
if, at this moment, he had undergone from the public of

* "Oh!" he exclaims, in a letter to Madame von Wolzogen, "you
cannot believe how *necessary* it is to me to find *noble* human natures!"

his fatherland the same fearful calumny and injustice which, in the anguish and the trial of existence, hooted Byron into exile? None of the earlier writings of Byron can be compared for a moment, in their offences against settled opinions, to those which the youth of Schiller sent forth to agitate society and inflame the mind. "The Robbers," "Fiesco," "Cabal and Love," are, one and all, defiances of Prescription. The revolutionary stamp is upon each. To ordinary observers they might well appear the more dangerous from the systematic purpose which seemed to pervade them all. In England, such works would have given impunity to the slander of literary envy, and the bigotry of political hate. But there was a nobler temper in the German public;—there was granted to Schiller what, despite the greater temptations of birth, and beauty, and prevalent example, was never conceded to our immortal countryman—the allowance for unsettled youth and imperfect education;—and the result should be a lesson to the public in all lands. His manhood was the splendid redeemer of his youth.

Suddenly, in the midst of Schiller's anxious gloom and conflicting emotions—at the very moment when hypochondria was fast darkening over his heart and unnerving his intellect—the sun broke out upon him. The Duke of Würtemberg, whose resentment never seems to have been ungenerous or vindictive, tacitly relinquished all thoughts of persecuting a man in whom the whole of Germany began to feel a romantic interest. The courtier Dalberg perceived that the time was come when, without imprudence, he might bring to the aid of his theatre the author of the most popular drama of the time. He invited Schiller to Mannheim. The young Poet's plays were to be produced upon the stage—the object of an ambition, modest as to temporal means, vast as to intellectual empire, was attained. He was appointed, with a fixed, though very limited salary, Poet to the Theatre at Mannheim, then the first in Germany. On the evening of the 22nd July, 1783, he arrived at the town in which the foundations of his dramatic glory had been laid; and, at the house of Meier he was once more beheld—but, this time, with a cheerful and radiant countenance — by his faithful Streicher.

CHAPTER VI.

But it is one thing to print a drama—another to represent it. "Fiesco" still required great alterations to adapt it to the stage. One essential cause of the theatrical success of Schiller, was the earnest readiness with which he lent himself to the suggestions of practical criticism. He was not like many of our young authors who write for the stage, and will not sacrifice a passage to what they call the arrogant ignorance of managers and actors. Unless the Poet obtains and follows the advice of manager and actor, he may depend upon it that he will never command an audience. While employed upon the task of revising "Fiesco," and its companion Drama, Schiller was seized with fever, which exhausted his strength and protracted his labours. But, in nothing is Schiller more au example to us than in his iron perseverance and diligent industry. These were the very elements of his genius. Perhaps they are so of all genius that accomplishes what is great and lasting. Through weakness and through sickness he toiled on.

"Fiesco" was not so successful at Mannheim as had been anticipated. Schiller complained that the public of the Palatine could not understand it; that with them Republican Liberty was an empty sound. But, in Berlin and Frankfort, it produced a considerable sensation, which reacted on the Mannheim audiences, and soon secured its fame. It was followed, in March or April,[*] by "Cabal and Love," which obtained the most brilliant reception.

On the first representation of this drama, Streicher found his reward for all his friendship. He sate by the side of Schiller; he heard the rapturous applauses it excited; he

---

[*] On the 9th of March, according to Schwab; somewhere in April, according to Hoffmeister.

saw all eyes turned to the Poet; he had shared the adversity—he participated in the triumph.*

Schiller's existence was now assured. He had found a country, as well as confirmed his fame. He was acknowledged a subject of the Elector Palatine. He had no longer any cause of apprehension from the Duke of Würtemberg. He was elected a member of the German Literary Society established at Mannheim. The circle of his intimates was thus enlarged amongst men of the same pursuits, and his ambition corrected and guided, by comparison between himself and others. New resources were opened to him; and his ambition could not readily settle upon any one of the numerous objects by which it was allured. He proposed at first to translate "Timon of Athens," and "Macbeth," but ultimately returned to "Don Charles." This was the first drama, commenced in the retirement of Bauerbach, which he had attempted in verse; and herein he first ascended, though with an uncertain step, towards the higher and purer realm of ideal fiction, in which his genius finally fixed its home. A marked change, indeed, was now visible in his modes of thought. He took loftier conceptions of the aims and duties of the Poet. He became aware of the moral deficiencies of " The Robbers;" he meditated a sequel to that play, which should be an ample apology for its predecessor, and in which " all immorality should be resolved into the highest moral."† He reassumed his early instincts of the preacher; not indeed as from the pulpit, but from the boards. He laid down to others and to himself the principle, that the Stage should take its rank with the Church and the School amongst the primary institutions of a state. In proportion as representation must be more vivid than dead book-lore and cold narration, so assuredly might he think that the stage should work lessons deeper and more lasting than mere moralising systems.‡ Whether he did not over-estimate the possible influence of the theatre in modern times, may be reasonably doubted. But that very ex-

* At the end of the second act the audience shouted applause so much more emphatically than usual, that Schiller, taken by surprise, rose and bowed.
 † Schiller's " Brief an Dalberg," s. 85, &c.
 ‡ Hoffmeister.

aggeration could only serve to purify his ambition and elevate his aims.

Meanwhile, his pecuniary circumstances, though improved, and though, perhaps, sufficient for a strict economist, were not adequate to the wants of a man so liberal, so charitable, and so careless of detail and method. Wrapt in his ideal realm, he forgot the exigencies of practical life. "Hogarth," says his biographer, "might have been inspired by the disorder of the young Poet's chamber." His debt at Stuttgart still weighed upon him, till at length his landlord lent him the money to defray it. He resolved upon new efforts to emancipate himself from all difficulties. He undertook a periodical called the "Rhenish Thalia," from which he anticipated to reap an independence. In the announcement of this work he speaks thus of his own views and hopes: "I write as a Citizen of the World who serves no prince. Early I left my father-land, exchanging it for the great world, *Dec. 1784.* which I only beheld at a distance, and through a glass." He proceeds to speak of his education; his poetic enthusiasm; his "Robbers;" his flight from Würtemberg; and thus continues:—"All my former connexions are dissolved. The Public has become my all, my study, my sovereign, and my confidant. To the Public alone henceforth I belong. Before this tribunal, and this tribunal only, I take my stand. Something of greatness hovers over me as I resolve to know no restraint but the sentence of the world—appeal to no throne but the soul of Man!"

This frank and stately egotism was thoroughly characteristic of Schiller. And the reader will readily understand how much, as in the case of Byron, the admiration for the Poet became associated with interest in the Man. Grave men, whom he did not know, wrote to offer him their homage; fair maidens, whom he had not seen, transmitted to him their miniatures. But in the midst of his labours and his increasing fame, his heart was lonely. He pined for love and for female society. In the bustle of the town he recalled with a sigh the retirement of Bauerbach. Forgetful of the gloom which had, there, so often overshadowed his solitude, he looked self-deludingly back to the winter months he had spent amidst its pine-trees as amongst the happiest of his life. The image of Charlotte von Wolzogen haunted him; but it was rather as the ideal Egeria of the nympholept than as the one living woman who renders all others charmless and indifferent. "To be linked to one," he says, "who shares with us joy and sorrow; who meets us in our emotions, and accommodates her mood to our humours; at her breast to release our souls from the thousand distractions, the thousand wild wishes and unruly passions; and drown all the bitterness of Fortune in the enjoyment of domestic calm;—ah! such were the true delight of life." He proposed openly to Madame von Wolzogen for her daughter Charlotte; but, thoroughly convinced at last of the hopelessness of that pursuit, his desire for love in the abstract soon found its object elsewhere. Margaret, the daughter of Schwan the bookseller, was one in whom he might woo an equal, and reasonably hope to find a return for his affection. She possessed great personal beauty, and a lively turn of mind; "rather devoted," say, with some malice, the good German biographers, "to the world, to literature, and to art, than to the tranquil domestic duties." She was then nineteen years old, and the death of her mother had placed her at the head of the household. Schiller's literary intercourse with her father necessarily drew him much into her society; and about the autumn of 1784, the fair Margaret gained possession of a heart still somewhat too inflammable for constancy.*

With the new love he resumed the new drama; and the passion for Margaret burns in many a line which proclaims the affection of the ill-fated Carlos.

1785.

But new circumstances began to conspire against the repose of Schiller, and his continuance at Mannheim. The periodical he had commenced, without greatly increasing his resources, embroiled him with the actors. Those worthy personages were mightily concerned at the freedom of his criticisms; he in turn was no less aggrieved

---

* It appears, indeed, that in the interval Schiller had admitted the influence of some wilder and less refined passion than either Margaret Schwan or Charlotte von Wolzogen had inspired, and to which he alludes with frank regret, in a letter some years afterwards to the lady whom he married. The object of this passing fancy has apparently baffled the research of his biographers.

by their slovenly repetition of his verses, and their irre-
verent treatment of himself. His ambition had been
diverted into new paths, by the dignity of Councillor* of
the Duchy of Weimar, conferred upon him by the Duke,
who in a visit to Mannheim had granted him an audience.
The honour in which literary men were held in the court
of Weimar inflamed his imagination. He had not yet
entirely resigned the practical world for the ideal ; and in
Schiller, despite his want of economy and method, there
were talents and capacities which were not restricted solely
to the pen. One of those who knew him best says of
him, no doubt with truth, "that if he had been withheld from the destiny of a great poet, he could not have
failed, perforce, to have become a remarkable man of
action.† For action Schiller certainly possessed those
peculiar qualities which usually ensure success in a career
once fairly opened ;—indomitable will—the power of
earnest application—inflexible honour—and a strong sense
of justice.

The rank of Councillor to the Duchy of Weimar
thus opened to him a path more alluring than that in
which he passed, not over the flowers his youth had
fancied, as Poet to a Theatre. After much consultation
with some friends at Leipsic, and with Schwan, and in the
midst of all kinds of disgusts and difficulties in his residence at Mannheim, it was determined that he should
remove to Leipsic. He resolved there to devote himself
to Jurisprudence, and to use Poetry, if we may borrow the
admirable saying of Sir Walter Scott, "as his staff, not
his crutch." He communicated these intentions to
Streicher, who shared his new enthusiasm. What might
not so much industry, in a mind already exercised in
severe thought and arduous studies, accomplish in a few
years ? Some honourable appointment at the least in one
of the small Saxon Courts. The friends grew warm over
their hopes, and agreed at last to suspend all correspondence till the Poet was Minister, and the Musician Chapel
Master ! Thus ends—amidst new projects, and on the

* A merely nominal dignity—but it is difficult for an Englishman to
comprehend the eagerness with which these petty distinctions are sought
for in Germany.
† Scharffenstein. At a later period Goethe expressed the same opinion.

eve of a new flight—the First Period in the life and career of Friedrich Schiller.

He was only in his twenty-sixth year—and how much had he effected! His name was already a household word in Europe. His genius had not been stationary; the most marked improvement in taste, in thought, in self-cultivation distinguished his more recent from his earlier compositions. Even at this time, the genial and gentle Wieland had prophesied that Friedrich Schiller would be the first man of his age. The very misfortunes, the very errors of his life, had served to augment the true knowledge of genius—viz., experience of the heart—its sufferings—its passions—its infirmities. In "Fiesco," as in "The Robbers," there is much that is distorted and exaggerated, but the characters move in a far higher atmosphere—the language is chaster and more severe—the descriptive passages want nothing but rhythm to have the beauty and the charm of poetry. All the men are drawn on the large scale of heroes. The magnificence of Fiesco, and the austerity of Verrina, are no doubt contrasted with too distinct a force for the delicacy of art, but the fault is that of a giant, who has not yet learned to subdue and regulate his strength. Still more promise of real and permanent excellence is to be found in "Cabal and Love;" for, to idealise common life is impossible, save to those who have already perceived the great truths in which high Poetry moves and breathes. In these plays, the influences which we have noticed in our brief sketch of the state of German Literature, are visible. Through the lurid and stormy phantasies of French republicanism—through the hazy mists of Rousseau's passionate sentiment—may yet be discovered glimpses of the robust humanity of Herder—the noble earnestness of Lessing—the last especially. "Emilia Galotti" speaks in the Domestic Tragedy of "Cabal and Love," and its Odoardo transfuses something of his high spirit into the Verrina of "Fiesco." Yet finer influences than even these were now at work upon a mind ever shooting onward, or mounting upward. The study of Shakspeare — necessarily intense to one meditating the translation of "Timon" and "Macbeth"—led Schiller, not indeed to *imitate* a genius wholly dissimilar to his own, but to ponder upon the

1785.

attributes of that genius which were within his reach. He began the transition from what may be called the passionate and declamatory drama to the intellectual and analytical. He says of the hero of the tragedy on which he was now employed, " Carlos has the soul from Shakspeare's Hamlet—the pulse from me." There is little in common, it is true, between Carlos and Hamlet; but Schiller had made a great progress in his conceptions of art, when he studied a Hamlet, in order to create a Carlos.

But in this, as in the several periods of his life, the mirror of his heart and his genius is to be found in his minor poems. In their fervour and exaggeration—their beauties and defects — lives immortally the youth of Schiller.

CHAPTER VII.

Schiller's arrival at Leipsic—Proposes for Margaret Schwan—Removes to Dresden—His habits, studies, &c.—His infatuation, and departure for Weimar.

SCHILLER arrived at Leipsic in the midst of its famous Fair. His name was soon bruited abroad, and the throng pressed to see him. But though Schiller was not without that noble vanity which pants for applause, and takes enjoyment in renown, the curiosity of idlers could only offend his taste, and wound his pride. "It is a peculiar thing," he says, writing to Schwan, "to have an Author's name. The few men of worth and mark who on this account offer their acquaintance, and whose esteem confers pleasure, are too greatly outweighed by the swarm who, like flesh-flies, buzz around the Author as a monster, and claim him as a colleague on the strength of a few sheets of blotted paper. Many cannot get it into their heads that the author of "The Robbers" should be like any other mother's son. They expected at least a crop, the boots of a postilion, and a hunting-whip!"

Meanwhile Schiller continued his contributions to "The Thalia," in which a considerable portion of "Carlos" appeared; laboured with assiduity at the completion of that drama; and composed, in a happy moment, "The Hymn to Joy," by far the noblest lyrical poem he had yet achieved. Insensibly the more worldly ambition with which he had quitted Mannheim, died away. The profession of Jurisprudence was not adopted; but, still anxious to found a livelihood upon some basis more stable than Literature, he meditated a return to Medicine; and, encouraged, perhaps, by the attention and respect he received at Leipsic, he ventured now to demand the hand of Margaret Schwan. After a preface at once modest and manly, he thus opened himself to her father: "My free and unconstrained access to your house afforded me the opportunity of intimate acquaintance with your amiable daughter; and the frank kind treatment with which both you and she honoured me, tempted my heart to entertain the bold wish of becoming your son. My prospects have hitherto been dim and vague; they begin now to alter in my favour. I will strive with more continuous vigour when the goal is clear. Do you decide whether I can reach it, when the dearest wish of my heart supports my zeal. Yet two short years, and my whole fortune will be determined. . . . The Duke of Weimar was the first person to whom I disclosed myself; his anticipating goodness, and the declaration that he took an interest in my happiness, induced me to confess that that happiness depended on a union with your noble daughter. He expressed satisfaction at my choice. I have reason to hope he will do more, should it come to the point of completing my happiness by this union. I shall add nothing further. I know well that hundreds of others might offer your daughter a more splendid fate than I at this moment can promise her; but that any other heart can be more worthy of her, I venture to deny." *

A bookseller is generally the last person to choose, as his son-in-law, an Author. He has seen too much of the vicissitudes of an Author's life, and of the airy basis of an Author's hopes in the future, to be flattered by the proposals of a suitor who finds it easier to charm the world than to pay the butcher. He wrote to Schiller a refusal, implying that his daughter's character was not in unison with her wooer's. Till then, a correspondence had been carried on between the young persons; this, Schiller properly and honourably now broke off, to Margaret's surprise, and apparently to her grief, for her father had not communicated to her Schiller's proposal,—a discreet reserve which seems to prove that he did not reckon on her free acquiescence in his reply. The friendship between Schiller and Schwan, however, still continued, and the remembrance of Margaret never wholly faded from Schiller's heart. "Like all noble and manly natures," says Madame von Wolzogen, "Schiller ever retained an affectionate remembrance of the woman who had inspired him with

* We have borrowed the translation of this extract from Carlyle's "Life of Schiller"—the *Boston* edition, 1833.

tender emotion. These recollections moved him always, but he rarely spoke of them; for love with him was always earnest and solemn; not the sensual and fickle boy, but the young Divinity,—who unites himself with Psyche."

Perhaps, to dissipate his disappointment by new change, Schiller yielded to the invitation of friends he had secured at Dresden, and at the end of the summer he repaired to that city, and made a home in the house of Körner, lately appointed Councillor of Appeals * (*Appellations-Rath*), and newly married to Minna Stock, an enthusiastic admirer of Schiller.†

Körner's house was placed on the banks of the Elbe, near Loschwitz. A summer-house in the garden, surrounded by vineyards and pine-woods, was soon surrendered to the Poet, and became his favourite retreat. Here "Don Carlos" made effective, though not rapid progress. This Tragedy, the first (as we have before observed) in which Schiller superadded the purer form and the more refined delineations of Poetry to the vigour and effect of the Drama, put the seal upon his fame. Hitherto, with all the admiration of the many, he had not won to himself that more durable, that more enviable reputation, which is maintained and confirmed by the graver few. But judges, the most critical and refined, shared for "Don Carlos," in the closet, the enthusiasm it excited on the stage.

But, while engaged in the completion of this Drama, Schiller's prodigious activity had already extended the realm his genius was destined to subdue and overspread. Besides the sketch of a Play—"The Misanthrope"—never finished, he conceived the idea of his Romance, called "The Ghost Seer," and collected materials for the historical works he began to meditate. For History, indeed, his mind was already prepared by the earnest and thoughtful study of character, and of the philosophy of events, which had been brought to bear on "Don Carlos." And now this restless and ever-inquiring mind arrived at that stage in which, between the enthusiasm of youth, and the wisdom of manhood, is so often placed the transition-

---

* Father to the poet Theodor Körner.

† Minna Stock was one of the young ladies who had honoured Schiller with their miniatures.

interval of Doubt. That intensity of religious faith and conviction which had characterised his boyhood, had, perhaps, been somewhat roughly shaken by the hard bigotry of his teachers at the Stuttgart Academy; but there is evidence to show that it existed during the composition of the "Robbers." Amongst his earlier Poems is one called "Letter from Julius to Raphael, from an unpublished Romance." This Romance afterwards took the shape and title of "Philosophical Letters between Julius and Raphael," of which only a fragment was printed, but in which the scepticism of the Author is first apparent. There is no doubt that this work was remodelled and rewritten during Schiller's sojourn at Dresden, and no reason to suppose that, in its earlier form, it contained the matter for just offence, subsequently admitted.

In these letters appears a crude and wavering conflict between Spinozism and Kantism. With Kant's great work on "Pure Reason," Schiller seems to have been first acquainted, but only by hearsay, at Leipsic or Dresden, between 1785-87. It was not till some years afterwards, in 1791, that he studied Kant at the fountain-head, and learned from him, if not a precisely orthodox Christianity, at least that æsthetical form of religion to which the great German has led so many, who would otherwise have been lost in the pathless wilds of infidelity. But now, much that Schiller composed, shows the doubt and conflict of his mind—a state, to one so constitutionally devout, of great anguish and despondency, and to which, in his later writings, he has many solemn and pathetic allusions. In the "Philosophical Letters" is to be found the illogical yet brilliant fallacy of Pantheism, which bewildered hopelessly the more erratic intellect of Shelley, but which did not long delude the robust understanding of Schiller. In the Poems which he composed at this time, denominated by critics the Second Period of Schiller, the conflict is visible, though subdued. It was in conformity with this state of mind that Schiller—in whom the intellect was no less strong than the imagination—should turn to that positive and actual Something which is found in the external history of man., Plans too large for one writer to accomplish, hovered before his ambition—some history that might be to practical narrative what the vast conccption of Herder suggested to the theory in which history should be told.

He meditated, and, in part, undertook, what, indeed, if ever accomplished suitably, would be one of the greatest records in the world—"A History of all the more remarkable Conspiracies and Revolutions of Modern Times." Meanwhile his private life had at once its charms and its sorrows. The love of solitude still clung to him. He was seen in the morning, wandering along the banks of the Elbe, thoughtful and alone ; or, like Byron at Venice, when the lightning flashed and the storm burst, tossed in his gondola upon the waves. He disliked, and sought to shun, miscellaneous, and especially what is called fashionable society ; he carried his earnest mind, and his love of freedom, into all circles,—impatient of the talk that was frivolous, and the etiquette that was restrained. But he generally devoted some portion of the day to the interchange of mind with the congenial ;—artists, men of letters, or even those who, simple and unaffected, interested his heart, if they could not appeal to his intellect.

Shy and silent in the crowd, he was eloquent with those familiar to him, and his conversation was yet more charming from his simple kindliness, than from the stores which it displayed : this was the bright side of his private life, —the reverse of the medal is only darkly shadowed out. Before his visit to Dresden, Schiller had formed an acquaintance with a young woman named Sophy Albrecht, intended for the stage ; he had taken a strong interest in her professional career, and he met her again at Dresden, as one of the most celebrated actresses of the day. He visited at her house on familiar terms, and there, one evening, after the play was over, he saw a young, blue-eyed stranger, who made upon him an impression equally deep and sudden. This girl was the eldest daughter of a Saxon widow, who lived upon a small pension, and whose husband had been an officer in the army. He afterwards encountered the fair Julia (such was the young lady's name) at the "Redoute," and ventured to accost her. The mother was, by all accounts, an artful and abandoned person, who did not scruple to put to profit the beauty of her daughter. She saw, in the admiration of so distinguished a poet, the means of widening Julia's already lucrative notoriety. Schiller was accordingly lured into an intimacy which occasioned the most serious anxiety to his friends.[*] It seems uncertain whether Julia, who appears to have followed her mother's depraved counsels with something of reluctant shame, returned the passion she had inspired. There was that in Schiller to have won a worthier affection, despite the unflattering portrait which Sophy Albrecht, in her coarse taste of actress, has drawn of the young Poet.

Schiller, no doubt, at that time, and indeed from his entrance into youth, had lost the mere physical beauty which he seems to have possessed as a child, when his sister compared his countenance, shaded with locks of gold, "to an Angel's head." He was tall, extremely thin, though muscular, and large of bone; his neck was long (a noble defect, which is never without dignity), and his dress was rude and neglected. His face was not handsome, perhaps, in the eyes of actresses,—whose profession leads them to admire show and colour in all things,—but so noble a countenance has rarely been given to the sons of Genius; true, the complexion was pale, the cheeks somewhat hollow, and the dark auburn hair, though rich and profuse, had a deep tinge of red, but the forehead was lofty and massive, somewhat receding towards the temples when regarded in profile (a peculiarity found in most men of characters brave and determined). His eyes, described variously as blue, brown, and dark gray, and probably shifting in colour with the light,[†] were, though deep-sunken, singularly brilliant and expressive; and his nose, if too large for perfect symmetry of feature, was finely formed. His personal appearance, in short, harmonised with his intellectual character: and as, in Goethe, the pre-eminent attribute both of outward form and mental accomplishment was beauty;[‡] so, in Schiller, the pre-eminent attribute in both

* Döring, Madame von Wolzogen, Hoffmeister, Schwab.

† Madame von Wolzogen says their colour was undecided, between blue and light brown. His sister calls them blue: one of his College friends, dark gray.

‡ Goethe was, perhaps, the handsomest poet of whom we have any record. With a beauty of face not inferior to that of Milton or Byron, he had advantages of stature denied to either,—and that air of majestic dignity which is beauty in itself. We remember being very much struck with a comparison between two portraits of Byron and Goethe, taken when each was about the same age, viz., twenty-one. There was a strong likeness between the two, though Goethe's features, not less symmetrical, were larger and more manly: but the contrast in the expression was startling. The Ger-

was nobleness. If, as one who remembered him well declares, the colossal bust of Dannecker alone shows him as he really was in life, no one who has ever seen that likeness will deny, that it is a countenance which strikingly arrests the admiration, and deeply engrosses the interest—a certain grandeur, both of outline and expression, dwarfs into effeminacy whatever portraits of more justly proportioned beauty may be placed beside it. But the actress, describing Schiller at this time, could see only, as was natural to such an observer, the gray, threadbare frock—the general disdain of the toilette—the awkwardness given by pride and reserve to the movements of the tall figure—the indulgence of Spanish snuff—and the stoop of the " ever-thoughtful head." . . Whether or not the fair Julia regarded Schiller with the same eyes as the actress is a matter, however, of very little importance:—not so the love felt by Schiller, since it not only gave rise to some of his poems, but coloured many immortal pages in the "Ghost-seer." His friends did their best to dispel his infatuation, and tear him from a connexion which they considered disgraceful to his name, ruinous to his means, and injurious to his prospects; finally, they succeeded in their appeals. He appears, indeed, to have become aware of the treachery * practised on him; and, after many a struggle between reason and passion, at last he tore himself away.

He had long meditated a journey to Weimar—then to Germany what Athens, in the time of Pericles, was to Greece; he now accepted a cordial invitation from a friend of his, Madame † von Kalb; and, in the month of July, 1787, he arrived at the little Court, brightened by a constellation of Art and Genius, before which the wealth and splendour of every capital in Europe was, at that day, but as foil and tinsel.

man lady who showed us the portraits, observed with truth,—" What dejection and discontent with the world is already stamped on Lord Byron's face !—What calm, yet sanguine energy—what hopeful self-confidence in Goethe's !" The several expression in either countenance seemed almost like a prophecy of either fate.

    * Julia had directed Schiller not to enter the house when a light was to be seen in a certain chamber, upon pretence of being then engaged in the domestic circle, while in truth she was receiving some more favoured admirer.

    † We have preferred (in this, and other instances), as more familiar to the English ear, the title of *Madame* to that of *Frau*, which is of course more rigidly correct.

CHAPTER VIII.

Goethe was absent from Weimar,—in " those fair Ausonian climates," the influence of which so powerfully affected his plastic genius, and served **1787.** to give to his after-creations that severe and statue-like repose which has, with all the beauty, something of the coldness and the terror, of Medusa :—Goethe was absent ; but at Weimar were Herder, Wieland, Böttiger, and other eminent men. Schiller was not disappointed in the charm of the place. " I think here," he writes, " at least in the territory of Weimar, to end my days—and at last, once more, to find a country." And yet Schiller was not at first fully appreciated at the court to which he was admitted. The Augustan character which Weimar had obtained, originated in the tastes and the talents of Amelia, mother to the reigning Duke. Her especial favourite was the polished and graceful Wieland, whom she had appointed tutor to her son, Karl August. She had been left a widow at the age of nineteen ; and fulfilled the duties of Regent during the minority of the young Prince.

To considerable talents for public business, and intuitive knowledge of the world, this remarkable woman added a strong affection for art ; and blended a thorough enjoyment of society with a keen thirst for knowledge. She acquired some acquaintance with the learned languages from Wieland, and translated Propertius. The circle of eminent men that she drew around her was attracted no less by her manners than her information and her abilities. But Schiller's genius, as yet made manifest, was not very congenial to a taste half French and half classical; and the Duchess-Mother does not seem to have been aware that, in the rude strength of the young Suabian, Germany had secured a classic author of her own.* Of all the literary men then at Weimar, the amiable Wieland was the most cordial to Schiller. Herder welcomed him, "but without warmth." Not till a much later period does the Duke himself appear to have taken any very vivid interest in his great visitor. The style of conversation, though intellectual and refined, was not that which Schiller was likely to enjoy —it was too critical, and perhaps too courtly—"more was babbled than was thought." But nothing is more beneficial to a man of genius, yet young, than to frequent society in which he is not over-estimated;—nothing more injurious than to be the sole oracle of his circle. From that period we date a purer and more dignified taste in Schiller—the tone of good society henceforth entered into his writings, and improved his manners: without weakening the one, it brought ease; without marring the simplicity of the other, it served to soften and make social.

At the end of October, Schiller made an excursion to Meiningen, on a visit to his eldest sister, who had lately married Reinwald. Madame von Wolzogen was also at Meiningen; at her house he found his old college friend, Wilhelm; and, with this companion he returned towards Weimar. They took the journey on horseback, and proposed by the way to visit some relations of M. von Wolzogen —a memorable visit; for now Schiller approached that bright period of his life when his wanderings and apprenticeship of mind and heart were alike to cease—when his genius settled into art—when his affections were concentered in a home.

At Rudolstadt, on the banks of "the soft winding Saale," in a valley bounded by blue mountains and sloping woodlands, lived a Madame von Lengefeld, with two daughters; the elder, Caroline, married to M. von Beulwitz, Hofrath of Rudolstadt, to whom (more distinguished by the name she acquired in a second marriage,

---

* Schiller attributes to the good offices of Goethe (despite his absence) the access to the Duchess Amelia.

von Wolzogen) we are indebted for a delightful, though somewhat high-flown Biography of Schiller; and the younger, Charlotte, unmarried, and then in her twenty-first year. The father had died when the children had severally arrived at the ages of thirteen and ten. Till that time they had been brought up in close retirement. But a situation at the Court of Weimar being destined for Charlotte when she should arrive at a fitting age, Madame von Lengefeld deemed it advisable to remove for a short time into Switzerland, as affording better facilities for the kind of education necessary for a girl intended to mix in the society of a brilliant and polished court. Three years before the date on which we now enter, the two sisters, who were related to the Wolzogens, had seen Schiller for the first time at Mannheim, and been favourably struck by his appearance. Madame von Lengefeld was then on her return from Switzerland; and the marriage of her elder daughter to M. von Beulwitz, served to settle her residence at Rudolstadt. The younger daughter, Charlotte, was highly prepossessing both in form and face. To borrow the description of her sister, " the expression of the purest goodness of heart animated her features; and her eye beamed only truth and innocence." She had a talent for landscape-drawing, and wrote poetry with grace and feeling. But above all, she had sympathy with whatever, in others, was noble in character, or elevated in genius;—her temper was sweet, and her disposition affectionate, faithful, and sincere.

At that time, however, Charlotte von Lengefeld was suffering under the melancholy which succeeds to the first fair illusions of life. Her early affections had been given to one from whom Fate had divided her. Her lover was in the army, and his duties called him to a distant part of the globe. Whether there were other obstacles, besides those of the young man's precarious profession, does not appear clear; but the family were opposed to the connection, and Charlotte von Lengefeld obeyed their wishes in struggling against the inclination she had formed.

Nothing could be more solitary and remote than the little valley in which the Lengefelds dwelt. No high-road intersected it: a stranger was a phenomenon. The appearance of two horsemen along the straggling street, one dark November evening, sufficed to create curiosity and interest. One of the riders, as he presented himself to the Lenge-felds, playfully concealed his face in his mantle, but the ladies recognised their cousin, Wilhelm von Wolzogen.

1787. The other was unknown or unremembered, till his companion announced the already famous name of Schiller. The simple and shy Suabian, usually distant with strangers, found himself at home at once in the family circle he had entered. The conversation fell on his recent publication, "The Philosophical Letters," and on his earlier poems. The earnest Schiller wished the Lengefelds to become acquainted with his "Carlos." A single evening sufficed to form an intimacy. On his departure, Schiller had already conceived the project of spending the next summer at Rudolstadt.

It so chanced that Wilhelm von Wolzogen had, from the early period of his student life at Stuttgart, cherished a romantic attachment to his fair cousin, Caroline von Lengefeld—now Madame von Beulwitz. Her marriage was not happy, and her health was delicate and infirm. Perhaps these circumstances served to confirm in Wolzogen an affection that then seemed hopeless, and was only nursed in secret. But as the two friends rode to Weimar, there was no doubt much in Wolzogen's conversation that found an echo in Schiller's breast. An impression more deep, and yet more calm, than woman had hitherto made upon him, recalled to the poet, amidst the distractions of Weimar and the labour of his occupations, the image of the soft and pensive Charlotte. Fortune smiled upon the dawn of this affection. Charlotte came to Weimar that very winter, on a visit to Madame von Stein, a friend of her family, and Schiller met her in the society of the place, but not frequently. Still he con-trived to approach her, as nearly as his delicacy and the consciousness of his precarious worldly circumstances would allow to his pride. He supplied her occasionally with his favourite authors ; she undertook the commission to find him a lodging at Rudolstadt for the summer. Occasion was thus found for the interchange of notes. On his part the correspondence was frank, but respectful; it proclaimed friendship and esteem—it did not betray more.

"There breathes," in these letters, says an eloquent biographer, "a noble, mild, discreet inclination, without a trace of passion;"—and here the writer we quote adds finely, "Our love is generally the effigy of the one we love. Schiller's present love was the gold, purified from the sensual passion which had mastered him at Dresden." It seems probable, however, that in neither was the memory of the previous love yet effaced : and this, while it served to invest their feeling for each other with a certain tranquillity, allowed them both more sensibly to perceive the remarkable congeniality between their minds, tastes, and tempers. Thus, as it were, the soul began to love, before the heart was thoroughly moved. Schiller's fame, and his somewhat graver years, permitted him to assume with his young friend a certain tone of warning and advice. That court life, to which she seemed then destined, was opposed to all his ideas of true dignity and pure happiness. And, in the lines closing the second division of his poems, he expresses, in verse, the ideas often repeated in his correspondence.*

In the midst of May, the following year, we find Schiller settled in the valley of Rudolstadt. 1788. He lodged in a house, half-an-hour's walk from the town,† and his chamber overlooked the banks of the Saale, flowing through meadows, and under the shade of venerable trees. There, on the opposite side of the river rose a hill, clothed with woods, at the foot of which lay tranquil villages; — there, high above the landscape, towered the castle of Rudolstadt. A small monument, crowned with a bronze copy of Dannecker's bust of Schiller, yet commemorates his sojourn in this happy valley, recalling Goethe's lovely words—

"The place that a good man has trod, remains hallowed to all time." ‡

It is thus that the elder sister speaks of those days — the fairest, perhaps, in the life of Schiller : — " How welcome was it, after some tedious visit,§ to see our genial friend approaching, beneath the fair trees that skirt the

* Lines to a Female Friend, written in her Album.
† In the village of Volkstädt.   ‡ Hoffmeister.
§ "*Kaffee-Visite*"—Coffee-visit: we should say Tea-party.

banks of the Saale!   A forest brook, that pours itself into that river, and was crossed by a little bridge, was the meeting-place at which we awaited.   When we beheld him in the twilight, coming towards us, a serener, an ideal life entered within us ; a lofty earnestness, and the graceful ease of a mind pure and candid, ever animated Schiller's conversation.   One seemed, as one heard him talk, to wander as it were between the immutable stars of heaven, and yet amidst the flowers of earth."

But Schiller, during this holiday of existence, was not idle in that solemn vocation of Author—of Instructor—of High Priest in Literature—to which he was sworn.   His evenings were devoted to Charlotte and her family, his mornings to study.   Here he laboured at his "History of the Revolt of the Netherlands"—at the correction of the tale so well known in England, "The Ghost Seer,"—here were concluded his "Letters upon Don Carlos"—and here was composed the first portion of the finest Poem written at this period of his life, "The Artists."   In the house of the Lengefelds, Schiller too, for the first time, met Goethe, on his return from Italy.   With the works of Schiller hitherto published, Goethe had no sympathy ; they contradicted his own theories of art, and they revolted his serene taste.   His manner to the Suabian was reserved and cold ; the pride of Schiller forbade him to make the first advances ; and though, as he wrote word to his friend Körner, the great idea he had formed of Goethe was not lessened by this first personal contact, he doubted if they could ever come into close communication.   "Much which is yet interesting to me — that which I yet wish and hope for — has had its epoch for him.   His whole being is, from its origin, constructed differently from mine ; his world is not my world ; our modes of conceiving things are essentially different : from such a combination, no secure substantial intimacy can result.   Time will try." *

About this time, at the instigation of the friendly and learned Wieland, Schiller turned his attention to the literature of Greece, with which he had hitherto

* Correspondence with Körner: Carlyle's "Life of Schiller."

but a very slight and superficial acquaintance. Nothing ever produces a more durable influence upon an author's genius, than the deliberate and systematic recurrence to Hellenic Poetry and Letters. Studied too early, they may often correct the taste at the expense of the fancy; but, studied with the mature thought of manhood, they only strengthen by purifying the inventive faculties. From that time Schiller began to comprehend true art, the vivifier of nature. From that time he became *an Artist*. Homer first engrossed his reverent delight; he passed to the Greek Tragedians; and the character of his mind, which inclined to philosophy, and the tendency of his genius, which was essentially pathetic and humane, rendered ample justice to the still wronged Euripides.*

From these new sources of inspiration came his noble Poem on the "Gods of Greece," and the classical perfection to which he brought "The Artists," before begun. The former of these Poems, which appeared in the "Mercury," superintended by Wieland, occasioned much offence to those who sought orthodoxy, even in the wildest dreams of the Poet. Although Schiller's mind at that time was certainly still unsettled, he yet grieved at an interpretation which he appears not to have foreseen; and at a subsequent period, he sacrificed many of his most brilliant stanzas, in order to purify the whole from whatsoever sincere and liberal piety could reasonably revolt at or regret. The remarkable frankness of his genius often, it is true, led him to depict or to imply his own struggles, and his own errors; but, in his stormiest interval of doubt, Schiller never contemplated the dangerous and dark ambition of unsettling the religious convictions of others.

Charlotte's admiration of "The Artists" greatly and seasonably served to cement the affection now ripening daily between them.† In fact, that fine poem no vulgar mind could really relish and admire. In one whom so elevated an appeal to the intellectual faculties could move

---

* We must not, however, suppose that Schiller ever attained to the facility of a *scholar* in Greek. . . In translating Euripides, he had constant need of the Latin version, and even the French of Brumoy.

† Madame von Wolzogen.

and animate, a lover might well behold the true companion of a poet's life, the true sympathiser in a poet's labours.

. This summer, otherwise so happy, was however darkened by the death of Madame von Wolzogen—Schiller's earliest protectress and second mother. He felt this affliction most deeply — his letter to her son, stillextant, is full of tender grief and delicate consolation.

In November, Schiller returned to Weimar, and occupied himself with the conclusion of his "Ghost Seer," and translations from Euripides. His chief relaxation and luxury were in his letters to Charlotte—letters unequalled in their combination of manly tenderness, confiding frankness, and refined yet unexaggerated romance ; still, though they now betrayed his own love, they did not formally hazard a declaration, or press for a return.

But early in the following year he was called to a new and more active career. Considerable portions of his history of the "Revolt of the Netherlands" had already appeared in Wieland's "Mercury," and excited considerable sensation. His friends wished to see him in one of those honourable situations, which, to the credit of Germany, afford shelter and independence to so numerous and brilliant a host of literary men. Goethe (though still not intimate with Schiller) displayed the calm magnanimity towards a rival natural to one in whom meanness was impossible, and employed the interest of his rank and his fame on behalf of the young historian.

1789.

Ætat. 30. Schiller was finally summoned to take the chair of Historical Professor at the University of Jena. It was not without modest reluctance, and a sense of his own deficiences in the details of history, that he undertook this office. His reception was such as might be anticipated—Four hundred students crowded to the Lecture-room—their presence and applause animated him—and his voice, naturally not strong, filled the Hall.

Amongst the German youth of this day, Schiller is the favourite ; he was then, says Hoffmeister, "the idol." His very defects as a Lecturer were not those on which young men would be severe or discriminating critics. Through the fire and the vigour which animated his language and his delivery, his ardent listeners were not likely to detect that redundant rhetoric, in which genius is too apt to conceal deficient information. He came too fresh to his task. He was acquiring one day, the knowledge he imparted the next. His facts had not been sufficiently meditated, nor his views sufficiently sobered down.

The society of Jena was more congenial to Schiller than that of Weimar—here nothing was courtly and restrained; here manners were diversified and opinions uncontrolled. To this illustrious University flocked the Professors and the Students from so many quarters, that each part of Germany found its representatives. The streets swarmed with all varieties of costume; the halls resounded with all differences of dialect. From the coarsest manners to the most super-refined; from the most limited information and the narrowest prejudice, to the profoundest wisdom— to the most liberal knowledge of the world; all forms of intellect were here mixed and confounded. What a school for a man, who had yet to complete his education by the study of his kind—not in books, but in actual life! The true poet must divide his existence between solitude and the crowd.

Schiller's correspondence with Charlotte continued; and his chivalrous devotion, the habitual intercourse with his noble and beautiful nature, had produced, at last, its full effect upon his young admirer. The old affection was effaced—the new affection confirmed. Charlotte owned to her sister, "that she had so lived in Schiller—he had so contributed to the formation of her mind, and to her happiness—that it seemed to her impossible to separate her lot from his."

The sisters were now staying at Lauchstädt: thither Schiller (escaping from Jena) visited them; a full explanation of what indeed must have been long since clear to both hearts, took place. Charlotte confessed that the love she had inspired was not unreturned, and promised, one day or other, to become his wife. True, as yet, it was hope deferred,—the fortunes of Schiller were still to be confirmed—the consent of Madame von Lengefeld still to be obtained. But it was enough for the present to feel that love was won. "How different," thus writes Schiller himself to Charlotte, on his return to Jena—"how different is all around me now, since in each step of my life thine image meets me: like a halo thy love hovers over me; like a fair mist does it clothe the face of Nature. I return from a walk: in the vast space of Nature, as in my lonely chamber, it is ever the selfsame atmosphere in which I move; and the fairest landscape serves but for the fairer mirror of one ever-enduring image. The remembrance of thee leads me back to the All; the All reminds me, in turn, of thee. Never so freely and so boldly could I traverse, in my enthusiasm, through the world of Thought as now that my soul has found a possession—a home; and no longer incurs the danger to lose itself in its wanderings: I know where again to find myself—in thee!"

At last came the long-yearned-for holidays. Schiller was released from his task; he fled back to the neighbourhood of Rudolstadt; he occupied his old chamber; he lived back his old life,—but in the brighter air of hope assured and of love returned. As yet, however, the lovers could only hold unwitnessed interviews by stealth; and to this date we must refer the exquisite love poems of the "Mystery" and the "Assignation." At last, but not till after long and severe probation, Schiller's hopes were crowned. After the failure of various schemes and projects, he obtained from the Duke of Saxe Weimar an appointment as Professor Extraordinary, with a salary of 200 rix dollars; and he now boldly applied to Madame von Lengefeld for the hand of her daughter. His suit was supported with zeal and earnestness by Madame von Stein, who had great influence with Madame von Lengefeld, and by M. von Dalberg,* elder brother to the Superintendent of the Mannheim stage, a nobleman of the highest rank, and the most admirable character. Madame von Lengefeld was moved by these instances; her prejudices gave way before the happiness of her daughter and the distinction of the suitor.

The title of Höfrath, conferred on Schiller by the Court of Meiningen, in the beginning of 1790, perhaps served yet more to content the good lady with her daughter's choice; and on the 20th February,

1790.

---

* Often confounded with Wolfgang von Dalberg, the Mannheim Baron; but an infinitely better person. It was to the elder brother that Schiller addressed the verses which accompanied the copy of "William Tell;" not, as Mr. Carlyle supposes, to Wolfgang, who deserved no such honour.

1790, after an intimate acquaintance of three years, the lovers were united.

Never was marriage, if we except only the narrowness of pecuniary circumstances, formed under more favourable auspices. The very age of the parties was that, in each, in which affection promises to be most durable, and the choice best considered. Schiller was about one-and-thirty, Charlotte about four-and-twenty: the length of the courtship had but served to found attachment upon esteem, while it augmented it by delay. The characters of bride and bridegroom were in the most perfect harmony; where they differed, it was but for each to improve the other; the refinement of the woman softened the impetuous man; the noble fire of the man warmed and elevated the gentle woman. Schiller was now really formed for the home he had so long sighed for. With all that depth of feeling and singleness of heart which are common to those fond of solitude, he now combined much which intercourse with mankind alone can give. As all misanthropy had fled from his heart, so all cynicism was now banished from his manners and his dress. He could no longer have been open to the caricature of the Dresden actress; and, independently of his fame, his genius, and his noble heart, a vainer woman than Charlotte von Lengefeld might have been proud of her choice.

CHAPTER IX.

SCHILLER was not disappointed in the hopes he had formed of domestic happiness. A few months after his marriage he exclaims in his correspondence: "Life is quite a different thing by the side of a beloved wife, than so forsaken and alone—even in summer. . . . The world again clothes itself around me in poetic forms; old feelings are again awakening in my breast. . . . Fate has conquered the difficulties for me. From the future I expect everything. . . . I think my very youth will be renewed, an inward poetic life will give it me again." * But, alas! even as these lines were written, that bodily enemy for which the mind so rarely prepares itself was at hand. Disease struck root into a constitution always delicate; he was attacked with a disorder in the chest; and though he recovered from its immediate severity, the head of the shaft was left behind. He never entirely recovered his health—from that time consumption rankled within.

1791.

He had been labouring more intensely than ever: to such a man, the consciousness that on his toils rested the worldly comforts of a wife who had resigned a Court for a scholar's roof stimulated industry into fever. He was immersed in severe studies connected with the historical pursuits to which he was now devoted, but the first and most peremptory injunction of his physician was repose to his intellect. . . . . . Repose—and his very subsistence rested on activity! At this crisis, however, one of those rare acts of munificence which are the god-like prerogatives of wealth, came to brighten poverty and comfort genius. A report of Schiller's death had been spread abroad: it had

* Extracted from the translation in Carlyle's "Life."

reached Denmark, at the moment when a princely circle of the Poet's admirers had resolved to repair to Hellebeck, near Copenhagen, and, amidst it sublime and enchanting scenery, to hold a court in his honour, and chant his "Hymn to Joy." Amongst these were the Danish Poet, Baggesen; the Count Ernest von Schimmelmann; the Prince Christian von Holstein Augustenburg and his Princess. Their grief, as enthusiastic as their admiration, changed the meditated festivities into a funeral solemnity.

They met at Hellebeck, on the shore of the sea, opposite the high rocks of Sweden, and Baggesen began to read the hymn. Clarinets, horns, and flutes chimed in to the song of the chorus; two additional stanzas, in honour of the supposed dead, were chanted, and may be thus translated :—

> " Hail to a friend, O choir of friends !
>   The dead we love shall live once more ;
> Bright to the bowers of heaven ascends
>   His soul : our lives it hovers o'er.

> *Chorus.*—Lift your attesting hands on high ;
>   Swear by this wine from lands made free,*
> Till found once more in yonder sky,
>   Faith to our brother's memory."

As the song ceased, all eyes wept.

Homage to the dead is a vulgar and idle tribute, if it come after neglect or injury to the living. The heart sickens at that mockery of admiration, which allowed Spenser to die of a broken heart, and threw copies of verses into his grave,—which suffered political vengeance to reduce Dryden to a bookseller's drudge, and insisted on burying his dust in the sepulchre of kings. To Schiller's biographers belongs the pleasing task of commemorating the only true homage ever rendered to a dead poet,— simply because the poet was *not* dead ! No sooner was the report confuted, than the noble mourners exulted to exchange ceremonial honours to the lifeless, for practical benefits to the living. A letter, from which we extract the purport, was sent to Schiller by the Prince von Augustenburg and Count Schimmelmann.

"*27th Nov.* 1791.

"Two friends, united through the citizenship of the

* *i.e.* French wine.

world, send this letter to you—noble man! Both are un-known to you—both love you and revere. They find in your recent works the mind and the enthusiasm which knit the bond of their own friendship; by the perusal of those works they accustom themselves to regard the author as a member of their own union. Great was their grief at the report of his death; their tears were not the scantiest of those which flowed from all good men by whom he was known and loved. The lively interest with which you have inspired us must excuse us from the appearance of officious importunity. They tell us that your health suffers from too severe an application, and needs for some time an entire repose. This repose your pecuniary circum-stances alone forbid you to enjoy. Will you grudge us the delight of contributing to your relief? We entreat you to receive, for three years, an annual gift of a thousand dollars." * The writers proceed with dignity to touch upon their rank, and to imply a delicate hope that it may not prove an obstacle to their request; they desire not to wound his spirit of independence, or parade the ostenta-tion of patronage. "We know no pride but this,—to be men!—citizens in that great Republic whose boundaries extend beyond single generations—beyond the limits of earth itself." They proceed to invite him into Denmark: " For we are not the only ones here who know and love you; and if, after the restoration of your health, you desire to enter into the service of our state, it would be easy for us to gratify such an inclination. Yet think us not so selfish as to make such a change in your residence a condition : we leave our suggestion to your free choice; we desire to preserve to Humanity its instructor, and to this desire every other consideration is subordinate."

There may be in this letter—which the gratitude of Literature should render no less imperishable than the works of him to whom it is addressed—something of the romantic exaggeration, in tone and phrase, which betrays the influence of the French cosmopolites; but that in-fluence here affected men of noble hearts, who desired to have an excuse in philanthropy for individual beneficence; not, as with the maudlin confraternities of France, an

---

* A sum which, at Weimar, would go perhaps three times as far as it would in England.

excuse, in the citizenship of the world, from doing good to a single creature !

The effect such a letter produced on Schiller no one can describe—every one can imagine. Nothing but the declaration of his physicians that a visit to so northern a climate would be fatal, prevented him from hurrying to benefactors so delicate and so munificent. In a letter to Baggesen, the depth and manliness of his gratitude are apparent; and this letter is the more interesting, inasmuch as it expresses those views of the dignity of letters, and that repugnance to regard art as a *livelihood*, which may serve the ambition of youthful genius at once with warning and emulation.

"From the cradle of my intellect till now," writes Schiller, "have I struggled with Fate; and since I knew how to prize intellectual liberty, I have been condemned to want it. A rash step, ten years since, divided me from every other practical livelihood, but that of a writer. I had given myself to this calling before I had made proof of its demands, or surveyed its difficulties. The necessity of pursuing it befel me before I was fitted for it by knowledge and intellectual maturity. That I felt this—that I did not bound my ideal of an author's duty to those narrow limits within which I was confined—I recognise as a favour of Heaven. As unripe, and far below that ideal which lived within me, I beheld all which I gave to the world." With feeling and with modesty Schiller proceeded to enlarge upon the conflict between his circumstances and his aspirations, to touch upon the melancholy with which he was saddened by the contemplation of the great masterpieces of art, ripened only to their perfection by that happy leisure denied to him. "What had I not given," he exclaims, "for two or three tranquil years; that, free from all the toils of an author, I could render myself only to the study, the cultivation of my conception,—the ripening of my ideal!" He proceeds to observe that in the German literary world, a man could not unite the labour for subsistence with fitting obedience to the demands of lofty art; that for ten years he had struggled to unite both; and that the attempt to make the union only in some measure possible, had cost him his health . . . . "In a moment when life began to display its whole value—

when I was about to knit a gentle and eternal bond between the reason and the phantasy—when I girded myself to a new enterprise in the service of art, death drew near. This danger indeed passed away; but I waked only to an altered life, to renew, with slackened strength and diminished hopes, my war with Fate. So the letter received from Denmark found me! I attain at last the intellectual liberty so long and so eagerly desired. I win leisure, and through leisure I may perhaps recover my lost health; if not, at least for the future, the trouble of my mind will not give nourishment to disease. If my lot does not permit me to confer beneficence in the same manner as my benefactors, at least I will seek it where alone it is in my power,—and make that seed which they scatter, unfold itself in me, to a fairer blossom for humanity." And he did so!

Thus enabled to enrich while he relaxed his mind, Schiller devoted himself with ardour to the study of Kant.* With the closer knowledge of this philosopher—who, whatever his defects, certainly did more than any other reasoner to counteract the hard and narrow scepticism of the French Encyclopædists,—to bring imagination to the aid of Faith, and at once to enlarge the tolerance of the sectarian and to calm the doubts of the seeker—really commences the Third Period of Schiller's intellectual career, though his biographers postpone its date to the time when its fruits became practically apparent.

In June, 1792, Schiller and his wife visited Körner at
1792.   Dresden: On their return, they received Schiller's mother and youngest sister, Nannette, whom he had not seen for eight years. The tender associations thus revived led the mind of the exile back to his Suabian home. In August, 1793, the Schillers, therefore, commenced an excursion to the Poet's father-land.† At

---

* Conz, Professor of Poetry and Eloquence at Tübingen, who visited Schiller in 1792, says that he was then thoroughly absorbed in Kant. Conz gives a charming picture of Schiller's simple and frugal life. "He was," says the Professor, "Humanity itself, and his excellent wife a pattern of complaisance and modesty."

† About this time Schiller's sister-in-law, according to the German law, annulled her marriage with M. von Beulwitz. She afterwards married Wilhelm von Wolzogen, attached to her, as we have before said, from his earliest youth. She also joined the Schillers at Heilbronn.

Heidelberg, Schiller met once more the object of his early love, Margaret Schwan, now like himself married to another; he saw her with a deep emotion, which his wife comprehended too well to resent; he who sees, unmoved, the one in whom he formerly garnered up his hopes of home, can never constitute the happiness of the home he has found with another.

At Heilbronn, unsurpassed, even in Germany, for the peculiar beauties of its landscape, the family of Schiller met the long-lost wanderer. He stood *1793.* amongst them no longer a rude stripling, a penniless exile; —but the favourite of princes, the idol of a people—his hopes fulfilled—his destiny assured; crowned already with renown, and calm in the certainty of triumphs more splendid yet to come. He had reached the time when, without humiliation, he could humble himself to his native sovereign. With Schiller's wild love for liberty, he never was without that loyalty, which is almost inborn with the children of the North. He wrote to the Duke of Würtemberg such a letter as that loyalty might dictate; he received no direct reply, but was informed, privately, " that the Duke would be ignorant of his movements if he reentered Würtemberg." Schiller then repaired to Ludwigsburg, where he was in the immediate neighbourhood of his father's house, and under the medical care of one of his early friends, von Hoven, now Court physician. *Sept. 14,* Here he first enjoyed the happiness he had *1793.* long coveted; he became a father. His earnest, manly, and affectionate nature was precisely that which finds children at once a charge and a blessing. Now he would play for the hour together with his " Gold-son, his heart's Karl," * as he named his firstborn; now shut himself up to study Quintilian, on the plan of education to be pursued.

Those who remembered the youth of Schiller were startled by the change which years and circumstance had effected; all that was sharp and hard in his character was gone. His early fire was softened—it warmed more and alarmed less; there was far greater grace in his demeanour. His ancient neglect of appearance and dress was replaced

* Conz. Schwab. Hoffmeister.

by a decent elegance; his even humour scarcely allowed them to recognise the impetuous and stormy stripling they had known ten years before.* But, alas! with the mental change had come the physical; the features were drawn and hollow, the complexion wan and haggard. Illness frequently confined him to his bed—Kant and Homer his companions; and at this time the grand outline of "Wallenstein," before chalked out, began to receive colour and fullness; he devoted himself to its composition principally at night, diversifying the poetical task with the first sketch of his "Philosophical Essay upon Æsthetical Cultivation."

During his residence at Ludwigsburg the Grand Duke Karl died.†   Schiller was asked by his father to congratulate the Duke's successor in a poem—we need scarcely say that he refused. He could not seem to rejoice at the death of a man who had been both his benefactor and his persecutor. Schiller was never more himself than when, standing by his sovereign's grave, with von Hoven, he spoke thus touchingly:—"Here rests this once active restless man! He had great faults as a Prince, greater yet as an individual. But the first were overwhelmed by his high qualities, and the remembrance of the last must be buried with the dead. I say to thee, therefore, if thou hearest one speak of him disparagingly, as he lies there—trust that man *not !*—he is no good, at least, he is no noble man." •At Ludwigsburg he formed an acquaintance with Cotta the bookseller, which had considerable influence on his later labours. In connection with this publisher, a new literary periodical, the "Horen," was chalked out, and a new political journal, intended to take the lead over all its German contemporaries. Of this last Schiller proposed to assume the editorship; but his growing disinclination for objects less noble than the art of which Philosophy had brought

Oct. 24, 1793.

---

* Von Hoven, ap. Mad. von Wolzogen.

† Biographers have raised a doubt if Schiller had removed from Heilbronn to Ludwigsburg before the Duke's death. But it seems quite clear that he was at Ludwigsburg early in September, since von Hoven, who resided at Ludwigsburg, attended his wife in her confinement,—Sept. 14th.

him clearer and sublimer views, induced him happily
to resign this notion. The political journal was, however, set up by the publisher, and exists to-day in high
repute, under the well-known name of the "Allgemeine
Zeitung."

CHAPTER X.

THIRD PERIOD.

The Horen and Musenalmanach—Two deaths in Schiller's family—Return
from philosophy to poetry—The summer-house—Influence of Goethe on
Schiller's genius— Appearance of Wallenstein.

In May, 1794, Schiller returned to Jena, his body
worn to a shadow; * his mind more than ever vigorous
and resolved. Here he found the charm of a friendship
more complete, and more sympathetic alike in intellect and
in taste, than he had yet known. Wilhelm von Humboldt
had settled at Jena, with a charming wife, whom he had
lately married;—the two families contracted the closest
intimacy. The undertaking of the " Horen " was now
seriously commenced, as a monthly Periodical, with the
assistance of the greatest names in Germany,—Goethe,
Herder, Jacobi, Matthisson, &c. In this journal Schiller
desired to consummate an idea which had long haunted
him, and which had been but imperfectly developed in the
"Thalia." It may be said that this idea had grown out
of the vast and luminous humanity of Herder, and ripened
under the influence to which Herder was most opposed—
that of Kant. The journal was intended to merge all that
belonged to sect, to party, and the day, and devote itself
to all that could interest the common family of man ; so
far, this was akin to Herder ; but Schiller sought the
interest, not in broad and popular topics, but in that
æsthetical cultivation—that development of ideal beauty,
which, since his study of Kant, he regarded as the flower
and apex of human accomplishment. But the enterprise
of this periodical, memorable in much, is so principally on
account of the union it established between Goethe † and
Schiller—an union inestimable to both, and therefore to

* Goethe thought, on seeing Schiller, that he had scarcely a fortnight's
life in him.—Hoffmeister. Eckermann.

† We need scarcely say that Goethe's fame and position had prodigiously
increased since the publication of Schiller's " Robbers."

tho world. Hitherto, these eminent men had moved in separate orbits; and Goethe's calm kindness to his great rival had not advanced to intimacy; but now the friendship Goethe felt for Schiller's wife, whom he had known from her childhood; the ties formed by acquaintances in common; and that power of attracting others to his designs, which Goethe himself has remarked in Schiller; drew them closely together, and served to form a bond which death only could dissolve. Goethe says, with noble candour, in his corrrespondence, "I really know not what might have become of me, without the impulse received from Schiller;"—and he procceds to enumerate the writings which had never been produced but for the co-operation of the only man from whom—had Goethe been one fraction less than Goethe—he would have been kept aloof by jealousy and alarm. Into this journal Schiller, appointed chief editor, poured some of the finest thoughts to be found in his prose writings; embodied in the form of philosophical criticism. Here too, and in the "Musenalmanach," an annual publication, also undertaken in conjunction with Goethe, somewhat later, appeared tho immortal lyrics, which perhaps established the most popular and indisputable of Schiller's claims to admiration, purely and singly as the Poet. In this last periodical finally flashed forth those Epigrams, under the name of Xenien; sometimes personal and caustic, sometimes thoughtful and ideal, which set the literary world of Germany in a blaze. The connection between Goethe and Schiller had excited much jealous hostility amongst many lesser writers; an hostility wreaked upon the "Horen," and avenged in the "Musenalmanach" by these laconic sarcasms. The sensation they excited was prodigious; though they can inspire but a lukewarm interest in the public of a foreign country.* Many of the more personal epigrams Schiller had the grace to withdraw from the subsequent collection of his poems; and in

* Nevertheless, their effect upon German literature yet endures. Mr. Carlyle observes—("Miscellanies," vol. i. p. 67)—that "the war of all the few good heads in the nation with all the many bad ones, began in Schiller's Musenalmanach for 1767;" and adds that, "since the age of Luther, there has scarcely been seen such strife and stir in the intellect of Europe." We do not quite subscribe to Mr. Carlyle's admiration for "the new critical doctrine," which dates from the Xenien.

this withdrawal he could afford to sacrifice what critics have termed his best. In the midst of these labours he had the misfortune to lose his youngest sister, Nannette, a girl of promise and beauty; and in the same year, after a lingering disease, his father. He felt both losses acutely; the last perhaps the most: but in his letters it pleases us to see the philosopher return to the old childlike faith in God, the reliance on Divine goodness for support in grief, the trust in Divine mercy for the life to come. For it has been remarked with justice that, while Schiller's *reason* is often troubled in regard to the fundamental truths of religion, his *heart* is always clear. The moment death strikes upon his affections, the phraseology of the schools vanishes from his lips—its cavils and scruples from his mind: and he comforts himself and his fellow-mourners with the simple lessons of Gospel resignation and Gospel hope.

About this period Schiller began to turn wearily from the studies which had for years occupied his intellect and influenced his genius. He felt that he had given himself too much to abstract speculation, too little to the free poetic impulse. "It is high time," he says, in a letter to Goethe, "that for a while I should close the Philosophy Shop." He returned with ardour to the grand outline of his "Wallenstein," commenced years ago; long suspended, never forgotten. He yearned for some escape from the learned and arid atmosphere around him, some quiet retreat in which he could be alone with his genius—a summer-house with a garden! At length, this modest desire which literally seemed to haunt him was realised. Not far from Jena, to the south-west of the town, he purchased a garden, and built himself a kind of pavilion, with a single chamber. The site commanded a wide and noble prospect. Placed on the brow of a hill, up which the garden climbed, the summer-house overlooked the valley of the Saale, and the hanging pines of a neighbouring forest.* "There," says Goethe, in his Prologue to the "Lay of the Bell"—

---

* The house exists no more; upon its site is placed an urn dedicated to the memory of the poet.—*Doring.*

> " There, deck'd he the fair garden watch-tower ; whence
> Listening he loved the voice of stars to hear,
> Which to the no less ever-living sense
> Made music, mystic, yet through mystery clear ! "

Here then, in the summer months, did he devote himself, with a passion more fervent than in youth, to the divine faculty of creation. Often was the light seen at night streaming from the window, and the curious might even catch a glimpse of his tall shadowy figure walking to and fro the chamber ; now halting to write down the verses which he first declaimed aloud, or to support the overstrained physical power with the fatal excitements, for which our own Byron had more excuse, and has found less mercy. It was his custom to have placed on the table not only strong coffee and chocolate, but champagne, and the far more irritating and pernicious wines of the Rhine. Thus would he labour the night through, till sleep, or rather exhaustion, came on at morning ; and he never rose till late. Dearly purchased, indeed, was the luxury of these midnight watches ; but who shall conceive their intense delight ? Thus he speaks himself in his letter to Goethe, May, 1797, on his first occupation of his new abode :—" I greet you from my garden, on which I entered this day : a fair landscape surrounds me ; the sun goes gently down ; and the nightingales begin their warbles. All around serves to render me serene ; and my first evening in my own ground and soil is of the fairest omen ! "

It happened, perhaps fortunately, that, in the summer of 1797, Wilhelm von Humboldt left Jena for Italy. The influence that this eminent but over-refining intellect had exercised on Schiller, had not been on the whole favourable to his poetical genius ; * it had withdrawn him too much from the broad and popular field in which poetry, of the highest order and most extended empire, should seek its themes, into the "Realm of Shadow,"—an obscure and metaphysical ideal. With the departure of Humboldt, a new and far happier direction was given to Schiller's eager

---

* W. v. Humboldt, who was a devoted Kantian, seems to have supposed that poetry should be a riddle. It is always in the Abstract that he searches for the Beautiful. ·

energies. More delivered to the luminous influence of Goethe, he became more imbued with his art. A friendly emulation with Goethe led to the production of Schiller's greatest, though simplest poetical productions—his Ballads. Goethe had already shown what epic interest and what subtle wisdom might be given to this form of verse: Schiller caught the inspiration, and composed his "Diver," the sublimest ballad in the German language. This was followed by "The Glove," "The Cranes of Ibycus," &c., &c. The years 1797-98 were signalised by these performances, in which the ripest art of Goethe seems united with the earliest force of Schiller.

Meanwhile, "Wallenstein" still, though slowly advanced to its elaborate completion. Schiller grudged no pains, and neglected no study, which might serve to fulfil in this great work, that ideal of excellence, for the achievement of which the necessary leisure had been so desired. He plunged into the recesses of astrology and consulted the dreams of the Cabalists, in order to treat with conscientious accuracy, and invest with solemn dignity, the favourite superstition of his hero.* Finally, in January, 1799, after great preparation, the first portion of "Wallenstein," the "Piccolomini," was produced at Weimar. This was followed by the "Death of Wallenstein," in April. If on the boards the interest of these several parts of the great whole was not so intense as Schiller's earlier dramas, he was fortunate in the cordial support of the few who ultimately decide the judgment of the many : the perusal of the work, subsequently published entire, served to deepen and to widen general admiration : the more "Wallenstein" was examined and discussed, the more its profound beauty grew upon the world. Long after its publication, Goethe compared it to a wine, which wins upon the taste in proportion to its age. "This work," says Tieck, "at once rich and profound, is a monument for all times, of which

1799.
Ætat. 40.

---

* Schiller was fond, for their own sake, of such ultra-philosophical inquiries. When at Heilbronn, 1793, he took much interest in animal magnetism.

Germany may be proud; and a national feeling—a native sentiment—is reflected from this pure mirror, teaching us a greater sense of what we are, and what we were." In fact, from that time Schiller became the National Poet of all Germany.

CHAPTER XI.

In the same year, 1799, by the advice of his physicians, Schiller removed to Weimar; the Grand Duke awarded him a pension, of 1000 dollars, with a declaration that it should be doubled if illness should interfere with his other resources. His pecuniary circumstances were now competent to his moderate wants. "Wallenstein" had brought him ample remuneration; the periodicals with which he was connected yielded a regular and liberal income. Nevertheless, his activity increased as the ruder necessities for exertion were diminished. Vast schemes were constantly before him. His genius itself became to him that spur which Poverty is to the genius of less earnest men. His play of "Maria Stuart," and "The Lay of the Bell," long premeditated, were his next productions; the last the greatest of his lyrics; the first the poorest of the dramas conceived in his riper years. To an Englishman nothing can be less satisfactory than Schiller's character of our great Elizabeth; and history is violated for insufficient causes, and from an indistinct and imperfect ideal. Madame de Staël thought more highly of the tragedy than it deserved, precisely because of its defects. The Mary and the Elizabeth of Schiller have much of the shallowness and the tinsel of French heroines.* The public for once judged accurately in admiring the scattered beauties of the piece, and condemning it as a whole. But sickness of body may perhaps have conduced to the faults of this play. After Schiller's death, this note, in his handwriting, was found: "The year 1800 I was very ill. Amidst pain was 'Mary Stuart' completed."

---

* A. W. Schlegel, nevertheless, preferred, or affected to prefer, in many important respects, the "Maria Stuart" to the "Wallenstein."

But from this single fall Schiller's genius recovered itself with the bound of a Titan. The lovely image of the "Maid of Orleans" haunted him. Already, with the commencement of the new year, 1801, three acts of this masterpiece of elevated romance were composed. In the autumn of the same year, during a visit to his friend Körner at Dresden, he laboured at the no less magnificent "Bride of Messina," unequalled as a lyrical tragedy. From Dresden he went to Leipsic, and was present at the performance of the "Maid of Orleans." Here one of those signal triumphs, which so rarely await living genius, awaited him. Scarce had the drop-scene fallen on the first act, than the house resounded with the cry, "*Es lebe Friedrich Schiller!*" The cry was swelled by all the force of the orchestra. After the performance the whole crowd collected in the broad place before the theatre to behold the Poet. Every head was bared as he passed along; while men lifted their children in their arms, to show the pride of Germany to the new generation —crying out, "*Dieser ist es*"—"That is he!"

From Leipsic Schiller returned to Weimar, where "The Maid of Orleans" soon found its way to the boards; but its most gorgeous representation was at Berlin, where the New Theatre commenced with its performance on a scale of grandeur unprecedented on the German stage.

Schiller and Goethe were now almost inseparable. Together they directed the management of the Weimar Theatre, in which Schiller still entertained ideas of dramatic dignity too lofty for the social life of the moderns. Still did his manhood desire that for which his boyhood had been destined—the vocation of the Preacher;—and the stage still but suggested to him the office of the pulpit. "The pulpit and the stage are the only places for us," said he. He loved the Theatre; it was the sole public entertainment he habitually frequented. He was fond of the society of actors. He used to invite them to supper at the Stadthause, after the first, or even a more than usually successful, performance of one of his pieces. But generally, on returning from the Theatre, his mind was excited, and his emulation fired. And the midnight lamp at Weimar, as at Jena, attested that prodigious energy, which no infirmity slackened, and no glory could appease.

At this time he purchased a small house on the Esplanade—associated indeed with melancholy auspices : the same day he entered it his mother died. He felt in this affliction the rupture of the last tie of youth. He wrote to his sister—" Ah, dear Sister, so both the beloved Parents are gone from us, and the oldest bond that fastened us to life is rent ! O let us, we three (including his other sister), alone surviving of our father's house, let us cling yet closer to each other ; forget not that thou hast a loving brother. I remember vividly the days of our youth when we were all in all to each other. From that early existence our fate has divided us ; but attachment—confidence, remain unchanged—unchangeable."

In his own circle lay his purest and best comfort. He loved to associate himself with the infant sports of his children. Many a time was he found with his boy playing* on the floor. Around him were assembled such friends as Genius rarely finds—men dear alike to his heart, and worthy of his intellect. At the Court he was grown familiar, and, though he frequented it less than his royal friends desired, it was no longer made displeasing to his tastes by the reserve of his earlier pride.

To his intellectual life Goethe had grown necessary,— while his more household friends were his old College acquaintance, Wilhelm von Wolzogen, and Wolzogen's wife, —the eloquent and enthusiastic sister of his own. But, withal, his passion for solitary wanderings was unabated. Often was he seen in the lonely walks of the Park, stopping abruptly to note down his thoughts in his tablets ; often seated amidst the gloomy beeches and cypresses that clothe the crags, leading towards the Royal Pleasure House (the Römische Haus), and listening to the murmur of the neighbouring brook.

In 1802 he received from the Emperor of Austria a patent of nobility ; it was obtained through the unsolicited influence of the Duke of Weimar. He esteemed the honour at its just price—not with the vulgar scorn of the would-be cynic, still less with the elation of a vain convert from Republicanism. It pleased " Lolo and the children."

* At the game called " Lion and Dog," on all fours.

In the following year Madame de Staël visited Weimar, where her unequalled powers of conversation were more appreciated than in London. She herself has, in her "Allemagne," given us an interesting sketch of Schiller. He seems at first to have been more startled with the readiness of her powers, than charmed with their brilliancy, or penetrated with their depth. He says of her, not without justice, that her "*Naturel* and her feeling were better than her metaphysics." He is not quite pleased with that French clearness of understanding that made her averse to the Ideal Philosophy, which she believed led only to mysticism and superstition. He asserts somewhat too positively, "for what we call Poetry, she has no sense." He complains that "she can appreciate only in such works, the passionate, the rhetorical, the universal or popular. She does not prize the false, but she does not always recognise the true."

In a subsequent letter to his sister, Schiller appears to have found the illustrious Frenchwoman improved upon acquaintance, for he there expresses his admiration with more cordiality and less reserve. He now finds her a Phenomenon in her sex—for *esprit* and eloquence equalled but by few men—uniting with all the delicacy or finesse, obtained by intercourse with the great world, that rare earnestness and depth of mind obtained by most only through solitude.* In truth, whatever were the errors of Madame de Staël, there was in her character and her genius, a genuine nobleness akin to Schiller's; and though much of her fame, founded on her conversational eloquence, passed away with herself, her works still attest that union of imagination with intellect—enthusiasm with sense, which is never found but in minds of a great order, and in hearts which may indeed be misled by passion, but in which honesty and goodness are as instincts.

---

* In the sixth volume of the "Correspondence between Goethe and Schiller," and in Goethe's own "Tag-und Jahres-Heft," we may nevertheless perceive that Madame de Staël was to both these illustrious Germans somewhat too oppressively brilliant and loquacious—somewhat approaching occasionally to that social infliction for which we have no phrase so expressive as that which one of our most eminent Englishmen somewhat bluntly applied to her:—"The cleverest woman in the world for such a bore, and the greatest bore in the world for so clever a woman."

CHAPTER XII.

AND now, in that mysterious circle in which the life of genius so frequently appears to move, Schiller, nearing the close of his career, returned to the inspirations with which it had commenced. His first rude Drama had burned with the wild and half-delirious fever of Liberty ;—Liberty, purified and made rational, gave theme and substance to his last. The euthanasia of the genius which had composed "The Robbers," was the "Wilhelm Tell." Goethe has observed, indeed, that, although the idea of freedom runs through all the works of Schiller, the earlier embodied the physical freedom, the later the ideal. But this cannot fairly be regarded as the distinction between "The Robbers" and "Wilhelm Tell." It is no ideal liberty for which the simple mountaineers, whom Schiller has drawn in outlines so large and muscular, aspire and struggle; it is physical, practical, homely liberty—liberty of life and soil. It is this very practicability which really divides the "Tell" from "The Robbers:" in the last heaves the perturbed sigh for a social revolution,—for some liberty contrary to all the forms and the very substance of the organised world; it is an unreasoning passion that would risk a chaos for the chance that again may go forth the words—"Let there be light!" But in "Tell" the idea of liberty, intense and visible in itself, is yet circumscribed to the narrowest possible boundaries; it is but the struggle of an honest and universal people for independence, without one whisper of ambition, without one desire of revenge : it is a revolution portrayed in an anti-revolutionary spirit; throughout the whole breathes the condemnation of the French anarchy; it is an evoking of the true Florimel, that, beside her living and human Beauty, the false Florimel may dissolve into snow.*

In the spring of 1804 Schiller visited Berlin, at which city he was received with signal honours ; in July we find him at Jena, where, while his wife was happily confined of her youngest daughter, his constitution was severely shaken by a feverish cold. He suffered much and frequently during the rest of the year, but his mental activity was undiminished : besides some of his minor poems, such as " The Alp Hunter," and " The Lay of the Hill," he was employed on a translation of Racine's " Phèdre," and the outline of the tragedy of " Demetrius," never completed.

He also, about this time or very little later, conceived the scheme of a Drama which, if suitably executed, would have been, perhaps, the most extraordinary of all his various compositions. The subject was to be the *French Police*—and the plot to have embraced all the evils and abuses of modern civilization. Such a work would indeed be of wide compass and noble uses, but it seems to require the space of a prose fiction, and it is difficult to comprehend how it could have been contracted into the limits, and expressed in the form, of a Poetical Drama. It is noticeable, that the singular sympathy with mankind which Schiller possessed, often makes him the father of ideas in others with whom no direct communication can be traced,—the seeds that spring up so lavishly in his humane intellect are dispersed by invisible winds to grow on every soil. This idea of depicting, by literary portraiture, the social ills of Civilization and France, is the main stock of more than half the French writers of our own day.—In Balzac, in Sand, in Sue, in Souvestre, living in the midst of the great whirlpool—are heard the echoes of the Thought which was only breathed inaudibly within the heart of the Poet-student of the tranquil Weimar. And with these recurrences to the peculiar inspirations of his youth, the desire of travel returned prophetically to one about to depart for ever from all earthly homes. He traced routes upon the chart, and spoke of plans and pilgrimages never to be realised.

* See Schiller's own poem, entitled " William Tell," in which his object is briefly and simply explained.

The reperusal of Herder's "Ideas on the History of Man"—to which (though he was often largely indebted to it) he did not before do justice °—seems also to have deepened his meditations upon Life, Nature, and Eternal Providence. "Christianity," he said to his gifted sister-in-law, "has stamped a new impression on Humanity, while it revealed a sublimer prospect to the soul." According to this witness, Madame von Wolzogen—the best, for the most household, evidence—his faith increased as his life drew nearer to its goal.

At length, after many preparatory warnings—visitings, under the name of catarrhal fever, of his constitutional pulmonary disease—Schiller was stricken with his last illness on the 28th of April, 1805; Goethe, who was just recovering from a dangerous illness, called on Schiller, whom he found leaving his house for the theatre. He was too unwell to accompany, too polished to detain him,—they parted for the last time at the threshold of Schiller's door. At the close of the performance Schiller felt himself seized with a feverish attack. A young friend, Henry Voss (son of the celebrated author of "Luise," &c.,), led him home. On calling the next morning, Voss found him stretched on the sofa between sleep and waking. "Here I lie again!" he said in a hollow voice. As yet, however, he had no conception of his danger; he thought to have discovered a treatment to ensure his recovery. His mind for some days continued clear, and the chief regret he expressed was for the interruption to "Demetrius." But on the 6th of May he began to wander: on that day Voss, visiting him again, observed that his eyes were deep sunken; every nerve twitched convulsively: they brought him some lemons, at which he caught eagerly, but laid them down again with a feeble hand. Delirium came on: he raved of soldiers and war; the word Lichtenberg, or Leuchtenburg (the former the name of an author whom he had been lately reading, the latter of a castle which he had long desired to visit),

---

* He said to Madame von Wolzogen, "I know not how it is, but this Book speaks to me after quite a new fashion." Herder and Schiller were not very familiarly intimate—they were *too like each other* for cordial concurrence. Both were essentially earnest, and therefore the differences between them resisted compromise.

came often to his lips. On the evening of the 7th, his mind recovered; he wished to renew his customary conversations with his sister-in-law upon the proper theme and aims of tragedy; she prayed him to keep quiet; he answered, touchingly—"True; now, when no one understands me, and I no more understand myself, it is better that I should be silent." Shortly before, he had concluded some talk on death with these striking words: "Death can be no evil, for it is universal." And now the thought of eternity seems to have occupied his mind in its dreams; for in sleep he exclaimed, "Is that your hell?—is that your heaven?" He then raised his looks, and a soft smile came over his face. It was, perhaps, on awaking from this sleep that he used those memorable words— "Now is life so clear!—so much is made clear and plain!"

In the evening he took some broth, and said to his friends that "he thought that night to sleep well, with God's will." His faithful servant, who watched him, said that, during the night, he recited many lines from "Demetrius," and once he called on God to preserve him from a long and tedious death-bed.

On the morning of the 8th of May he woke up composed, and asked for his youngest child. She was brought to him. He took the infant's hand in his own, and gazed at her long with a look of unspeakable sorrow. He then began to weep bitterly, kissed the young face with emotion, and beckoned to them to remove the child.

Towards the evening his sister-in-law approached his bed, and asked how he felt. "Better and better, calmer and calmer," was his answer. He then longed once more to see the sun; they drew aside the curtains; he looked serenely on the setting light. Nature received his farewell.

His sleep that night was disturbed; his mind again wandered; with the morning he had lost consciousness. He spoke incoherently, and chiefly in Latin. His last drink was champagne. Towards three in the afternoon came on the last exhaustion; the breath began to fail. Towards four, he would have called for naphtha, but the last syllable died on his lips;—finding himself speechless, he motioned that he wished to write something; but his hand could trace only three letters, in which was yet recognisable the distinct character of his writing. His wife knelt by his side; he pressed her hand. His sister-in-law stood with the physician at the foot of the bed, applying warm cushions to the cold feet. Suddenly a sort of electric shock came over his countenance; the head fell back; the deepest calm settled on his face. His features were as those of one in a soft sleep.

The news of Schiller's death soon spread through Weimar. The theatre was closed; men gathered together in groups. Each felt as if he had lost his dearest friend. To Goethe, enfeebled himself by long illness, and again stricken by some relapse, no one had the courage to mention the death of his beloved rival. When the tidings came to Henry Meyer, who was with him, Meyer left the house abruptly, lest his grief might escape him. No one else had the courage to break the intelligence. Goethe perceived that the members of his household seemed embarrassed, and anxious to avoid him. He divined something of the fact, and said, at last, "I see,—Schiller must be very ill." That night they overheard him—the serene man, who seemed almost above human affection, who disdained to reveal to others whatever grief he felt when his son died—they overheard Goethe weep! In the morning he said to a friend, "Is it not true that Schiller was very ill yesterday?" The friend (it was a woman) sobbed. "He is dead," said Goethe faintly. "You have said it," was the answer. "He is dead!" repeated Goethe, and covered his eyes with his hands.

The body was dissected; and it was some consolation to the mourners to know that much prolongation of life would have been beyond the art of medicine; the left lung was destroyed, the ventricles of the heart wasted, the liver indurated, the gall-bladder extremely swelled. A son of the great Herder, one of the physicians who examined the body, thought it impossible that, under any circumstances, he could have lived half a year, nor that without great suffering.

Schiller was buried in the night of the 11th of May; twelve young men of good family bore the coffin; the heavens were clouded, but the nightingales sang loud and full. As the train proceeded, the sound of a horse's hoofs was heard; a rider dismounted and followed the procession—it was Wilhelm von Wolzogen, who had heard the fatal news at Naumburg, and hastened to pay the last respect to the remains of his college friend. As the bier was lowered, the wind suddenly scattered the mists, the moon broke forth, and its light streamed upon the coffin. When all was over, the skies were suddenly obscured again.

CONCLUDING CHAPTER.

So, at the early age of forty-five, closed the earthly career of Friedrich Schiller. In this brief epitome of his life the reader will not fail to perceive the peculiar distinctions of his character and mind : his singular ardour for Truth; his solemn conviction of the duties of a Poet; his prevailing idea, that the Minstrel should be the Preacher, —that Song is the sister of Religion in its largest sense,— that the Stage is the Pulpit to all sects, all nations, all time.   No author ever had more earnestness than Schiller, —his earnestness was the real secret of his greatness ; this combination of philosophy and poetry, this harmony between genius and conscience, sprang out of the almost perfect, almost unrivalled equality of proportions which gave symmetry to his various faculties.*   With him the imagination and the intellect were so nicely balanced, that one knows not which was the greater ; owing, happily, to the extensive range of his studies, it may be said that, as the intellect was enriched, the imagination was strengthened. Unlike Goethe's poet in "Wilhelm Meister," he did not sing " as the bird sings," from the mere impulse of song, but he rather selected Poetry as the most perfect form for the expression of noble fancies and high thoughts.   "His conscience was his Muse."†   It was thus said of him with truth, "that his poetical excellence was of later growth than his intellectual;" and as the style of Lord Bacon ascended to its sonorous beauty in proportion as his mind became more stored, and his meaning more profound, so

* Hence Mr. Carlyle well observes, " Sometimes we suspect that it is the very grandeur of his general powers which prevents us from exclusively admiring his poetic genius.   We are not lulled by the siren song of poetry, because her melodies are blended with the clearer, manlier tone of serious reason, and of honest though exalted feeling."—Carlyle's *Life of Schiller.*

† " Sa conscience étoit sa Muse."—De Staël,

the faculty of expression ripened with Schiller in exact ratio to the cultivation of his intellect. His earliest compositions were written with difficulty and labour, and he was slow in acquiring thorough mastery over the gigantic elements of his language. Perhaps this very difficulty (for nothing is so fatal to the mental constitution as that verbal dysentery which we call facility) served both to increase his passion for his art, and to direct it to objects worthy the time and the care which, in his younger manhood, he was compelled to bestow upon his compositions. From this finely poised adjustment between the reasoning and the imaginative faculties, came the large range of his ambition, not confined to Poetry alone, but extending over the whole fields of Letters. We can little appreciate Schiller, if we regard him only as the author of " Wallenstein," and the " Lay of the Bell; " wherever the genius of his age was astir, we see the flight of his wing and the print of his footstep. While, in verse, he has made experiments in almost every combination, except the epic (and in that he at one time conceived and sketched a noble outline), embracing the drama, the ode, the elegy, the narrative, the didactic, the epigrammatic, and in each achieved a triumph,—in Prose, he has left monuments only less imperishable in the various and rarely reconcilable lands of romance, of criticism, of high-wrought philosophical speculation, and impartial historical research. His romance of the " Ghost-Seer " is popular in every nation, and, if not perfect of its kind, the faults are those of a super-exuberant intellect, which often impedes, by too discursive a dialogue, the progress of the narrative, and the thread of the events. In this he resembled Godwin rather than Scott. If with " St. Léon " and " Caleb Williams " the " Ghost-Seer " rests in the second class of popularity, it is because, as with them, it requires a reflective mind to seize all its beauties, and yield to all its charms.

In History, if Schiller did not attain to the highest rank, it was not because he wanted the greatest qualities of the historian, but because the subjects he selected did not admit of their full development. But while his works in that direction are amongst the most charming, impartial, and justly popular, of which his nation boasts, he has shown, in the introductory Lecture, delivered by himself at Jena, how grand his estimate of history was. His notions on history are worth whole libraries of history itself.* As a Philosophical Essayist, he is not perhaps very original (though in borrowing from Kant he adds much that may fairly be called his own), and rigid metaphysicians have complained of his vagueness and obscurity.† But his object was not that of severe and logical reasoning; it was to exalt the art to which most of his essays were devoted; to make the great and the pure popular; to educate the populace up to purity and greatness. The ideal philosophy, as professed by Schiller, was, in fact, a kind of mental as well as moral Christianity, which was to penetrate the mind as well as the soul—extend to the arts of man as well as his creeds; to make all nature a temple —all artists priests: Christianity in spirit and effect it was —for its main purpose was that of the Gospel faith, viz., to draw men out of this life into a purer and higher air of being—to wean from virtue the hopes of reward below— to make enjoyment consist in something beyond the senses. What holy meditation was to the saints of old, the ideal of Æsthetic art was to the creed of Schiller. Therefore, his philosophy, in strict accordance with his poetry, was designed not so much to convince as to ennoble;—and, therefore, though in the wide compass of Schiller's works there are passages which would wound the sincere and unquestioning believer; though in his life there were times when he was overshadowed by the doubts that beset inquiry; though, in the orthodox and narrower sense of the word Christian, it would be presumptuous to define his sect, or decide on his belief; the whole scope and tendency of his works, taken one with the other, are, like his mind, eminently Christian. No German writer—no writer, not simply theological—has done more to increase, to widen, and to sanctify the reverent disposition that inclines to Faith.

---

* Of this lecture—"What is universal History, and with what views should it be studied?"—Mr. Carlyle observes justly, "There perhaps has never been in Europe another course of history sketched out on principles so magnificent and philosophical."—Carlyle's *Life of Schiller*.

† Mr. Carlyle, however, estimates the logical precision of Schiller more highly than many of Schiller's own countrymen; and speaks of the Æsthetic Letters as "one of the deepest, most compact pieces of reasoning he is anywhere acquainted with."—*Miscell.* p. 62.

As Schiller's poetry was the flower of his mind, so in his poetry are to be found, in their most blooming produce, all the faculties that led him to philosophy, criticism, and history. In his poetry are reflected all his manifold studies. Philosophy, criticism, and history pour their treasures into his verse. One of a mind so candid, and a life so studious, could not fail to be impressed by many and progressive influences. Schiller's career was one education, and its grades are strongly marked. Always essentially humane, with a heart that beat warmly for mankind, his first works betray the intemperate zeal and fervour of the Revolution which then in its fair outbreak misled not more the inexperience of youth than the sagacity of wisdom; a zeal and fervour increased in Schiller by the formal oppression of academical tyranny;* a nature unusually fiery and impatient; and a taste terribly perverted by the sentiment of Rousseau and the bombast of Klopstock. Friendship, love, indignation, poverty, and solitude, all served afterwards to enrich his mind with the recollection of strong passions and keen sufferings: and, thrown much upon himself, it is his own life and his own thoughts that he constantly reproduces on the stage. The perusal of Shakspeare has less visible and direct influence on his genius than he himself seems to suppose;—the study of History has far more. From the period in which he steadily investigated the past, his characters become more actual; his *Humanity* more rational and serene. He outgrows Rousseau; the revolutionary spirit fades gradually from his mind; he views the vast chronicle of man not with the fervour of a boy, but the calm of a statesman. At this time he begins to deserve the epithet Goethe has emphatically bestowed on him—he becomes "*practical.*" But with the study of history comes the crisis of doubt, the period of his scepticism and his anguish. From this influence he emerged into the purer air, which he never afterwards abandoned, of the ideal Philosophy. Here he found a solution of his doubts—a religion for his mind. Almost at the same time that his intellect is calmed and deepened by philosophy, his taste acquires harmonious symmetry and repose from the study of the ancient masterpieces. From that period, his style attains its final beauty

* Thus Schiller himself calls his "Robbers" a "monster produced by the unnatural union of Genius with Thraldom."

of simplicity combined with stateliness, and vigour best shown by ease. A happy marriage, a fame assured, an income competent to his wants, serve permanently to settle into earnest and serious dignity a life hitherto restless—an ambition hitherto vague and undefined. Thenceforth he surrenders himself wholly to the highest and purest objects human art can attain. His frame is attacked, his health gone for ever; but the body has here no influence on the mind. Schiller lives in his art; he attains to the ideal existence he has depicted; he becomes the Pure Form, the Archetype, the *Gestalt*, that he has described in his poem of the "Ideal and the Actual;" living divorced from the body—in the heavenly fields a spirit amongst the gods. It is now that we trace in his works the influences of two master-minds with which he lived familiarly—William von Humboldt and Goethe.* The first we see in his mystical, typical, and Kantian compositions; the last in the more lucid and genial spirit of his lyrics and his narratives. By degrees, the latter happily prevailed. As Humboldt receded from the scene, and his intercourse with Goethe mellowed, Schiller comes out of the cloud into the light. He recognises the true ideal of art; the clear expression of serene thought; the Grecian Athenè prevailing over the typical Egyptian Naith. The last influence produced on him by profane literature was in the works of Calderon, then just translated; and which, according to the testimony of Goethe, deeply and sensibly impressed him. But he did not survive long enough for that impression to become apparent in his own compositions.

We omit all detailed criticism of Schiller's Dramas; for they have been made more or less familiar to the reader, by various translations, by repeated notices in our popular journals, and by the attention they have received in the biographical work of Mr. Carlyle. Our limits would not permit us to do justice to works requiring lengthened and elaborate considerations, or to enter into a controversy with other critics, from whom we may differ as to their merits or defects. Briefly, it appears to us, that, like the dramas

* The intimacy between Goethe and Schiller was the more remarkable, because it was almost purely intellectual. Goethe says, in a conversation with Eckermann, "that there was no necessity for especial friendship between them—their common efforts made their noblest bond."

of many great poets, from Byron up even to Shakspeare, their highest merit is not that purely dramatic. Perhaps of *this* quality there is more in the earlier than the later Tragedies. "The Robbers" is still upon the whole the most frequently acted of all Schiller's Plays.* Glancing over his riper performances, his grandest, in point of intellect, is "Wallenstein:" in point of verbal poetry, of music and expression, "The Bride of Messina" is the loveliest: in point of feeling and conception "The Maid of Orleans" most engrosses the heart and enlists the fancy. But the one in which Schiller, with the fullest success, emancipates his art from himself—in which his own individuality the least moulds and influences his creations—seems to us the "Wilhelm Tell." As his chief merit, whether as Man or Artist, lay in his earnestness, so in that earnestness lay his main defect as a writer for the Stage. He could not, as the stage-writer really ought, reflect indifferently—*veluti in speculum*—vice and virtue†—the mean and the sublime. He could not escape the temptation of placing in the mouths of his characters the sentiments he desired to enforce upon the world—even though the occasion was inappropriate. All his favourite characters talk too much—and too much as Schiller thought and Schiller felt. Morally one of the least selfish of men,—intellectually he is one of the most egotistical. Who that held the doctrine that the Dramatist, the Poet, should be the Preacher, could fail to be so? He loved Truth too much to suffer her to be silent, whenever he had occasion to make her oracles be heard. The complex varieties—the sinuous windings of human character, are, for the most part, without the pale of his conscientious and stately

---

* The true test of the *Dramatic* faculty, apart from the Poetical, is its practical adaptability to the stage. A play of very inferior literary merit may keep its hold on the boards, to the exclusion of works infinitely more poetical, by its dramatic qualities;—viz., by the correspondence between the action of its plot and emotions the most generally popular. . . . Hence the vitality on the stage of plays that are almost despised in the library—such as the "Stranger," "Pizarro," &c. Kotzebue's dramatic talent, as separate from intellectual excellence or poetic inspiration, is positively wonderful, and deserves the minutest study of all practical writers for the stage. Of this, Schiller was fully aware.

† Thus Madame de Staël well observes, "that he lived, spoke, and acted as if the wicked did not exist; and when in his works he described them, it was with more exaggeration and less depth than if he had really known them."

genius. He thus avoids (at least in his later works) the vulgar reproach attached to Goethe, and which might with equal truth be urged against Shakspeare, viz., that he makes error amiable, and clothes crime with charm. His characters are, for the most part, embodiments of great principles and great truths, rather than the flexible and multiform representations of human nature, which, while idealised into poetry, still render the creations of Shakspeare so living and distinct.

Schiller is thus, on the whole, greater as a Poet than a Dramatist—so, indeed, is Shakspeare, but from entirely different and opposite causes: Shakspeare, from the exquisite subtlety of his imagination, which, in a Caliban, an Ariel, a Titania, escapes the grossness of representation; Schiller, from too statuelike a rigidity and hardness: we do not see the veins at play beneath his marble.

It is in the Collection of his Minor Poems that Schiller's true variety is best seen—a variety not of *character*, but of thought, of sentiment, of fancy, of diction, and of metre. In those poems are the confessions of his soul, as well as the exercises of his genius. For, with a little modification, what Jean Paul said of Herder, may be said of Schiller, "that he was less a Poet than a Poem,"—and therefore, all his poetry should be studied as illustrations of the Human Poem—Schiller himself!

Any comparison between Goethe and Schiller would be, and has been, but a futile attempt at comparing dissimilarities.* We shall waste no time in attempting to show where one is greater or the other less. Brothers they were in life—let them shine together in equal lustre—the immortal Dioscuri—twin stars! Nor shall we touch upon those theories of art which the mention of Schiller and Goethe calls into discussion amongst the metaphysical critics of their country. We cannot invent a set of school terms to prove, without farther discussion, that one poem is great because objective—another not so great because subjective. Beauty escapes all technical definitions; the art of estimating beauty—viz., *criticism*—must follow the genius it would examine through all its capricious wind-

* Goethe himself is reported to have said, " The Germans are great fools to quarrel which should take the prior rank, Schiller or myself—they ought only to be too happy that they have us both."

ings, and admire equally, Milton where subjective,—and where objective, Shakspeare.

There is a class of poets in which self-consciousness is scarcely perceptible; another in which it is pervading and intense. In the former class, Shakspeare and Homer tower pre-eminent; in the latter, we recognise Dante and Milton—Schiller, Byron, and Burns.

To the last two, Schiller, in some attributes of his genius, bears a greater resemblance * than perhaps to any of his own countrymen; resembling them in the haunting sense of individuality—in the power of blending interest for the poet with delight in the poem—in the subordination of sentiment to feeling—in the embodiment of what is peculiar in forms the most widely popular;—resembling them in these points, differing from them no less widely in others, according as the different modifications of life, habits, education, heart, and conscience, differ in the English noble, the German student, the Scotch peasant. But in all three there is this characteristic of a common tribe—their poetry expresses themselves. To borrow the idea of Schiller himself, they seek truth in the heart within—others in the world without,—by each order of inquirer can truth equally be found : Or, to avail ourselves again of Schiller's accurate and noble distinction, whether light breaks into the variety of colours in which its individuality is lost, or unites the colours into a single shimmer, it is still the light which vivifies and illumes the world.

Mr. Carlyle quotes, with some approval, a dogmatic assertion, "that readers till their twenty-fifth year usually prefer Schiller; after their twenty-fifth year, Goethe." † If Herder and Novalis are right in their belief that the true elements of wisdom and poetry are found freshest and purest in the young, this is no disparagement to Schiller. It is, certainly, only in proportion as the glow for all that is noble in thought and heroic in character fades from the weaker order of mind, amidst the cavils, disgusts, and scepticism of later life, that the halo around the genius of Schiller, which is but a reflection of all that is noble and

---

* Goethe himself has remarked the similarity in some points between Byron and Schiller.

† Carlyle's Miscellanies, vol. iii. p. 65.

heroic, wanes also into feebler lustre. For the stronger nature, which still " feels as the enthusiast, while it learns to see as the world-wise," * . . . there is no conceivable reason why Schiller should charm less in maturity than youth.

Finally, as, in the life of Schiller, the student may gather noble and useful lessons of the virtue of manly perseverance—of the necessity of continued self-cultivation—of the alliance between labour and success—between honesty and genius ;—so in his Poems will be found, living and distinct, a great and forcible intellect ever appealing to the best feelings—ever exalting those whom it addresses —ever intent upon strengthening man in his struggles with his destiny, and uniting with a golden chain the outer world and the inner to the celestial throne.

* Schiller, " Light and Warmth."

ON THE CAUSES OF HORACE'S POPULARITY.*

No one denies that there are greater poets than Horace ;
and much has been said in disparagement even of some of
the merits most popularly assigned to him, by scholars who
have, nevertheless, devoted years of laborious study to the
correction of his text or the elucidation of his meaning.
But whatever his faults or deficiencies, he has remained
unexcelled in that special gift of genius which critics define
by the name of charm.   No collection of small poems,
ancient or modern, has so universally pleased the taste of
all nations as Horace's Odes, or been so steadfastly secure
from all the capricious fluctuations of time and fashion. In
vain have critics insisted on the superior genius evinced in
the scanty relics left to us of the Greek lyrists, and even on
the more spontaneous inspiration which they detect in the
exquisite delicacy of form that distinguishes the muse of
Catullus.   Horace still reigns supreme as the lyrical singer
most enthroned in the affections, most congenial to the
taste, of the complex multitude of students in every land
and in every age.

It is an era in the life of the schoolboy when he first commences his acquaintance with Horace.   He gets favourite
passages by heart with a pleasure which (Homer alone
excepted) no other ancient poet inspires.   Throughout
life the lines so learnt remain on his memory, rising up
alike in gay and in grave moments, and applying themselves to varieties of incident and circumstance with the
felicitous suppleness of proverbs.   Perhaps in the interval
between boyhood and matured knowledge of the world, the

* [Prefixed to Lord Lytton's translations of the Odes and Epodes of
Horace, published in 1869, after having appeared in the pages of " Blackwood's Magazine."]

attractive influence of Horace is suspended in favour of some bolder poet adventuring far beyond the range of his temperate though sunny genius, into the extremes of heated passion or frigid metaphysics—

> "Visere gestiens
> Qua parte debacchentur ignes,
> Qua nebulæ pluviique rores."*

But as men advance in years they again return to Horace—again feel the young delight in his healthful wisdom, his manly sense, his exquisite combination of playful irony and cordial earnestness. They then discover in him innumerable beauties before unnoticed, and now enjoyed the more for their general freedom from those very efforts at intense emotion and recondite meaning for which, in the revolutionary period of youth, they admired the writers who appear to them, when reason and fancy adjust their equilibrium in the sober judgment of maturer years, feverishly exaggerated or tediously speculative. That the charm of Horace is thus general and thus imperishable, is a proposition which needs no proof. It is more interesting and less trite to attempt to analyse the secrets of that charm, and see how far the attempt may suggest hints of art to the numberless writers of those poems which aim at the title of lyrical composition, and are either the trinkets of a transitory fashion, or the ornaments of enduring vogue, according as they fail or succeed in concentrating the rays of poetry into the compactness and solidity of imperishable gems.

The first peculiar excellence of Horace is in his personal character and temperament rather than his intellectual capacities ; it is in his genial humanity. He touches us on so many sides of our common nature ; he has sympathies with such infinite varieties of men ; he is so equally at home with us in town and country, in our hours of mirth, in our moments of dejection. Are we poor ? he disarms our envy of the rich by greeting as a special boon of the Deity the suffisance which He bestows with a thrifty hand ; and, distinguishing poverty from squalor, shows

---

* ["...bounding blithely to visit
Either pole, where the mist or the sun
Holds the orgies of water or fire."]

what attainable elegance can embellish a home large
enough to lodge content. Are we rich? he inculcates
moderation, and restrains us from purse-pride with the
kindliness of a spirit free from asceticism, and sensitive to the true enjoyments of life. His very defects
and weaknesses of character serve to increase his attraction; he is not too much elevated above our own
erring selves.

Next to the charm of his humanity is that of his inclination towards the agreeable aspects of our mortal state.
He invests the virtues of patience amidst the trials of
adversity with the dignity of a serene sweetness, and exalts
even the frivolities of worldly pleasure with associations of
heartfelt friendship and the refinements of music and song.
Garlands entwined with myrtle, and wine-cups perfumed
with nard, seem fit emblems of the banqueter who, when
he indulges his Genius, invokes the Muse and invites the
Grace. With this tender humanity and with this pleasurable temperament is blended a singular manliness of
sentiment. In no poet can be found lines that more rouse,
or more respond to, the generous impulse of youth
towards fortitude and courage, sincerity and honour,
devoted patriotism, the superiority of mind over the
vicissitudes of fortune, and a healthful reliance on the
wisdom and goodness of the one divine providential
Power, who has no likeness and no second, even in the
family of Olympus.

Though at times he speaks as the Epicurean, at other
times as the Stoic, and sometimes as both in the same
poem, he belongs exclusively to neither school. Out of
both he has poetised a practical philosophy which, even in
its inconsistencies, establishes a harmony with our own
inconsistent natures; for most men are to this day in
part Epicurean, in part Stoic. Horace is the poet of
Eclecticism.

From the width of his observation, and the generalising
character of his reasoning powers, Horace is more emphatically the representative of civilisation than any other
extant lyrical poet. Though describing the manners of his
own time, he deals in types and pictures, sentiments and
opinions, in which every civilised time finds likeness and
expression. Hence men of the world claim him as one of

their order, and they cheerfully accord to him an admiration which they scarcely concede to any other poet. It is
not only the easy good-nature of his philosophy, and his
lively wit, that secure to him this distinction, but he owes
much also to that undefinable air of good-breeding which is
independent of all conventional fashions, and is recognised
in every society where the qualities that constitute good-
breeding are esteemed. Catullus has quite as much wit,
and is at least as lax, where he appears in the character of
a man of pleasure—Catullus is equally intimate with the
great men of his time, and in grace of diction is by many
preferred to Horace; yet Catullus has never attained to
the same oracular eminence as Horace among men of the
world, and does not, in their eyes, command the same rank
in that high class of gentlemen—thorough-bred authors.
For if we rightly interpret genius by *ingenium*—viz., the
inborn spirit which accommodates all conventional circumstances around it to its own native property of form and
growth—there is a genius of gentleman as there is a genius
of poet. That which his countrymen called *urbanitas*, in
contradistinction to provincial narrowness of mind or vul-
garity of taste, to false finery and affected pretence, is the
essential attribute of the son of the Venusian freedman.
And with this quality, which needs for brilliant development familiar converse with the types of mind formed by
a polished metropolis, Horace preserves, in a degree unknown to those who, like Pope and Boileau, resemble him
more or less on the town-bred side of his character, the
simple delight in rural nature, which makes him the
favourite companion of those whom cool woodlands,
peopled with the beings of fable, "set apart from the
crowd." He might be as familiar with Sir Philip Sidney
in the shades of Penshurst, as with Lord Chesterfield in
the saloons of Mayfair. And out of this rare combination
of practical wisdom and poetical sentiment there grows
that noblest part of his moral teaching which is distinct
from schools and sects, and touches at times upon chords
more spiritual than those who do not look below the surface would readily detect. Hence, in spite of his occasional
sins, he has always found indulgent favour with the clergy
of every Church. Among the dozen books which form the
library of the village *curé* of France, Horace is sure to be

one; and the greatest dignitaries of our own Church are among his most sedulous critics and his warmest panegyrists. With all his melancholy conceptions of the shadow-land beyond the Grave, and the half-sportive, half-pathetic injunction, therefore, to make the most of the passing hour, there lies deep within his heart a consciousness of nobler truths, which ever and anon find impressive utterance, suggesting precepts and hinting consolations that elude the rod of Mercury, and do not accompany the dark flock to the shores of Styx:

> "Virtus recludens immeritis mori
> Cœlum negata tentat iter via." *

Thus we find his thoughts interwoven with Milton's later meditations; † and Condorcet, baffled in aspiration of human perfectibility on earth, dies in his dungeon with Horace by his side, open at the verse which says, by what arts of constancy and fortitude in mortal travail Pollux and Hercules attained to the citadels of light.

It is, then, mainly to this large and many-sided nature in the man himself that Horace owes his unrivalled popularity —a popularity which has indeed both widened in its circle and deepened in its degree in proportion to the increase of modern civilisation. And as the popularity is thus so much derived from the qualities in which the man establishes friendly intimacy with all ranks of his species, so it is accompanied with that degree of personal affection which few writers have the happiness to inspire. We give willing ear to the praise of his merits, and feel a certain displeasure at the criticisms which appear harshly to qualify and restrict them; we are indulgent to his faults, and rejoice when the diligent research and kindly enthusiasm of German scholars redeem his good name from any aspersions that had been too lightly credited. It pleases us to think that most, perhaps all, among his erotic poems which had left upon our minds a painful impression, and which a decorous translator shuns, are no genuine expressions'of the poet's own sentiment or taste, but merely a Roman artist's translation or paraphrase from the Greek originals.‡ We

* ["Virtue essays her flight through ways to all but her denied;
   To those who do not merit death she opes the gates of heaven."]
† See Milton's Sonnet, xxi., To Cyriac Skinner.
‡ The opinion at which most Horatian scholars have now arrived is well

readily grant the absurdity of any imputation upon the personal courage of Brutus's young officer, founded upon the modest confession, that on the fatal field of Philippi, when those who most vaunted their valour fled in panic or bit the dust, he too had left his shield not too valiantly behind him; he who, in the same poem, addressed to a brother soldier, tells us that he had gone through the worst extremities in that bloody war. For those panegyrics on Augustus which, in our young days, we regarded as renegade flattery bestowed upon a man who had destroyed the political liberties for which the poet had fought, we accept the rational excuses which are suggested by our own maturer knowledge of life and of the grateful human heart, and our profounder acquaintance with the events and circumstances of the age. We see in the poems themselves, when fairly examined, with what evident sincerity Horace vindicates his enthusiastic admiration of a prince whom he identifies with the establishment of safety to property and life, with the restoration of arts and letters, with the reform of manners and the amelioration of laws. We can understand with what genuine horror a patriot so humane must have regarded the fratricide of intestine wars, and with what honest gratitude so ardent a lover of repose and peace would have exclaimed,—

> " Custode rerum Cæsare, non furor
> Civilis aut vis exiget otium." *

If to the rule of one man this blessed change was to be ascribed, and if public opinion so cordially endorsed that assumption, that the people themselves placed their ruler in

expressed by Estré in his judicious and invaluable work, " Horatiana Prosopographeia:" " Credo Horatium prorsus abstinuisse a puerorum amoribus, etiamsi ipse, jocans, aliter de se profiteatur. Distabant, si quid judico, Horatii tempore, puerorum amores tantum a persona sancti castique vi·i quantum libera venus nostris temporibus abest. Novi autem hodiè quoque, quis ignorat, juvenes virosque vel castissimos et sanctissimos, inter amicos, animi causa, ita jocantes, quasi liberam venerem ardentissime sectarentur. Nec Libri iv. carm. i. curo, scriptum, uti egregie observavit Lessingius, post legem Juliam latam de pudicitia quum nemo amplius amorem in puerum palam celebrare ausus fuisset."—P. 524.

       * [" Cæsar our guardian, neither civil rage
         Nor felon violence scares us from repose."]

the order of Divinities—it scarcely needs even an excuse for the poet that he joined in the general apotheosis of the great prince, who to him was the benignant protector and the sympathising friend. When the population have once tested the security of established order, and, with terrified remembrance of the bloodshed and havoc of a previous anarchy, felt the old liberty rather voluntarily slip than be violently wrenched from their hands, a benevolent autocracy that consults the public opinion which installs it seems a blessing to the many, and is accepted as a necessity by the few. And if the professed statesmen and political thinkers of the time—the Pollios and the Messalas, the most eminent partisans of M. Antony, the noblest companions of Brutus—acquiesced, with the more courtly and consistent Mæcenas, in the established government of Augustus, it would indeed be no reproach to a man whose mind habitually shunned gloomy anticipations of the distant future, that he could not foresee the terrible degeneration of manners and the military despotism which were destined to grow out of the clement autocracy of that accomplished prince who had won the title of "father of his country," and who might be seen on summer evenings angling in the Tiber, or stretched upon its banks amidst a ring of laughing children, with whom the Emperor whose word gave law to the Indian and the Mede was playing with nuts and pebbles.

What Horace was as man, can, however, furnish but little aid to those who desire to rival him as poet—little aid, indeed, except as it may serve to show how far a genial and cordial temperament, an independent and manly spirit, and a fellowship with mankind in their ordinary pursuits and tastes, contribute to the culture and amenities of the poet who would make his monument more lasting than bronze and more lofty than the pyramids. But in Horace, as artist, we may perhaps, on close examination, discover some peculiarities of conception and form sufficiently marked and pervasive to evince that with him they were rules of art; so successful as to make them worthy of study, and hitherto so little noticed, even by his most elaborate critics, as to justify an attempt to render them more generally intelligible and instructive.

In what I am about to say on this head, I confine my

remarks to the short lyrical pieces to which commentators
after his time gave the name of Odes, and on which his
eminence as a poet must mainly rely. Whatever merit
be ascribed to his Satires, it is scarcely in the power
of genius to raise satire to an elevated rank in poetry.
Satire, indeed, is the antipodes of poetry in its essence and
its mission. Satire always tends to dwarf, and it cannot
fail to caricature ; but poetry does nothing if it does not
tend to enlarge and exalt, and if it does not seek rather to
beautify than reform. And though such didactic and
moralising vein as belongs to the Epistles of Horace be in
itself much higher than satire, and in him has graces of
style that, with his usual consummate taste, he rejects for
satire, which he regards but as a rhythmical prose, still,
the higher atmosphere in which the genius of lyrical song
buoys and disports itself is not within the scope of that
didactic form of poetry which "walks highest but not
flies." Hegel, in his luminous classification of the various
kinds of poetry, has perhaps somewhat too sharply drawn
the line between its several degrees of rank ; yet every one
acquainted with the rudimentary principles of criticism
must acknowledge, that just as it requires a larger combination of very rare gifts to write an epic or a drama
which the judgment of ages allows to be really great, than
to write a lyrical poem, so it demands a much finer
combination of some of the rarest of those rare gifts to
write a lyrical poem which becomes the song of all times
and nations, than to write a brilliant sarcasm upon human
infirmities, or an elegant lecture in the style of an Epistle.
These last require but talents, however great, which are
more or less within the province of prose-writers. The
novel of "Gil Blas" or the Essays of Montaigne evince
qualities of genius equal at least to those displayed in
Horace's Satires and Epistles. But if you were to multiply
Lesages and Montaignes *ad infinitum*, they could not accomplish a single one of Horace's nobler odes.

Now, the first thing that strikes us in examining the
secrets of Horace's art in lyrical poetry—and which I venture humbly to think it would be well for modern lyrists to
study—is his terseness. Terseness is one of the surest
proofs of painstaking. Nothing was ever more truthful in
art than the well-known reply of the writer to the friendly

critic, who said, "You are too prolix:" "I had not time to be shorter."

We know from Horace himself that he bestowed upon his artist-work an artist's labour—"Operosa carmina fingo." He seems to have so meditated upon the subject he chooses as to be able to grasp it readily. There is no wandering after ideas—no seeking to prolong and over-adorn the main purpose for which he writes. If it be but a votive inscription to Diana, in which he dedicates a tree to her, he does not let his command of language carry him beyond the simple idea he desires to express. He seems always to consider that he is addressing a very civilised and a very impatient audience, which has other occupations in life besides that of reading verses; and nothing in him is more remarkable than his study not to be tedious. Perhaps, indeed, it is to this desire that some of his shortcomings up to the mark which very poetical critics would assign to lyrical rapture are to be ascribed; but it is a fault on the right side.

The next and much more important characteristic of Horace as a lyrical artist is commonly exhibited in his grander odes, and often in his lighter ones; and to this I do not know if I can give a more expressive word than picturesqueness. His imagination, in his Odes, predominates over all his other qualities, great as those other qualities are; and that which he images being clear to himself, he contrives in very few words to render it distinct and vivid to the reader. When Lydia is entreated not to spoil Sybaris; by enumerating the very sports for which her lover has lost taste, he brings before us the whole picture of an athletic young Roman noble—his achievements in horsemanship, swimming, gymnastics; when, in the next ode, he calls on the Feastmaster to heap up the fagots, and bring out the wine, and enjoy his youth while he may, he slides into a totally different picture. Here it is the young Roman idler, by whom only the mornings are devoted to the Campus Martius, the after-noons to the public lounge, the twilights to amorous assignations; and the whole closes still with a picture, the girl hiding herself within the threshold, and betrayed by her laugh, while the lover rushes in and snatches away the love token from the not too reluctant finger. When he invites Tyndaris to his villa, the spot is brought before the eye: the she-goats browsing amid the arbute and wild thyme; the pebbly slopes of Ustica; the green nook sheltered from the dog-star; the noon-day entertainment; the light wines and the lute. The place and the figures are before us as clearly as if on the canvas of a painter. He would tell you that he is marked from childhood for the destiny of poet; and he charms the eye with the picture of the truant infant asleep on the wild mountain-side, safe from the bear and the adder, while the doves cover him with leaves.

With a rarer and higher attribute of art Horace introduces the dramatic element very largely and prominently into his lyrics. His picture becomes a scene. His ideas take life and form as personations. Does he wish to dissuade his countrymen from the notion of transferring the seat of government from Rome to Asia, or perhaps, rather, from some large emigration and military settlement in the East? He calls up the image of the Founder of Rome borne to heaven in the chariot of Mars; ranges the gods in council on Olympus; and puts into the lips of Juno the warning which he desires to convey. Does he seek to discourage popular impatience for the return of the Parthian prisoners—viz., the soldiers of Crassus who had settled and married in the land of the conqueror? He evokes the great form of Regulus urging the Senate to refuse to ransom the Roman captives taken by Carthage—places him as on a visible stage—utters his language, describes his looks, and shows him departing to face the tormentors, satisfied and serene. Would he console a girl for the absence of her lover, and hint to herself a friendly caution against an insidious gallant? In eight short stanzas he condenses a whole drama in personages and plot. Does he paint the reconciliation of two jealous lovers? He makes them speak for themselves; and their brief dialogue is among the most delightful of comedies. Would he tell us that he is going to sup with convivial friends? He suddenly transports us into the midst of the scene, regulates the toasts, calls for the flowers and music, babbles out his loves. The scene lives.

Not to weary the reader with innumerable instances of this art of picture and of drama, so sedulously cultivated

by Horace, I will only observe that the various imitators
of Horace have failed to emulate this the most salient characteristic of his charm in construction; and that even his
numerous commentators have but slightly noticed it—nay,
some have even censured as a desultory episode that which,
according to Horace's system of treating his subject, is the
substance of the poem itself.   For the commencing stanzas
sometimes only serve as a frame to the picture which he
intends to paint, or a prologue to the scene which he
proposes to dramatise.

Thus he begins a poem by an invocation to Mercury and
the lyre to teach him a strain that may soften the coy heart
of a young girl; passes rapidly to the effect of music even
upon the phantoms in the shades below; the Danaides rest
their urn, and then, as if the image of the Danaides spontaneously and suddenly suggested the idea, he places on the
scene the sister murderesses at night slaughtering their
bridegrooms—and the image of Hypermnestra, the sole
gentle and tender one, waking her lord and urging him
to fly.

So, again, when his lady friend, Galatea, is about to
undertake a voyage, he begins by a playful irony about
omens, hastens to the reality of stormy seas—and suddenly
we have the picture of Europa borne from the field-flowers
to the midst of the ocean.   We behold her forlorn and alone
on the shores of Crete—hearken to the burst of her despair
and repentance—and see the drama conclude with the con-
solatory appearance of Venus, and Cupid with his loosened
bow.   To some commentators these vivid presentations of
dramatic imagery have appeared exotic to the poem—
episodes and interludes.   But the more they are examined
as illustrative of Horace's peculiar culture of lyric art, the
more (in this respect not unimitative of Pindar) they stand
out as the body of his piece, and the developed completion
of his purpose.   Take them away, and the poems themselves would shrink into elegant *vers d'occasion.*   Horace, in
a word, generally studies to secure to each of his finer and
more careful poems, however brief it be, that which play-
writers call a "backbone."   And even where he does not
obtain this through direct and elaborate picture or dramatic effect and interest, he achieves it perhaps in a single
stanza, embodying some striking truth or maxim of popular

application, expressed with a terseness so happy, that all times and all nations adopt it as a proverb.

We see, then, how much of his art in construction depends on his lavish employ of picture and drama—how much on compression and brevity. We must next notice, as constituent elements of Horace's peculiar charm, his employment of playful irony, and the rapidity of his transitions from sportive to earnest, earnest to sportive; so that, perhaps, no poet more avails himself of the effect of "surprise"—yet the surprise is not coarse and glaring, but for the most part singularly subdued and delicate—arising sometimes from a single phrase, a single word. He has thus, in his lyrics, more of that combination of tragic and comic elements to which the critics of a former age objected in Shakspeare, than perhaps any poet extant except Shakspeare himself. The consideration of this admirably artistic fidelity to the mingled yarn of life, leads us on to the notice of Horatian style and diction.

The character of the audience he more immediately addresses will naturally have a certain effect on the style of an author, and an effect great in proportion to his practical good sense and good taste. No man possessed of what the French call *savoir vivre*, employs exactly the same style even in extempore discourse, whether he addresses a select audience of scholars or a miscellaneous popular assembly. The readers for whom Horace more immediately wrote were the polite and intellectual circles of Rome, wherein a large proportion were too busy, and a large proportion too idle, to allow themselves to be diverted very far, or for long at a stretch, into poetic regions, whether of thought or diction, remote from their ordinary topics and habitual language. Horace does not, therefore, in the larger number of songs composed—some to be popularly sung and all to be popularly read—build up a poetic language distinct from that of conversation. On the contrary, with some striking exceptions, where the occasion is unusually solemn, he starts from the conversational tone, seeks to familiarise himself winningly with his readers, and leads them on to loftier sentiment, uttered in more noble eloquence—just as an orator, beginning very simply, leads on the assembly he addresses. And possibly Horace's manner in this respect —which, though in a less marked degree, is also that of

Catullus in most of the few purely lyrical compositions the latter has left to us—may be traced to the influence which oratory exercised over the generation born in the last days of the Republic. For in the age of Cicero and Hortensius it may be said that the genius of the Roman language developed itself rather in the beauties which belong to oratory than those which lie more hidden from popular appreciation in the dells and bosks of song.

And as the study of rhetoric and oratory formed an essential part of education among the Roman youths contemporary with Horace, so that study would unconsciously mould the taste of the poet in his selection and arrangement of verbal decorations. Be the cause what it may, nothing is more noticeable in Horace's style than its usual conformity with oratorical art, its easy familiarisation with the minds addressed, its avoidance of over-floridity and recondite mysticism, and its reliance for effects that are to fascinate the imagination, touch the heart, rouse the soul, upon something more than the delicacies of poetic form. His reliance, in short, is upon the sentiment, the idea, which the glow of expression animates and illumes. Thus that *curiosa felicitas verborum* justly ascribed to Horace has so much of the masculine, oratorical character —so unites a hardy and compact simplicity of phrase with a sentiment which itself has the nobleness or grace of poetry (as oratorical expression of the highest degree ever has)— that of all ancient poets Horace is the one who most furnishes the public speaker with quotations sure of striking effect in any public assembly to which the Latin language is familiar. Take one example among many. Mr. Pitt is said never to have more carried away the applause of the House of Commons than when, likening England—then engaged in a war tasking all her resources—to that image of Rome which Horace has placed in the mouth of Hannibal —he exclaimed :—

> " Duris ut ilex tonsa bipennibus
> Nigræ feraci frondis in Algido,
> Per damna, per cædes, ab ipso
> Ducit opes animumque ferro." *

---

* [" Even as the ilex, lopped by axes rude,
Where rich with dusky boughs, soars Algidus,
Through loss, through wounds, receives
New gain, new life—yea, from the very steel."]

Now, this passage, when critically examined, does not owe its unmistakable poetry to any form of words, any startling epithet, inadmissible in prose, but to an illustration at once very noble and yet very simple; and, in rapidity of force, in the development and completion of the idea, so akin to oratory, that an impassioned speaker who had his audience in his hands might have uttered the substance of it in prose.

I may perhaps enable the general reader to comprehend more clearly what I mean by Horace's art in diction as starting from the conversational tone, and, save on rare occasions, avoiding a style antagonistic to prose, by a reference to the two loveliest, most elaborate, and most perfect lyrics in our own language—"L'Allegro" and "Il Penseroso." In these odes Milton takes for representation the two types of temperament under which mankind are more or less divisibly ranged—viz., the cheerful and the pensive. But he treats these two common varieties of all our race as a poet, of a singularly unique temperament himself, addressing that comparatively small number of persons who are *poetically* cheerful or *poetically* pensive. And in so addressing them his language is throughout essentially distinct from prose : it is, like most of his youthful poems, the very quintessence of poetic fancy, both in imagery and expression. Perfectly truthful in itself, the poetry in these masterpieces is still not of that kind of truthfulness which comes home to all men's business and bosoms. Like the poet's own soul, it is "a star, and dwells apart." It may be doubted whether Horace, in his very finest odes, ever, in his maturest age, wrote anything so exquisitely poetical, regarded as pure poetry addressed to poets, as these two lyrics written by Milton in his youth. But then the difference between them and Horace's Odes is, that out of England the former are little known—certainly not appreciated.* Their beauty of form is so delicate, that it is only the eye of a native that can detect it—their truthful-

* It may be said in answer to this, that on the Continent Latin is more read than English. True ; but that does not prevent those English poets who address themselves to a cosmopolitan audience, as Shakspeare, and I may add Byron, being as well appreciated on the Continent as any Latin author is ; and I doubt whether even in England there be as many readers of poetry familiar with "L'Allegro" and "Il Penseroso" as there are with the Odes of Horace.

ness to nature so limited to a circumscribed range of mind, that, even in England, neither the mirthful nor the melancholy man, unless he be a poet or a student, recognises in either poem his own favourite tastes and pleasures. But where Horace describes men's pleasures, every man finds something of himself; the familiar kindliness of his language impresses its poetry upon those who have no pretension to be poets. Had Horace written with equal length and with equal care an "Allegro" and a "Penseroso," not only the poet and the student, not only the man of sentiment and reflection, but all varieties in our common family—the young lover, the ambitious schemer, the man of pleasure, the country yeoman, the city clerk, even the rural labourer —would have found lines in which he saw himself as in a mirror.

Thus, then, Horace's exquisite felicity of wording is for the most part free from any sustained attempt at a language essentially distinct from that of conversation; and for that very reason its beauties of poetical expression both please and strike the more, because they have more the air of those spontaneous flashes of genius which delight us in a great orator or a brilliant talker.

I cannot pass by without comment a characteristic of "form" which, though found more or less in other ancient Poets, and not least in Virgil, is too strikingly conspicuous in Horace to escape the notice of any ordinary critic; yet no critic has attempted satisfactorily to define the principles of art to which its peculiar fascination may be traced. It is in the choice of epithets derived from proper names, or rather the names of places, by which "generals" are individualised into "particulars." The sea is not the sea in general—it is the Hadrian, or the Myrtoan, or the Caspian sea; the ship is not a ship in general—it is the Cyprian or the Bithynian ship; the oaks, which are not always shaken by the blast, are not the oaks in general— they are the oaks upon Garganus; the ilex, which thrives by being pruned, is not an ilex in general—it is the ilex upon Algidus; and so forth, through innumerable instances. That in this peculiarity there is a charm to the ear and the mind of the reader, no one acquainted with Horace will deny. But whence that charm? Partly because it gives that kind of individuality which belongs to

x

personation—it takes the object out of a boundless common-place, and rivets the attention on a more fixed and definite image; but principally because, while it thus limits the idea on the prosaic side of the object, it enlarges its scope, by many vague and subtle associations, on the poetic side. When a proper name is thus used—a proper name suggesting of itself almost insensibly to the mind the poetic associations which belong to the name —the idea is enlarged from a simple to a complex idea, adorned with delicate enrichments, and opening into many dim recesses of imagination. The keel of a ship suggests only a keel; but the Cyprian keel connects itself with dreamy recollections of all the lovely myths about Cyprus. The ilex unparticularised may be but an ilex by a dusty roadside, or in the grounds of a citizen's villa; but the ilex of Algidus evokes, as an accompanying image, the haunted mountain-top sacred to Diana. The verse of Milton is largely indebted to such recourse to poetic proper names for the delight it occasions, not more by melodious sounds than by complex associations. Walter Scott owes much of the animation of his lyrical narratives to his frequent use of proper names in scenery connected with historic association or romantic legend; and Macaulay's Roman Lays push the use of them almost to too evidently artificial an extreme, savouring a little overmuch of elaborate learning and perceptible imitation. But on the whole this exquisite beauty—in lyrical composition especially— is rare among later poets and may be safely commended to their study. It is noticeable that Horace has little or nothing of it in the Epodes (his earliest published poems, except the First Book of the Satires). Perhaps he thought it more especially appropriate to purely lyrical composition, such as the Odes, than to the Epodes, which are not lyrical in form, and, with one exception, Epode xiii., are but partially lyrical in spirit. For it might be wrong to infer that it only occurred to him in the riper practice of his general art as poet, since some of the Odes in which it is found, though not published till after the Epodes, must have been composed within the period to which the latter are assigned.

The defects or shortcomings of Horace as a poet are, like those of all original writers, intimately connected with his peculiar merits. His strong good sense, and that which may be called the practical tendency of his mind in his views both of life and art, while they serve to secure to him so unrivalled a popularity among men of the world, not only deter him from the metaphysical speculation which would have been not less wearisome to the larger portion of his readers than distasteful to himself, as appertaining to those regions beyond the province of the human mind, "at which Jove laughs to see us outstretch our human cares,"—but rarely permit him to plumb very far into the deeps of feeling and passion. Marvellously as he represents the human nature we have all of us in common, each thoughtful man has yet in him a something of human nature peculiar to himself, which, like the goal of the Olympian charioteer, is sometimes almost grazed, but ever shunned, by the rapid wheels of the Venusian.

It may also be said that his turn for irony, or his deference to the impatient taste of a worldly audience, while serving to keep the attention always pleased, and contributing so largely to his special secrets in art, sometimes shows itself unseasonably, and detracts from the effect of some noble passage, or interrupts the rush of some animated description.

Take but one instance among many. In an ode which is among his grandest— Book IV., Ode iv., "Qualem ministrum fulminis alitem "—when he comes, after imagery of epic splendour, to the victory of Drusus over the Vindelici, he checks himself to say, with a sort of mockery which would have been well in its place at a supper-table, that where the Vindelici learned the use of the Amazonian battle-axe he refrains from inquiring, for it is not possible to know everything. No doubt there was some "hit" or point in this parenthetical diversion which is now lost to us; possibly it was a satirical allusion to some pedantic work or antiquarian speculation which was among the literary topics of the day; but every reader of critical taste feels the jar of an episodical levity, inharmonious to all that goes before and after it.* It is like a sarcasm of Voltaire's thrust into the midst of an ode of Pindar's.

* Some critics have indeed proposed to omit these digressive verses altogether, and consider them an impertinent interpolation by an inferior hand. But this is an audacity of assumption forbidden by the authority of manu-

From causes the same or similar, Horace's love-poetry has been accused of want of deep feeling, and compared in this respect, disadvantageously, to the few extant fragments of Sappho. But here it may be observed, that in the whole character of Horace there is one marked idiosyncrasy which influences the general expression of his art. Like many men of our day, who unite to familiar intercourse with fashionable and worldly society an inherent sincerity and a dread of all charlatanic pretences, Horace is even over-studious not to claim any false credit for himself—not to pretend to anything which may not be considered justly his due; he will not pretend to be better born or richer, wiser or more consistent, or of a severer temper than he is. In his Satires and Epistles he even goes out of his way to tell us of his faults.' In his Odes themselves—with all his intense and candidly uttered convictions of their immortality—he seizes frequent occasion for modest reference to the light and trivial themes to which his lyre and his genius are best suited. A man of this character, and with a very keen susceptibility to ridicule, would perhaps shun the expression of any feeling in love much deeper in its sentiment, or much more devoted in its passion, than would find sympathy with the men of the world for whom he principally wrote. If he ever did compose love-poems so earnest and glowing, I think it doubtful whether he would have prevailed on himself to publish them. To a poet who so earnestly seeks to inculcate moderation in every passion and desire, there would have seemed something not only inconsistent with his general repute as writer, but perhaps something offensive to his own sense of shame and the manliness of his nature, in that passionate devotion to the charms of a Cynthia to which Propertius refers the source of his inspiration and his loftiest pretension to the immortality of renown. And Horace is so far right, both as man and as artist, in the mode in which he celebrates the smiling goddess round whom hovers Mirth as well as Cupid, that, as man, one really would respect him less if any of those young ladies, who seem to have been too large-hearted to

scripts, and justly denounced by the editors and critics whose opinions on such a subject Horatian students regard as decisive.

confine their affection to a single adorer, had inspired him
with one of those rare passions which influence an entire
existence. We should feel as much shame as compassion
for any wise friend of ours whom Venus linked lastingly in
her brazen yoke to a Lydia or a Pyrrha. And as an artist,
Horace appears so far right in his mode of dealing with
erotic subjects, that, despite all this alleged want of deep
feeling and passionate devotion, Horace's love-poetry is
still the most popular in the world—the most imitated, the
most quoted, the most remembered. The reason, perhaps,
is, that most men have loved up to the extent that Horace
admits the passion, and very few men have loved much
beyond that limit.

Notwithstanding the amazing pains taken by grave professors and erudite divines to ascertain the history of
Horace's love-affairs—to tell us who and what those young
beauties were—whom he loved first and whom he loved
last—how many of them are to be reduced to a select few,
one being sung under different names lending their
syllables to the same metrical convenience, so that Cinara,
Lalage, Lydia, are one and the same person, &c.—the question remains insoluble. Some scholars have had even the
cold-blooded audacity to assert that, with the single exception of Cinara, and some strange sort of entanglement
with the terrible sorceress to whom he gives the name of
Canidia, all these Horatian beauties are myths and fig-
ments—as purely dreams as those out of the ivory gate—
many of them, no doubt, translations, more or less free,
from the Greek.

The safest conjecture here, as in most cases of disputed
judgment, lies between extremes.

It is probable enough that a man like Horace—a man of
wit and pleasure—thrown early into gay society, and of a
very affectionate nature, as is evinced by the warmth of his
friendships—should have been pretty often in what is commonly called "love" during, say, thirty-nine years out of
the fifty-seven in which he led a bachelor's life. And as
few poets ever have been more subjective than Horace—
ever received the aspect of life more decidedly through the
medium of their own personal impressions—or more regarded poetry as the vehicle of utterance for their opinions
and doctrines, their likings and dislikings, their joys and

their sorrows—so it may be reasonably presumed that in many of his love-verses he expresses or symbolises his own genuine state of feeling. Nor if in some of these there be detected imitations from the Greek, does such imitation suffice to prove that the person addressed was imaginary, and the feeling uttered insincere. Nothing is more common among poets than the adaptation of ideas found elsewhere to their own individual circumstances and self-confessions. When Pope paraphrases Horace where Horace most exclusively personates himself, Pope still so paraphrases that the lines personate Pope and not Horace; and one would know very little of the subjective character of Pope's mind and genius who could assert that he did not utter his own genuine feelings in describing, for instance, his early life and his early friendships, because the description was imitated from a Latin author.

On the other hand, it is impossible to distinguish with any certainty what really does thus illustrate the actual existence of Horace, and does utter the sounds of his own heart, from those purely objective essays of his genius (for, like all poets who have the dramatic faculty strongly developed, he is objective as well as subjective) which were the sportive exercises of art, and the airy embodiments of fancy. It is safest here to leave an acute reader to his own judgment; and it is one of those matters in which acute readers will perhaps differ the most.

Among the faults of Horace may also be mentioned his marked tendency to self-repetition, and especially to the repetition of what one of his most admirable but least enthusiastic editors bluntly calls his "commonplaces:" viz., the shortness of life; the wisdom of seizing the present hour; the folly of anxious research into an unknown future; the vanity of riches and of restless ambition; the happiness of a golden mediocrity in fortune, and an equable mind in the vicissitudes of life. But these iterations of ideas, constituting the body of his ethics, if faulty —inasmuch as the *ultima linea* of his range may therein be too sharply defined—are the inseparable consequence of the most beautiful qualities of his genius. They mark the consistent unity and the sincere convictions of the man— they show how much his favourite precepts are part and parcel of his whole moral and intellectual organisation.

Whether conversing in his Satires, philosophising in his Epistles, giving free play to invention in his Odes—still he cannot help uttering and re-uttering ideas the combination of which constitutes HIMSELF. And as the general effect of these ideas is soothing, so their prevalence in his verse has a charm of repose similar to the prevalence of green in the tints of nature: we greet the constant recurrence of the soft familiar colour with a sensation of pleasure even in its quiet monotony.

Perhaps in most writers who have in a pre-eminent degree the gift of charm, there is, indeed, a certain fondness for some peculiar train of thought, the repetition of which gains the attraction of association. We should be disappointed, in reading such writers, if we did not find the ideas which characterise them, and for which we have learned to seek and to love them, coming up again and again like a refrain in music. It is so with some of our own poets—Goldsmith, Cowper, and Byron—who, alike in nothing else, are alike in the frequent recurrence of the ideas which constitute the characteristic colourings of their genius, and who, in that recurrence, deepen their spell over their readers.

I believe, then, that the attributes thus imperfectly stated are among the principal constituent elements of Horace's indisputable charm, and of a popularity among men of various minds which extends over a wider circle than perhaps any other ancient poet commands, Homer alone excepted. It is a popularity not diminished by the limits imposed on the admiration that accompanies it. Even those critics who deny him certain of the higher qualities of a lyrical poet, do not love him less cordially on account of the other qualities which they are pleased to accord to him. It is commonly enough said that, either from his own deficiencies or those of the Latin language, he falls far short of the Greek lyrical poets in fire, in passion, in elevation of style, in varied melodies of versification. Granted: but judging by the scanty remains of those poets which time has spared, we find evidence of no one— unless it be Alcœus, and conjecturing what his genius might have been as a whole less by the fragments it has left than by Horace's occasional imitations—no one who combines so many excellences, be they great or small, as even a very qualified admirer must concede to Horace ; no one who blends so large a knowledge of the practical work-day world with so delicate a fancy, and so graceful a perception of the poetic aspects of human life ; no one who has the same alert quickness of movement "from gay to grave, from lively to severe ;" no one who unites the same manly and high-spirited enforcement of hardy virtues, temperance and fortitude, devotion to friends and to the native land, with so pleasurable and genial a temperament ; no one who adorns so extensive an acquaintance with metropolitan civilisation by so many lovely pictures of rural enjoyment ; or so animates the description of scenery by the introduction of human groups and images, instilling, as it were, into the body of outward nature the heart and the thought of man.   So that where his genius may fail in height as compared with Pindar, or in the intensity of sensuous passion as compared with Sappho, it compensates by the breadth to which it extends its survey, and over which it diffuses its light and its warmth.

Of all classical authors Horace is the one who has most attracted the emulation of editors and commentators. Students, indeed, have some reason to complain of the very attempts made by learning and ingenuity to determine his text and interpret his meaning.   No sooner have they accustomed themselves to one edition than a new one appears to challenge the authority they had deferred to, and disturb the reading they had accepted.   Paraphrases and translations are still more numerous than editions and commentaries.   There is scarcely a man of letters who has not at one time or other versified or imitated some of the Odes ; and scarcely a year passes without a new translation of them all.   No doubt there is a charm in the proverbial difficulty of dealing with Horace's modes of expression ; but perhaps the true cause which invites translators to encounter that difficulty has been sufficiently intimated in the preceding remarks—viz., the comprehensive range of his sympathy with human beings.   He touches so many sides of character, that on one side or the other he is sure to attract us all, and we seek to clothe in his words some cherished feeling or sentiment of our own. Be that as it may, an unusual degree of indulgence has by tacit consent been accorded to new translations from Horace. Readers unacquainted with the original are disposed to welcome every fresh attempt to make the Venusian Muse express herself in familiar English; and Horatian scholars feel an interest in examining how each succeeding translator grapples with the difficulties of interpretation which have been, as many of them still are, matters of conjecture and dispute to commentators the most erudite, and critics the most acute.

May a reasonable share of such general indulgence be vouchsafed to that variety in the mode of translation of which I now propose to hazard the experiment.

I have long been of opinion that the adoption of other rhymeless measures than that to which we at present confine the designation of blank verse would be attended with especial advantage in translations from the classical poets, and, indeed, in poems founded upon Hellenic and Roman myths, and treated in the classical character and spirit. In that belief I began many years ago these translations from Horace, and more recently submitted to the public the experiment of the metres employed in the " Lost Tales of Miletus." I will not lengthen this preface by any definition of the general rhythmical principles upon which, in my judgment, lyrical measures that, taking the form of strophe or stanza, dispense with rhyme, should be invented and framed. Should any writer be tempted hereafter to repeat and improve on my experiments, he will easily detect the laws I have laid down for myself, and adopt, modify, or reject them, according to his own idiosyncrasies of ear and taste.

So far as these translations are concerned, it will be seen that I have shunned any attempt to transfer to our own language the exact form of the original metres. I have rather sought to construct measures in accordance with the character of English prosody, akin to the prevalent spirit of the original, and of compass sufficient to allow a general adherence to the rule of translating line by line, or at least strophe by strophe, without needless amplification on the one hand, or harsh contraction on the other.

The same licence of diversifying the metres employed in translation, according as the prevalent spirit of the ode demands lively and sportive, or serious and dignified expression, in which most of the rhyming translators unscrupulously indulge, must be conceded to him who rejects rhyme from his version. We have no English metres, rhymed or unrhymed, so supple for the expressing of opposing sentiment or emotion as are the Alcaic, and even the Sapphic, in the hands of Horace;· and if we desire to be true to the spirit of Horace, we have no option but to vary his form, and not always preserve for loose and sprightly movement the same mechanical arrangement of syllables which accords with the march of the serried and the grave.

For the Alcaic stanza I have chiefly employed two different forms of rhythm; the one, which is of more frequent recurrence, as in Ode ix.—the other, as in Odes xxxiv.-xxxv., Book I. But in both these forms of rhythm I have made occasional variations.

For the Sapphic metre, in which Horace has composed more odes than in any other except the Alcaic, I have avoided, save in one or two of the shorter poems, any imitation of the chime rendered sufficiently familiar by Canning's "Knife-grinder," not only because, in the mind of an English reader, it is associated with a popular burlesque, but chiefly because an English imitation of the Latin rhythm, with a due observance of the trochee in the first three lines of the stanza, has in itself an unpleasant and monotonous sing-song. In my version of the Sapphic I have chiefly employed two varieties of rhythm: for the statelier odes, our own recognised blank verse in the first three lines, usually, though not always, with a dissyllabic termination; and, in the fourth line, a metre analogous in length and cadence to the fourth line of the original, though, of course, without any attempt at preserving the Latin quantity of dactyl and spondee. In fact, as Dr. Kennedy has truly observed, the spondee is not attainable in our language, except by a very forced effort of pronunciation. That which passes current as an English spondee is really a trochee. For the lighter odes of the Sapphic metre, a more sportive or tripping measure is adopted.

I must leave my versions of the other metres which Horace has less frequently employed to speak for themselves.

In the Latin version, placed side by side with the English, I have generally adopted the text of Orelli. The rare instances in which I have differed from it for that of another editor are stated in the notes. For the current punctuation—which in Orelli, and indeed in Macleane, is so sparse as not unfrequently to render the sense obscure to those not familiarly intimate with it—I am largely indebted to the admirable edition of Mr. Yonge. The modes of spelling preferred by Ritter and Mr. Munro as more faithful transcripts of the ancient MSS., involve questions of great interest to professional scholars, but are as yet too unfamiliar to the general reader for adoption in a text especially designed for his use, and annexed to the English translation for the convenient facilities of reference and comparison.

My objects in the task I have undertaken have compelled me to add in some degree the labour of a critic to that of a translator. The introductions prefixed and the notes appended to the several odes are designed not only to serve for readers unacquainted with the original, but to bring, in a terse and convenient form, before such students of Horace as may not have toiled through the many and often conflicting commentaries of the best editors, the opinions of eminent authorities upon difficult or disputed questions of interpretation. In my notes will be seen the extent to which I am indebted not only to Dillenburger, Orelli, Ritter, but to our own recent English editors, Macleane and Yonge—and, on certain points of controverted interpretation, to Mr. Munro's erudite and valuable introduction to the beautiful edition illustrated from antique gems, by Mr. King.

The majority of critics concur in the doctrine that all the Odes in Horace, differing in this respect from the Epodes, consist of stanzas in four lines, as the Alcaic and Sapphic do. This opinion has been ably controverted by Ritter. Munro declines either to affirm or deny it. But conformably to the general opinion, I have treated, and so translated, the Odes as quatrains, with four exceptions, for which I subjoin my reasons.

Odes i. Book I., xxx. Book III., and viii. Book IV., are
in the same metre, and the only ones that are; but Ode viii.
Book IV. consists of thirty-four lines, and cannot therefore be reduced to quatrain stanzas; and the supposition
that two verses required for such subdivision have been
lost—no evidence of such loss appearing in the oldest
MSS. or being intimated by the early commentators—is a
hazardous basis on which to rest the theory that the poem
must have been originally composed in quatrain. It is also
to be observed that Ode i. Book I. so little adapts itself to
the division of four-line stanzas with a suitable pause, that
Mr. Yonge follows Stallbaum in printing the first two
lines as prefatory to the rest, and the last two lines as the
complement of the stanza. But it is a somewhat bold
proceeding, for the sake of establishing an arbitrary system, thus to cut a stanza in half, placing one half at the
beginning and the other half at the end of a poem; nor
does the arrangement entirely effect the object aimed at,
if, as Macleane and Munro contend, a full stop should be
placed at the end of the fifth line—"nobilis." Even the
remaining ode in this metre—Ode xxx. Book III.—does
not readily flow into quatrain, the pause not occurring at
the fourth and eighth lines, but at the fifth and ninth. I
have not, therefore, in my translation, divided these three
odes into stanzas. Lastly, I have followed Dillenburger,
Orelli, Macleane, Munro, in the arrangement of Ode xii.
Book III. as a stanza of three lines, instead of adopting
the quatrain arrangement of Kirchner, to be found in the
excursus of Orelli, and favoured by Mr. Yonge.

The Secular Hymn I have printed in its proper chronological place, between Books III. and IV.

I concur in the reasons which have led recent editors to
reject the headings to the Latin version, which are found
in the MSS.; but I have given headings to the translation,
for the convenience of reference which they afford to
English readers.

It remains for me only gratefully to acknowledge my
obligations to the distinguished scholars who have permitted me to consult them in the course of this translation. Many years ago I submitted the earliest specimens
of my attempts to my valued friend Dr. Kennedy. His
encouragement induced me to proceed with my under-

taking, while his advice and suggestions enabled me materially to improve it. With no less liberal a kindness another friend, the Rev. F. W. Farrar, has permitted me to encroach on his time, and profit by his taste and his learning. Much more could I say in gratitude, as to the services so generously rendered me by these eminent scholars, were it not for the fear that I might seem in so doing to shelter my defects and shortcomings under the authority of their names. It is enough for me to acknowledge that to them must be largely ascribed any merit which may be accorded to my labours, and that without their aid my faults would have been much more numerous and grave.

ON ART IN FICTION.

Art is that process by which we give to natural materials the highest excellence they are capable of receiving.

We estimate the artist, not only in proportion to the success of his labours, but in proportion to the intellectual faculties which are necessary to that success. Thus a watch by Breguét is a beautiful work of art, and so is a tragedy by Sophocles:—The first is even more perfect of its kind than the last, but the tragedy requires higher intellectual faculties than the watch, and we esteem the tragedian above the watchmaker.

The excellence of art consists in the fitness of the object proposed with the means adopted. Art carried to its perfection would be the union of the most admirable object with the most admirable means: in other words it would require a greatness in the conception correspondent to the genius in the execution. But as mechanical art is subjected to more definite and rigorous laws than intellectual art, so, in the latter, a comprehensive critic regards the symmetry of the whole with large indulgence towards blemishes in detail. We contemplate mechanical art with reference to its utility—intellectual art with reference to its beauty. A single defect in a watch may suffice to destroy all the value of its construction;—a single blemish in a tragedy may scarcely detract from its effect.

In regarding any work of art, we must first thoroughly acquaint ourselves with the object that the artist had in view. Were an antiquarian to set before us a drawing, illustrative of the costume of the Jews in the time of Tiberius, we should do right to blame him if he presented to our eye goblets in the fashion of the fifteenth century; but when Leonardo da Vinci undertook the sublime and moving representation of the Last Supper, we feel that

* [Original appeared in 1838, in two instalments, headed "The Critic," No. I. and No. II. in the first of the seven volumes of *The Monthly Chronicle*, published by the Messrs. Longman,]

his object is not that of an antiquary; and we do not regard it as a blemish that the Apostles are seated upright instead of being recumbent, and that the loaves of bread are those of an Italian baker. Perhaps, indeed, the picture affected the spectators the more sensibly from their familiarity with the details; and the effect of art on the whole was only heightened by a departure from correctness in minutiæ. So, in an anatomical drawing that professed to give the exact proportions of man; we might censure the designer if the length of the limbs were disproportioned to the size of the trunk : but when the sculptor of the Apollo Belvedere desired to convey to the human eye the ideal of the God of Youth, the length of the limbs contributed to give an additional and superhuman lightness and elasticity to the form ; and the excellence of the art was evinced and promoted by the sacrifice of mechanical accuracy in detail. It follows, therefore, that Intellectual Art and Technical Correctness are far from identical; that one is sometimes proved by the disdain of the other. And, as this makes the distinction between mechanical and intellectual art, so is the distinction remarkable in proportion as that intellectual art is exercised in the highest degree— in proportion as it realises the Ideal. For the Ideal consists not in the imitation, but the exaltation, of Nature ; and we must accordingly inquire, not how far it resembles what we have seen so much as how far it embodies what we can imagine.

It is not till we have had great pictures, that we can lay down the rules of painting ;—it is not till we have had great writers in a particular department of intellect, that we can sketch forth a code of laws for those who succeed them : For the theory of art resembles that of science ; we must have data to proceed upon, and our inductions must be drawn from a vast store of experiments.

Prose fictions have been cultivated by modern writers of such eminence, and now form so wide and essential a part of the popular literature of Europe, that it may not be an uninteresting or an useless task to examine the laws by which the past may be tested, and the labours of future students simplified and abridged.

PROSE FICTIONS.

The novelist has three departments for his art—*Manners, Passions, Character.*

MANNERS.

The delineation of manners embraces both past and present; the Modern and Historical Romance.

The Historical.

We have a right to demand from the writer who professes to illustrate a former age a perfect acquaintance with its characteristics and spirit. At the same time, as he intends rather to interest than instruct us, his art will be evinced in the illustrations he selects, and the skill with which they are managed. He will avoid all antiquarian dissertations not essentially necessary to the conduct of his tale. If, for instance, his story should have no connection with the mysteries of the middle ages, he will take care how he weary us with an episodical description that changes his character from that of a narrator into that of a lecturer. In the tale of "Notre Dame de Paris," by Victor Hugo, the description of the Cathedral of Notre Dame is not only apposite, but of the deepest interest; for the cathedral is, by a high effort of art, made an absolute portion of the machinery of the tale. But the long superfluous description of the spectacle with which the story opens is merely a parade of antiquarian learning, because the Scholars and the Mysteries have no proportionate bearing whatever in the future development of the tale.

The usual fault of the historical novelist is over minuteness in descriptions of dress and feasts, of pageants and processions. Minuteness is not accuracy. On the contrary, the more the novelist is minute, the more likely he is to mar the accurate effect of the whole, either by wearisome tameness or some individual error.

An over antiquated phraseology is a common and a most inartistical defect: whatever diction the delineator of a distant age employs can never be faithful to the language of the time, for, if so, it would be unintelligible. So, in the German novels that attempt a classical subject, there is the prevalent vice of a cold imitation of a classic epistolary style. It is the very attempt at resemblance that destroys the illusion, as it is by the servility of a copy that we are most powerfully reminded of the difference between the copy and the original. The language of a former time should be presented to us in the freest and most familiar paraphrase we can invent. Thus the mind is relieved at once from the task of forming perpetual comparisons, and surrenders itself to the delusion the more easily, from the very candour with which the author makes demand on its credulity. In selecting a particular epoch for illustration, an artistical author will consider well what is the principal obstacle in the mind of his audience to the reception of his story. For instance, if he selects a story of ancient Greece, the public will be predisposed to anticipate a frigid pedantry of style, and delineations of manners utterly different from those which are familiar to us now. The author will, therefore, agreeably surprise the reader, if he adopt a style as familiar and easy which a Greek would have used in common conversation; and show the classical spirit that pervades his diction, by the grace of the poetry, or the lightness of the wit, with which he can adorn his allusions and his dialogue. Thus, the very learning he must evince will only be but incidental and easy ornament. On the other hand, instead of selecting such specimens and modifications of human nature as are most different from, and unfamiliar to the sympathies of modern times, he will rather prefer to appeal to the eternal sentiments of the heart, by showing how closely the men of one age resemble those of another. His hero, his lover, his epicure, his buffoon, his miser, his boaster, will be as close to the life as if they were drawn from the streets of London. The reader will be interested to see society different, yet men the same; and the Manners will be relieved from the disadvantage of unfamiliarity by an entire sympathy with the humours they mark, or the passions on which they play.

Again, if the author propose to carry his readers to the time of Richard I., or of Elizabeth, he will have to encounter a universal repugnance from the thought of an imitation of "Ivanhoe" or "Kenilworth." An author who was, nevertheless, resolved to select such a period for his narrative would, accordingly, if an artist of sufficient excellence, avoid, with care, touching upon any of the points which may suggest the recollection of Scott. He would deeply consider all the features of the time, and select those neglected by his predecessor;—would carefully note all the deficiencies of the author of "Kenilworth," and seize at once upon the ground which that versatile genius omitted to consecrate to himself.

To take the same epoch; the same characters, even the same narrative, as a distinguished predecessor, is perfectly allowable; and if successful, a proof at once of originality and skill. But if you find the shadow of the previous work flinging itself over your own,—if you have not thoroughly escaped the influence of the first occupant of the soil—you will only invest your genius to unnecessary disadvantage, and build edifices, however graceful and laboured, upon the freehold of another.

In novels devoted to the delineation of existing manners, the young author will be surprised to find, that exact and unexaggerated fidelity has never been the characteristic of the greatest novelists of their own time. There would be, indeed, something inane and trifling, or mean and vulgar, in Dutch copies of the modern still life. We do not observe any frivolity in Walter Scott, when he describes with elaborate care the set of the ruffle, the fashion of the cloak of Sir Walter Raleigh, nor when he catalogues all the minutiæ of the chamber of Rowena. But to introduce your hero of "May Fair," with an exact portraiture of the colour of his coat or the length of his pantaloons, to item all the commodes and fauteuils of a Lady Caroline or Frances, revolts our taste as an effeminate attention to trifles.

In humbler life the same rule applies with equal strength. We are willing to know how Gurth was dressed or Esmeralda lodged, but we do not require the same minuteness in describing the smock frock of a labourer, or the garret of the girl who is now walking upon stilts for a penny. The greatest masters of the novel of modern life have usually availed themselves of *Humour* as the illustration of manners; and have, with a deep and true, but perhaps unconscious, knowledge of art, pushed the humour almost to the verge of caricature. For as the Serious Ideal requires a certain exaggeration in the proportions of the Natural, so also does the Ludicrous. Thus Aristophanes, in painting the humours of his time, resorts to the most poetical extravagance of machinery, and calls the clouds in aid of his ridicule of philosophy, or summons frogs and gods to unite in his satire on Euripides. The Don Quixote of Cervantes never lived, nor, despite the vulgar belief, ever could have lived, in Spain; but the art of the portrait is in the admirable exaltation of the Humorous by means of the Exaggerated. With more qualification the same may be said of Parson Adams, of Sir Roger de Coverley, and even of the Vicar of Wakefield.

Where the author has not adopted the Humorous as the best vehicle for the delineation of manners, he has sometimes artfully removed the scene from the country that he seeks to delineate, so that he might place his portraitures at a certain, and the most advantageous, distance from the eye. Thus, Le Sage obtains his object, of a consummate and masterly picture of the manners of his own land, though he has taken Spain for the theatre of the adventures of Gil Blas; and Swift has transferred all that his experience or his malice could narrate of the intrigues of courts, the chimeras of philosophy, the follies and vices of his nation and his time, to the regions of Lilliput and Laputa.

It may be observed, that the delineation of manners is usually the secondary object of a novelist of high power. To a penetrating mind manners are subservient to the illustration of views of life or the consummation of original character. In a few years the mere portraiture of manners is obsolete. It is the knowledge of what is durable in human nature that alone preserves the work from decay. Lilly and Shakspeare alike painted the prevailing and courtly mannerism of their age. The Euphues rests upon ourselves—Don Armado will delight us as long as pedantry exists.

Character.

An author once said, "Give me a character, and I will find the play ; " and, if we look to the most popular novels we shall usually find, that where one reader speaks of the conduct of the story, a hundred readers will speak of the excellence of some particular character.

An author, before resolving on the characters he designs to portray, will do well to consider maturely, first, what part they are designed to play in his performance ; and, secondly, what is the precise degree of interest which he desires them to create. Having thus considered and duly determined, he will take care that no other character in the work shall interfere with the effect each is intended to produce. Thus, if his heroine is to be drawn gentle and mild, no second heroine, with the same attributes, should distract the attention of the reader, a rule which may seem obvious but which is usually overlooked. When the author feels that he has thoroughly succeeded in a principal and predominant character, he will even sacrifice others, nominally more important, to increase the interest of the figure in the foreground. Thus, in the tale of "Ivanhoe," Rowena, professedly the heroine, is very properly sacrificed to Rebecca. The more interesting the character of Rowena, the more pathetic the position she had assumed, the more we should have lost our compassion and admiration of the Jewess, and the highest merit of the tale, its pathos, would have been diminished. The same remark will apply to the Clementina and Harriet Byron of Richardson.

The author will take care not to crowd his canvas. He will select as few characters as are compatible with the full agency of his design. Too many plants in a narrow compass destroy each other. He will be careful to individualise each ; but if aspiring to the highest order of art, he will yet tone down their colours by an infinite variety of shades. The most original colours are those most delicately drawn, where the individual peculiarity does not obtrude itself naked and unrelieved. It was a very cheap purchase of laughter in Sir Walter Scott, and a mere trick of farce, which Shakspeare and Cervantes would have disdained, to invest a favourite humorist with some cant phrase, which he cannot open his mouth without disgorging. The "*Prodigious*" of Dominic Sampson, the "My Father the Baillie," of Nichol Jarvie, the "*Provant*" of Major Dalgettie, the "*Déjeûner* at Tillietudlem," of Lady Margaret Bellenden, &c., all belong to one source of humour, and that the shallowest and most hackneyed. If your tale spread over a considerable space of time, you will take care that your readers may note the change of character which time has necessarily produced. You will quietly show the difference between the boy of eighteen and the man of forty; you will connect the change in the character with the influence of the events you have narrated. In the novel of "Anastasius," this article of composition is skilfully and· delicately mastered, more so than in "Gil Blas."

If you bend all your faculties to the development of some single character, and you make us sensible that such is your object, the conduct of your story becomes but a minor consideration. Shakspeare probably cared but little whether the fencing scene in "Hamlet" was the best catastrophe he could invent; he took the incidents of the story as he found them, and lavished his genius on the workings of the mind, to which all external incidents on this side the grave had become trivial and uninfluential—weary, unprofitable, stale.

It must rest entirely on the nature of the interest you desire it to effect, whether you seek clearly to place before us, or dimly to shadow out, each particular character. If you connect your hero with supernatural agency, if you introduce agents not accounted for by purely human means, if you resort to the Legendary and Mysterious, for the interest you identify with any individual character, it may be most artistical to leave such a character vague, shadowy, and half-incompleted. Thus, very skilfully is the Master of Ravenswood, over whose head hang ominous and weird predictions, left a less distinct and palpable creation, than the broad-shouldered and much-eating heroes whom Scott usually conducts through a labyrinth of adventures to marriage with a wealthy Ariadne.

The formation of characters, improbable and grotesque, is not very compatible with a high conception of art, unless the work be one that so avowedly deals with beings different from those we mix with, that our imagination is prepared as to the extent of the demand upon its faith. Thus, when Shakspeare introduces us at once to the Enchanted Island, and we see the wand of the magician, and hear the song of Ariel, we are fully prepared to consider Caliban a proper inhabitant of such a soil; or when the "Faust" opens with the chorus of angels, and the black dog appears in the chamber of the solitary student, the imagination finds little difficulty in yielding assent to the vagaries of the witches, and the grotesque diablerie of the Hartz Mountains; but we are wholly unprepared to find a human Caliban in the bell-ringer of a Parisian cathedral; and we see no reason why Quasimodo should not have been as well shaped as other people. The use of the grotesque in "The Abbot," where Sir Percy Shafto is killed and revived, is an absurdity which is as gross as can well be conceived.

In the portraiture of evil and criminal characters lies the widest scope for an author profoundly versed in the philosophy of the human heart. In all countries, in all times, the delineation of crime has been consecrated to the highest order of poetry. For as the emotions of terror and pity are those which it falls to the province of the sublimest genius to arouse, so it is chiefly, though not solely, in the machinations of guilt that may be found, the source of the one, and in the misfortunes, sometimes of the victim of the guilt, nay, sometimes of the guilty agent himself, that we arrive at the fountain of the softer passion. Thus, the murder of Duncan rouses our compassion, through our admission to all the guilty doubts and aspirations of Macbeth; and our terror is of a far higher and more enthralling order, because it is reflected back upon us from the bared and struggling heart of the murderer, than it would have been if we had seen the physical death of the victim. It may be observed, indeed, that, in a fine tragedy, it is the preparation to the death that is to constitute the catastrophe, that usually most sensibly excites the interest of terror, and that the blow of the murderer and the fall of the victim is but a release to the suspense of fear, and changes the whole current of our emotions. But the grandest combination is when the artist unites in one person the opposite passions of terror and pity—when we feel at once the horror of the crime, yet compassion for the criminal. Thus, in the most stirring of all the ancient dramas, the moment that we discover that Œdipus has committed the crimes from which we most revolt, homicide and incest, is the very moment in which, to the deepest terror of the crimes is united the most intense compassion for the criminal. So again before the final catastrophe of the mystic fate of Macbeth, when evil predictions are working to their close, and we feel that his hour is come, Shakspeare has paused, to draw from the dark bosom of the fated murderer those moving reflections, "My way of life," &c., which steal from us insensibly our hatred of his guilt, and awaken a new and softer interest in the approaching consummation of the usurper's doom. Again, in the modern play of "Virginius," when the scene opens and discovers the avenging father upon the body of the murdered Appius, it is in Virginius, at once criminal and childless, that are concentrated our pity and our terror.

In the portraiture of crime, however dark, the artist will take care to throw some redeeming light. The veriest criminal has some touch and remnant of human goodness, and it is according as this sympathy between the outcast and ourselves is indicated or insinuated, that the author profanes or masters the noblest mysteries of his art. Where the criminal be one so resolute and hardened, so inexorable and preterhuman, in his guilt, that he passes the bounds of flesh and blood inconsistencies and sympathies, a great artist will bring forth intellectual qualities to balance our disgust at the moral. Thus, in "Richard III.," it is with a masterly skill that Shakspeare relieves us from the revolting contemplation of unmingled crime, by enlisting our involuntary and unconscious admiration on the side of the address, the subtle penetration into character, the affluent wit, the daring energy, the royal will, with which the ruthless usurper moves through the bloody scenes of his treachery. And at the last, it is, if not by a relic of human virtue, at least by a relic of human weakness, by the working conscience, and the haunted pillow, that we are taught to remember that it is a man who sins and suffers, not a beast that ravages and is slain. Still, despite all the subtle shadings in the character of Richard, we feel that the guilt is overdrawn—that the dark spirit wants a moral as well as intellectual relief. To penetrating critics, it has always, therefore, been the most coarse of all the creations of Shakspeare, and will never bear a comparison, as a dissection of human nature, with the goaded and writhing wickedness of Macbeth.

In the delineation of a criminal, the author will take care to show us the motives of the crimes—the influences beneath which the character has been formed. He will suit the nature of the criminal to the state of society in which he is cast. Thus he will have occasions for the noblest morality. By concentrating in one focus the vicious influences of any peculiar error in the social system, he will hold up a mirror to nations themselves.

As the bad man will not be painted as thoroughly and unredeemably bad, so he whom you represent as good, will have his foibles or infirmities. You will show where even the mainspring of his virtues sometimes calls into play a counter vice. Your just man will be sometimes severe; your generous man will be sometimes careless of the consequences of generosity. It is true that, in both these applications of art, you will be censured by shallow critics and pernicious moralists. It will be said of you in the one case, "He seeks to interest us in a murderer, or a robber, an adulterer, or a parricide;" it will be said of you in the other, "And this man whom he holds up to us as an example, whom he calls wise and good, is a rascal who indulges such an error, or commits such an excess." But no man can be an artist who does not prefer experience and human nature to all criticism, and for the rest he must be contented to stand on the same ground, or to have filled his urn from the same fountains, as Shakspeare and Boccaccio, as Goethe and Schiller, Fielding and Le Sage. If it be, however, necessary to your design to paint some character as almost faultless, as exempt from our common infirmities and errors, you will act skilfully if you invest it with the attributes of old age. When all the experience of error has been dearly bought, when the passions are laid at rest, and the mind burns clear as the night deepens, virtue does in fact become less and less wavering and imperfect. But youth without a fault would be youth without a passion; and such a portrait would make us despair of emulation, and arm against reverence and esteem all the jealousies of self-love.

THE PASSIONS.

Delineation of passions is inseparable from the delineation of character. A novel admirable in character, may, indeed, be drawn, in which the passions are but coldly and feebly shadowed forth. "Gil Blas" is an example. But either such novels are intended as representations of external life, not of the metaphysical operations of the inner man, or they deal with the humours and follies, not the grave and deep emotions, of our kind, and belong to the *Comedy* of Romance.

But if a novel of character can be excellent without passion, it would be impossible to create a novel of passion without character. The elementary passions themselves, like the elements, are few: it is the modifications they take in passing through different bodies that give us so inexhaustible a variety of lights and shadows of loveliness and glory.

The passion of Love is not represented by a series of eloquent rhapsodies, or even of graceful sentiments. It is represented in fiction by its effects on some particular character; the same with Jealousy, Avarice, Revenge, &c. Therefore, in a certain sense of the word, all representations of passion in fiction may be considered *typical*. In Juliet it is not the picture of love solely and abstractedly, it is the picture of love in its fullest effect on *youth*. In Antony it is love as wild, and as frantic, and as self-sacrificing; but it is love, not emanating from the enthusiasm of youth, but already touched with something of the blindness and infirmity of dotage.

In Macbeth it is not the mere passion of ambition that is portrayed, it is ambition operating on a man physically daring, and morally irresolute; a man whom the darkest agencies alone can compel, and whom the fullest triumphs of success cannot reconcile to crime. So, if we review all the passionate characters of Shakspeare, we shall find that the passion is individualised and made original by the mould in which the fiery liquid is cast. Nor is the language of that passion declamation upon the passion itself, but the revelation of the effect it produces on a single subject. It is accordingly in the perfect harmony that exists between the character and the passion, that the abstract and bodiless idea finds human force and corporeal interest. If you would place the passion before us in a new light, the character that represents it must be original. An artistical author, taking advantage of the multiform inconsistencies of human nature, will often give to the most hackneyed passion a thoroughly new form, by placing it in a character where it could least be looked for. For instance, should you desire to portray avarice, you will go but on worn-out ground, if you resort to Plautus and Molière for your model. But if you find in history the record of a brilliant courtier, a successful general, marked and signalised by the vice of Harpagon, the vice itself takes a new hue, and your portraiture will be a new addition to our knowledge of the mysteries of our kind. Such a representation, startling, untouched, and truthful, might be taken from the character of the Duke of Marlborough, the hero of Blenheim. In portraying the effect of a passion, the rarest art of the novelist is to give it its due weight, and no more. Thus, in love novels we usually find nothing but love; as if in the busy and complicated life of man, there were no other spring to desire and action but

"Love, love——eternal love."

Again, if an author portrays a miser, he never draws him otherwise than as a miser. He makes him, not the avaricious miser, but abstract avarice itself. Not so Shakspeare when he created Shylock. Other things, other motives occupy the spirit of the Jew besides his gold and his argosies; he is a grasping and relentless miser, yet he can give up avarice to revenge. He has sublime passions that elevate his mean ones.

If your novel be devoted to love and its effects, you will act more consistently with the truths of life, if you throw the main interest of the passion in the heroine. In the hero you will increase our sense of the power of the passion, if you show us all the conflicting passions with which in men it usually contends—ambition, or honour, or duty: the more the effect of love is shown by the obstacles it silently subdues, the more triumphant will be your success. You will recollect that in the novel, as in the drama, it is in the *struggle* of emotions that the science of the heart is best displayed; and in the delineation of such struggles, there is ground little occupied hitherto by the great masters of English fiction. It was not in the province of Fielding or Smollett, and Scott but rarely indulges, and still more rarely succeeds, in the metaphysical operations of stormy and conflicting feelings. He rather seems to have made it a point of art to imitate the ancient painter, and throw a veil over passions he felt inadequate to express. Thus, after the death and burial of Lucy, it is only by the heavy and unequal tread of Ravenswood, in his solitary chamber, that his agonies are to be conjectured. But this avoidance of the internal man, if constant and systematic, is but a clever trick to hide the want of power.

The Sentiment.

The Sentiment that pervades a book is often its most effective moral, and its most universal charm. It is a pervading and indescribable harmony in which the heart of the author seems silently to address our own. Through creations of crime and vice, there may be one pervading sentiment of virtue; through the humblest scenes, a sentiment of power and glory. It is the sentiment of Wordsworth of which his disciples speak, when they enlarge upon attributes of holiness and beauty, which detached passages, however exquisite, do not suffice to justify. Of all the qualities of fiction, the sentiment is that which we can least subject to the inquiries or codes of criticism. It emanates from the moral and predominant quality of the author—the perfume from his genius: and by it he unconsciously reveals himself. The sentiment of Shakspeare is in the strong sympathies with all that is human. In the sentiment of Swift, we see the reflection of a spirit discontented and malignant. Mackenzie, Goldsmith, Voltaire, Rousseau, betray their several characters as much in the

prevalent sentiments of their writings as if they had made
themselves the heroes. Of all writers of great genius,
Shakspeare has the most sentiment, and, perhaps, Smollett
and Defoe the least. The student will distinguish between
a work of sentiment and a sentimental work. As the
charm of sentiment in a fiction is that it is latent and indefinite, so the charm vanishes directly it becomes ob-
truding and importunate. The mistake of Kotzebue, and
many of the Germans, of Metastasio and a feeble and
ephemeral school of the Italians, was in the confounding
sentiment with passion.

Sentiment is capable of many classifications and sub-
divisions. The first and finest is that touched upon—the
sentiment of the whole work: a sentiment of beauty or of
grandeur—of patriotism or of benevolence—of veneration
of justice, or of piety. This may be perfectly distinct
from the character or scenes portrayed: it evinces itself
insensibly and invisibly: and we do not find its effect till
we sum up all the effects that the work has bequeathed.
The sentiment is, therefore, often incorporated and identified with the moral tendency of the fiction.

There is also a sentiment that belongs to style, and gives
depth and colouring to peculiar passages. For instance, in
painting a pastoral life in the heart of lonely forests, or by
the side of unpolluted streams, the language and thoughts
of the author glide into harmony with the images he
creates; and we feel that he has, we scarcely know by
what art, penetrated himself and us with the Sentiment of
Repose.

A sentiment of this nature will be felt at once by the
lovers of Spenser, and of Ariosto and Tasso. In the entrance to the domains of Death, Milton breathes over the
whole description the Sentiment of Awe.

The Sentiments are distinct from the Passions: sometimes they are most eloquent in the utter absence of passion itself; as the sentiment that pervades the poem of
"The Castle of Indolence;"—at other times they are the
neighbours, the intervening shades, between one passion
and another; as the Sentiment of a Pleasing Melancholy.
Regret and Awe are sentiments; Grief and Sorrow,
passions.

As there is a sentiment that belongs to description, so

there are characters in which sentiment supplies the place of passion. The character of Jacques, in "As You Like It," is purely one of sentiment. Usually sentiment is, in character, most effective when united with humour, as in Uncle Toby and Don Quixote, and, to quote a living writer, some of the masterly creations of Paul de Kock. For the very delicacy of the sentiment will be most apparent by the contrast of what seems to us at first the opposite quality, as the violet we neglect in the flower-bed, enchants us in the hollow of a rock.

In the subsequent part of this paper it is proposed to enter upon the construction of the fiction itself—the distinctions between the Drama and the Novel—and the mechanism, conduct, and catastrophe of the different species of Invented Narrative.

THE CONCEPTION.

A story may be well constructed, yet devoid of interest; on the other hand, the construction may be faulty and the interest vivid. This is the case even with the drama. "Hamlet" is not so well constructed a story as the "Don Carlos" of Alfieri; but there is no comparison in the degree of interest excited in either tragedy. Still, though we ought not to consider that excellence in the technical arrangement of incidents as a certain proof of the highest order of art, it is a merit capable of the most brilliant effects when possessed by a master.

An exquisite mechanism in the construction of the mere story, not only gives pleasure in itself, but it displays other and loftier beauties to the best advantage. It is the setting of the jewels.

It is common to many novelists to commence a work without any distinct chart of the country which they intend to traverse—to suffer one chapter to grow out of another, and invention to warm as the creation grows. Scott* has confessed to this mode of novel writing; but Scott, with all his genius, was rather a great mechanist

* See Mr. Lockhart's Life of Scott, vol. v. p. 232: "In writing I never could lay down a plan," &c. Scott, however, has the candour to add, "I would not have young writers imitate my carelessness."

than a great artist. His execution was infinitely superior to his conception. It may be observed, indeed, that his conceptions are often singularly poor and barren, compared with the vigour with which they are marked out. He conceives a story with the design of telling it as well as he can, but is wholly insensible to the high and true aim of art, which is rather to consider for what objects the story should be told. Scott never appears to say to himself, " Such a tale will throw a new light upon human passions, or add fresh stores to human wisdom : for that reason I select it. He seems rather to consider what picturesque effects it will produce, what striking scenes, what illustrations of mere manners. He regards the story with the eye of the *property man*, though he tells it with the fervour of the poet. It is not thus that the greatest authorities in fiction have composed. It is clear to us that Shakspeare, when he selected the tale which he proposed to render χρῆμά ἐς ἀεί—the everlasting possession of mankind, made it his first and paramount object to work out certain passions or affections of the mind, in the most complete and profound form. He did not so much consider how the incidents might be made most striking, as how the truths of the human heart might be made most clear. And it is a remarkable proof of his consummate art, that though in his best plays we may find instances in which the mere incidents might be made more probable, and the theatrical effects more vivid. We can never see one instance in such plays where the passion he desired to represent could have been placed in a broader light, or the character he designed to investigate could have been submitted to a minuter analysis. We are quite sure that "Othello" and "Macbeth" were not written without the clear and deep and premeditative *conception* of the story to be told us. For with Shakspeare the conception itself is visible and gigantic from the first line to the last. So in the greatest works of Fielding a very obtuse critic may perceive that the author sat down to write in order to embody a design previously formed. The perception of moral truths urged him to the composition of his fictions. In Jonathan Wild, the finest prose satire in the English language, Fielding, before he set pen to paper, had resolved to tear the mask from False Greatness. In his conception of the characters and histories of Blifil and Jones, he was bent on dethroning that popular idol—False Virtue. The scorn of hypocrisy in all grades, all places, was the intellectual passion of Fielding; and his masterpieces are the results of intense convictions. That many incidents never contemplated would suggest themselves as he proceeded—that the technical plan of events might deviate and vary according as he saw new modes of enforcing his aims, is unquestionable. But still Fielding always commenced *with* a plan, with a conception —with a moral end, to be achieved by definite agencies, and through the medium of certain characters preformed in his mind. If Scott had no preconcerted story when he commenced chapter the first of one of his delightful tales, it was because he was deficient in the highest attributes of art, viz., its philosophy and its ethics. He never seems to have imagined that the loftiest merit of a tale rests upon the effect it produces, not on the fancy, but on the intellect and the passions. He had no grandeur of conception, for he had no strong desire to render palpable and immortal some definite and abstract truth.

It is a sign of the low state of criticism in this country, that Scott has been compared to Shakspeare. No two writers can be more entirely opposed to each other in the qualities of their genius, or the sources to which they were applied. Shakspeare, ever aiming at the development of the secret man, and half disdaining the mechanism of external incidents. Scott, painting the ruffles and the dress and the features and the gestures—avoiding the movements of the heart—elaborate in the progress of the incident. Scott never caught the mantle of Shakspeare, but he improved on the dresses of his wardrobe, and threw artificial effects into the scenes of his theatres.

Let us take an example : we will select one of the finest passages in Sir Walter Scott, a passage unsurpassed for its mastery over the *Picturesque.* It is that chapter in "Kenilworth" where Elizabeth has discovered Amy, and formed her first suspicions of Leicester.

"Leicester was at this moment the centre of a splendid group of lords and ladies assembled together under a portico which closed the alley. The company had drawn together in that place to attend the commands of her Majesty when the hunting party should go forward, and their astonishment may be imagined, when, instead of seeing Elizabeth advance towards them with her usual measured dignity of motion, they beheld her walking so rapidly, that she was in the midst of them ere they were aware, and then observed, with fear and surprise, that her features were flushed betwixt anger and agitation, that her hair was loosened by her haste of motion, and that her eyes sparkled as they were wont when the spirit of Henry VIII. mounted highest in his daughter. Nor were they less astonished at the appearance of the pale, attenuated, half-dead, yet still lovely female, whom the queen upheld by main strength with one hand, while with the other she waived aside the ladies and nobles who pressed towards her, under the idea that she was taken suddenly ill. 'Where is my Lord of Leicester?' she said, in a tone that thrilled with astonishment all the courtiers who stood around. 'Stand forth, my Lord of Leicester!'

"If in the midst of the most serene day of summer, when all is light and laughing around, a thunder-bolt were to fall from the clear blue vault of heaven, and rend the earth at the very feet of some careless traveller, he could not gaze upon the smouldering chasm which so unexpectedly yawned before him, with half the astonishment and fear which Leicester felt at the sight which so unexpectedly presented itself. He had that instant been receiving, with a political affectation of disavowing and misunderstanding their meaning, the half-uttered, half-intimated congratulations of the courtiers upon the favour of the queen, carried apparently to its highest pitch during the interview of that morning; from which most of them seemed to augur, that he might soon arise from their equal in rank to become their master. And now, while the subdued yet proud smile with which he disclaimed those inferences was yet curling his cheek, the queen shot into the circle, her passions excited to the uttermost, and supporting with one hand, and apparently without an effort, the pale and sinking form of his almost expiring wife, and pointing with the other to her half-dead features, demanded, in a voice that sounded to the ears of the astounded statesman, like the last dread trumpet-call that is to summon body and spirit to the Judgment-seat, 'Knowest thou this woman?'"

The reader will observe that the whole of this splendid passage is devoted to external effects: the loosened hair and sparkling eyes of Elizabeth—the grouping of the courtiers—the proud smile yet on the cheek of Leicester—the pale and sinking form of the wife. Only by external effects do we guess at the emotions of the agents. Scott is thinking of the costume and postures of the actors, not the passions they represent. Let us take a parallel passage in Shakspeare, parallel, for in each a mind disturbed with jealousy is the real object placed before the reader. It is thus that Iago describes Othello after the latter has conceived *his* first suspicions.

> "Look where he comes! Not poppy nor mandragora,
> Nor all the drowsy syrups of the world,
> Shall ever medicine thee to that sweet sleep
> Which thou ow'dst yesterday.
>   *Othello.*   Ha! ha! false to me?"

Here the reader will observe that there is no attempt at the Picturesque—no sketch of the outward man. It is only by a reference to the woe that kills sleep that we can form any notion of the haggard aspect of the Moor. So, if we compare the ensuing dialogue in the romance with that in the tragedy, we shall remark that Elizabeth utters only bursts of shallow passion, which convey none of the deep effects of the philosophy of jealousy, none of the sentiments that "inform us what we are." But every sentence uttered by Othello penetrates to the very root of the passion described: the farewell to fame and pomp, which comes from a heart that, finding falsehood in the prop it leaned on, sees the world itself and all its quality and circumstance, crumbled away; the burst of vehement incredulity; the sudden return to doubt; the intense revenge proportioned to the intense love; the human weakness that must seek faith somewhere, and, with the loss of Desdemona, casts itself upon her denouncer; the mighty knowledge of the heart exhibited in those simple words to Iago, "I greet *thy* love!"—compare all this with the mere words of Elizabeth, which have no force in themselves, but are made effective by the picturesque grouping of the scene, you will detect at once the astonishing difference between Shakspeare and Scott. Shakspeare could have composed the most wonderful plays from the stories in Scott; Scott could have written the most excellent stage directions to the plays of Shakspeare.

If the novelist be contented with the secondary order of Art in Fiction, and satisfied if his incidents be varied, animating, and striking, he may write from chapter to chapter and grope his way to a catastrophe in the dark; but if he aim at loftier and more permanent effects, he will remember that to execute grandly we must conceive nobly. He will suffer the subject he selects to lie long in his mind, to be revolved, meditated, brooded over until from the chaos breaks the light, and he sees distinctly the highest end for which his materials can be used, and the best process by which they can be reduced to harmony and order.

If, for instance, he found his tale upon some legend, the author, inspired with a great ambition, will consider what will be, not the most vivid interest, but the loftiest and most durable *order* of interest, he can extract from the incidents. Sometimes it will be in a great truth elicited by the catastrophe, sometimes by the delineation of one or more characters, sometimes by the mastery over, and development of, some complicated passion. Having decided what it is he designs to work out, he will mould his story accordingly; but before he begins to execute he will have clearly informed his mind of the conception that induces the work itself.

INTEREST.

No fiction can be first-rate if it fail to create Interest. But the merit of the fiction is not by any means proportioned to the *degree* of excitement it produces, but to the quality of the excitement. It is certainly some merit to make us weep; but the great artist will consider from what sources our tears are to be drawn. We may weep as much at the sufferings of a beggar as at the agonies of Lear; but from what sublime sympathies arise our tears for the last! What commonplace pity will produce the first! We may have our interest much more acutely excited by the "Castle of Udolpho" than by "Anastasius," but in the one, it is a melodramatic arrangement of hair-breadth escapes and a technical skill in the arrangement of other mysteries—in the other it is the consummate knowledge of actual life that fascinates the eye to the page. It is necessary, then, that every novel should excite interest; but one novel may produce a much more gradual, gentle, and subdued interest than another, and yet have infinitely more merit in the *quality* of the interest it excites.

TERROR AND HORROR.

True art never disgusts. If in descriptions intended to harrow us, we feel sickened and revolted by the very power with which the description is drawn, the author has passed the boundary of his province, he does not appal—he shocks. Thus nothing is more easy than to produce a feeling of intense pain by a portrait of great bodily suffering. The vulgarest mind can do this, and the mistaken populace of readers will cry, "See the power of this author." But all sympathy with bodily torture is drawn from our basest infirmities, all sympathy with mental torture from our deepest passions and our most spiritual nature. Horror is generally produced by the one, Terror by the other. If you describe a man hanging by a breaking bough over a precipice—if you paint his starting eyeballs, his erect hair, the death-sweat on his brow, the cracking of the bough, the depth of the abyss, the sharpness of the rock, the roar of the cataract below, you may make us dizzy and sick with sympathy; but you operate on the physical nerves, and our sensation is that of coarse and revolting pain. But take a *moral* abyss, Œdipus, for instance, on the brink of learning the awful secret which proclaims him an incestuous parricide. Show the splendour of his power, the depth of his wisdom, the loftiness of his pride, and then gradually, step by step, reveal the precipice on which he stands—and you work not on the body but the mind, you produce the true tragic emotion—*terror.* Even in this you must stop short of all that could make terror revolt while it thrills us. This Sophocles has done by one of those fine perceptions of nature which open the sublimest mysteries of art; we are not allowed time to suffer our thoughts to dwell upon the incest and self-assault of Œdipus or upon the suicide of Jocasta, before, by the introduction of the children, terror melts into pity, and the parricide son, assumes the now aspect of the broken-hearted father. A modern French writer, if he had taken the subject, would have disgusted us by details of the incest itself, or forced us from the riven heart to gaze upon the bloody and eyeless sockets of the blind king; and the more he disgusted us, the more he would have thought he excelled the tragedian of Colonos. Such of the Germans, on the contrary, who follow the school of Schiller, will often stop as far short of the true boundaries of Terror as the French romanticists would go beyond it. Schiller held it a principle of art never to leave the complete and entire effects of a work of art, one of pain. According to him the pleasure of the art should exceed the sympathy with the suffering. He sought to vindicate this principle by a reference to the Greek drama, but in this he confounded the sentiments with which we moderns read the works of Æschylus and Sophocles, with the sentiments with which a Greek would have read them. No doubt, to a Greek religiously impressed with the truth and reality of the woes or the terror depicted, the "Agamemnon," of Æschylus, the Œdipus Tyrnanus of Sophocles, and the Medea of Euripides, would have left a far more unqualified and overpowering sentiment of awe and painful sympathy, than we now can entertain for victims, whom we believe to be shadows, to duties and destinies that we know to be chimeras. Were Schiller's rule universally adopted, we should condemn Othello and Lear.

Terror may then be carried up to its full extent, provided that it work upon us through the mind, not the body, and stop short of the reaction of recoil and disgust.

DESCRIPTION.

One of the greatest and most peculiar arts of the novelist is description. It is in this that he has a manifest advantage over the dramatic poet. The latter will rarely describe scenery, costumes, *personals*, for they ought to be placed before the eyes of the audience by the theatre and the actors. When he does do so, it is generally understood by an intelligent critic to be an episode introduced for the sake of some poetical beauty which, without absolutely carrying on the plot, increases the agreeable and artistical effect of the whole performance. This is the case with the description of Dover Cliff in "Lear," or with that of the chasm which adorns by so splendid a passage the monstrous tragedy of "The Cenci." In the classical French theatre, as in the Greek, description, it is true, becomes an essential part of the play itself, since the catastrophe is thrown into description. Hence the celebrated picture of the death of Hippolyte in the "Phedre" of Racine—of the suicide of Hæmon in the "Antigone" of Sophocles. But it may be doubted whether both Sophocles and his French imitator did not, in this transfer of action to words, strike at the very core of dramatic art, whether ancient or modern, for it may be remarked—and we are surprised that it has not been remarked before—that Æschylus preferred placing the tragedy before the eyes of the reader, and he who remembers the sublime close of the Prometheus, the storm, the lightning, the bolt, the shivered rock, and the mingled groans and threats of the Titan himself, must acknowledge that the effect is infinitely more purely tragical than it would have been if we had been told how it all happened by the Aggelos or Messenger. So in the "Agamemnon" of the same sublime poet, though we do not see the blow given, the scene itself, opening, places before us the murderess and the corpse. No messenger intervenes,—no description is required for the action. "I stand where I struck him," says Clytemnestra. "The deed is done!" *

But without recurring farther to the Drama of other nations, we may admit at once that, in our own, it is the received and approved rule that Action, as much as possible, should dispense with Description. With Narrative Fiction it is otherwise; the novel writer is his own scene painter; description is as essential to him as canvas is to the actor,—description of the most various character.

In this art none ever equalled Scott. In the comparison we made between him and Shakspeare, we meant not to censure the former for indulging in what

* Even Sophocles in one of his finest tragedies has not scrupled to suffer the audience to witness the last moments of Ajax.

the latter shunned; each did that which his art required.
We only lament that Scott did not combine with external
description an equal, or, at least, not very inferior, skill in
metaphysical analysis. Had he done so, he would have
achieved all of which the novelist is capable.

In the description of natural scenery the author will
devote the greatest care to such landscapes as are meant
for the localities of his principal events.

There is nothing, for instance, very attractive in the
general features of a common; but if the author lead
us through a common, on which, in a later portion of
his work, a deed of a murder is to be done, he will strive
to fix deeply in our remembrance the character of the
landscape, the stunted tree, or the mantling pool, which he
means to associate in our minds with an act of terror.

If the duration of time in a fiction be limited to a
year, the author may be enabled artfully to show us
the progress of time by minute descriptions of the
gradual change in the seasons. This is attempted to
be done in the tale of "Eugene Aram;" instead of telling us when it is July and when it is October, the author
of that fiction describes the signs and characteristics of
the month, and seeks to identify our interest in the
natural phenomena with the approaching fate of the
hero, himself an observer and an artist of the " clouds
that pass to and fro," and the " herbs that wither and
are renewed." Again, in description, if there be any
natural objects that will bear upon the catastrophe—if,
for instance, the earthquake or the inundation be intended as an agent in the fate of those whose history
the narrative relates, incidental descriptions of the state
of the soil, frequent references to the river or the sea,
will serve to make the elements themselves minister to
the interest of the plot, and the final catastrophe will
be made at once more familiar, yet more sublime, if we
have been prepared and led to believe that you have
from the first designed to invoke to your aid the awful
agencies of Nature herself. Thus in the Œdipus at
Colonos, the Poet at the very opening of the tragedy
indulges in the celebrated description of the seats of
the Dread Goddesses, because the place, and the deities
themselves though invisible, belong yet more insensibly

to the crowning doom of the wanderer than any of the characters introduced.

The description of feelings is also the property of the novelist. The dramatist throws the feelings into dialogue —the novelist goes at once to the human heart, and calmly scrutinises, assorts, and dissects them. Few indeed are the writers who have hitherto attempted this—the master mystery of the hierophant. Godwin has done so the most elaborately, Goethe the most skilfully. The first writer is indeed so minute, that he is often frivolous,—so lengthened, that he is generally tedious; but the cultivator of the art, and not the art itself, is to be blamed for such defects.

A few words will often paint the precise state of emotion as faithfully as the most voluminous essay; and in this department condensation and brevity are to be carefully studied. Conduct us to the cavern, light the torch, and startle and awe us by what you reveal; but if you keep us all day in the cavern, the effect is lost, and our only feeling is that of impatience and desire to get away.

ARRANGEMENT OF INCIDENTS.

Distinctions between the Novel and the Drama.

In the arrangement of incidents the reader will carefully study the distinctions between the novel and the drama, —distinctions the more important because they are not at the first glance very perceptible.

In the first place the incidents of a play must grow progressively out of each other. Each scene should appear the necessary consequence of the one that precedes it. This is far from being the case with the novel: in the last it is often desirable to go back instead of forward,—to wind, to vary, to shift the interest from person to person —to keep even your principal hero, your principal actor, in the background. In the novel you see more of Frank Osbaldistone than you do of Rob Roy; but bring Rob Roy on the stage, and Frank Osbaldistone must recede at once into a fifth-rate personage.

In our closets we should be fatigued with the incessant rush of events that we desire when we make one of a multitude. Oratory and the drama in this resemble each other —that the things best to hear are not always the best to read. 'In the novel we address ourselves to the one person, —on the stage we address ourselves to a crowd; more rapid effects, broader and more popular sentiments, more condensed grasp of the universal passions, are required for the last. The calm advice which persuades our friend would only tire out the patience of the crowd. The man who writes a play for Covent Garden ought to remember that the Theatre is but a few paces distant from the Hustings: success at either place, the Hustings or the Theatre, will depend upon a mastery over feelings not perhaps the most common-place, but the most commonly felt. If with his strong effects on the stage, the dramatic poet can, like Shakspeare, unite the most delicate and subtle refinement, like Shakspeare, he will be a consummate artist. But the refinement will not do without the effects. In the novel it is different: the most enchanting and permanent kind of interest, in the latter, is often gentle, tranquillising, and subdued. The novelist can appeal to those delicate and subtle emotions, which are easily awakened when we are alone, but which are torpid and unfelt in the electric contagion of popular sympathies. The most refining among us will cease to refine when placed in the midst of a multitude.

There is a great distinction between the plot of a novel and that of a play—a distinction which has been indicated by Goethe in the "Wilhelm Meister." The novel allows *accident*, the drama never. In the former your principal character may be thrown from his horse, and break his neck; in the latter this would be a gross burlesque on the laws of the drama; for in the drama the incidents must bring about the catastrophe; in the novel there is no such necessity. Don Quixote at the last falls ill and dies in his bed; but in order that he should fall ill and die in his bed, there was no necessity that he should fight windmills, or mistake an inn for a castle. If a novelist had taken for his theme the conspiracy of Fiesco, he might have adhered to history with the most perfect consistency to his art. In the history, as Fiesco, after realising his ambitious projects, is about to step into the ship, he slips from the plank, and the weight of his armour drowns him. This is accident, and this catastrophe would not only have been admissible in the novel, but would have conveyed, perhaps, a sublimer moral than any that fiction could invent. But when Schiller adapted Fiesco for the stage, he felt that accident was not admissible,* and his Fiesco falls by the hand of the patriot Verrina. The whole dialogue preceding the fatal blow is one of the most masterly adaptations of moral truth to the necessity of historical infidelity in European literature.

In the "Bride of Lammermoor" Ravenswood is swallowed up by a quicksand. This catastrophe is singularly grand in romance; it could not be allowable on the stage; for this again is accident and not result.

The distinctions, then, between the novel and the drama, so far as the management of incidents is concerned, are principally these: that in the one the interest must always progress—that in the other it must often go back and often halt; that dealing with human nature in a much larger scale in the novel, you will often introduce events and incidents, not necessarily growing one out of the other, though all conducing to the completeness of the whole; that in the drama you have more impatience to guard against—you are addressing men in numbers, not the individual man; your effects must be more rapid and more startling : that in the novel you may artistically have recourse to accident for the working out of your design, in the drama never.

The ordinary faults of a play by the novelist,† and of a

---

* "The nature of the Drama," observes Schiller in his preface to Fiesco, and in excuse for his corruption of history, "does not admit the hand of Chance."

† "Why is it that a successful novelist has never been a successful play writer?" This is a question that has been so often put that we have been frightened out of considering whether the premises involved in the question are true or not. It is something like the schoolboy question, "Why is a pound of feathers heavier than a pound of lead?" It is long before Tom or Jack ask—is it heavier? *Is* it true that a successful novelist never has been a successful play writer? We will not insist on Goldsmith, whose comedy of "She Stoops to Conquer" and whose novel of the "Vicar of Wakefield" are alike among the greatest ornaments of our language. But was not Goethe a great play-writer and a great novelist? Who will decide whether the palm in genius should be given to the "Tasso" or the "Wilhelm Meister" of that all-sided genius? Is not the "Ghost Seer" a successful novel? Does it not afford the highest and most certain testimony of what Schiller could have done as a writer of narrative fiction, and are not

novel by the play writer, will serve as an illustration of the principles which have insensibly regulated each. The novelist will be too diffuse, too narrative, and too refined in his effects for the stage; the play writer will be too condensed, abrupt, and above all, too exaggerated, for our notions of the Natural when we are in the closet. Stage effect is a vice in the novel; but how can we expect a man trained to write for the stage to avoid what on the stage is a merit? A certain exaggeration of sentiment is natural, and necessary for sublime and truthful effect, when we address numbers; it would be ludicrous uttered to our friend in his easy-chair. If Demosthenes, urging a young Athenian to conduct himself properly, had thundered out * that sublime appeal to the shades of Marathon, Platea and Salamis, which thrilled the popular assembly, the young Athenian would have laughed in his face. If the dialogue of "Macbeth" were the dialogue of a romance on the same subject it would be equally good in itself, but it would seem detestable bombast. If the dialogue in Ivanhoe, which is matchless of its kind for fire and spirit, were shaped into blank verse, and cut up into a five act play, it would be bald and pointless. As the difference between the effective oration and the eloquent essay—between Pitt so great to hear, and Burke so great to read, so is the difference be-

"Wallenstein," and "Fiesco" and "Don Carlos" great plays by the same author? Are not "Candide" and "Zadig" imperishable masterpieces in the art of the novelist? Are not "Zaire" and "Mahomet" equally immortal? The three greatest geniuses, that in modern times the continent has produced, were both novelists and dramatists—equally great in each department. In France at this day Victor Hugo, who, with all his faults, is immeasurably the first writer in the school he has sought to found, is both the best novelist and the most powerful dramatist. That it has not happened *oftener* that the same man has achieved equal honour in the novel and the play is another question. But we might just as well ask why it has not happened oftener that the same man has been equally successful in tragedy and epic—in the ode and the didactic—why he who is sublime as a poet is often tame as a prosewriter, and *vice versá*—why the same artist who painted the "Transfiguration" did not paint the "Last Day." Nature, circumstance, and education have not fitted many men to be great except in one line. And least of all are they commonly great in two lines, which, though seemingly close to each other, run in parallel directions. The more subtle the distinction between the novel and the play, the more likely are they to be overlooked by him who attempts both. It is the same with all departments of art: the closer the approximation of the boundaries, the more difficult the blending.

* Dem. de Cour.

tween the writing for the eye of one man, and the writing
for the ears of three thousand.

Mechanism and Conduct.

The Mechanism and Conduct of the story ought to depend upon the nature of the preconceived design. Do you
desire to work out some definite end, through the passions
or through the characters you employ? Do you desire to
carry on the interest less through character and passion
than through incident? Or, do you rather desire to entertain and instruct by a general and wide knowledge of
living manners or human nature? Or, lastly, would you
seek to incorporate all these objects? Are you faithful to
your conception, will you be attentive to, and precise in
the machinery you use? In other words, your *progress*
must depend upon the order of interest you mean to be
predominant. It is by not considering this rule that critics
have often called that episodical or extraneous, which is,
in fact, a part of the design. Thus, in "Gil Blas," the
object is to convey to the reader a complete picture of the
surface of society : the manners, foibles, and peculiarities
of the time ; elevated by a general, though not very profound, knowledge of the more durable and universal
elements of human nature in the abstract. Hence the
numerous tales and nouvelletes scattered throughout the
work, though episodical to the adventures of Gil Blas, are
not episodical to the design of Le Sage. They all serve to
complete and furnish out the conception, and the whole
would be less rich and consummate in its effect without
them. They are not passages which lead to nothing, but
conduce to many purposes we can never comprehend,
unless we consider well for what end the building was
planned. So, if you wish to bring out all the peculiarities
of a certain character, you will often seem to digress into
adventures which have no palpable bearing on the external
plot of incident and catastrophe. This is constantly the
case with Cervantes and Fielding ; and the critic who
blames you for it, is committing the gross blunder of
judging the novel by the laws of the drama.

But as an ordinary rule, it may be observed that, since
both in the novel and the play human life is represented by

an epitome, so in both it is desirable that all your characters should more or less be brought to bear on the conclusions you have in view. It is not necessary in the novel that they should bear on the physical events; they may sometimes bear on the mental and interior changes in the minds and characters of the persons you introduce. For instance, if you design in the life of your hero to illustrate the Passion of jealousy upon a peculiar conformation of mind, you may introduce several characters and several incidents, which will serve to ripen his tendencies, but have not the least bearing on the actual catastrophe in which those tendencies are confirmed into deeds. This is but fidelity to real life, in which it seldom happens that they who foster the passion are the witnesses or sufferers of the effects. This distinction between interior and external agencies will be made apparent by a close study of the admirable novel of "Zeluco."

In the mechanism of external incidents, Scott is the greatest model that fiction possesses; and if we select from his works that in which this mechanism is most artistical, we instance not one of his most brilliant and popular, but one in which he combined all the advantages of his multiform and matured experience in the craft: we mean the "Fair Maid of Perth." By noting well the manner in which, in this tale, the scene is ever varied at the right moment, and the exact medium preserved between abruptness and *longueur*—how all the incidents are complicated, so as to appear inextricable, yet the solution obtained by the simplest and shortest process, the reader will learn more of the art of *mechanical* construction, than by all the rules that Aristotle himself, were he living, could lay down.

DIVISIONS OF THE WORK.

In the drama the Divisions of the plot in *Acts* are of infinite service in condensing and simplifying the design of the author. The novelist will find it convenient to himself to establish analogous divisions in the conduct of his story. The division into volumes is but the affair of the printer, and affords little help to the intellectual purposes of the author. Hence most of our greatest novelists have had recourse to the more definite sub-partition of the work into *Books;* and if the student use this mode of division, not from capricious or arbitrary pleasure, but with the same purposes of art for which, in the drama, recourse is had to the division into Acts, he will find it of the greatest service. Properly speaking, each Book should be complete in itself, working out the exact and whole purpose that the author meditates in that portion of his work. It is clear, therefore, that the number of his Books will vary according to the nature of his design. Where you have shaped your story after a dramatic fashion you will often be surprised to find how greatly you serve to keep your construction faithful to your design, by the mere arrangement of the work into the same number of sub-divisions as are adopted in the drama, viz., five books instead of five acts. Where, on the other hand, you avoid the dramatic construction, and lead the reader through great varieties of life and action, meaning in each portion of the history of your hero to illustrate separate views of society or human nature, you will probably find a much greater number of sub-divisions requisite. This must depend upon your design. Another advantage in these divisions consists in the rules that your own common sense will suggest to you with respect to the introduction of characters. It is seldom advisable to admit any new Characters of importance after the interest has arrived at a certain point of maturity. As you would not introduce a new character of consequence to the catastrophe, in the fifth act of a play, so with more qualification and reserve it will be inartistical to make a similar introduction in the corresponding portion of a novel. The most illustrious exception to this general rule is in "Clarissa," in which the Avenger, the brother of the heroine, and the executioner of Lovelace, only appears at the close of the story, and for the single purpose of revenge; and here the effect is heightened by the lateness and suddenness of the introduction of the very person to whom the catastrophe is confided.

The Catastrophe.

The distinction between the novel and the drama is usually very visible in the Catastrophe. The stage effect of bringing up all the characters together in the closing chapter, to be married or stabbed, as the thing may require, is to a fine taste eminently displeasing in a novel. It introduces into the very place where we most desire verisimilitude, a clap-trap and theatrical effect. For it must be always remembered, that in prose fiction we require more of the Real than we do in the drama (which belongs of right to the regions of pure poetry), and if the very last effect bequeathed to us be that of palpable delusion and trick, the charm of the whole work is greatly impaired. Some of Scott's romances may be justly charged with this defect.

Usually the author is so far aware of the inartist-like effect of a final grouping of all the characters before the fall of the curtain, that he brings but few of the agents he has employed to be *present* at the catastrophe, and follows what may be called the wind-up of the main interest by one or more epilogical chapters, in which we are told how Sir Thomas married and settled in his country seat, how Miss Lucy died an old maid, and how the miser Grub was found dead on his money-chest; disposing, in a few sentences, of the lives and deaths of all to whom we have been presented—a custom that we think might now give place to less hacknied inventions.

The drama will bear but one catastrophe; the novel will admit of more. Thus, in "Ivanhoe," the more vehement and apparent catastrophe is the death of Bois Guilbert; but the marriage of Ivanhoe, the visit of Rebecca to Rowena, and the solemn and touching farewell of the Jewess, constitute, properly speaking, a catastrophe, no less capital in itself, and no less essential to the completion of the incidents. So also there is often a moral catastrophe, as well as a physical one, sometimes identified each with the other, sometimes distinct. If you have been desirous to work out some conception of a principle or a truth, the design may not be completed till after the more violent effects which form the physical catastrophe. In the recent novel of "Alice, or the Mysteries," the external catastrophe is in the vengeance of Cæsarini and the death of Vargrave, but the complete denouement and completion of the more typical meanings, and ethical results of the fiction, are reserved to the moment when Maltravers recognises the Natural to be the true Ideal, and is brought, by faith and beauty of simple goodness, to affection and respect for mankind itself. In the drama it would be necessary to incorporate in one scene all the crowning results of the preceding events. We could not bear a new interest after the death of Bois Guilbert; and a new act of mere dialogue between Alice and Maltravers, after the death of Vargrave would be insufferably tame and frigid. The perfection of a catastrope is not so much in the power with which it is told, as in the feeling of completeness which it should leave on the mind. On closing the work we ought to feel that we have read a *whole*—that there is a harmonious unity in all its parts—that its close, whether it be pleasing or painful, is that which is essentially appropriate to all that has gone before: and not only the mere isolated thoughts in the work, but the unity of the work itself, ought to leave its single and deep impression on the mind. The book itself should be a thought. There is another distinction between the catastrophe of a novel and that of a play. In the last it ought to be the most permanent and striking events that lead to the catastrophe, in the former it will often be highly artistical to revive for the consummating effect many slight details—incidents the author had but dimly shadowed out—mysteries that you had judged till then, he had forgotten to clear up, and to bring a thousand rivulets, that had seemed merely introduced to relieve or adorn the way into the rapid gulf which closes over all. The effect of this has a charm not derived from mere trick, but from its fidelity to the natural and life-like order of events. What more common in the actual world than that the great crises of our fate are influenced and coloured, not so much by the incidents and persons we have deemed most important, but by many things of remote date, or of seeming insignificance. The feather the eagle carelessly sheds by the wayside plumes the shaft that transfixes him. In this management and combination of incidents towards the grand end, knowledge

of Human Nature can alone lead the student to the knowledge of Ideal Art.

These remarks form the summary of the hints and sug-
gestious that, after a careful study of books, we submit to
the consideration of the student in a class of literature
now so widely cultivated and hitherto almost wholly un-
examined by the critic. We presume not to say that they
form an entire code of laws for the art. Even Aristotle's
immortal treatise on Poetry, were it bequeathed to us complete, would still be but a skeleton ; and though no poet
could read that treatise without advantage, the most
glorious poetry might be, and has been written in defiance
of nearly all its laws. Genius will arrive at fame by the
light of its own star; but Criticism will often serve as a
sign-post to save many an unnecessary winding, and indicate many a short way. He who aspires to excel in that
fiction which is the glass of truth may learn much from
books and rules, from the lecturer and the critic ; but he
must be also the Imaginer, the Observer. He will be ever
examining human life in its most catholic and comprehensive aspects. Nor is it enough to observe,—it is necessary
to feel. We must let the heart be a student as well as the
head. No man who is a passionless and cold spectator,
will ever be an accurate analyst, of all the motives and
springs of action. Perhaps if we were to search for the
true secret of Creative Genius, we should find that secret
in the intenseness of its Sympathies.

THE END.

BRADBURY, AGNEW, & CO., PRINTERS, WHITEFRIARS.

www.ingramcontent.com/pod-product-compliance
Lightning Source LLC
Chambersburg PA
CBHW051136120726
47905CB00005B/1567